SAVING THE KARAMAZOVS

SAVING THE KARAMAZOVS

BY GARY GOLDSTICK

CITIOFBOOKS, INC.
3736 Eubank NE Suite A1
Albuquerque, NM 87111-3579
www.citiofbooks.com
Hotline: 1 (877) 389-2759
Fax: 1 (505) 930-7244

Ordering Information:
Quantity sales. Special discounts are available on quantity purchases by corporations, associations, and others. For details, contact the publisher at the address above.

Printed in the United States of America.

ISBN-13:   Softcover   979-8-89391-938-7
                  eBook   979-8-89391-932-5

Library of Congress Control Number: 2025920260

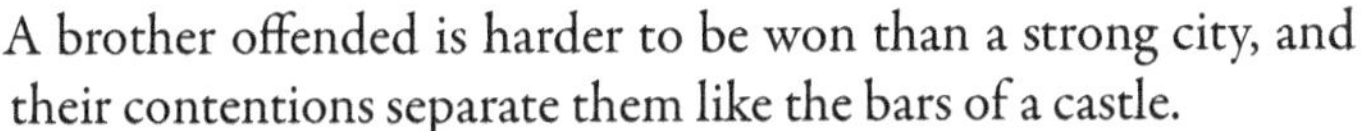

A brother offended is harder to be won than a strong city, and their contentions separate them like the bars of a castle.

—Proverbs 18:19

1

APRIL, 1970

Jeff Bascomb, twenty-seven, 1st Lieutenant in the 173rd Airborne Brigade, lay in his bunk. He had been marking the passage of time by frequently checking his watch. Sleep had not materialized by the time he looked at his watch again, 2100. Showtime. He breathed a sigh of relief. He rotated his legs over the bunk, sat up, and began to dress. He emerged from the bunker and felt his boots sink into the muck. The night was dark and stifling hot. Sergeant Flores was with the assembled patrol. Flores was forty-two years old, tall, and black, and had the build of an NFL linebacker.

"Ready?" Jeff adjusted his belt and holster.

"Yes sir, Lieutenant." Flores stood at attention.

"How many?" Jeff looked down the line of troops.

"Nine plus the two of us. Sergeant Leroy, Smith, Conners, Calhoon, Rodrigues, Miller, Simpson, Baker, and Doc."

"Too many. I need you to stay in the compound. I smell an attack in the wind."

"You smell it?" Flores allowed himself a hint of a smile.

"Intuition, Sergeant. And I'm not crazy about taking Rodrigues. I haven't been impressed with what I've seen." Jeff looked over to the line of troops and focused on Rodrigues, who was fidgeting with his rifle.

"He knows that," said Flores looking directly at Jeff. "He wants a chance to prove himself. I recommend that he go."

"Tell him to stick close to Corporal Smith and make sure Smith knows that he's to look after him. Okay?"

"Yes sir."

Jeff turned toward the bunker and began to unbuckle his belt. "I need ten minutes to put my stuff together. Use the time to check their gear. I want two M-60s and one M-79. We'll need twenty-four hundred rounds for the 60s and forty rounds for the 79. Make sure everything is taped. Navarro almost got us all killed the other night."

"Yes sir."

He headed for his bunker dogged by a mini-pang of guilt. He should have had his gear ready to go. Too much Wild Turkey last night. He checked through his pack to make sure he was carrying what he needed: a compass, maps, codebooks, binoculars, a strobe light, a .45 caliber pistol, three ammunition clips for the .45, an M-16 and twenty-five ammunition clips for the M-16. Each magazine was loaded with eighteen rounds. Every fifth round was a tracer. He checked to see that his dog tags and any other thing that could go clink in the night were taped. He deposited the book he had been reading in his footlocker and made up his bunk. He laced his boots, put on his helmet, grabbed his M-16, and walked back to the command post. He looked up at the moonless sky and checked his watch: 0110. He spoke briefly to Flores, putting him in command while he was on patrol, and then signaled to Sergeant LeRoy to move the men out.

The platoon could not afford to remain inside their triangular home. If they did, the initiative would be vouchsafed to the Vietcong, who would be able to pick at and probe the compound until they were in a position to overwhelm it. And of all the activities to which you could assign a soldier, the night patrol was the most dangerous. Of the twenty serious casualties the platoon had sustained, seventy-five percent had occurred during a night patrol. This translated into a probability of about a serious casualty every ten night patrols. Jeff ensured that he assigned himself at least fifty percent more night patrols than any soldier in the platoon. That was the least he could do to protect his men.

Their mission was to set an ambush for a North Vietnamese Army patrol that had been operating in the area. The designated ambush area was about two kilometers southwest of the compound. The terrain between the compound and the ambush area was laced with rice paddies. The only way across the rice paddies were the dikes, dirt mounds that afforded walkways no more than a foot wide. Contiguous to the paddies was underbrush that offered good cover for an enemy who might be lying in wait to ambush the prospective ambushers. Since it was impossible to hack your way through the underbrush at any reasonable rate, Jeff opted to cross the paddies by walking along the dikes—single file—with at least ten feet separating each man so as to present only small targets. The good news about the dikes was that they were unlikely to be booby-trapped. Small consolation.

They headed to the south compound exit, and single file, the men moved through the wire into the hostile terrain. Each man wore a flak jacket and carried an M-16 rifle, his own ammunition, several fragmentation grenades, and some smoke grenades.

Jeff was particular. He studied his men and kept a ledger in his head, strengths against weaknesses. In a night patrol walking single file, they would be positioned in the column to exploit their experience, capitalize on their strengths and, he hoped, mitigate the potential downside of their weaknesses.

Calhoon, the twenty-one-year-old graduate of Michigan State, had nine months in country and excellent reflexes. He would lead the column. Corporal Smith had almost as much experience and would follow. Rodrigues would stay between Smith and himself so that he could watch him. His RTO, Baker, would follow. Conners, Simpson, and Miller, all of whom had less than three months under their belts, would be next, followed by Doc. Sergeant LeRoy, career noncom, who would bring up the rear.

Jeff looked up at the clear moonless sky. Good. A slight improvement in the patrol's odds. They reached a north – south trail, the designated target, at 0220 without incident. Jeff sent Calhoon, Conners, and Simpson with an M-60 and a claymore mine fifty meters up the trail to set up the north killing position, and LeRoy, Miller, and Smith fifty meters down the trail to set up the south killing position. At the north killing position, Calhoon, who was the designated hit man, emplaced his claymore to the side of the trail, securing it to a tree and covering it with loose vegetation. He then moved down the trail on the friendly side of the mine fifteen to twenty meters, and then concealed himself in a position from which he could electrically detonate the claymore when the enemy appeared. The Conners – Simpson machine gun team concealed themselves similarly on Calhoon's uphill flank. Upon detonation of the claymore, it would hurl seven hundred hardened steel balls weighing 10.5 grams each in a sixty-degree arc, usually killing everything therein up to a distance of one hundred meters. The machine gun team would engage the enemy, denying him the ability to maneuver until the rest of the platoon moved forward to reinforce the killing position.

Sergeant LeRoy took on the role of hit man in the south killing position. The balance of the platoon—Jeff, Baker, Doc, and Rodrigues—went into a tight perimeter defense across the trail midway between the two ambushes so that they could reinforce either of the committed positions. Jeff and Baker positioned themselves on the west side of the road and Rodrigues and Doc positioned themselves on the east side.

Jeff checked his watch: 0235. So far so good. No problems. Rodrigues had performed well on the march to the ambush zone. No one had clinked or clattered. There was just enough starlight so that he could observe Smith and Rodrigues on the other side of the trail.

God, he hated the waiting—what a shitty job for a guy with a really low threshold for boredom. At 0247, he still had almost four hours 'til dawn. He would maintain the ambush until 0545 and then pack up shop and go home. Another three hours and...

Shadows moved on the other side of the trail. He grabbed Baker's arm and pointed. His heart started to race. If the shadows were NVA or Vietcong that had outflanked them, the platoon was doomed.

"What the fuck," whispered Baker. "It's Smith and Rodrigues—they're moving."

Jeff breathed a momentary sigh of relief. At least he didn't see any enemy. But the feeling of relief was soon overshadowed by the realization that in the absence of an enemy, there was absolutely no reason for either of them to be moving. "Wait here," said Jeff.

He leaped over the trail and ran after Smith who was running after Rodrigues. He raced ahead, blindly. The grass was waist high and wet and slapped against his hands and wrists. Jeff pushed past Smith and overtook Rodrigues. Rodrigues started to scream. Jeff pulled the bandana from his head and plunged it into Rodrigues' mouth and drove his head into the grass and placed his knee in the small of Rodrigues' back, further driving Rodrigues down into the ground. No more noise. Smith kneeled at Jeff's side.

"Sorry, Lieutenant. He started to freak out. Mumbling that he knew he was going to die and that he had dreamed he was dying. I tried to quiet him but he stood up, dropped his gear, and started running."

Jeff's heart pounded.

"Okay, you need to get back to support Baker—assuming that all this noise hasn't compromised our position. I'll deal with Rodrigues. Maybe I can calm him down."

Smith ran back to the support position next to Baker. Jeff was about seventy-five meters from the trail, exposed, and vulnerable. He took his knee off of Rodrigues' back and turned him over. The bandana was still stuffed in his mouth. His eyes were wide, and his face was twisted and sweating.

"Okay, Rodrigues. Let's do this real slow. If you promise not to scream, I'll take the bandana out. Hear me? If you agree, nod yes." No sign. Jeff put his finger to Rodrigues' carotid artery and felt for a pulse. None. "Holy shit." He felt nauseated. He suppressed the urge to vomit. He pulled the bandana out of Rodrigues' mouth, ripped Rodrigues' jacket off, opened his shirt, checked his mouth, and started CPR. Five minutes into CPR, a claymore detonated, followed by the rhythmic pounding of the M-60, which was followed by several M-16 rounds. Seven minutes in, he felt something crack dully in Rodrigues' chest.

Ten minutes, still no pulse and there never would be one. Jeff slowly rose to his feet. His hands and elbows wanted to stay locked from pressing on Rodrigues' chest. He massaged his forearms to relieve the cramping. He took the bandana from around his neck and wiped away the tears that were streaming down his face. He ran back to the trail and found the patrol inspecting the results of their efforts. Five NVA regulars, or what was left of them, were sprawled around the trail near the southern killing point. The troops were jubilant. They were high-fiving each other. Several were smoking. LeRoy was eating.

"Goddamn," said Conners.

"This here is a fucking mess," said Simpson. "Glad I don't have to clean up after us."

"Sweet mother of God," said Miller. "That claymore's bad."

"No," said LeRoy. "That claymore's good."

He found Baker. "Call for a Medvac for Rodrigues," said Jeff, loud enough for all the men to hear. "There's no pulse." The celebration quickly subsided. One of their own had become a statistic.

Jeff carried his cup of coffee to the command post and watched the red sun rise over the canopy of the Vietnam landscape, ushering in another hot, sticky day.

He tried to employ every sensory capacity he could muster to absorb the scene—to be in the moment. There was a very real probability that this would be the very last time that he saw it. He was resigned to the fact that he would not survive his first command.

Eight of his men had been killed, nine counting Rodrigues, and another twelve maimed with virtually nothing to show for their deaths and wounds. Nine of the casualties occurred within and just outside the compound. From where he sat right now, he could pick out the locations where each one happened—or was still happening, in a way, in his horrified memory. They had been living in a hostile, equilateral triangle of dirt, fifty meters on a side. At that wall right there, Jennings had taken a direct hit by a mortar round as he smoked a cigarette. And over there, near those sandbags, Boles was shot in the head on his way to the latrine. Carter took a fifty caliber round in his throat during the bombardment two weeks ago. One minute he was a funny, enthusiastic, highly competent soldier, and the next minute he was an ex-person, a statistic, sprawled on the dirt. And then there was Rodrigues, last night. His body was still waiting for the helicopter.

Their so-called home in the jungle, this mass grave, was located adjacent to the village of Trueng Lam in Binh Dinh province and was situated about seven kilometers east of North – South Highway 1 and three kilometers west of the South China Sea. The company command post was three kilometers south, and another American unit lay four kilometers to the west. The NVA and the Vietcong owned all other territory fifty meters outside of the perimeter. Hence, the platoon's position was fortified by six rolls of concertina barbed wire, coiled wire with razor-edged protrusions all along its length. Amid the wire were punji stakes, bamboo poles honed to a fine point and then hardened in fire. Only two layers of sandbags rose above ground level.

Forty feet overhead, adjacent to the command position was a bamboo tower. One very brave observer served as a lookout. Jeff tilted his gaze above the sun and saw the hunkered form of one of his men up there now. At the moment, he was the only other human in sight—temporarily safe, but for how long? Their mission was to deprive the Vietcong and North Vietnamese Army of the sanctuary of the village, maintain security around the village, and win the hearts and minds of the inhabitants. Yet Jeff no longer believed in The Mission—to win the "hearts and minds" of the Vietnamese. The only real estate the army controlled in the boondocks of Vietnam was located within the heavily fortified compounds and bases. And when the sun went down, the Vietcong and NVA held sway over all the ground outside the wire—including the villages. There was nothing out here worth dying for.

When he graduated West Point, he had assumed that his training, dedication, empathy, and physical strength would give him the edge to protect his men and himself. But after five months in Vietnam, he had concluded that the ubiquitous booby traps and the army's inability to constrict the flow of weapons into the area. Safety and survival had less to do with being a good soldier and a lot more to do with fate and luck. The best he could do under the circumstances was to keep his casualties low and get his guys back home in one piece—this was *his* mission, and he was failing.

He grew up wanting to be a soldier. The photos and memorabilia of his father's service in World War II and Korea and his grandfather's service in World War I had been all over the house. He loved hearing the stories his father told about the battles, the camaraderie, the pranks, and the heroism. And he remembered his grandfather telling him that there was no higher calling and no greater honor than fighting for your country. Those were the forces that motivated him to join the Army out of high school, volunteer for service in Vietnam, and then seek an appointment to West Point. But that was sixty-seven night patrols and thirty-eight senseless casualties ago.

Now, his men struggled to contain and manage their fear. He knew the terror that they experienced as they moved through the wire for a night patrol, wondering whether this would be the night that the bullet comes, or the mine explodes, rearranging their anatomy or ending their lives. He experienced the fear. He would no longer describe himself as fearless. He still had not desensitized himself to being surprised at how quickly one of his soldiers could be transformed from a son and or husband into whom years of education, experience, and training were poured, and who expected to change some aspect of the world, into torn flesh and blood that rapidly screamed itself out of existence.

He suppressed a flutter of nausea as he remembered the circumstances of Rodrigues' death and once again he reviewed every detail of the patrol that might provide some insight as to what he did or failed to do that caused the tragedy. His CO had advised him that there would be an investigation and that he should cooperate fully. He had no intention of doing otherwise.

He watched the sun move higher in the clear sparkle of an apparently calm Vietnam morning and recalled that his twelfth-grade English teacher had him memorize a speech by Macbeth and deliver it in front of the class as part of the final exam. She would be amused to learn that it took ten years and an eight-thousand-mile journey for him to make it relevant.

> *Life's but a walking shadow, a poor player*
> *That struts and frets his hour upon the stage,*
> *And then is heard no more; it is a tale*
> *Told by an idiot, full of sound and fury,*
> *Signifying nothing.*

❖

Twelve night patrols later.

The Boeing 707 taxied down the long runway of Bangkok's Don Muang airport. Jeff shrouded his eyes against the searing late afternoon sun. He was conscious of his garish flowered shirt, great white hunter jungle pants, and the local variety of sandals that he'd purchased yesterday upon arriving in Bangkok. The aircraft taxied to the gate, and the ground crew pushed the stairs into position. As he was watching the door open, he caught sight of a lithe woman dressed in the traditional *ao dai*, a patterned tunic, over white trousers.

He sauntered over to her. "*Bonjour.*"

She turned to him and smiled. She had perfect teeth. He pointed to himself.

"*Je m'appelle Jeff. Quel est votre nom?*"

She shifted the bag she was carrying to her left hand and extended her right hand to him. "No need to struggle. I speak English. My name is Thuy Do."

He took her hand in a firm clasp. "It wasn't a struggle. *Enchanté de faire votre connaissance.*"

Her smile broadened. "That was really good. You have the accent, how do you say it, 'nailed.'"

He gently shook her hand. "Thanks, I'm really working on it. Jeff Bascomb. I'm very happy to meet you."

"What brings you to Bangkok, Mr. Bascomb?"

"The US Army. I'm stationed in Binh Dinh province. I'm here to meet my father, General Sid Bascomb, who is theoretically on that plane." He gestured at the aircraft that was just beginning to disgorge its passengers. "And you?"

"I live here. I'm attending the university. My girlfriend is also on that plane, theoretically." She smiled, this time with her eyes and her lips.

Jeff's eyes darted toward the gate door just as his father emerged—in uniform. As he shifted his gaze back to Thuy Do, he took a deep breath. "I see my father. His arrival is no longer theoretical. Why don't the four of us go to dinner tomorrow night? You and your friend can play tour guides. My father and I would be honored and grateful to have the pleasure of your company." He made a point of timing his most ingratiating smile to coincide with "grateful."

She hesitated, as if she were evaluating several other options. "I have to speak with my friend." She pulled out a card from her handbag and handed it to Jeff. "Call me tonight." She turned to the gate door and waved. "I see my friend. We will speak later, *A bientôt.*" She glided off toward her friend.

Jeff put the card in his shirt pocket. He placed the thumb and middle finger of his right hand in his mouth and blew. When Sid Bascomb heard the familiar whistle, he turned his head toward Jeff.

"Dad, Dad, over here."

Sid Bascomb had just reached the bottom of the stairs. He was lugging a bulging cordovan briefcase. The three silver stars on each shoulder glistened. He held himself erect looking taller than five-nine. Jeff's eyes started to tear. It was as if his house, parents, brothers, high school teammates, teachers, and girlfriends had all arrived to remind him who he was and what he had been fighting for.

Sid dropped his briefcase and clasped Jeff in a bear hug.

"It's good to see you, Dad." He untangled himself from his father.

Sid wrapped his arms around Jeff again. "I need to hold you, Jeff. I really missed you." After he released him, he stepped back and scrutinized Jeff's tanned and lithe body. "Say, you've lost a lot of weight."

"That's what happens when you eat crappy rations, don't sleep, and are scared shitless most of the time. Say, you've gained weight."

Sid patted his gut that was hanging over his belt, pleading for release from his shirt. "It's an occupational hazard. Too many diplomatic dinners with rich food and no exercise. My waist is up two inches since I redeployed."

"Too bad you can't grow your cock that easily."

Sid placed his hand on his hips and pursed his lips in mock indignation. "Now Jeff, what would I possibly do with a ten-inch cock? Your mother can hardly accommodate what I have."

Jeff laughed. His father's humor was crass, blunt, and typical for their family. God, he had missed it. "Are you sure that you're not measuring in centimeters?" He picked up Sid's briefcase. "Let's get your bags and get a drink. I know you need one."

"Amen." They headed along the corridor toward the baggage claim area.

"How is Mom, anyway?" said Jeff, as they waited for Sid's luggage.

"She's fine. She keeps busy with her charity work. She's president of the local United Way Chapter now."

"How's her health?" said Jeff.

"Still drinking too much. Always has a glass of white wine in her hand. Always. I've tried to get her to cool it. But every time I say something, she says, 'Unlike you, General Bascomb, this is my only vice!'"

Jeff laughed. "Well, Dad, she does have a point."

Sid ignored the comment, perhaps on purpose. "There's my stuff." They walked over to the luggage rack and pulled down a matching cordovan suitcase. As they walked out of the terminal and toward the parking lot, Jeff asked about Kevin and his family.

"Kevin's real busy. He's working on a new recon system that the Agency hopes to deploy within the next year. It's top secret, so I can't really tell you the details. He's the project manager of the whole enchilada. I'm really proud of him." Sid was beaming. "Carolyn is a typical suburban housefrau. Spends most of her time driving the kids from one activity to another. Dance lesson to music lesson to football practice to God knows what. Your mother never had to do that."

"Different era, Dad. The three of us thrived on benign neglect."

They arrived at Jeff's rented car. They put Sid's bag and briefcase in the trunk and got in. The comment lingered, unanswered except for the humorless line of a smile on his father's lips.

Jeff pushed away his half-eaten Sangkhaye. "I've had it. I'm stuffed."

"I've never seen you eat so much and so fast. It's like the last meal before your execution." Sid wiped his mouth with the cloth napkin and placed it on the table next to his empty plate.

"It could be," said Jeff. "Tomorrows are never guaranteed—and that's certainly true in Vietnam." He took out a folded sheet of paper from his breast pocket and placed it on the table next to his brandy snifter.

"Aren't you being overly morbid?"

"It's an occupational necessity. You know, I mean, I'm doing the same damn thing you did in WWII and Korea. I deal in death. I'm a trained killer. I train my men to be killers. I keep a tally of how many gooks we kill, and how many of our men are killed or wounded. And I will do it day-in and day-out until I'm killed, seriously wounded, or until these six months are over."

Sid appeared to feel Jeff's stare. He moved his chair back slightly and repositioned himself. "You chose the Army, Jeff. That is what the Army does. It destroys things and it kills people."

"I didn't have any comprehension what it would be like. I know that sounds dumb. And it is dumb." He hesitated, sat back in his chair, and looked up as if he were trying to find his words on the ceiling. His eyes returned to Sid. "I was plain, fucking dumb." He wiped his eyes with his hand and remained silent.

Sid's big hand closed over Jeff's. "You okay, son?"

Jeff pulled his chair closer to the table, leaned his elbows on it, and peered directly into Sid's eyes. He spoke just above a whisper. "Dad, the Army never prepared me for the experience of holding the hand of a screaming nineteen-year-old kid from Birmingham, Alabama who had his legs, balls, and half of his face blown off, knowing that there was nothing I could have done to prevent it, and there is nothing that I can do to fix it; or humping through the brush scared to death that each step I take may trigger a booby trap, drop me into a punji pit, or bring me face to face with a gook whose only purpose is to shoot me and my men; or bedding down for the night with the full knowledge that most of the territory outside my tiny compound is controlled by the NVA who, if they wanted to, could wipe us out."

He stopped. His face was flushed. He pushed his chair back, stood, up, and announced: "I've got to pee." He came to attention, threw his shoulders back, turned on his heel, and marched off to the bar where the restroom was located.

He entered a large, gleaming black slate restroom that appeared to have just been cleaned. He relieved himself in the sparkling urinal and moved to the sink counter that was stocked with toiletries, towels, and combs. He looked into the mirror to see a dejected Jeff with bloodshot eyes and disheveled hair. The faucet was positioned high enough above the sink so that he could place his head under it and allow the cold water to soak his hair and face. He dried his face and then toweled and carefully combed his hair and left the restroom.

"I'm sorry. I didn't ask you to come eight thousand miles to hear me whine. This is the first time in six months that I've really been relaxed and my censoring systems are down."

"You don't need to censor anything with me. I've been there. I know what you're going through."

Jeff took a sip from his brandy snifter. "Right. I'll get through this, and like you, I'll have some great stories to tell my kids."

Sid smiled. "So why did you have me haul my ass out here?"

Jeff looked around and behind, and satisfied that he would not be overheard, he turned back to Sid. "In a minute," he said. "First I want to talk with you about this."

He slid the folded sheet of paper across the table. Sid unfolded the paper. Jeff followed Sid's eyes, and it was clear that Sid had seen the contents before. He held the sheet loosely in his left hand. He reached for the water glass and took a long drink. He coughed and then cleared his throat. He re-folded the sheet, placed it on the table, and slid it back to Jeff. His lips formed into a faint smile.

"I was hoping that the story hadn't reached you." Sid was attempting to be casual. "How did you get it?"

"My company commander sent the *Times* article to me." Jerry's face was circled and his name was underlined. "It was attached to a note asking whether I was related to this 'traitor' who is leading the parade of war protesters in Stockholm. I haven't answered him yet. I assume the question was rhetorical." Jeff could no longer suppress the anger that had been building. He slapped his hand on the table, shaking it so that the ice cubes clinked against the sides of the glasses. "What was the little fucker thinking?"

Sid steadied the table and pulled his chair in. "Come on, Jeff, he's just a kid. He protests everything and marches for anything. Civil rights, save the whales, women's rights, and free speech. He'll get over it."

"Bullshit!" Jeff could barely suppress his fury. "You know, I mean, he was in a foreign country organizing a protest against his own country—and me, his brother, and you, his father—when thousands of kids not much older than him are risking their lives and dying." He slapped the table again, toppling the floral centerpiece. "He's undermining the war effort. He's helping the enemy. He's a fucking traitor and if I could get my hands on him, I'd kick the shit out of him."

Some of the patrons had turned to stare at him. He took a deep breath.

"I'm through venting," said Jeff. His voice was hoarse. His anger was spent. He wet his lips and spoke as if he were reporting the weather. "You and I have never agreed on anything where Jerry is concerned—so I don't expect you to agree with me now. Just warn the little fucker that I'm going to wring his neck if I get back with all my parts intact."

Sid sat back in his chair. He righted the centerpiece as an afterthought. "Let's talk about what you brought me out here for."

Jeff repeated his routine of looking around and behind to ensure that no enemy was lurking. The restaurant had thinned out. Most of the tables within twenty-five feet were empty. The waiters and waitresses languished at their wait stations, chatting and laughing. Jeff pulled his chair close to Sid and in a very low voice told him the story of the patrol and the death of Private Emilio Rodrigues. When he finished, he leaned back in his chair and motioned to the waitress for another round of Courvoisier. Sid's sober expression conveyed his complete understanding of the implication of Rodrigues' death. He released a long breath.

"What's the status?"

"They're conducting an inquiry."

"Who?"

"CID, the criminal investigation guys."

"What's your risk?"

The waitress arrived with the drinks and removed the empty glasses. Jeff took a sip. He looked to each side and then turned so that he could see behind his chair. The restaurant was almost empty. One of the waiters had started to sweep the floor. He leaned into the table. "Runs the gamut—reprimand to the equivalent of a criminal indictment and a General Court-martial. At this point, I don't have a clue as to how this is going to go down."

"Have you been assigned an attorney?"

"No," said Jeff. "Not yet."

They sat in silence. Finally Sid said, "Ever since Mai Lai, the brass is hair-trigger sensitive—they recently charged fourteen officers with obstruction and they just charged Calley's company commander. They may give you the option of an administrative discharge to avoid a court-martial and a full airing of the sordid details. Why don't I sniff around and see what I can find out. Maybe there's a wrinkle in the deal that could help you."

Jeff put his hand on his father's arm. "No, Dad, absolutely not. You're in line for your fourth star, and I do not want you to put it at risk. Get too close and the stink will taint you. You stay away from this. I know you're stubborn, so I'm giving you an order, General." Jeff continued to hold his father's arm and stare intently into his eyes. "What I need from you now is just some advice. That's all, advice. What do I do if they do give me the option of an administrative discharge to avoid a court-martial?"

Jeff loosened his grip of Sid's arm and pushed his chair away from the table. Sid stood up. "Tell the waiter that we're going to take a stroll on the deck. I'll meet you out there. Bring your brandy." Sid strode over to and then passed through the double doors to the deck.

Jeff motioned to the waiter who came over to the table. "*Combien coûte?*"

The waiter held up eight fingers. Jeff handed him a ten-dollar bill, stood and picked up his brandy snifter, and quickly followed Sid to the deck. The restaurant was located in a marina that berthed boats and yachts ranging from twenty-foot sloops to fifty-foot schooners. They stood at the rail, looking at the boats and the reflection of the moon off the water. The only sounds came from the sloshing of wakes against the hulls.

Sid shook his head. "I can't believe you'd even consider giving up your career and let the Army use you to cleanse itself of Mai Lai. It's not like you. You've always been a fighter. You're the guy who never gives up. Remember your hero, Winston Churchill. Never, never, never, never, never give up! You're a survivor."

"I've survived so far. I may not survive the next patrol, the next firefight, the next bombardment."

Sid smiled. He reached over and placed his hands on Jeff's shoulders and looked him directly in the eyes. "Well, if you don't survive, you don't have any decision to make. Come on. You saved the lives of seven soldiers. Rodrigues was a war casualty. If they start throwing shit at you, pick if up and throw it back. Get a lawyer and fight it. You owe it to yourself, to me, to Mom, and Kevin—even to Jerry. If you slink off into the twilight, it will look like an admission of guilt and you'll regret it the rest of your life." He held Jeff in his grip for a few moments and then let go.

Jeff put his head back and inhaled the rest of the Courvoisier. Then he threw the brandy snifter into the water, smiled, and then put his arms around his father and kissed him on the cheek.

"Thanks. You really helped me. I know what I need to do. What a terrific night." Jeff let out a loud whoop. "I feel great. Thanks, Dad."

Sid slapped him on the back. "You'll do fine. You are a fucking rock!"

"Finish your drink," said Jeff. "And let's walk for a while."

They walked in silence around the deserted deck. "Since we've completed the business part of the trip," continued Jeff. "Let's focus on the R-and-R portion. I've arranged for us to have dinner with two attractive Vietnamese women that I met at the airport. Interested?" He was apprehensive as he waited for his father's reaction, not absolutely sure Sid would go.

"I'm not really into that anymore, Jeff. I promised your mother that I'd follow the straight and narrow."

Jeff stopped walking, grasped Sid's shoulder, and turned him around so that they were facing. He laughed. "Don't bullshit me. You can't expect me to believe that with all your traveling and wheeling and dealing with the Agency types, you don't get extracurricular pussy from time to time?"

The faint glimmer of a sheepish smile enveloped Sid's face. "Only on very rare occasions, Jeff. Very rare."

"Well," said Jeff, removing his hand from his father's shoulder. "Let this be one of those rare occasions. Look at it as an act of mercy. You're going to help your son get what he can before the VC deprives him of his manhood—or his life. And, I'll make it easy for you. I'll pay for dinner and your room."

Sid frowned, but the frown shifted to one of feigned indignation. "Lieutenant, are you implying that a three-star general can be bribed with a dinner and a room? I'm shocked."

"Okay," said Jeff. "I'll add two bottles of Dom Perignon."

Sid's face transformed into a bright smile. "I think that will work just fine."

Six patrols after Sid's visit, a CID investigator came to the compound and interviewed all the men who had been on the patrol the night Rodrigues died. The captain confided to Jeff that based on the reports he had received from Battalion Headquarters, he expected Rodrigues' death to be ruled an accident. His father had been right. Stick to your knitting, do your job, kill VC, forget Rodrigues, and protect the men. It paid off. Jeff felt recharged, almost buoyant.

He lay in his bunker and attempted to sleep. The trip to Bangkok had refreshed him. He couldn't say whether he had Sid to thank or the wildly satisfying two days with Thuy Do.

Just then, a series of explosions shook the bunker. RPGs. He rolled out of his cot, put on his helmet and flack jacket, grabbed his M-16, and scrambled outside. His RTO, Baker, was on his knees gasping for breath. A round hit ten meters away. He fell to the ground, and it shuddered beneath him.

There was no point in yelling. Mortar rounds were falling all over the compound. Jeff ran over to the injured Baker, unstrapped the unit from his back and tried to call company headquarters to request immediate air support. Static, no response. "Fuck!" He took a deep breath and called Platoon Bravo. "Come on, answer, dammit."

"Bravo Platoon, this is Corporal Maser."

"Lieutenant Jamison!" said Jeff. He held the hand set in a death grip. The bombardment continued unabated.

"Who's this?"

"Lieutenant Bascomb. I need to talk to Jamison pronto!" Jeff struggled to keep his voice even and professional.

"Jamison's dead. Sergeant Frazier's in command."

"Can you get him?"

Five explosions later, Frazier was on the phone. "Frazier here."

"We're under heavy attack and company headquarters isn't responding. Have you called them?"

"Several times with no response. We're getting clobbered, too."

"Keep trying. Let them know that we need immediate air. My number one RTO is down and I can't locate my backup."

"Will do, Lieutenant. Good luck."

Jeff picked up the unit and sprinted back to the command bunker. He put the unit inside the bunker and climbed ten feet up the tower ladder to assess his defenses. Squads B and C covered the northwest and southeast legs. They were still at full strength and holding their positions. Squad A was covering the south leg and posed a big problem. Nine guys were covering just over one hundred yards. And there were only eight guys in the D backup squad. Bill Calhoon, leader of D squad, was down and being worked on by Doc.

"How you doing, Bill?"

Calhoon bit his lip. "Not good, Lieutenant. I can't feel nothin' below my right thigh."

Jeff looked at the twisted wreckage that once was the leg of an athlete. Calhoon was looking at his face.

"You've got some damage, but all the parts are there. Doc's got it in a splint. Try to stay calm. We'll call in a Medvac." He turned to Doc. "You need to look at Baker. He's about fifteen meters from the command bunker."

An explosion was immediately followed by a scream. Jeff turned around to see the sickening sight of what was left of three bodies that ten seconds ago were one third of alpha squad. A mortar round had directly hit their hole. Simultaneously about two dozen NVA regulars stood up and prepared to charge the undefended section of the perimeter.

"Fuck." He clutched the medic's shoulder. "Follow me. Calhoon will have to wait. You'll feed and I'll shoot. Load up on ammo. Quickly." Jeff grabbed the squad D's M-60, and he and the medic ran to the foxhole that had just been involuntarily vacated.

"Help me stack these guys," he said as he grabbed one of the dead soldiers by the legs and pulled him to the front of the foxhole. The medic stood frozen, staring at him.

"Now, you son of a bitch! Move or we're all dead."

The medic dropped the ammo and helped stack the other two bodies on the first one adjacent to the trench. Jeff set up the M-60, so that the barrel was just above the stacked bodies. Then he and the medic crouched behind the gun and the dead bodies. The medic opened the ammo box, fed the belt into the chamber, and Jeff started firing at the regulars as they crossed the third wire perimeter. Jeff, Doc and the six remaining members of alpha squad fired continuously for about a minute. The assault stalled and the NVA retreated, leaving eight of their comrades behind.

"Get Jones and LeRoy."

The medic hesitated. "But you?"

"I'll be fine. You'll be back before they regroup. Move fast and don't you get killed or I'm fucked. Get it?"

Fortunately Doc was five-eight and 145 pounds and did not offer a very large target. He zigzagged in a crouch to the adjacent bunker thirty meters northwest of Jeff's position.

Minutes later Doc, Jones, and Leroy slid next to Jeff.

"What's happening in your sector?"

"It's gotten real quiet," said Jones.

"Let's hope it stays that way for a few more minutes," said Jeff. "Maybe there is a God. Jones, you handle the M-60. Doc will feed. Leroy, you're the new RTO. The unit's in my bunker."

Jones winced. He had just become aware that his former comrades were propping up the M-60.

"Focus on the NVA, Jones. You know, I mean, these guys are still putting out for the platoon. Doc is here to look after them."

As he and Leroy moved to his command post the first flight of Phantoms started their strafing run two hundred meters north of the compound.

2

MONDAY, JUNE 25, 1990

A sharp buzz startled him. He disentangled his right arm from under Helen's body, fumbled with his watch, and turned off the alarm.

She laughed. "Christ, Jeff. Were you timing that?"

"Sorry, honey, I have a meeting at noon with Kevin and our lawyer about the bank problem. I've got to go." Jeff rolled off her and made his way across the king size bed, and got up. He stooped down to gather up his clothes that were spread all over the floor. He disentangled his trousers from his briefs and held them up along with his shirt for inspection, shaking his head and grinning.

"The result of passion is wrinkles. I can't go looking like a bagman. Where's your iron and ironing board?"

"Give them to me. I'll do it. This is a full service establishment. We provide food, drinks, sex, and valet services."

Helen jumped out of bed, took the clothes from him, put her arm around his neck, kissed him, and then gently pushed him away. "You better take a shower. Kevin bought me the perfume I'm wearing." She covered herself with his clothes in a gesture of coy modesty, and as she brushed passed him, he again felt himself rising. He glanced at his watch and realized that he would have to hustle to make the bank meeting on time. He walked up behind Helen as she was levering open the ironing board and kissed the warm, smooth flesh of her shoulder.

"You're more addictive than a damn drug," he said.

"Go," she said, pushing him away. "Take a shower and cool down that package."

He turned up the shower pressure to the max and allowed a cold stream to blast against his face. How long had it been? Five months? Six?

Yeah, six. He knew how a heroin addict must feel. What a piece of work she was. Firm, tight, thin, tits like grapefruits and no silicone. And those white-white teeth. As he worked the lather over his body, he was getting turned on again.

He shut off the water and reached for the towel she had placed by the shower door. I've got to focus, he thought. He turned on the shower radio and stood in front of the full-length mirror, drying himself off. His attention lingered on his biceps and washboards—muscles as hard as the day he finished West Point and shipped out to Nam. He moved closer to the mirror and noticed a hair in his left nostril. He rummaged through the drawers until he found the type of scissors he needed and carefully snipped it off. The radio grumbled the news, and he stopped to listen. One of his ex-military buddies predicted that Saddam was planning trouble in the Gulf, but the media reported nothing.

He shut off the news. In the spare bedroom, he approached Helen from behind and wrapped his arm around her chest and caressed her left breast. He glanced at his watch. Eleven twenty. If he left by eleven forty-five he'd only be fifteen minutes late...

He whispered in her ear. "I've got twenty-five minutes."

"Animal..." she whispered back.

"Right."

She set down the iron, turned around, and kissed him. Then she reached down and very gently grabbed him and slowly, slowly led him back to the bedroom.

Three time zones away, a gust of cool air came through the open window of the Upper East Side apartment and passed across Jerry's bare skin. It took his attention away from the immediate task, namely holding back his orgasm until he knew that Lisa had come. She was slow tonight.

She made the moan he loved. Good, she was close. Hallelujah. His reputation for stamina had a great deal to do with his success with women. Lisa was moaning louder and in a higher key. Jerry shifted his weight, placed his hands under her buttocks and plunged into her as deeply as he could. It only took five or six thrusts and Lisa was digging her nails into his forearms and yelling, "Oh God, oh God..." Simultaneously with the second, "Oh God," the telephone rang and the answering system engaged.

"Alyosha! Ivan here. Hey, bro, hey, we really need to talk. We've got some serious problems here and…uh…I need your input. It's 8:40 here, so call me whenever you get in, any time…"

"Answer that now and I'll kill you," yelled Lisa.

Jerry wasn't paying any attention to Lisa or to the telephone. He heard the urgency in Kevin's voice just as his orgasm started and then all of his faculties were focused on the moment.

Jerry sprawled across Lisa's legs and slowly stroked her back.

"You were great again," she said.

"I know, but it's nice to hear it."

"How do you manage to hold back? What's your secret?"

"I've studied Zen."

She grabbed the pillow and brought it down hard on his head, pushing his face into the covers. "That's bull. Come on, tell me how you do it." He turned to ward off the next blow and she lunged at him again, but he moved away.

"Trade secret," he said. "It's my competitive advantage and I don't intend to share it. Any woman who wants to enjoy me has got to shop in my store."

"Chauvinist!"

"Guilty as charged.

"Who is Alyosha?"

"It's my nickname, or the nickname my brother uses, anyway. It's a family thing."

"I thought 'Jerry' was your nickname, you know, for Gerome?"

"Right, but when I was in high school, I read *The Brothers Karamazov*. I saw the similarities between the Karamazovs and our family." Lisa nodded at the book's title, but Jerry could see that she hadn't actually read it. "There were three Karamazov brothers and a domineering father. So I started using the names of the brothers and the father as alternatives to our real names. Kevin caught on to the game and we still play it."

"What's his name?"

"Ivan."

"How many brothers do you have?

"Just two, Kevin and Jeff. Kevin's four years older than me and Jeff's eight years older." He rolled off of her and out of bed and started for the kitchen. "You hungry?"

"What's available?"

He opened the refrigerator and studied its contents. When he returned to the bedroom, Lisa was in the same position, arms and legs spread wide, half-dozing.

"Vegetarian frozen pizzas or leftover Chinese food from Ying Lee's, and lots of frozen yogurt."

She opened her eyes. "How old is the Chinese?"

"Yesterday."

"I'll take it—but heat it up. I'm going to sleep for a few minutes." She turned on her side. Jerry covered her with the comforter and left the bedroom. He inserted a CD of *Don Giovanni* in the entertainment unit and stooped down to pet Chelsey, his Golden Retriever, whose head was collapsed on her big front paws in front of the fireplace. He retrieved the chow mein from the refrigerator, dumped it into a bowl, and microwaved it. The pause while he waited for the food brought him back to Kevin's call. He reached for the telephone and replayed the call.

Kevin sounded anxious, more so than usual. He took the chow mein out of the microwave, put it on a tray with a fork and a napkin, and walked it back to the bedroom, humming along with Plácido Domingo.

"Soup's on."

She sat up and locked her elbows, breasts hanging between them. "Are both your brothers cocksmen like you?"

He was still feeling a twinge of guilt over not having called Kevin yet, and didn't answer her flirting. "Not anymore. They're both married." He gave her the bowl of chow mein. "I really have to call Kevin back. I may be tied up for a while. Do you want to sleep over? We can have breakfast tomorrow at Nate's before we go to work."

Lisa braced her back with a pillow and settled the tray on her lap. "No, I'll go home. I can't sleep when you go into your wheeling and dealing mode. The call from your brother didn't sound like he wanted to discuss your mother's birthday present." She tossed a bolster at him, hitting him in the crotch.

Jerry laughed, picked up the pillow, and tossed it back on the bed. "Okay, enjoy your midnight snack." He felt a twinge of regret over sending her home and forfeiting the balance of a night of guaranteed great sex. But he would not have been able to keep his mind on screwing her, knowing that his brother was waiting for his call.

Kevin picked up on the second ring.

"Jerry?"

"Yeah, how you doing, bud?" Jerry punched the speakerphone button and headed toward the entertainment unit.

"Not so good. We're in deep shit."

Jerry turned off the entertainment unit, covered his naked body with a burgundy afghan and walked to the kitchen. "Kevin, you and National are always in deep shit, or doo-doo, or ka-ka, or whatever."

"It's different this time. It's serious."

"Okay, what do you think the problem is?" Jerry started to load the dishwasher.

"Think is not the operative word, Jerry." Kevin's voice stretched tighter. "We know what the problem is. Our chief financial officer and our vice president of manufacturing have been cooking the books since February. Our financial condition is upside-down. The bankers are furious and want to cut off our balls and hang them from the company flagpole."

Jerry stopped loading the dishwasher and moved in the direction of the phone.

"Jerry, are you still there?"

He sat down in the chair next to the phone, picked up the receiver, and took the phone off of speaker mode. "Yeah, I'm here. How the hell did this happen? Where were you and Jeff?"

"It's complicated. It's hard to discuss over the phone. I need you to come to LA and meet with Jeff, Richard, and the family." He coughed and blew his nose. "Sorry, I'm catching a cold. I really need your input, Jerry. I can't think clearly anymore. This whole thing has shaken me."

"Who the hell is Richard?"

"He's the bankruptcy attorney we hired. Will you come out?"

"You hired a bankruptcy attorney?" He groaned. "I guess it's serious. When do you want me to come?"

"As quickly as you can. Tomorrow if possible. I wouldn't ask if it wasn't critical."

Jerry thought through his schedule and which partners might pick up his slack. "I think I can get there by Wednesday. I'll call the airlines and get back to you later tonight."

"Thanks, Alyosha, I'm feeling better already."

Jerry cleared the line and then quickly made his reservations to leave on a 9:05 a.m. Delta flight out of Kennedy on Wednesday morning and called Kevin back with the information.

He knocked on the bathroom door.

"Lisa, honey, you out of the shower?"

The toilet flushed. "Be out in a minute."

"Good, I need to go over some things with you. We need to juggle."

Lisa walked back into the bedroom, wearing nothing but her smile.

"I'll be happy to help you juggle your schedule, Mr. Bascomb, sir, but I'm afraid I won't be able to concentrate until you help me out with something..."

She came over to the chair next to the bed where Jerry had sat down, climbed up on it, straddled his legs and pressed her pelvis against him, all the while moving her hips to the rhythm of *Don Giovanni*.

3

TUESDAY JUNE 26, 1990

"You unmitigated asshole!"

Sheila Crown's complexion had, in a brief moment, transformed from bland, pale and colorless to bright crimson. She delivered the line at screech. This was no act. The banker was a very unhappy camper and she didn't give a damn who knew it and who heard it.

Her voice moved up an octave. "You don't really expect us to believe that bullshit!"

The conference room was darkening. The late afternoon sky was overcast and the lack of light added to the funereal atmosphere. No one moved to turn on a light. Sheila's attorney, Bill Bromfield, was sitting to her left. He stifled a smile; he'd been through scenes like this before.

"There is nothing to smile about, Bill. I'm fucking pissed—no, I'm furiously pissed. For Christ's sake, how did those guys in the Torrance branch let these assholes into the bank?" She encompassed the assholes with a gesture across the table, aimed at the group from National Technology.

Bill Bromfield, senior partner at McCallaster and Reardon, merely looked down at his papers and organized them into two neat piles. The room grew very quiet.

Jeff, the CEO and fifty percent shareholder of National Technology, stared at Sheila as if playing "made-you-blink." This was one of the few times he did not know either what to say or how to say it. The rest of the National Technology team consisted of Kevin, who was the chairman and the other fifty-percent shareholder, Richard Krimble, a bankruptcy attorney, and Cecil Watson, the company's independent accountant. Kevin slumped down in the chair as if he were trying to make himself less obtrusive, despite his bulk. Krimble's fingers remained positioned on the keyboard of his laptop. They all sat pinned to their respective chairs, waiting for the next round to explode.

Jeff's heart beat at what seemed like twice its normal rate; his throat was dry and a lump prevented him from swallowing. He tried to look directly into the pupils of Sheila's eyes, but he simply couldn't cope with all that righteous indignation. He had to perform; this was his play. The rush of energy that usually sustained him when he was under pressure was absent. Reaching down into his soul for it would not help. It simply was absent. But he had to speak.

"Sheila, could you arrange to bring this thirsty asshole a glass of water?"

Bromfield giggled and Sheila actually laughed. Krimble removed his fingers from the keyboard. Sheila suggested a break, and the room quickly emptied. Bullet dodged.

In his Vietnam days, his platoon's position had been fortified by concertina wire punctuated by punji stakes, trip flares, claymore mines, and M-60 machine guns. Considering the enemy that made these provisions necessary, and comparing the enemy to Sheila's tenacity now, he thought maybe he had not lost his survival instinct, as he sometimes feared. He still didn't know where that joke had come from.

Fifteen minutes later, after the secretary had left, everyone was back in his or her chairs. Sheila, somewhat more composed, but still very stern, looked across the table at Jeff.

"Okay, Jeff, in your own words, tell me how fifteen percent of your inventory disappeared?"

The sweat ran down his neck. His throat was still parched, the water having had little effect. The survival of the company and the financial well-being of his family and his brother's family, and perhaps even his freedom, depended on his ability to persuade Sheila that he and Kevin were not crooks. Incompetent, yes! Negligent, yes! Perhaps even stupid—but honest. He looked directly at Sheila, this time at her pupils.

"Sheila, I know that you will find what I tell you hard to believe. I don't believe it myself and I was running the damn place. But I did not know that it was going on. Potter and Johnson did it on their own. They thought that they were helping the company over a rough spot. These guys are experienced executives. We never suspected."

Jeff took a breath and made sure he was holding eye contact with Sheila and Bromfield. He dwelled a bit longer on Sheila, who looked attentive. It was about the most he could hope for at this stage.

"It was excruciatingly simple," he said. "We had more orders for our new ACS system than we had the cash to fill. So rather than turn down business, Potter and Johnson got creative and started shipping units that were in for repair. They cleaned them up, stuck on a new serial number, and shipped them as new. They figured the profits from these borrowed units would cover the cost of building replacements for the customers waiting on repairs."

"And how many 'borrowed' units were shipped between April and last Monday, when Cecil here blew the whistle?"

"About one thousand," Cecil answered. "We're still working on it."

"How come you had so many units running through your repair operation?" Bromfield asked.

Jeff said, "Why don't you respond to that, Kevin. You're the technical guru."

Kevin sat up in his chair and for the first time during the meeting appeared alert. He was the only participant not wearing a coat. Both his white shirt and pale blue tie were stained, and he wore a pocket protector. "We were shipped a bunch of bad memory chips by Intel." His voice was slow and confident. "The bad chips caused intermittent failures in the field after the equipment was shipped. At first we couldn't figure what the hell was wrong and we busted our asses for two weeks twenty-four hours a day until we sorted the thing out. We went back to Intel and finally traced the glitch to a quality control problem. They agreed to replace the chips, but we had to recall the units and invest the labor to retrofit the units."

Jeff nodded. "We were halfway through the repairs when the new order rate went through the roof. Potter saw all those fresh units in the repair shop, and he came up with the plan to use them to fill the new orders."

"I see," said Sheila. Her face expressed something between humor and ridicule. "And since starting that practice, you have been scrounging for parts to build for both the new orders and replace the units that you stole."

Richard Krimble was on his feet, all six-feet-four of him, and he knocked the table with his knuckles. "Damn it, Sheila, you know that there was no criminal intent."

"I don't know that and neither do you," she said. A no-nonsense banker face had replaced her sarcasm. Yet, in an instant, the consummate actress was smiling. "But since this is a fact-finding meeting, I will give your client the benefit of the doubt and use the word 'converted.' So, Potter has been replacing the converted units while trying to keep up with new orders."

"Right," Jeff said. He overcame the urge to shift his position, assuming that Sheila would interpret it as squirming.

"And you didn't have a clue, a tiny fucking clue that this was happening in your company. Christ, Jeff, do you have a bridge you want to sell me, too?"

Jeff allowed his eyes to drop ever so slightly. "No, I didn't have a clue and neither did Kevin."

Kevin was turning paler. "I didn't know either, I didn't."

"And what about the controller, Howard—did he know?"

"He should have," said Kevin. "But he's a new employee. I think that he just didn't recognize the anomaly."

Sheila turned to the CPA. "What did Johnson say to you, Cecil, when you confronted him with the discrepancies?"

Cecil shrugged with one hand. "What could he say? He didn't say anything. He just stared at me and nodded. He went directly to his office and shut the door. He exited the building about forty-five minutes later with a box of personal belongings. He left a one-line letter of resignation on his desk. I don't think anyone has spoken with him since."

Bill Bromfield fingered the neat stacks of papers in front of him. He cleared his throat. "This is a very interesting story, and perhaps you might be willing to sell me the rights to the movie. But you still haven't explained the missing inventory. What happened to the $926,000 of missing inventory?"

Jeff glanced at Kevin and saw that Kevin wanted him to carry the ball. Jeff drank from the water glass, looked at Sheila, and then Bromfield. "It never existed, Bill. It was the labor cost of repairing the defective units that should have been expensed as warranty repairs, but were added to the cost of goods. Cecil, why don't you fill in the blanks?"

Cecil began passing around copies of a worksheet. When everyone had received a copy, Cecil said, "As you can see, as of June 30, the repaired units amounted to an inventory increase of $961,000. Since the bank advances 65 percent of inventory, including work in process, the company borrowed $624,000 for the 'excess' inventory." He paused. "On collateral that doesn't exist."

Kevin spoke up. "The repair should have only cost about $100 per unit and would have if they had been shipped to our facility in Mexico. It was crazy to fix them here in LA. Christ, the labor on a new unit is just under $800."

Sheila abruptly stood and started to pace around the conference room. No one else moved. "I just may throw up. I feel that I'm attending the Mad Hatter's tea party." She completed the circuit in silence and then sat down again. "So tell me, why the hell didn't you ship the units to Mexico for repair?"

"I think I can answer that," said Jeff. "I've known Potter for almost twenty years. He probably did not want to let the units out of his hands, since he was changing serial numbers. I'm sure he never thought that it would be so expensive to fix them in LA."

"That's bullshit, Jeff," said Kevin, his voice rising in frustration and anger. "Potter knows what everything costs down to the last grommet. The goddamn son-of-a-bitch just did not think it through. Once he got into it and figured out what it was costing us, there was no way to stop. And I'm sure he never shared the real numbers with Johnson."

Jeff was surprised at Kevin's outburst. But there was nothing he could do except nod in agreement.

Sheila turned to Cecil. "Is that the extent of the problem?"

"Not quite," said Cecil. "After the inventory adjustment, the company's loss in the first six months is about one million six. That compares to a profit of about one million three in the first six months of last year. Even discounting the excess inventory problem, the company experienced a negative profit swing of almost three million dollars despite an increase of fifteen percent in the shipment rate. That's huge." Cecil paused. "And of course there is the matter of the borrowed units. I estimate that it will cost the company almost three million to replace the customer units, assuming they can still build them at their historical margins—which appears unlikely."

Sheila made notes on her yellow pad.

"What about Potter?" asked Bromfield.

"He gave us the entire story Monday night," Jeff said. "He's very contrite. He said he did it for the company, and for Kevin. He did not want to leave—he's been here since Kevin started—but he knew he was a dead player, so he resigned."

"Anyone else in on it outside of Potter's and Johnson's departments?" asked Bromfield.

Jeff did not respond immediately. He allowed Bromfield's statement to hang while he mustered up his indignation. "No," replied Jeff. "We've interviewed the middle managers, and they all appear to have been as surprised as we were."

"Do you have anything to add?" Sheila asked Kevin.

"Jeff pretty much covered it all." He sat up in the chair, placed both hands on the table, and splayed his fingers as if he were trying to tap into a hidden source of energy. "I just want to say that as the founder of the company, I am mortified over what happened, and I want to assure you that we'll do whatever it takes to make this thing right. We just need some time to work things out." He pulled a handkerchief from his pocket and wiped his eyes. He blew his nose and took a deep breath. "I've given my life and my health to this company. This is a good company. We make a great product. We've got a great reputation and triple-A customers. What's happened is a fluke, an aberration. We can fix it." He stopped and looked from Sheila to Bromfield. "All we need is a chance and some time. That's all I have to say."

The room was very quiet. Jeff was embarrassed for his brother.

Sheila was unmoved. She looked over to Bill Bromfield and motioned to him to respond. "The bank will have to examine the situation and review its options. I don't have to tell you, Richard," he said, looking at Krimble. "What has happened here is serious. Your client's firm has converted property of its customers, offered bogus collateral, submitted fraudulent financial statements…And your chief financial officer has submitted fraudulent certificates of compliance. Your firm is in default of virtually every covenant of the loan agreement. And what is the most disturbing aspect of the entire sorry situation, your two principals, both of whom are highly educated and well experienced, appear to have been asleep at the helm. He continued, "The bank is very concerned that when your supposed triple-A customers find out what your clients have done, you will not have much of a business left." He looked back to Sheila, who was already standing.

Fully composed, she walked around the conference table and smiled as she shook hands with each member of the National team.

Kevin walked slowly along the aisle formed by the windowed offices of the attorneys and the tiny cubicles of the clerks and secretaries. He negotiated his way through the corridors to the elevators and stood, slouching. When Jeff and Cecil stopped beside him, he was holding his scarred and battered attaché case loosely against his leg and staring at his shoes, what he could see of them. They were in need of a shine. Jeff and Cecil kept up their conversation, not paying much attention to Kevin, until Jeff noticed that the call light for the elevator was not lit. He glanced over to Kevin and then walked over to push the elevator button. Kevin did not notice.

"Well, it wasn't as bad as I expected," Jeff said to Cecil. "Sheila is a real ball breaker, but she mellowed toward the end. Don't you think so, Kev?"

"It was no Sunday afternoon picnic," said Kevin. "And I expect that we haven't seen the worst of it. And I don't think it was an act. I think she's reflecting the bank's attitude. Shit, I don't want to talk about it now."

Jeff threw his arm around Kevin's back and gently shook him. "Let's not hang the black crêpe until we talk with Richard. I told him we'd wait for him downstairs at the bar and grill. He doesn't expect to be more than a half hour."

As the elevator descended the thirty-five floors, Jeff felt nauseated. Kevin was too depressed to be scared, but he was scared enough for both of them. Then there was the guilt—the goddamn guilt over the fact that he was asleep at the helm. It was his responsibility to know what the hell was going on, and he wasn't paying attention. He wasn't paying attention because he was too busy screwing his wife's sister. He was busy screwing her during lunch, after work, on the weekends, and every spare minute he could arrange. He looked over at Kevin—poor dejected, depressed Kevin. Kevin's world was crumbling because his brother's life was consumed with screwing their sister-in-law.

The elevator stopped. Kevin headed for the parking lot and said over his shoulder, "You guys wait for Richard. I don't feel so hot, so I'm going to head home. Call me later and let me know what happened. Regards to Salli, Jeff."

His voice was flat. No surprise. Kevin had almost broken down in the meeting. He was beaten, a casualty of war.

"Richard, it's your meeting." Sheila smiled. He had remained behind after the National team left. "I trust that you'll provide some enlightened interpretation of the bullshit that we've listened to for the past half-hour."

"I hope to."

Richard was across the table from Sheila and Bill Bromfeld, but the atmosphere was more relaxed. He closed his laptop and returned it to his briefcase. The only items on the table in front of him was his coffee mug and the coaster on which it sat, and a neat pile of yellow paper about a quarter of an inch high. "I can understand why you have trouble believing the principals' story. Frankly, I did not believe it either. So I spent three days interviewing a total of twenty-one employees—middle managers, engineers, secretaries, and production supervisors. I even interviewed the janitor. I think I got the real story." He gestured over to the pile of typed yellow sheets. "Bill, I'd like a gentleman's agreement that if this deal ends up in litigation, I won't read what I'm going to tell you in a fucking affidavit. I'm taking a risk by laying this mess out on the table, but I think the company's worth saving and I'd like to work something out. Do we have a deal?"

Bill looked at Sheila, who nodded. He had his customary tablet and uncapped pen on the table in front of him.

Richard hesitated. "No notes, Bill. Please don't take offense." He looked at Sheila. "I don't have any experience in situations that could result in a criminal charge, so I need to be very careful."

Bill placed his pad back in his briefcase and put it on the floor. He put his pen in his jacket pocket.

Richard took a deep breath and thumbed the edges of yellow papers. "The company's current problems stem primarily from the fact that Kevin has been depressed and non-functioning for at least the past year and has abdicated all executive and operational duties to Jeff. It's not that Kevin doesn't want to work and be involved—it's just that he can't. I met with him privately a few days ago, and he simply can't focus on what is going on. He can't make decisions, can't function. So there's been a vacuum, and Jeff has filled the vacuum even though he doesn't have the technical background, people skills, or industry smarts that Kevin has when he's functioning. There is no question in my mind that if Kevin had been involved, he would have understood that the numbers didn't make sense and would have investigated. He simply has not been involved. Kevin has been seeing a psychiatrist for the past six months and is on antidepressants."

"Okay," said Sheila, "Kevin's *non compos mentis*. What about Jeff?"

"He lacks the business insight to see that the reports didn't make sense. Of course he would never admit it. The operational reports generated by accounting and production don't jive—there wasn't enough money being spent on the inventory that they were supposedly buying."

Bromfield shook his head and leaned into the table. "What about the other managers who looked at the reports, the ones who weren't perpetrating the scam? Didn't they notice?"

"They did, and at least three of them said they tried to bring it to Jeff's attention. But Jeff was either preoccupied with other problems or didn't take the time to understand what he was being told. Jeff has very little rapport with the troops. Most of the middle managers regard him as a megalomaniac martinet and try to minimize their involvement with him. The culture that developed at National during the last six months created the perfect environment for a gigantic management screw-up. Kevin and Jeff are guilty of stupidity, dereliction of duty, and gross mismanagement, but they are not crooks." Richard looked directly into Sheila's eyes. "You have my word on it. They are not crooks."

"But the result is the same," said Sheila. She pushed back her chair, stood up, and started pacing. She stopped and leaned on the table. Her voice conveyed the depth of her exasperation. "The company is financially upside down and over a million dollars of our collateral doesn't exist. What difference does it make whether they stole the money or squandered it? It's still gone. And we have a company that is being run into the ground by a Laurel and Hardy management team." She pointed her finger at Richard. "You tell me why I should feel better."

Richard placed his large boney fingers on the table and looked first at Bill and then at Sheila. He kept his voice calm. "You should feel better because the bank has options that it would not have if Kevin and Jeff were crooks. If they had been stealing, you would have to foreclose, I'd have to file a Chapter 11 to protect the company, and you would have to move to install a trustee, which Jeff and Kevin would fight but would not be able to prevent. The negative publicity and the installation of a trustee would spook our customers and our engineers, many of whom would walk. The company would not be able to survive. The bank would incur a huge loss in the liquidation. Kevin would lose, Jeff would lose, and the vendors would lose. A disaster."

Bill's face remained expressionless.

"And what's my option?" said Sheila. She sat, clasping her hands together. "I'm certainly not going to sit by and let those idiots run the company. If I recommended that to the loan committee, they'd send *me* to a psychiatrist."

"I'm not suggesting that. My point is that I believe the company is basically sound, and with proper leadership could be turned around, so that nobody gets hurt. Bill, you and I have worked on these deals before. Remember the plumbing equipment distributor? What the hell was its name?"

"Reliable Plumbing," said Bromfield.

"Yeah, Reliable," said Richard. "Five years ago, the partners were in a pissing contest because of some family dispute."

Bromfield laughed and turned to Sheila. "The partners were brothers-in-law, and one of the partners was screwing the accounts receivable manager. They stopped talking to each other and the business turned to shit. Richard told them that they had to get a consultant in there pronto to fix the problem or you were going to call the loan. They hired Farmer, didn't they?"

"Yes," said Sheila. "He did a hell of a job. Turned the company around so that it was making more money than it ever had, and structured a deal, so that one partner bought the other one out. The bank didn't lose a penny. We got all of our interest, attorney fees, and accounting fees. Farmer made me a hero."

"That's what I have in mind," said Richard. "We need them to stay with the company. Kevin's technical expertise and Jeff's relationships with the customers are crucial. They'll have jobs and salaries—but they won't sign the checks, and they won't make policy."

Sheila studied the table in front of her hands for a long moment. Behind the gaze was a silent conversation, and finally she sighed. "You think that they'll agree to that?"

"I believe I can persuade them that it would be in their best interest," said Richard.

Sheila pushed her chair back and stood up. She straightened her skirt and whisked her hair away from her face. She seemed to be pulling off some of the ball-breaker façade that had carried the meeting. "It's been a long morning," she said. "I'm drained. We need some quite time to talk this through. Call me tomorrow morning. I appreciate your hard work."

4

Delta Flight 27 roared down the runway. Jerry stuffed his novel in the seat pocket, put his seat back, and closed his eyes. His first thoughts were of Lisa humping him on the chair to the beat of *Don Giovanni*. How much he loved his twin demons, work and sex. But another five hours and he'd be in Kevin's time and seeing Mom and Dad, Carolyn, the kids, and good old Salli. He hadn't seen Salli in two years, the same time he saw Jeff.

Wonder how Jeff reacted to the fact that Kevin called me—if Kevin told him. *Shit, five hours and I'm back in that mire...*

He closed his eyes and tried to resurrect that final meeting at National.

The sparsely furnished conference room had felt crowded that day, even though there were only five of them. The air was thick. Jeff was smoking a pungent President cigar even though he knew the smoke pissed Jerry off. Jerry remembered how he had sat quietly at the end of the table, listening to Kevin recount how he and Jeff had hiked twenty-two miles from the Big Kern Lake to the trailhead when the wrangler failed to show up with their horses.

"We left the lake at noon," said Kevin. "And we arrived at the trail head about nine. Damn good thing we had a flashlight or we'd still be out there."

"What happened to the wrangler?" said Johnson.

Jeff blew a perfect circle in Jerry's direction and grinned.

"He forgot the day he was supposed to pick us up," said Kevin, and laughed.

"Daniel Boone here shot a rattler on the trail," said Jeff. "Knocked his head off from twenty feet."

Kevin shuffled the papers on his desk. He held up a photo and passed it over to Johnson. "Here's the evidence."

Jerry had seen the photo of Kevin holding the dead rattler in one hand and his revolver in the other. Jerry wished he had been there to see the action, but work had kept him in LA.

Kevin had started the meeting and invited Jerry to express his concerns over the fact that engineering on the Hughes and Boeing projects were overrunning their budgets. He'd barely spoken two sentences when Jeff swaggered in, already on the attack, saying, "If you don't have enough fucking good engineers to do the job, I'll hire some for you." Jerry had really tried to remain calm and explained that at least half of the over-runs arose from freebees that Jeff had promised his buddies at Boeing. He was upset and had been loud, and Kevin had shouted at him. The cigar smoke and the tension were fusing into the same substance in his memory, weaving around the table, thickening.

"Stop yelling," said Kevin. "This is supposed to be a business meeting. And sit down. I've reviewed the memo, Jerry. You've got more detail, but it covers the same basic issues that were discussed two weeks ago. Why agonize over it. Jesus."

Jerry took a deep breath against the side of his fist, but the smoke made him dizzy. His notes and the points he needed to make swam a little. He said, "Each time I talk to Boeing, I find out some more things we have to do. The tasks keep expanding because Jeff negotiated such a nebulous contract."

Jeff pounded his fist on the table. "What the hell do you know about selling or negotiating? You couldn't sell lemonade in the desert."

Bill and Doug observed the altercation with the indifference of bored judges used to seeing lawyers insult each other. Only Kevin was upset. Logical, even-tempered Kevin. Jerry couldn't recall exactly how the meeting ended. But the fact that Kevin would not support him was seared in his memory, and he left the meeting, knowing that he was going to leave National. He was going to do something else with his life as far away from his brothers as he could go.

"Breakfast, sir?"
Jerry felt a hand on his arm and awoke.
"Breakfast, sir?"

Jerry looked up at the smiling flight attendant and realized that he had dozed off.

"Yeah, yeah." He sat up in his seat and lowered the tray table. He tried to recall what he had been dreaming about, but the aroma of ham and eggs diverted his attention. He attacked the mediocre airline food with more gusto than it deserved.

❖

The Delta 737 touched down at 11:35 a.m. LA time. The cabin was up and pressing forward. Jerry closed *The Brothers Karamazov*. He'd stopped reading at the end of the closing argument of Ippolit Kirrillovitch, the prosecuting attorney. A phrase lingered—*They have their Hamlets, but we still have our Karamazovs.* Jerry stuffed the book into his briefcase and muttered to himself, "We certainly do!"

As he emerged from the plane, he noticed Kevin at the fringe of the gate crowd. The lingering phrase transposed itself into their old family custom, and Jerry yelled, "Ivan! Ivan! Over here."

His brother had turned into a hulk, a flabby one. With slack jowls and red rimmed eyes, Kevin looked ten years older than forty-four. As he lumbered over to Jerry, he flashed a toothy smile. "Alyosha, it's good to see you!" Jerry set down his carry-on bag and his briefcase and put his arms around his brother. When he stepped back, Kevin's cheeks were wet.

"You came out on such short notice. You're a prince, no, a king. Jerry, thanks, thanks." He gripped Jerry's right hand and continued to shake it.

Jerry took his other hand and grabbed Kevin's elbow to stop the shaking and pulled his hand away. He looked around to see if anyone was watching. "Okay already, no big deal. You need me, so I'm here. Stop crying, Kevin. Things will work out. They always have." Jerry dug around in his pocket, found a packet of tissues, and handed them over.

Kevin stood back from Jerry and looked him over slowly. "You look fantastic. What do you weigh now? One seventy-five?"

"Nope, one sixty-nine, same as when I ran track for Mira Costa High."

"You work out?"

The attention was getting awkward. "Yeah, maybe four or five times a week. It depends."

"Maybe you'll inspire me, Jerry." He addressed the floor in front of his feet. "I feel like shit and I know I look like shit. I spend all my time and effort working and worrying. Carolyn's sick of me and I don't blame her."

His voice started to crack. "It seems as though things have been going downhill for the last three years. Christ, I'm glad you're here."

Jerry handed Kevin his carry-on bag. "Come on, big fellah, give me a hand. Let's go get something to eat and you can tell me the whole sordid story."

They drove south on Pacific Coast Highway through El Segundo, Manhattan Beach, Hermosa Beach, and Redondo Beach. The sky was clear, the sun bright and the ocean glistening. Jerry devoured the scenery as each building and landscape stimulated recollections—the shop where he bought his first surfboard, the park where he played little league baseball, and the auditorium where he was awarded soccer trophies. He recalled the evening when his team was awarded a trophy for winning the thirteen to fourteen division championship and he came away carrying the MVP trophy for the championship game—a heavy, shiny armful that seemed to promise more of the same for the rest of his life. He and his brothers were damn lucky.

"How are Mom and Dad? I spoke with them a few days ago, and they sounded fine. They haven't been sucked into this mess, or have they?"

"They're okay. I've kept Dad informed. I mean, he and Mom are major creditors. He's having a little difficulty with his gall bladder, and he might have to have it removed. He tells me that it's a minor operation, and you don't need a gall bladder to survive. He's playing golf three days a week and shooting in the low eighties. Mom's doing her hospice thing. She's real active and I expect she'll be on the board next year."

"They have enough money?"

"Money's not a big deal. The combination of his Army and Lockheed pensions and social security are almost equal to what he was earning at Lockheed." He laughed. "And their expenses are zilch. Where do you want to eat?"

"Something light—pasta, soup, salad." He wasn't sure if Kevin was trying to change the subject. "How are Carolyn and the kids?"

He hesitated as if getting together the exact words he wanted. "Carolyn's fine. She's into country western music and line dancing. Keeps her busy. She's lost a lot of weight. She and Salli could pass for sisters. You'll be surprised. Mary's finishing her junior year. She's a good student. She thinks she wants to go to law school."

Okay, he thought, let him change it, then. "Have her call me and I'll give her some ideas on where to apply. What about John and Kevin, Jr.?"

"John's still struggling. He moved up to San Francisco. He's currently working at a bookstore and taking some courses at San Francisco State. We don't talk much."

Jerry noted disappointment.

"And Kevin, Jr.? Is he still seeing the same girl?"

Kevin perked up. "Yeah. They're starting to talk wedding bells. I think she'd be great for him. Provide some ballast. Help him to focus. He's so damn smart—but can't focus."

Kevin took a right turn off of Pacific Coast Highway and drove over to the Redondo Beach Pier. They parked the car and walked over to Beachbum Bob's Restaurant that was located on the water and had a 180-degree panoramic of the ocean.

The waitress brought Kevin a beer and Jerry a Diet Coke. Jerry ordered angel hair pasta with sun-dried tomatoes and clams and a dinner salad. Kevin ordered a steak and French fries. During the next half-hour, Kevin told Jerry the recent history of National, its dealings with the bank, and yesterday's big meeting *cum* crucifixion by Sheila Crown. As Kevin spoke, Jerry could not help but focus on the speed at which Kevin's fork shoveled the food from the plate into his mouth. He was eating to dull his pain, and ordered another beer to wash it down.

As he sawed into another bite of steak, he said, "Why do I feel embarrassed eating steak and potatoes in front of you? I shouldn't eat this crap, but I can't help myself. Who says that being depressed ruins your appetite? Do you have any vices, Jerry?"

"Sure."

"Name one."

"I love sex. If I didn't have to earn a living, I would devote my life to achieving the maximum number of orgasms with the maximum number of women."

"Sounds more like an addiction than a vice. It must take a lot of effort. It's all I can do to try keeping one woman satisfied, and I'm not doing very well. It must take a lot of your time."

"It takes all my time except when I'm playing investment banker and working out. I don't have time to play the piano anymore, and I only read one book a week. It's like having a second job."

"How many women are you seeing?"

"You mean how many women am I screwing?"

"Whatever."

"At any given time, it's in the range of three to five. That's my rule—not fewer than three and not more than five. Three girlfriends keep me from getting too serious with any one and five is the limit that I can handle logistically."

"What about AIDS?"

"I usually wear a condom, and I pray a lot. If I get it, I won't put on the Magic Johnson act. Those NBA guys piss me off. What hypocrites. They screw any woman that's breathing, and when they're diagnosed with HIV, they appear on television, holding their wife's hand and imply that they got it from a toilet seat." He pulled his napkin off of his lap and threw it on the table. It fell on the floor. "I'll go quietly. What do the criminals say? If you can't do the time, then don't do the crime."

Kevin leaned down to retrieve Jerry's napkin and put it on the table. "I worry about you, Jerry. Don't you want to settle down, have kids, play daddy?"

"Maybe, when my testosterone level drops. Anyway, I didn't come three thousand miles to talk about me. Does old Dimitri Fyodorovich know I'm here?"

"I called him this morning."

"What did he say?"

"You know Jeff. It's not what he says, but what he doesn't. He was noncommittal. We're going to have a meeting at my house after dinner tonight. Richard Krimble, our attorney, is going to join us." He reached over and patted Jerry's hand, smiling broadly. "Incidentally, Helen's going to be there."

"Helen?"

"Salli's kid sister. She was living in Paris. Came back to the U.S. after her divorce. She's working in LA trying to get her new life started."

"I can't remember the last time I saw her. Maybe Jeff and Salli's wedding." He tried to recall what she had looked like. He shook his head. "I don't remember her. What does she do?"

"She's in the art business—galleries, you know. She's an absolute knockout, a ten-plus."

Jerry laughed. "You're kidding—or are you? You don't have to sell me, Kevin. I'm in LA already."

"I'll put ten bucks on your seeing her as a ten-plus."

"You're on, Kevin, but I need to warn you that I'm very particular."

Kevin glanced over the check, pulled some bills from his wallet, and left them on the table. They walked outside.

"How are you feeling?" said Kevin. "You look beat."

"I am. I was up into the wee hours getting stuff organized for my staff. I could use a shower and some sleep."

"Then let's go! We'll visit a few minutes with Carolyn, and then you're on your own until dinner." He slapped Jerry on the back and led him out into the perfect California day.

Kevin's house was the same one he'd been living in fifteen years ago when Jeff and Salli got married, but the landscaping was new. Sharp yucca leaves and acacia saplings glowed orange in the evening light, set amid generous heaps of mulch. The grass glittered with a recent rain from the irrigation system. Jerry climbed the few front steps, hands empty except for the rental car keys, thinking how grateful he was for his efficient little apartment.

The front door made a solid click and whooshed open. Jeff was wearing chinos and a collared cotton shirt, looking ready to step onto the first hole at Pebble Beach.

"Jerry, you little fucker, how ya doing?" He came toward him with outstretched arms, embraced Jerry in a bear hug, and kissed him smack on the lips. "Damn, it's good to see you! What's it been, at least three years? You look terrific! Still working out?"

Tears welled up in Jerry's eyes. He was incredulous that he still felt so much emotion for his brother. Into his mind flashed the old memory of Jeff flattening him when they met at Jeff's return-from-Vietnam party. Jeff had called him a traitor. It was a long time ago, but his brother's fist still lingered at the front of his memory's filing cabinet. And here he was, choking up, letting himself be led toward the foyer.

"It's good to see you too, Jeff." He squinted. Jeff's head eclipsed the reddish setting sunlight that streamed through the window over the front door, creating a halo effect.

"Hit me in the stomach," Jeff boasted. "Just hit me. I'm still a rock. Work out six days a week for an hour and a half a day—mostly on the gut. Come on, hit."

Jerry was embarrassed. His brother was as coarse and physical as ever. "Christ, Jeff!"

A woman said, "Jeff, why don't you take your shirt off and let Jerry feel the ripples on your stomach. Or better, strip down to your briefs and share your body with everyone."

She was wearing a beige fitted St. John dress that must have cost $1,500 and a small diamond heart that lay at the base of her throat. Her gleaming white smile lit up her face.

"Salli, how are you?" Jerry rushed over to Jeff's wife and hugged her, grateful for the reprieve.

"It's been quite some time, Jerry. My father tells me about the great things you're doing, but we never see or hear from you. We miss you." She held onto his hand and looked directly into his eyes.

In the time since he had last seen Salli, she had become even more beautiful than he had remembered. She was at least ten pounds lighter and all muscle.

"You're as smashing as ever."

"Good genes and a very expensive personal trainer. But I'm being impolite. You remember my sister Helen, don't you?"

Jerry was conscious of the fact that many of the people in the room were watching him, so he tried not to show the surprise that he experienced when Helen entered the foyer from the kitchen. Kevin had not overstated his case. She was a knockout, a definite ten. He started to extend his hand to her, but she brushed it away and hugged him, placing a discreet kiss on his cheek.

"No need to be formal, Jerry. We're all family."

"You've grown up since the wedding," said Jerry, hoping he appeared nonchalant. His whole family was there, but Helen was leaning in, speaking in a voice that was almost too soft for the room.

"That was two husbands and fifteen years ago, to be precise. Wall Street seems to agree with you. Jeff tells me you are quite the mover and shaker. Making lots of money?"

"Depends on what you mean by lots. I make more than I spend."

"That makes you a very unique member of this family. Sure you're not adopted? We can talk later—I must say hello to Carolyn and see if I can help. So good to see you again, Jerry." She floated off, flashing the famous pure white smile that was the trademark of Mrs. Knudsen's daughters. The feel of her hand on his arm lingered where she had squeezed it in parting.

The repartee had occurred at stock-ticker speed. Kevin came up to him holding a drink, wearing a loose fitting, garish blue and white Hawaiian shirt that was inappropriate for the host of even a casual dinner party. His face was red and blotchy.

"Try this. It should calm you down." Kevin handed him a large glass. "Well, admit it. I didn't oversell her, did I?"

Jerry took a large gulp, handed the drink back to Kevin, took out his wallet, and found a ten-dollar bill and handed it to Kevin. He nodded assent and watched Helen disappear into the kitchen.

Kevin introduced him to Richard Krimble, an Ichabod Crane of a man, and wandered off to pass out more drinks. Richard briefed Jerry on the status of discussions with the bank. He was concise, somewhat dry, and gave a clean summary of the situation. Jerry made a mental note to ask Birney to find out what he could about Richard's background and reputation. Mrs. Bascomb, who wanted to make sure that Jerry had everything he needed, interrupted them. Jerry assured his mother that he was fine and smiled—the youngest child syndrome. No matter how old you are she makes sure your nose is wiped and your fly is up.

Carolyn announced that dinner was ready. Kevin's description of Carolyn's metamorphosis from *hausfrau* to babe, was, once again, not overstated. She was a different woman from the one Jerry had seen years ago, and even though she was old enough to be in menopause, she could turn heads. She and Kevin led everyone into the brilliantly lit, formal dining room. Silver serving pieces and Waterford crystal reflected the light from the overhead chandelier and the twenty or so candles around the room. Fresh flowers, mostly irises and tulips, were arranged into elaborate centerpieces. Carolyn was the same in this one respect. She had always been elegant, even in the early days when the budget was tight.

Kevin and Carolyn sat at the ends. Jerry was seated between Helen and his mother and opposite Salli, who was seated next to Jeff. Kevin stood, struck his wineglass several times with the salad fork, and asked for order.

"I want to propose a toast—while I'm still capable. The advantage of entertaining at home is that you don't have to worry about driving." Kevin shifted his weight a little to avoid staggering. "To Jerry. I certainly never expected that when my little brother left National many years ago, thoroughly pissed at Jeff and me, that he'd go off and become a hero on Wall Street. Welcome back, little brother. We're grateful for your help."

Jeff rose and lifted his glass. "I second the toast. Here's to the return of the not-so-prodigal son."

There were a number of "here-heres" and "to Jerrys." During dinner he attempted to allocate his conversation and attention equally among his mother, Helen, Salli, and Jeff. However, he was drawn more and more into conversation with Helen; as if planned, his mother all but ignored him during the meal, choosing instead to hear all about Mrs. Krimble's recent tour of the Greek Islands, and Salli turned her attention to Carolyn. Jeff was dissecting his Saturday golf game for Richard and his father. The joviality of the evening, plus three glasses of wine and the absence of other distractions at the table, conspired to focus Jerry's attention on Helen. During the two hours of dinner, Jerry learned about the last several years of her life and her analysis as to why her two marriages failed. He could not take his eyes off her; his concentration was often so intense that he frequently missed a sentence or two. He noticed on two occasions that his father appeared to be staring at Helen. When their eyes locked, Sid just smiled and turned his attention back to Richard and Jeff.

Finally the wine, jet lag, and din caused him to feel slightly nauseated. He excused himself and navigated to the main bathroom to douse his head with cold water. Shortly after he returned to the table, Kevin announced that the men would be meeting in the den to discuss business.

"I really enjoyed talking with you and learning about your adventures in France," said Jerry as he pushed back his chair and stood.

A blush highlighted Helen's cheekbones. "I'm afraid I dominated the conversation." She made no movement to leave the table, but turned and looked up at him. Her gaze flicked to his crotch, then back at his face. "You're such a good listener. I hope I didn't bore you."

"Uh, not at all," he stammered. He sat back down in the chair. "You've led a very interesting life, but I want a turn. How about we have dinner tomorrow night and I'll tell you my story—which in comparison is dull and pedestrian."

"I'd love to, but I'm booked this rest of the week. What about next week?"

"I'm planning on returning to New York by the weekend."

Helen hesitated. "I'll see if I can free up my schedule for tomorrow. Call me before noon." She took out a card from her purse and handed it to him. He felt a hand on his back; behind his chair towered a ruddy-faced Kevin.

"Come on, Jerry, time to work."

Jerry turned to Helen and grabbed her hand. "I'm looking forward to our dinner."

She covered his hand with her left hand and squeezed it. "So am I."

Kevin's den was designed to create an old money club ambience like the ones in New York where the bankers and traders gathered at noon to lie to each other. The room was about sixteen by twenty and had ten-foot ceilings. One long side consisted of floor-to-ceiling bookcases. The other three walls were lined with dark paneling. Oil paintings, primarily landscapes and hunting scenes, broke up the paneling. The rug was the one Kevin and Carolyn purchased during a trip to Turkey. The furniture, several green and burgundy wing chairs and a large three-person burgundy sofa, were organized around a large circular glass coffee table. It was a man's space, but Jerry was pretty sure Carolyn decorated it.

Richard situated himself in one of the wing chairs. Jeff and Jerry took the other ones and Kevin and their father shared the sofa. Although Sid Bascomb was much shorter than Kevin, he had a bulldog build that he moved around with a general's swagger. He had a full head of white wavy hair. His face was more suntanned than Jerry had ever seen it—reflecting the many hours of his retirement that he invested in golf, hunting, and fishing.

"I've had a number of conversations with Bill Bromfield since our meeting on Wednesday," said Richard. "Bill is trying to be helpful, but the bank is taking a very hard position. We have very few options. What I want to do this evening is to set out the bank's current position and where I think our wiggle room is. I want you to realize," he said, looking first at Kevin and then at Jeff. "I am not optimistic that we will be able to materially affect the bank's position."

Sid interrupted. "How serious do you think they are about the criminal issues, Richard?"

"They are not talking at this time. They know that the threat of a criminal referral to the FBI for the violation of banking regulations is guaranteed to get our attention, but they are not about to put themselves into a situation where we can yell 'extortion.'

They've hired a criminal attorney to advise them whether they are obligated to report this matter to the regulators and if, by failing to report it, they will be violating the law. If they are advised that a report to the regulators is mandatory, they will do so, independent of any other considerations."

"So they're not holding out the notification to the regulators as a deal point?" asked Jeff.

"No," said Richard. "They can't do that. What they are saying is if they don't have to report it to the regulators, they may choose not to do so."

Kevin put his hand on his father's shoulder. "Don't worry about it, Dad—they don't want our hides. just the money."

"Jeez, I hope you're right." Sid did not appear reassured. "What's your take on this, Richard? I mean your opinion beyond the usual lawyer bullshit. I need to know."

Richard nodded. He sat back in his chair and closed his eyes for a minute. If it had been any of Jerry's New York banker friends, he'd think the gesture was affected. But Richard just opened his eyes when he was done thinking and said to Jerry's father, "No bullshit. Kevin and Jeff have every reason to be concerned. Having said that, there really is nothing any of us can do at this time to affect the outcome, other than to press on and attempt to work things out with the bank."

The room was silent for a minute, and Jeff spoke up. "Okay, Richard, so what's the deal, really?" He looked relaxed and immersed in the process of cleaning and paring his nails. "What's it going to take to get the bank out of our hair?"

Richard looked around the room, making sure that he was making eye contact with everybody. "Jeff, this is 'not a get the bank out of our hair' problem. This is an extremely serious matter and it's very important that everyone understands our situation. The bank is apoplectic, and they have every reason to be. The company has lost about one million dollars during the last six months, its liquidity ratios have deteriorated by 35 percent, the bank's collateral is underwater, the company owes its customers almost a thousand units, and the bank has lost confidence in the management skills of you and Kevin." He paused again. "And, what makes both of our situations untenable is that the bank has a concern that Kevin and Jeff may have known about or even condoned Potter and Johnson's actions."

Jerry sat upright in his chair. He hadn't expected this. He looked over to Kevin who just shook his head.

"That's a bunch of garbage and they know it," said Jeff, voice rising.

Richard ignored the outburst. "The bank is fully prepared to foreclose and liquidate the company's assets to satisfy their debt. It is currently owed about thirteen million; but even if they liquidate and sue Kevin and Jeff, both of whom guaranteed the loan, they will still have a shortfall of a least six million." He paused. "Any questions?" There was none. "So let me outline the bank's position. First, the bank wants all of the funds collected on the converted units that were financed to be paid to the bank."

"That will really screw up our cash flow," said Kevin. His face was less ruddy.

"Second, the bank wants Kevin and Jeff to pledge all their personal assets that are not already being used as collateral, specifically Kevin's residence, Jeff's residence, and the Lake Arrowhead cabin. The bank is willing to give Kevin and Jeff six months to either find another lender or sell the company. They are willing to extend on three month increments, provided the company is making progress."

"What do they mean by progress?" said Kevin. He closed his eyes. The last of the color had left his face.

"If they feel that the management is doing everything in their power to take them out or sell the company, and the value of their collateral is not deteriorating."

"Their call exclusively?" asked Jerry.

Richard nodded. "That's the way it works." Richard looked down at the pad on his lap. He flipped through a few pages and said, "In addition, Kevin and Jeff would have to give up operating control to a professional turnaround or workout manager who is acceptable to the bank. The turnaround manager would have all the authority of a CEO with full powers to manage the day-to-day operations of the company. He would not have the authority to enter into any financing agreements or sell the company; that authority remains with the board. The bank provided me with five names. I'm familiar with two of the guys on the list, and I'm checking with some bankruptcy attorneys who I know to get information about the other three. The bank wants Jeff and Kevin to start the interviewing process immediately."

"Would they consider people who are not on their list?" asked Kevin.

"Sure, if the bank interviews them and they're acceptable. This guy is going to work for National and be paid by National and theoretically be National's advocate. But, the reality is that his ultimate loyalty will be to the bank because that's where he will get his next assignment."

Jeff abruptly got out of his chair and walked behind it and leaned over the back. "Well what the fuck are Kevin and I supposed to do while this guru takes over the company?" He dug his fingers into the leather.

"I asked the same question," answered Richard. "And Sheila's answer was to quote Clark Gable in *Gone with the Wind*. She said to resolve that with the workout manager."

He squeezed harder. "That cunt!"

Sid jabbed his finger at the chair. "Jeff, shut up and sit down. That kind of an attitude is not going to help get us out of this mess."

Jeff returned to his seat, dug out his nail clippers from his pants pocket, and resumed paring his nails.

"Let's go on," said Kevin.

"The rest of the deal is pretty vanilla." He paused and looked over his notes. "Oh, I almost forgot. They handed me this list of reports that they want us to submit periodically. There are a bunch of them. Some are due weekly, some monthly, and some quarterly. Failure to submit a report on time will place the loan in default. You'll have to add some muscle to the accounting department to be able to produce those reports. And of course, you'll have to find a new CFO to replace Johnson."

As Richard completed his recitation of the bank's offer, a thick silence settled in the room. Kevin slouched down in the sofa. Sid's face was teary, and he looked as though he had aged during the meeting. He wiped his eyes, folded the tissue hard several times, and put it into his pocket. Jeff was back to his fingernails.

Jerry tented his fingertips on the bridge of his nose. Although he had talked to Kevin and to his partner Birney about the difficulty National was in, this was the first time the enormity of National's problem registered.

"Richard," he said. "How do you see our options for responding to the bank's offer?"

"I don't want to be flippant, but the answer is slim to none. We could refuse the offer and file a Chapter 11 petition in the bankruptcy court, but it wouldn't help."

"Why not?"

"Two reasons. One, the bank will be in the next day with a motion to appoint a Chapter 11 trustee, which will contain affidavits that lay out the whole sordid story of the Potter – Johnson scam. It's likely that the bank would win in court, a trustee would be appointed, and Jeff and Kevin would be out anyway. And the second reason is that all of National's customers will immediately become aware of the scam and the company's reputation will be permanently damaged."

"Any others?" asked Jerry.

"If we had a buyer or investor standing in the wings with substantial resources, and you could work out a satisfactory deal in the short term, we could probably persuade the bank to sit still until the investor did his due diligence."

"You're talking about a white knight," said Jerry.

"Right."

"Any ideas?" he said, looking over to Jeff and Kevin.

"Nothing comes to mind," said Jeff. Kevin merely shook his head.

Silence.

After several minutes, Jerry had worked through the situation again in his head. "It's obvious that accepting the bank's offer is the only viable alternative. So let's stop pissing and moaning about it and deal with it. Richard, what parts of the bank's offer are negotiable that could help us? Would they give us more time?"

"I don't think so, not initially. They want to keep the pressure on us."

"What about keeping the residences out of the collateral?"

"No way," said Richard. "That is a deal point."

"The workout manager?" asked Jerry.

"I guarantee you, that one is a deal point."

Kevin abruptly sat up straight and set his glass of burgundy down on the coffee table with a loud clink. "I have an idea," he announced. "What if we propose Jerry as the workout manager? That would at least ensure that we had some influence over the management of the company."

"You're kidding," said Jerry. Or too drunk to think clearly, he thought.

"I'm damn serious," said Kevin.

Jerry glanced over to Jeff. The expression on his face was unchanged, and he had begun to file his nails.

"What do you think?" Kevin asked Richard.

"It would be a tough sell, assuming Jerry would take the job. He's not a turnaround manager, and as your brother, he's hardly independent. It would take a lot of convincing."

"Right," said Jerry. "I don't want the job. I've got a job in New York. I've got responsibilities, commitments. I simply can't put my life on hold to..."

"Just hold on a minute," said Sid. "You stop whining, and, Kevin, give me the rationale behind your suggestion. Why would Jerry's involvement as CEO be so important?"

"Look, Dad," said Kevin. "We don't know shit about any of these workout artists.

I've heard lots of stories. I'm sure some of them are good, but the majority have egos the size of—well, the size of the Eiffel tower and the management style of Attila the Hun. We've got problems up the ass and the very last thing we need is some jerk who doesn't know shit about the industry, the company, and the people, taking over and fucking things up worse than they are. We'll lose key people; the engineers will get spooked. Trust me, Dad, it will be a disaster."

Sid folded his hands and leaned over the coffee table. "How do you feel about it, Jeff?"

"I would say Amen. Kevin's perceptions are right on. The workout guy could be a Dr. Jekyll, but it's more likely that we'll get Mr. Hyde because, you know, I mean, there are a higher percentage of Hydes in the workout business. Jerry is a known quantity. With him on board, at least things won't get any worse and with some luck they could improve."

Jerry's head was getting light, and not from the wine at dinner. "Thanks for the vote of confidence, Jeff, but I really, really, don't want the job and moreover..."

"You just stop right there," said Sid. "I hoped that I wouldn't have to be this blunt, but I've got a dog in this fight, too—in the form of a $750,000 subordinated note. Kevin's got $500,000 in the deal. Salli's got $1.25 mil in the deal. Kevin and Jeff have their life in the deal. If National blows up, your mother and I go with it." He rose from the chair, straightened to his full height, pushed out his chest, and walked over to Jerry. He stood in front of him, hesitating as if deciding what to do next. Then he pointed his finger. "You're making the big bucks now. And why? Due in large part to the money we gave you to go through Harvard. What was it, $75,000?" His voice was deep and gravelly, the way it got when he wanted to boss people around. It was the voice that used to grind down Jerry and his brothers. "Your mother and I never hesitated. You asked and we gave. Well, I'm calling in my marker, Jerry. Nobody freeloads. Not in my brigade, not in my business, and sure as hell not in my family. We are in trouble. If you have to put your life on hold for one year to help us out of this mess, so be it."

He turned and went back to his seat. His hand was shaking.

Jerry didn't move, and was suddenly damp and hot. His father had not attacked him with such vehemence since he was a child, and his face was burning. This was the Fydodor Pavlovich Karamazov he had loathed growing up. The humiliation felt like steel bands constricting his chest and his throat. His father was under a lot of pressure, okay. He was the escape valve, okay. He sat in silence, knowing that all eyes were on him. Finally, he found something to say.

"How do you really feel about this, Jeff? We've never been able to work together without a lot of Sturm and Drang, have we?"

"No," replied Jeff. He returned his nail clipper to his pants pocket. "But we don't have any alternative. If you choose to take on the job, and the bank approves, I'll work with you. You can count on me not to make your life difficult."

Jerry went back to his silence. He wanted to stand up and scream that he didn't create this problem, and he resented being drafted to solve it, but he was stuck. He slowly pushed himself out of the chair.

"I'm beat," he said. "Let me sleep on it. We'll talk in the morning."

He really was beat, and drained. He had tried to organize his thoughts during the meeting, as the momentum of the discussion was moving in a direction he did not anticipate and did not want. But he could not stop the train. His father's attack had shut down his brain and rerouted him straight back to age ten. As he emerged from the room, he noted that the women's conversation stopped and they turned toward the emptying den. He averted his eyes. He did not want to talk. He put a smile on his face and told himself that he needed to be polite and cordial, just for a minute or two. He went over to his mother and kissed her goodnight, and said his perfunctory goodnights to Salli, Carolyn, Helen, and Mrs. Krimble. He made it up the stairs to the guestroom, where he planned to explore every possible avenue to pull himself away from this tar baby of a problem without becoming a pariah to his entire family. As he opened the door to his room, he could not help but acknowledge the fact that he was trapped.

5

THURSDAY, JUNE 28, 1990

The situation lost some of the nightmare quality by morning. Jerry came downstairs to coffee and bagels and ate in a patch of sunlight at the breakfast island. The meal and warmth made the previous night's problem more solid, and he went upstairs and dressed in his best suit, feeling ready to meet Sheila Crown. He had finished reading *The Brothers Karamazov* and was standing at the window, thinking about his clients in New York.

He was still suffering from the hurt and shame of his father's attack. It had brought back so many memories of his youth, when his relationship was defined by his father's power and his own submissiveness. Except for that one time when he went to Stockholm for the anti-war rally, he was never able to stand up to his father. Not like Jeff or Kevin did, especially Jeff. He laughed silently. Boy, I stuck it to him then. He was so pissed at me, but I was six thousand miles away and didn't take his phone calls. Jeff never, never put up with his father's bullshit. But for Jerry, their father was "the General," and he was a raw recruit. His father knew exactly how to eviscerate him, and he had done it again last night. What could possibly be worse than a father who is both a general and a Karamazov!

His father's voice rose up the staircase, calling him down, so they could depart for the bank. And Jerry, hating himself, hopped to.

Sheila and Bill Bromfield emerged from a small conference room located adjacent to the bank's reception lobby.

"So sorry to keep you waiting." Sheila extended her hand to Richard, shook it firmly, and then turned to Jerry. "You must be Jerry. I've heard so much about you from Richard and Kevin and I'm so pleased to meet you."

Sheila had on her broad banker's smile and too much lipstick. But paired with the expensive suit and long scarf, the excessive makeup seemed intentional—she was rich and confident enough to not give a shit, even if it was out of vogue. Her demeanor would have been more appropriate had they been signing a new loan. Jerry returned the fake smile, took Sheila's extended hand and shook it.

"I really appreciate your rescheduling your day to accommodate my travel plans. I know that you must be very busy."

Sheila led them back into the conference room, silk scarf fluttering. Richard and Jerry sat on one side of the table and Sheila and Bromfield sat opposite.

Richard pulled a yellow legal tablet from his briefcase, placed it on the table, and said, "We are all under the gun on this deal, so I'll get directly to the issues. Last night, I met with the shareholders and explained the bank's position and offer in great detail. I believe they fully comprehend the seriousness of their situation and the risks they will face if they and the bank cannot accommodate each other. While they are not enthusiastic about the bank's offer, they recognize that they do not have a lot of options."

Sheila's smile lost some of its edge.

"Let me review the bank's proposal point by point," Richard said. "To make sure there is no misunderstanding among us." He talked through the plan that he had presented to the family the previous night. "Finally," he said. "The bank wants the company to retain a professional turn-around or workout manager who will take on the role of chief operations officer and be responsible for managing all day-to-day business matters, including signing all checks. In addition, he will also lead the effort to re-finance the company, so that the bank can be paid off. The bank provided the company with five names, all of whom are acceptable to the bank. As I stated to you on the phone, the shareholders are willing to accept the bank's proposal with regard to all aspects of the workout plan, provided the bank can see its way clear to approve Jerry Bascomb as the workout manager."

Sheila nodded. "Richard, I understand your position. The bank is delighted that the shareholders have decided to cooperate. However, as I explained to you during our phone conversation, the shareholder's request is highly unusual. I've reviewed Jerry's résumé and it reflects an excellent technical and legal background. And his investment banking experience and banking contacts would be very helpful in the refinancing effort. Also, I am sure he is honorable and has impeccable character. But—and it's a very big 'but'—he has no top management experience, the bank doesn't know him and cannot check out his experience working in similar situations because he has none. Moreover, as the brother of the two shareholders, he cannot qualify as an 'independent professional.' It would take an incredible leap of faith on my part to agree to your request, and I doubt that senior management would cotton such a leap."

Sheila had looked intently at Jerry as she delivered her last remarks. Jerry thought he detected a substantial component of empathy in both her speech and her stare. She was looking for a way to make it happen, but she couldn't see how to do it.

"This is not personal, Jerry, but blood is blood. If the chips were down and a conflict arose between the bank and your brothers, we could hardly expect you to align yourself with the bank's interests and oppose family." She looked over to Richard, who had continued to type on his laptop. "This is a high profile workout case, Richard. The bank can't—I can't—afford to take the risk." She looked back at Jerry. "I'm sorry."

No one spoke for a very long minute. Other than the sound of Bill Bromfield shuffling his papers, there was no sound. Jerry could not help but admire the degree to which Sheila had honed her inscrutable look. There was a part of him that wanted to jump for joy. A way out of the trap. All he had to do was say that he understood her position. If he had her responsibilities, he would do the same thing, and get up and leave and go back to New York and Lisa and his partners and resume his life that he loved. But that morning, he had made the promise to his father to take on responsibility for National's workout. Unlike Jeff, a promise meant something to Jerry. And unlike Kevin, he had the vision to see how difficult this promise was going to be. In his heart, he had always harbored Alyosha's monastic streak, and he had to follow through on his word.

Richard broke the silence. "Now, Sheila..."

Jerry reached over and grasped Richard's arm. "Richard, I think I should respond. After all, I'm the issue." Jerry put on his most ingratiating smile and looked first at Bromfield and then at Sheila. "If I put on my investment banker hat—after all I am a banker—I could not help but agree with you. Betting on Jerry Bascomb to pull the bank's fat out of the fire could certainly look like a high-risk bet to senior management." He paused. "But I believe it is absolutely the most prudent thing you can do. So let me outline your argument to senior management as to why you are not just willing, but are enthusiastic about approving me as the workout manager for National."

Sheila shuffled in her chair and folded her arms on the table. "Go on."

"First, I understand the technical and marketing aspects of National's business far better than any workout manager you are going to find. As you know, I was the chief engineer until I went to law school. The technology has changed somewhat since then, but not to the extent that I can't catch up. The marketing aspects of the product haven't changed much, and 70 percent of the sales are being made to the same customers I was dealing with when I was the chief engineer."

Sheila nodded and Bromfield took notes.

"Second, I understand the financing aspects of the business better than any turnaround guy you can find. I finance and refinance high tech companies for a living, and if you choose to review my personal financial statement, you will see that I have done very well since I graduated from law school. My involvement substantially improves the prospect of finding the money that will take the bank out."

Sheila nodded. "Go on."

"Third, I'm willing to do the deal for expenses only—travel, apartment, living expenses. I don't need any more money this year and I don't want to profit from the misery of my family. Any competent workout guy in the Los Angles area is going to cost from $25,000 to $40,000 a month in fees. By not paying those fees, the company preserves the bank's collateral and improves its liquidation position." He paused to give Bromfiled an opportunity to catch up with his note taking. "And finally, the key to this deal is being able to manage and control Kevin and Jeff. I certainly know my brothers better than anyone on this planet. I know their strengths, their weaknesses, and their idiosyncrasies. I know how to push their motivation buttons. Kevin is a brilliant technician, but an absolutely shitty manager and a weak leader. He cannot bring himself to discipline employees and doesn't know how to keep himself or his people focused. And Jeff is bright, articulate, and a wheeler-dealer of the highest magnitude. But he is a loose cannon. Kevin always under-reaches, Jeff always overreaches. I know how to work with Kevin and Jeff to dig the company out of the hole it's in." Jerry was aware that he was probably overselling in his assertions about his ability to "manage Jeff," but this aspect of the job was crucial to win Sheila's support.

Bromfield finally spoke up. "Your argument is cogent, Jerry, but you left out two important points. Why are you doing this, and how can we expect you to be independent?"

"The first question is easy: family loyalty. The family is in trouble. Kevin's, Jeff's, and my parents' entire net worth is at risk. My parents taught me that when anyone in the family was in trouble you circle the wagons. I can't let them go down without doing everything in my power to prevent it."

"And the second point," said Sheila. "The question of independence."

Jerry straightened. He looked directly into Sheila's eyes. They were paler than before, washed out by the light coming in from the conference room window, and the pupils were small. He spoke slowly and deliberately. "You will just have to accept it as a matter of faith that I am my own person and I will not allow anyone, including my brothers, to interfere with any job I undertake. My loyalty to my family, while very important to me, is second to my integrity and preserving my good name." Jerry delivered the last two lines as if he were speaking from a podium in a large auditorium. The certitude and volume of his voice was an attempt to fill the room so completely as to leave no more space for questions. It was the same technique that had given him confidence in Stockholm twenty years before. Accept the righteousness of your position, be passionate in its articulation, and allow no opening for dissent.

Sheila's eyes moved over Jerry's face as if searching for a clue that would decipher him—or for a crack in the argument. "Let's assume for argument's sake that I can sell you to senior management. What's your plan?"

Jerry smiled. He opened up his briefcase, pulled out three spreadsheets, and distributed them to Sheila, Bromfield, and Richard.

"The plan is fairly straightforward. We reduce the sales rate and the expenses to the 1989 levels and hopefully achieve the 1989 margins and profits. We keep the accounts payable level at about ten million—which should not prove too difficult with some professional vendor management. And we rebuild and return the customer units over the next three months. I estimate that the plan will require about a two-million-dollar cash infusion to implement."

Richard began to doodle. Jerry sat quietly, waiting for Sheila and Bromfield to complete their review.

Sheila looked up first. "You're going to provide a two-million-dollar line of credit to the company?" Finally, she looked incredulous.

"That's my proposal," said Jerry.

"Under what terms?"

"Interest rate at prime. The loan will be subordinate to the bank and will continue until the company is refinanced or sold. In addition, my loan is conditioned on the bank's continuing its credit at the current commitment level and the current rate of interest."

Bromfield began to speak, but Sheila interrupted him. "You must have an enormous amount of confidence in yourself, Jerry," she said.

"I do. And I have an enormous amount of confidence in the company, its employees, and its future."

Richard began to assemble his papers and deposit them into his briefcase.

"There's one more thing," said Jerry. "The houses will not be put up as specific collateral. This is real important to Jeff and Kevin and will not affect the bank's position. The bank will still control the collateral through their guarantees."

Sheila thought for a moment. "Will they agree that the bank gets to sign off in the event of a sale?"

"Sure," said Jerry.

Richard placed his last file into his briefcase. His voice was deliberately bored. "Sheila, I can't think of anything to add to what Jerry covered. Do you have any further questions?"

"No, I think you and Jerry were very thorough. Jerry, what time does your plane leave tomorrow?"

"About five in the afternoon."

"Good, we'll have an answer for you by 11 a.m. Thanks for coming in." Sheila stood. This time, her smile was genuine.

Jerry entered the Hungry Tiger Restaurant at the corner of Centenella and Sepulveda at 7:05 p.m. He'd kept his good tie on, but ditched the jacket on a hanger in the back of his rental car. He walked into the dim bar and scanned for her. After a few seconds, his eyes became accustomed to the low light and he made her out, a graceful figure at the far end. He walked over and sat down on the next stool.

"Waiting long?"

"Just a few minutes," said Helen.

"What are you drinking?"

"Pelforth's. It's French."

"Do you always support the home team?"

She turned to him and flashed the famous Knudsen smile. "I'm fiercely loyal."

"We certainly have that trait in common. I really appreciate your juggling your calendar, so that we could get together. I had such a great time at Kevin's, I wanted to keep the party going."

"So did I. I hear that you may be moving to LA shortly."

"It looks that way. I'll know definitely tomorrow."

She smiled again, leaned over, and squeezed his hand. "Well, I'm hoping you do."

Jerry turned to meet her smile and attempted to maintain a modicum of the cool demeanor that had served him so well in his transactions with women. He grinned ever so slightly. "I agree." He leaned over and kissed her on the cheek. He took her hand. It felt warm and smooth with just a touch of moisture. "Let's see if our table's ready."

In this handful of days, Jerry felt his life teetering on the apex of a sharp turn. The last time he had felt this way was before the US embassy in Stockholm, denouncing the newly appointed ambassador to Sweden and President Johnson, Robert McNamara, General Westmoreland, and the US military. God, had he been passionate! He had been a true believer that everything that was wrong in the world was somehow the fault of the United States. His life seemed to have rounded a bend from his youth, showing him a vista of unexpected meaning and good fortune beyond General Bascomb's tiny suzerain.

He had never felt so passionate about anything before Stockholm—or, for that matter, after Stockholm. In another handful of years after that, the meaning and fortune had failed to materialize.

Yet here it was again, the promise of something new and meaningful. Jerry sat alone in Kevin's office reviewing the remarks he planned to make at the company meeting that was due to start in five minutes. He would be batting third, after Kevin and then Jeff. So of necessity, his remarks would have to be brief. By the time he would get to speak, Jeff and Kevin would have conveyed the important facts about the status of the company and why Jerry was coming on board.

He needed to be convincing, to exude confidence, empathy, and competence. He, Jerry Bascomb, had been called to right the sinking ship that was National, and by God, he would do it. He'd been commissioned to save the Karamazovs. And by God he would do it.

Believe it!

Kevin knocked on the office door, opened it, and asked him if he was ready. He joined Kevin in the hallway, and together they walked to the nearby cafeteria.

The three brothers stood together on a hastily constructed podium in the National cafeteria. It had the hollow roughness of a high school stage, but a roll of beige carpeting and a bunch of National signboards from the trade show kit rescued it enough to pass for corporate quality. Jeff had just arrived and appeared warm and sweaty, as if he had been running to catch a train. But he was well dressed. He wore a dark gray glen plaid double-breasted suit with a red club tie, a white shirt, and oxblood wingtips. Jerry had exhausted his best suit the day before, and was dressed somewhat less formally in a single breasted blue blazer, blue shirt and a red and blue striped tie. Kevin, the perennial engineer, wore a white long sleeve shirt with several pencils, pens, and a small calculator protruding from his left breast pocket. Flanked by his brothers on the company podium, Jerry was full of nostalgia and warm feelings for the old National; it had been years, and he was surprised to feel so much at home. He could still identify familiar faces in the crowd. Every few minutes, someone came over to introduce himself, and he searched his memory for a tidbit of information that would help him recall exactly what that person did during the time he was chief engineer. Most of the time, he could find something.

The reluctance and resentment over being hijacked into this assignment were gone. He was back on the team. No, he was leading the team. The announcement was distributed to all employees at 11:15 a.m., fifteen minutes after Sheila's phone call. It stated only that there was to be an important company meeting at 1 p.m. in the cafeteria and all employees were urged to attend. The halls had been abuzz with speculation and rumor. No one in the company, other than Jeff, Kevin, and Howard, National's controller, were aware of the bank negotiations or that Jerry had been proposed and approved as the new Chief Operating Officer.

When Richard and Jerry had left the bank the previous day, Jerry told Richard that he believed the bank would approve him and they should prepare. Richard called Jeff and Kevin and arranged a meeting at Richard's office that afternoon. At the meeting, they drafted and reproduced a new organization chart and a memorandum to the employees, and also the story that would be put out to customers.

They had agreed that Kevin would make the announcement at the employee lunch. Jeff would then make a few remarks indicating his support for the change. Jeff's remarks would be key, since it would be clear to the employees and ultimately the customers that he was being demoted. Jerry would end the presentation by stating how happy he was to be back at National, how difficult it would be to achieve their objectives, and how confident he was that they would ultimately succeed. After extensive discussion, they also had decided to avoid any allusion to the precarious financial situation, since any hint of this reality could create panic and hasten the exodus of the best employees. Copies of the memo and the organization chart had been delivered to Howard with instructions to distribute the documents to everyone.

At a quarter after one, Kevin held up his hand to start the meeting. The buzz in the cafeteria began to ebb. He shouted, "Fellow employees, can I have your attention, please?"

The room grew quiet and soon a few hundred heads were turned toward Kevin and his brothers.

"Thank you for coming. I know that you are all very busy and we would not have dragged you to a Friday afternoon meeting unless it was important. I certainly do not need to tell you that National has been under some pressure during the past several weeks as a result of what can only be described as a total lapse of good judgment and ethics by two members of our senior management." His voice was firm and matter-of-fact. He spoke without emotion, like an anchor on the evening news. "As a consequence of their acts, the company produced financial statements that inflated the company's earnings. In substance, we produced reports that indicated that we were making more money than was actually the case. As you might expect, our bankers are upset over this situation because, among other things, it indicates that I did not have a handle on the problem and that our management control systems are defective."

He paused and looked into the crowd and made sequential eye contact with half a dozen employees. His forehead was getting damp. "As president, I am responsible for this fiasco. I cannot adequately express the hurt I feel over the fact that I let you down. I want to take this opportunity to personally apologize to each of you, because as a result of the situation we are in, you and I will all have to work harder and more diligently to turn this company around and regain our former stride."

Kevin touched a bead of sweat on his temple and flicked his hand against his trousers. He half-turned toward Jerry.

"In order to achieve these objectives and satisfy the concerns of our bankers, we have made a number of changes in the structure of the management team. My brother, Jerry, whom many of you know, has agreed to take on the job of President and Chief Operations Officer and will be responsible for the day-to-day management of the company. Jerry is taking a leave of absence from his position in a New York investment-banking firm to help us through this problem. The future of our business depends on our ability to create new customers and new markets for the products we've developed. Jeff will concentrate his efforts in this area in his role as Vice President of Marketing.

"I will focus my efforts on refinancing the company through an expanded bank line and new investment capital. I know that each of you is dedicated to the success of National and that you will give your total support to Jeff, Jerry, and me."

Kevin stepped away from the front of the lectern to make way for Jeff. Jeff slowly looked around the room, smiling and nodding at key employees and middle managers as if he was preparing to speak at a political rally. The only things missing, thought Jerry, were the placards, straw hats, and red, white, and blue bunting.

"Friends," boomed Jeff. "We have a challenge." Long pause. "We have an opportunity." Long pause. "We will be successful." Long pause. "We have the products, we have the production, we have the technology, but most important," and he started banging the lectern in time with his voice. "WE HAVE THE PEOPLE! YOU! RIGHT! RIGHT!"

The employees began to clap, whistle, stomp, and yell. Jerry wondered whether his surprise showed. Jeff had, in less than two minutes, turned a somber company meeting into an enthusiastic pep rally. After several minutes, Jeff raised his hand, and shortly the stamping and yelling subsided.

"We have a talented team, a dedicated team, and we will be successful. RIGHT!"

A whoop arose from the crowd and the stomping, clapping, and whistling resumed, and Jeff let it go on for a long time. Then he raised his hand again. "Thanks so much for your support. The management will need it as we move the ball down the field. It's not real comfortable having our backs to the goal posts, but we're fortunate that we've been able to acquire a new quarterback to lead our team, my brother Jerry. He's created quite a reputation in the Wall Street jungles, and we are very fortunate to have him back. Let's give him a rousing National welcome."

Jeff turned to face Jerry and started clapping, and soon the entire cafeteria was awash in applause. Jerry moved to the front of the lectern and shook Jeff's hand and then turned and waved to the employees, all of whom were now standing and clapping. As he smiled and nodded to the assembly, Jerry could not avoid thinking that this was another of the very few times in his life when he heard Jeff say something nice about him. Jerry raised his hand to ask for quiet, the clapping died down, and the employees returned to their seats.

"Thanks so much for the enthusiastic welcome." He looked over to Jeff. "My brother is a tough act to follow—and I know because I've been following it for most of my life."

A few titters and guffaws emanated from the crowd.

"My brothers have said most of what needs to be said. I am delighted to be back at National, working with so many of my former colleagues. This is a fine company. I know. I helped build it. I too am confident that we will be successful. Thank you." Jerry nodded and waved to the crowd. Kevin and Jeff both moved to the front of the lectern and took turns shaking Jerry's hand. The employees started to clap, and Kevin, Jeff, and Jerry stood at the front of the room, shoulder to shoulder waving at the clapping, whistling, stomping, and yelling employees. Jerry wondered whether this moment would turn out to be the high point of the assignment. He hoped it would not.

6

FRIDAY, JUNE 29, 1990

After the cafeteria meeting on Friday, Jerry changed his reservations to a Saturday flight. He spent the rest of Friday meeting with all the National managers to get up to speed on technical and personnel issues. At his suggestion, Jeff and Kevin had not attended in order to let him extract whatever critical comments managers wanted to share about his brothers. Jerry finally arrived back at Kevin's house at seven for a light dinner that Carolyn prepared. After dinner, he and Kevin talked and drank beer until late.

It had been a very long weekend since the telephone call that launched his rollercoaster ride. But he was comfortable with the way things had turned out. Despite all of his griping and the way his father had pressured him, he knew, deep down in his gut, that there was no way he could have turned his back on his family and allowed them to drown financially, while he racked up big bucks in New York. He was doing the right thing, and dammit, he would make it come out right for the family.

On Saturday, he spent the morning searching for a furnished condominium that he could lease on a short-term basis and would take Chelsey. He located a nine-hundred-square-foot apartment in Marina Del Rey on Bora Bora Way. The apartment was bright, airy, with white walls and had a large balcony that overlooked the boat slips. As a bonus, the condominium complex included a pool, spa, and a gym equipped with Nautilus equipment. As a double bonus, the pool area was teeming with very attractive women, most of whom, he assumed, were single. He went straight to the airport after signing the lease, taking with him a feeling of accomplishment and optimism.

He caught a plane for New York at two o'clock and arrived at one in the morning. He took a cab to his apartment, undressed, and fell into bed. As he was falling asleep, the sense of accomplishment waned, and he chastised himself for failing to complete more of the list of things he had to do by Tuesday, the day he was scheduled to return to California.

He spent Sunday packing and making flight reservations for Chelsey and himself. He called Lisa and told her his plans. She was surprised and upset—he expected as much. But she agreed to pick up the files on all his active deals and bring them over to his apartment, along with Chinese takeout dinners for both of them. He hung up the phone and crossed off the items on his list.

She arrived as promised in the mid-afternoon. Her eyes were red and watery, and she was sniffing and wiping her nose. She placed the files on the large desk in the living room and stood there staring at them. Jerry put his arms around her and pulled her close.

"I know you're upset, honey. I did not really want to do this, but my family really didn't give me a choice."

He moved his hand under her blouse and unsnapped her bra and started to kiss her. She put both of her hands on his chest and pushed him away with such force that he staggered backwards.

"Don't you fuck with me!" Her voice was so high and raw, it was unrecognizable. "I know better. No one tells you what to do. No one! Not Birney! Not Sheffield!" She took a breather, combed her hair down with her fingers, and wiped her nose. "I've seen you in action, Jerry, so don't fuck with me. I don't know why you're doing this, but I do know that you didn't give one second's thought to our relationship before you decided to do it. I feel like a dirty towel that's been tossed into the garbage." She started to crack again. "You are a shit! Shit!" Now she was completely out of control, screaming and crying.

Jerry stepped back, dumbfounded. He was fond of her and had just assumed they could continue the relationship after he returned from California. He raised his hands in front of him as if he were holding off an assault from his blind spot.

"Whoa, there. You are jumping to conclusions without knowing the facts. Calm down. Let's have a drink and talk about it." He grabbed her hand and led her toward the living room. "I've mixed up some margaritas."

She pulled her hand away and re-snapped her bra. "I don't want to calm down, Jerry. I want to vent. I'm hurt. You can't imagine how much I hurt. I thought we had something great going—but obviously I was mistaken. And it's going to take me some time to get used to the idea that it was all in my head and in your dick."

She started to weep again. Jerry walked back to her and held her in his arms. She remained rigid, unaffected by his efforts to comfort her. He whispered in her ear that he was very fond of her, but needed to go to California to rescue the business. He massaged her back, and she relaxed and put her arms around him. He kissed her and then steered her over to the couch. On the coffee table in front of the couch were two tumblers and a pitcher containing the margaritas. They sat down, and he poured her one of the glasses he'd prepared, and she took it from his hands.

On Monday, Jerry walked briskly through the revolving door at 40 Wall Street, nodded to the security officer at the reception desk, and headed for the elevator. He glanced at his watch and noted that it was a few minutes after nine. He rode the elevator with his eyes closed. He emerged, said hello to the receptionist, and quickly moved down the hall to his office. Lisa was at his desk organizing papers and files into neat piles. She was dressed in a conservative black suit with a white blouse and wore black high heels. She looked up at him and smirked.

"Sleep well?"

Jerry grinned and moved closer to her and pretended to look at one of the files she held. Speaking softly, he said, "How could I, after that workout last night?"

"I want you to think about me during those long, lonely nights in California."

With his back to the door of the office, he picked up her hand and looked into her eyes. "I'm sure I will." He lifted her hand to his lips and kissed it while still looking into her eyes. "I'm certain I will." He carefully lowered her hand and then asked her whether Birney was in.

"He's waiting for you. I didn't tell him the subject of the meeting. I thought I'd leave that unpleasant task to you."

"Okay, please call him and tell him I'll be down in a minute." Jerry left his office and walked down the long wide corridor. On his left were the windowed offices of the analysts and the brokers. On his right were the secretary cubicles and accounting offices. He nodded and said hello to everyone who caught his eye. The pace of Bricker and Weldon was usually too frantic to allow much time for small talk in the morning—everyone was engrossed in a deal. Every day the *Wall Street Journal*, *Barron's*, *The New York Times*, and *The Washington Post* reported events that changed the playing field for all the projects at Bricker. The nerdy junior analysts started work very early in the morning, scouring the TV reports, wire services, and newspapers for any morsel of information that might significantly affect the deals on which the senior analysts and bankers were working. Jerry loved the bustle, the action, the fast pace, and the wheeling and dealing of the investment banking scene. The fact that you could put a deal together and work on it for six months, make a few million dollars, and then move on to the next deal offended, at some level, Jerry's engineering background, That side of him, making so much money so quickly, based primarily on a great Rolodex, was almost cheating. Jerry still had a hard time believing that his success as an investment banker wasn't just a fantasy, a fluke that might suddenly end.

When he took the job with Bricker almost ten years before, he did not have a clue as to what an investment banking firm was really like or what an investment banker did. He was considered a trophy: a *cum laude* graduate of Harvard Law School with engineering undergraduate and master's degrees and extensive technical and management experience. Every day since day one, he walked into his office and thanked God for his good fortune in choosing a second career that so matched his interests, intelligence, and lifestyle.

So why was he leaving it and risking his carefully-honed reputation to take on Kevin and Jeff's mess? He thought he knew. Maybe when he explained it to Birney, he'd understand it better.

He arrived at the big office of Birney Schwartz, the managing partner. The door was open and Birney was on the phone having an animated conversation. All of Birney's conversations were animated. The television was blaring and Birney was talking loudly to compensate for the noise. Jerry stood at the doorway for a long moment until Birney noticed him and waved him in. He put his hand over the receiver and motioned again for Jerry to take one of the two chairs in front of his desk.

"I'm talking with Foster about the fees on the Carmichael deal. The son-of-a-bitch is squeezing us on our part of the fees." He took his hand off the receiver. "All right, all right, we'll agree to your terms, but I'm not happy about it. Just remember that what goes around comes around."

He slammed the phone down, leaped from his chair, and walked around the desk to Jerry. Jerry rose and they shook hands. Birney was a few years older and spent his spare time exercising and lifting weights. He bulged out of his shirt; the definition of his muscles was apparent even through his clothes.

"Sit down, Jerry. How are things? How's the dog? You were in LA?" He seated himself in the wing chair adjacent to Jerry's, crossed his legs, and waited.

"Chelsey's fine. I'm a little tired because the weekend was so chaotic. That's why I needed to see you."

"Before I forget," said Birney. "How is the Allied Electronics deal going? Are we going to close on schedule?"

"Yeah, everything is moving along per plan. City Bank completed its due diligence on Wednesday, and we expect the loan commitment in two weeks. Everyone is marching in lock step. No glitches."

"That's fantastic, Jerry, a great piece of work. It will make our quarter. You are the only guy who could have pulled that deal off—I mean the president, what's his name?"

"Koldoski."

"Yeah, Koldoski. What a schmuck! I could not have put up with him for fifteen minutes and you worked with him for five months. Incredible."

"Growing up with my brother, Jeff, was great training. He had to be the king of the schmucks. At least to me he was."

"This deal will get great press, Jerry. It will be a big notch in your belt."

"I had a lot of help from the staff, especially John and Marlene. When the kudos and bonuses are being handed out, they should be at the front of the line."

"Sure, sure, but you did it, Jerry. Christ, a five million fee. I love you, boychick."

Birney leaned over and engulfed Jerry's right hand in his two large paws and shook it.

"Great work! Great work!"

"Thanks, Birney. But I've got a problem that I need to talk with you about, and I'm going to need your understanding."

"Sure, sure. What's up?"

"I'm not sure you know or recall that my brothers have a business in California that develops hardware and software for access control security systems. The company's name is National Technology. I started there when I graduated from UCLA and was chief engineer before I went to Harvard. The company is having serious financial problems and my brothers have asked me to come to California to help them. I estimate it will take about six months to work things out, and I would like to take a leave of absence for that time. I've considered time-sharing between National and Bricker, but I've concluded that I would not be able to do justice to either job."

Jerry watched Birney's eyes for a forecast of his reaction. He could be volatile.

"How big is National?"

"Last year's sales were about 50 million."

"How big is the hole?"

"About six and one half million—plus or minus."

"Who's the bank?"

"California First."

"You'll be dealing with Sheila Crown. She's tough—and smart."

"I've already met her."

"So this thing has moved pretty far along."

"The announcement was made to the employees on Friday. I start tomorrow."

"As what?"

"President and chief operating officer."

Birney leaned back into the chair and reflected for a minute. Jerry waited and noticed how strong his fatigue was. It stirred in his body and weighed him down, and he was having trouble not slouching.

"Why are you doing this, Jerry? It's insane. You don't have any experience as an executive operating in a turnaround. These types of deals are always long shots. And you can't expect any quarter from Sheila. She can be ruthless. There must be something you are not telling me. Is it money? Is there a possibility of some huge payday if you pull it off?"

Jerry detected a gleam in Birney's eye. He needed to shut down Birney's malevolent interpretation immediately.

"I'm not going into competition with Bricker. In fact, there is no money—I'm doing it for expenses—and I've agreed to lend the company up to two million dollars."

Birney let out a long whistle—descending gradually in pitch until it faded. He stared at Jerry. "That cinches it. You are crazy. Working for nothing! Risking two million! You're going to bring disrespect to our noble profession."

"Birney, I know every argument against my doing this. I've already used it on myself. I need to do this for my family. I simply cannot let them twist in the wind when I believe I can help them."

"Jerry, you can't help them. You're not a professional turnaround manager. You've never been a COO or a CEO. You're an ex – chief engineer with a law degree and investment banking experience." Birney's voice began to rise. "It's like a father who can't swim jumping into a pool to save his drowning daughter. They both die." SMACK. He slammed his hand down on the arm of the leather wing chair. "The chances of your pulling this off are slim at best. And you're risking your reputation and career for a part in some—some fucking morality play!" Birney's voice continued to rise, ending in a shout. He paused and caught his breath.

"Now Birney," said Jerry. "I think you're being overdramatic and..."

"I know what this is. This is you getting to play the part of the hero child along with the chance to rub Jeff's nose in crap for good measure."

Jerry laughed and shook his head. "I can't say for sure that it's not the case, Birney, but I don't think so. Kevin and Jeff have put their lives and their assets into the business. My parents invested $750,000, which is about one half of their retirement nest egg. My brother Kevin and sister-in-law, Salli, have another $1.75 million in the company. My brothers have personal guarantees out the ying-yang. If this deal craters, Kevin and Jeff lose everything and my parents see their retirement lifestyle drastically curtailed. I simply cannot sit by and watch it happen. I have to do what I can. Otherwise, I won't be able to live with myself."

The conversation was drifting in an uncomfortable direction. Jerry sighed and sat back. He held out his hands as if offering his request to Birney in a shoebox.

"Birney," he said. "I'm not asking for your advice or your empathy. I'm asking for a six-month leave of absence and an advance on my end-of-the-year bonus. Kapish?"

Birney did not respond right away. He sat quietly flexing his muscles. "You've already made your decision. It's a *fait accompli*. If I say no, you'll quit and go to a competitor when your California deal is over. Let's not bullshit each other." He stood up and began to pace around the room.

"I'd rather not put it that way, Birney. I like the company, I like you. After all, you are my rabbi." He smiled. "I want to come back."

Birney walked over to Jerry and stood in front of him. "What about the Franklin deal? Isn't that starting up?"

"Give it to Josh. He can handle it."

"You're giving up a big fee."

"As I said, this is not about money. It's about loyalty and duty. I'm old-fashioned, I guess. Kevin and my parents made a great home for me and made sure I got a terrific education. This is payback time."

Birney smiled, finally. "Okay, we'll do whatever you need."

Jerry stood up. Birney threw his arms around him and gave him a bear hug. "Take care of yourself, boychick. We need your ass back here. You're our star, even if you are crazy. Coordinate with Joan. She'll make everything happen. We'll reassign the members of your team on a temporary basis, but you can continue to touch base with them while you're away. I'll brief the other partners at the meeting on Friday." He gripped Jerry's hand again. "Good luck. Call me if you need anything. You're a hell of a guy. I know I wouldn't do it."

7

THURSDAY, JULY 5, 1990

Kevin met Jerry at LAX and helped with the luggage, the dog, and the rental car, and they drove to Marina Del Rey together. Jerry tried to give him the grand tour, but Kevin faded quickly these days. He took off for home, and Jerry noticed for the first time that he had a calm set of hours, lying wide open before him.

He showered, set his alarm clock for 5:00 p.m., and fell into bed. The cool ocean air stirred over his nude body. He could not help turning over in his mind the sequence of events that had brought him to this spartan California condo. He was a reluctant warrior, truly an Alyosha at heart. Yet his good intentions held no real currency with National's bank, creditors, and customers. He could not afford to be as passive as the youngest Karamazov. His family's name was riding on his ability to be a rational Ivan and a charismatic Dmitri—to be all the brothers at once.

He started to organize his ideas about the pending manager's meeting when his alarm sounded. He bounded out of bed, refreshed, grateful for having slept and prepared for the ensuing battle.

National's executive conference room was jammed. Thirty-five supervisors, middle managers, and senior managers were crowded two-deep around the twelve-foot conference table. Although conversations were whispered, there were so many of them that the room was loud. At 5:45 p.m., the three brothers entered the room and took the three unoccupied places at the head of the table. Kevin motioned for silence and the din subsided.

"Thanks for giving up your evening. We know it is an inconvenience to you and I want to make sure you convey our appreciation to your children, wives, and significant others. We expect to conclude by ten o'clock, so that you can all get home at a reasonable hour. Jerry?"

Kevin sat down and Jerry stood up and walked back a few steps to the wall unit that contained the flip charts.

"These are the ground rules," said Jerry. "The objective of this meeting is to make sure that all of the problems that might prevent us from making the numbers on our business plan are identified. I'm counting on the fact that everyone has parked their titles, politics, and prejudices outside this room and will join with me in the search for the truth. We are operating on a very short and a very tight tether, and we do not have the luxury of time to get this company back on track. This meeting is critical. What I need from each of you is total candor in discussing each and every operational problem that is affecting our order rate, our production rate, or our operating costs. I'll play scribe." He held up the magic marker pen. "We'll list the problems with a few descriptive words. We won't have the time to talk about solutions this evening, but if we can identify the majority of the problems, we will be well on our way toward addressing them. Any questions before we start?"

One of the product line managers raised her hand. "What if the problems originate outside my group, but they affect my group's production?"

"Good question, easy answer. Tell us about it. Don't expect the other supervisor to bring it up. He or she might not recognize the issue you're talking about as a problem. Don't worry about embarrassing anyone. We're fighting for survival. Any more questions?" He looked around the room for a hand. "None. Okay. There are thirty-five people in this room not counting Kevin, Jeff, and myself. Everybody gets five minutes to talk. Who wants to go first?"

Jerry had planted three shills in the group to ensure that there was some initial momentum. One raised his hand. "Frank, go ahead."

"We have a major problem in the shipping department. We are being charged back by our customers for not following their routing instructions. The charge-backs are running from twenty-five to fifty dollars a shipment. I have no idea how much this totals every month."

Jerry wrote on the flip chart, "Failure to follow customer shipping instructions." He turned to Howard, the acting CFO, who until recently was the controller reporting to the recently departed Bill Johnson.

"Do you have any numbers for this, Howard?"

Howard thought for a few moments. "In the range of ten to twenty thousand a month."

Jerry wrote "10K to 20K per month" on the chart. He turned to Frank. "Why can't we follow the customer's shipping instructions?"

Frank shrugged. "We haven't had the manpower to update the shipping programs with the latest information from the customers. It's at least a six-man-month job and the software departments can't spare the help. We've been asking for almost a year."

"You mean the customer routing information is at least a year out of date?" said Jerry.

"You got it," said Frank.

Jerry looked over to Jeff and Kevin. Kevin smiled sheepishly. Jeff was impassive. Jerry turned his attention back to the managers and smiled.

"Good input, Frank. That's why we're here. Who wants to go next?"

Geoff Mullin, manager of the special project software group, raised his hand. Geoff was not one of the shills. Jerry had hired him right out of Berkley, a typical apolitical, iconoclastic engineer.

"There is a huge fuck-up in accounting," Geoff said. "I was talking with one of the engineers at Lockheed yesterday about some custom software they want on the iris scanner project. In order to scope out the amount of dollars that would be involved, I went over to accounting to review the charges and billings for the custom package we did for Hughes. In the process of reviewing the numbers, I noticed that all the charge codes had been changed from a 'custom software' billable charge to a 'warranty non-billable charge.' No one in accounting could give me an explanation. We had over one hundred and ten thousand of non-reimbursed software charges into the Hughes job."

Jerry wrote, "Invoice for Hughes custom software—$110K." He asked the entire group, "Does anyone have any information on this issue?" Howard averted his eyes. The room was quiet. Finally Jeff spoke up.

"I authorized the change. We were very late on delivery. We needed to provide some accommodation to the customer because he was upset."

What Jerry wanted to do was turn to Jeff and scream that he was a fucking idiot giving up over one hundred thousand in billable dollars to kiss a customer's ass. He checked on Kevin, who shrugged.

Geoff muttered under his breath, just loud enough for Jerry and the people surrounding him to hear: "No wonder we're in deep shit. We're giving away the fucking store."

Jerry ignored the comment and looked for another volunteer. Bill Franklin, the accounting manager, spoke up.

"I don't think we need to buy all those season tickets for the Dodgers, Angels, Lakers, and Kings that are supposed to be for customers. I understand that most of the time, we can't find a customer to give them to, so the employees wind up getting them."

"Good point, Bill," said Jerry. Jerry turned to the flipchart and was in the act of writing on the chart when Jeff spoke up.

"Don't even write it down, Jerry. It's not on the table. It's a marketing tool. It's nobody's business what we do with those tickets."

"Jeff, to be consistent with the spirit of the meet..."

Jeff stood. "Fuck the spirit of the evening. You can write anything you want and we'll talk about it later." He looked at his watch. He looked around the room and said, "I'm sorry folks, but I have an important meeting that I could not rearrange. Good hunting." He nodded at Jerry and Kevin and left the conference room.

No one spoke. Kevin shook his head in disbelief. All eyes were turned toward Jerry, and Jerry observed the anxiety and confusion that began to build among the employees. He had to take action to save the meeting. So he decided to lie. He smiled at the group of managers.

"Jeff is meeting a potential investor who is only in town for an evening. He'll be working later than any of us, if you want to call eating and drinking at Scandia 'working.'"

Howard supported Jerry's cover story, and the ice was broken. The managers started laughing and telling each other stories on how clever Jeff was in avoiding "hard duty." Jerry decided then and there to leave something to Howard in his will. He allowed the jocularity to go on for several minutes and then reeled everyone back into the process of identifying problems.

The meeting droned on for three more hours. But the employees really got into the flow. When Jerry and Kevin decided to call it quits at 10:30 p.m., Jerry's magic marker pen had densely covered fifteen sheets of flip chart paper, all of which were affixed to the walls with tape.

When the last manager had left the conference room, Kevin stood in front of the magic marker wall with his hands on his hips, shaking his head.

"There are so many problems. It looks overwhelming."

Jerry clapped his back and tossed the pens on the side table. "We're too tired to think or talk about it. I've got to get home and feed Chelsey. We'll talk tomorrow."

Kevin came over and gave Jerry his signature bear hug. "You're a wonder Alyosha, just a wonder."

Jerry smiled. "Thanks. I think the meeting went well." He started to pull down the charts from the wall and stack them on the table. "Also, this will do a lot for morale. The managers now know that you and Jeff are serious about fixing the company." He stopped and looked directly at Kevin. "I hope this will help you feel better about the whole situation. You need to show more enthusiasm, for your employees' sake."

A tear started to trickle down the left side of Kevin's face. He nodded. "I'll try," he said. "I'll really try." He hugged Jerry again and wandered off to talk with a small group of managers that had congregated at the back of the room.

As Jerry continued to pack the product of the evening's work into his large briefcase, he thought back to the first time that he talked to Kevin about *The Brothers Karamazov*. It was on a Saturday several months before his seventeenth birthday. His parents were away for the weekend. He and Kevin were in the family room, watching a college football game, drinking Coronas, and munching on chips. When the game ended, Kevin asked him how school was going and whether he had come to any decisions as to what he wanted to study in college. As Jerry was describing his courses and his interests, he told Kevin about his having read *The Brothers Karamazov* in his World Literature class and that he had been absolutely fascinated by the novel. He asked Kevin if he had read it.

"No," said Kevin. "But I read *Crime and Punishment*."

"You should read *The Brothers Karamazov*. It's fucking uncanny how the main characters, the three brothers and the father, have the same personalities as we do. I'm not kidding. He wrote the novel in the 1880s, and it's as if he had our family in mind. It's eerie."

Kevin smiled at him. "Really made an impression on you, huh?"

"It explains Dad's craziness and Jeff's impulsiveness."

"And what about me?" said Kevin.

"You're Ivan, the middle brother—the intellectual, mediator, and brooder."

Kevin laughed. "And you, who are you?

"I'm Alyosha. The hero."

❖

Jeff steered his white Lexus carefully through the winding streets of Brentwood, wary and watchful as he'd been on any night patrol in Nam, taking care to stop completely at every stop sign. He knew that his blood alcohol was well over 0.08, thanks to the two bottles of *Beaujolais* he and Helen had consumed. The very last thing he needed was a DUI. He glanced at his watch. Nine thirty-five. Not bad. A very reasonable time for the breakup of a business dinner and the ride home. Salli would not have anything to harangue him with tonight.

He turned into the driveway of the two-story French provincial that consumed two-plus acres of prime Brentwood real estate. Every time Jeff entered the mini-estate, he heard Salli's insistence on the pretentious property, the support and maintenance of which kept him on the verge of bankruptcy. "You want us to live in some kind of affected poverty?" she'd said a hundred times. "We need this." He had agreed to the purchase of the home five years before during one of the many attempts at reconciling and revitalizing their failing marriage. The house cost him six thousand a month by the time he paid for the utilities, gardener, and pool service—more than one half of his after-tax from National. And all Salli did was sit on her trust fund. So for five years, he'd had to supplement his income by consulting a few days a month to various government intelligence agencies in order to stay solvent.

He sighed. More reasons to resent his wife. He parked the car in the garage and entered the house through the laundry room. Salli was in the den, curled up on the sofa, engrossed in the latest from John Grisham. The room was dim except for the lamp at the end of the sofa. Jeff stood at the door to see if she would acknowledge his presence. She didn't.

"Hi."

"Oh, I didn't hear you come in. You're home early."

"Yeah."

Salli returned to her book.

"Where are the girls?"

"In their rooms." She turned a page.

"What's new?"

"Not much." She looked at him, smiled, and then looked down at her book.

He stood there watching her ignore him. Who the fuck did she think she was? He'd been gone since 6:00 a.m. It was all he could do to keep himself from blurting out, "I just spent the last two hours fucking your sister—and it was great." He took a deep breath and waited a few seconds.

"I'm going upstairs to see the girls."

Salli kept her eyes fixed on her book. "Fine."

Jeff turned away and walked out to the entry hall. He stopped at the small table. A large silver tray held the day's mail. Jeff thumbed through the envelopes. Other than his paycheck from the Defense Intelligence Agency, all were bills: phone, electricity, window cleaning, landscaping, Jessie's ballet teacher, rug cleaning, and the catering service. He shook his head and replaced them on the tray, and then climbed the spiral staircase to the second floor where two bedrooms contained the only benefits and pleasures he derived from his marriage. He stopped at the first door on the right and knocked.

"Who is it?" a small voiced asked.

"The very most important man in your life."

"Daddy!" she shouted.

The door opened abruptly and nine-year-old Michelle jumped into his arms and hugged him.

"How are you, princess?"

"Fine, Daddy, how are you?"

"Great! Maybe just a little tired. How was school today, princess?"

"Okay, but Mrs. Forsythe assigned a research paper and it's causing me fits."

Jeff chuckled. "What kind of research, honey?"

"We're studying the Old West and she wants us to write a paper." She shuffled around in her backpack and pulled out the assignment sheet and read from it. "About how the lack of government regulations and control caused bad things to happen to the environment. And I don't know what to write about and I thought about it all night. Can you help me, Daddy?"

"Did you ask your mom?"

"She said you know a lot more about the West than she does. She said to ask you."

It was nice to know that Salli placed some value on his opinion. "Okay, princess, let me say hello to Jessie, and I'll come back, and we'll talk about it before you go to bed."

Jeff left her planted on her bed in the middle of her unpacked backpack and knocked on the adjacent door.

"Jessie, it's your dad."

"Come in, and welcome to the pit."

Jeff opened the door and was greeted by total chaos. Every drawer of every dresser was open; clothes were tossed over both twin beds; several carton boxes partially filled with clothes were lying on the floor. Jessie was standing in front of the full-length mirror, smoothing out her skirt and turning from side to side.

"What happened?" said Jeff. "It looks like a robbery."

"I'm rearranging my clothes. I've decided I need a new look and I'm going to purge any vestige of the old Jessica Bascomb. Mom says I'm due for some new clothes, and we're outing at Nordstrom's."

She was growing up. No longer a string bean, long-legged tomboy he could roughhouse with. Her evolving breasts, hips, and buttocks would require him to post guards.

"How's school?"

"Terrific! Got an A-plus on my Keats paper and a perfect score on the Civil War test."

He smiled and made the thumbs up sign. "You're on a roll," he said.

"You betcha. Oh, have you talked to Mom about my clothing allowance for the semester? The situation is critical. You might have noticed that I'm quickly running out of things that fit." The latter statement was made with just the trace of a seductive smile.

The combination of the statement and the smile made him feel awkward. He turned away to look at the box of relatively new clothes that were destined for Goodwill.

"She hasn't mentioned it yet."

"Please, Daddy, discuss it with her. I really, really need clothes."

"I'll talk with her tonight. Now give me a kiss goodnight."

Jessica jumped across the twin bed and threw her arms around him, catching him by surprise. She planted a big kiss on his unsuspecting lips and said, "Good night, sweet prince. And flights of angels sing thee to thy rest."

He continued holding her. "Great line, sounds like Shakespeare."

"Correct. Hamlet, Act Five, Scene Two. Horatio's farewell to Hamlet. It doesn't quite fit this situation since Hamlet was dying. But I love the sound of it."

He set her down and kissed her lightly on her lips. "Did anyone ever tell you that you were smart, Jessie?"

"And pretty, and popular, and athletic. That's why I need clothes to sustain my image."

"Okay. Okay. Goodnight." He gave her one last hug and released her.

As he walked out the door, he could not help but tell himself again, as he had so many times in the past, that Jessie had certainly inherited her mother's ability to be persistent. As he passed Michelle's room, he opened the door and said, "Buffalos."

Michelle looked up from her homework. "Buffalos?"

"Yeah, buffalos. There was no Endangered Species Act or laws protecting the wildlife, so settlers, tourists, hunters, farmers, and ranchers destroyed the buffalo herds in the last part of the nineteenth century. Since the Plains Indians depended on buffalos for food, clothing, and building materials, their entire culture was affected. Look into the destruction of the buffalo herds. It should make a great paper."

"Thanks, Daddy, I knew you'd come through for me. I'll look it up."

"Goodnight, princess."

Jeff descended the oak staircase to the family room. He poured three ounces of Absolut into one of his grandmother's crystal tumblers and then filled the glass with ice from the bar refrigerator. He went into the den. Salli was still engrossed in the book.

"Is there any specific reason you're ignoring me tonight?"

She looked up. "No, Jeff, no new reasons."

"I'd like to talk."

"Why? What's the point?"

"We can't continue to grate on each other, Salli. It's not good for us, and it's not good for the kids. We've got to try to get along."

"Okay, we'll talk," she said, closing her book and placing it on the table. "Provided you promise not to scream at me when I say something you don't agree with."

Jeff sat down on the large sofa that faced Sally's chair. "I hear you."

She leaned toward him. "Jeff, I'm expected to manage the household, pay all the bills, shop for food, feed and clothe the children, see to it that they get to the music lessons, their soccer games, and their gym meets, hire and fire the servants, entertain our friends periodically, monitor the kids' educational progress, and maintain contact with the various family members. I am willing, no I am happy, to do all of these tasks and take on any other burdens that are appropriate—but I can't do it for the funds you are providing. The checkbook is always close to a zero balance and I literally have to dance on the head of a pin to maintain relations with our various creditors. Our credit cards are maxed out. I'm tired of it all, Jeff. We cannot maintain our lifestyle on the income you are providing."

"I know things have been tight, but..."

"No, Jeff, things are beyond tight. The financial situation of this family is in extremis." Salli leaned forward, her face contorted into an angry grimace. "We cannot go on this way. We are living way beyond our means. You need to do something." She pointed her finger at his chest. "We need more money. It's your job to provide it. The kids need new clothes; we have to make a deposit for our Thanksgiving vacation in Maui; the gardener presented me with an estimate of fifteen hundred dollars for the fall plantings." She ticked off the various expenses on her fingers. "I can't juggle any more." She leaned back into the sofa. "I need a drink. Please fix me a gin and tonic."

"You usually don't drink this late," he said.

"I need a palliative to deal with this unpleasantness."

Jeff went over to the bar, prepared Salli's drink, and brought it over to her.

She took the glass. "Thanks." She took a long drink that emptied one half of the tumbler. She set the glass down on the coffee table.

"Salli, we've talked about this before. I'm doing the best I can."

"That doesn't help. We created this lifestyle on the assumption that we could pay for it." She sat back in her chair and folded her hands across her lap.

"I'm happy to see you use the 'we' word."

"We did it together, on the assumption that your income would support it. It hasn't and it doesn't."

"Dammit Salli, between consulting and National, we are netting twelve thousand a month after taxes." He was talking too loud again. He stood up and pushed his hands in his pockets. "I can't get any more money now."

"What about a raise from National? It's been over three years since your last raise. I'm sure Kevin would agree."

"That's not possible. The bank agreement froze our salaries. Raises are deferred until we can refinance the company."

"What about increasing your consulting efforts? If you did another two days a month we could make it." She'd been thinking about this for a while, it seemed.

He sat back down in the chair. He took a sip of his drink. "Can't do it, Salli. The pressure at National is going to be super-intense during the next six months. I simply can't take any more time off."

"You're not helping, Jeff. Do you suggest I ask the girls to mow lawns? Or should we try to rent the spare room?"

"Come off it, Salli. You know you could use some of your trust income to carry us over the hump." As the words came out, he knew he was making a mistake. That remark was guaranteed to lead to a humungous argument, a period of stony silence, and a freeze on all sexual favors. But in the absence of any other creative idea, he pressed on. "You could give the family a small portion of the two hundred thousand a year you earn for a short period until we..."

Salli's eyes widened, her face turned red, and she clenched her jaw, so that her lower teeth protruded. "Forget it, Jeff. That is not going to happen. I already put one and a quarter million, over twenty percent of my trust fund, into National, and frankly, based on what's happened, I don't really expect to get it back. Not another fucking cent, Jeff."

"Why not? It doesn't make sense. You don't need the money. The family needs it. You know that I'll pay you back. It's logical."

Salli reached for her gin and tonic, lifted the glass to her lips and sipped it. Clutching the glass in her hand, she turned on him again. She spoke in a calm, deliberate, and controlled voice. "It's my money, Jeff, and it's being invested in accordance with the recommendations of my financial advisor. It's to ensure us a good retirement, assuming we're together in retirement." She took another sip of her drink. "And if we're not, it's to ensure me a good retirement. And it's to ensure that our two girls are independently wealthy and that they don't have to marry some testosterone-drunk bozo to survive." She drained the glass and returned it to the coffee table. "It is not going to be used to pay household bills or to bail you out of the financial morass you've gotten us into as a consequence of your mismanagement of National. My trust fund income is off the fucking table." She pointed her finger at him again. "You wanted to marry me. You wanted children, the country club, the big house, and all that goes with it. I bought your story, now make good on it. Provide or get the fuck out."

Salli had spoken the last four or five sentences slowly and in a steady voice. Only the intensity of her glare and the set of her jaw revealed how angry she was. She picked up her book and began reading again. Her hands didn't even shake.

Jeff stared at Salli. His faced flushed and his heartbeat accelerated. His palms were damp. He took a deep breath. "Okay. I don't agree with you. I don't like it, but it's your money. I just thought..."

"Stop talking about it, stop thinking about it. As far as you are concerned, my money doesn't exist." She had not looked up from her book.

He had agreed to provide for his family. Like he agreed to protect his men, like he agreed to make sure two hundred and fifty employees received their paychecks. He had done his job under worse conditions than these. He was more than just a good peddler.

"How much do we need?"

Like a light that had been switched off, Salli was again calm and spoke in her pronounce-every-syllable voice that was typical of every graduate of East Coast female prep schools.

"We need five thousand immediately. We will need about seventy-five hundred more by the end of August and another five thousand by the end of September. That should cover it."

Jeff swirled the ice in his glass and took a drink. He ran his hand across his brow and let out a sigh. "I'll talk to Kevin. I'm sure he will lend me the money until the company turns around."

"One other thing, Jeff. We need to make reservations for Maui. I've talked with Betsy, and she and Jim would like to stay at the Kanapalli Alihi during the week of November 25—the week of Thanksgiving. It's his fiftieth birthday, and she wants us to join them. We're going to take the kids out of school for the three days prior to the Thanksgiving recess. They are all top students, so I don't think the school will hassle us. We can get a three-bedroom condo. We'll each have a bedroom and the four girls can share a room. Does that work for you?"

"I may have a problem taking off, you know, considering the company's situation."

"Don't give me that crap. You will take that week off. Betsy and Jim are our best friends and it's very important to them. Just tell Kevin to plan on it."

"It's Jerry's call now."

"Well, tell Jerry, unless you want me to tell him."

It was all Jeff could do to avoid telling Salli to fuck off. "I'll take care of it." His voice trailed off and sounded so far away from him he didn't even recognize it.

"Everything is set then, right?"

"Yes."

Salli turned her attention back to her book. He had been dismissed. He stared at her for several moments. Then he got up and walked into the family room and turned on CNN. As he watched the late news, he slowly sipped his drink. He replayed the evening with Helen and slipped into the pleasant fantasy of her body, wishing she were with him now.

8

MONDAY, JULY 9, 1990

Jerry woke up groggy from the sleeping pill he'd taken at three in the morning, and punched at the numbers on the phone. Kevin, for once, sounded better than he did, and they set up a time that afternoon to hash out the management meeting data.

It was a Greek tragedy. The gods had conspired and made their decisions. He was just playing his part. He knew the drill; he just did not like the moves. The information that came to light during the meeting proved that the showdown with Jeff could not be put off any longer. The company was bleeding profusely due to Jeff's hubris and reckless management style. Same old shit, he thought. As he had told Sheila, nothing really had changed.

By four-thirty that afternoon, Jerry had drunk enough cups of coffee to feel like himself. He walked into Kevin's office, carrying several large notebooks and files. Jeff was sitting in front of Kevin's desk. His feet were propped up on the desk, and he was smoking a large cigar. He blew a smoke circle in Jerry's direction. "Hiya, bro, how ya doing?" he said. He clenched the cigar between his teeth, rose out of the chair, and helped Jerry deposit his books and files on the small conference table.

"Fine. How did your meeting work out last night?"

Jeff grinned. "Great, just great! We may get a new customer out of it."

Jerry continued to arrange the books on the conference table and did not look at Jeff. It was time to start pissing on each other's legs again, and he hoped that Kevin was up to keeping the peace.

"You know, you could have told us you planned to bail out of the meeting, Jeff. Kevin and I looked like a couple of jerks."

Jeff took the cigar out of his mouth and flicked off the ash into a Styrofoam coffee cup. "Slipped my mind, Jerry. It just slipped my mind. What are we meeting about? Kevin didn't seem to know."

Kevin was staring out the window. Jerry sighed and handed Kevin and Jeff several pages of computer spreadsheets and waited.

Several minutes passed and Jeff spoke. "Do you plan to decipher this for me, or are we going to play twenty questions?"

Kevin just continued to study the report.

"Let's look at Table One first," said Jerry. "This is a printout of all the problems that were identified by the managers and supervisors. The first column names the problem, the second identifies the supervisor or executive who raised it during the meeting, the third column identifies the person who is most knowledgeable about the problem, and the fourth column is an estimate of the lost revenue or increased cost that can be attributed to the problem over the past year. The last column contains a code that identifies the probable source of the problem.

"Table Two aggregates the dollar impact of each of the codes. You can see that the estimate of the total of all the codes is $2.45 million."

Jeff whistled. "No shit. That is a big number."

"It's about one half of next year's forecasted profit," said Jerry. Kevin continued to stare at the computer sheets with the same expression he'd given the view out the window and remained silent.

"Where's the explanation of the codes?" asked Jeff.

"I have them here." Jerry handed Kevin and Jeff an additional sheet.

Jeff looked at the new sheet for a moment and then a deep, angry scowl engulfed his face. Here it comes, Jerry thought.

"What kind of bullshit is this?" He threw the new sheet on the table. "You are out of your fucking mind and your numbers are off the wall." He got out of his chair and stalked toward the end of the table, turned and faced Jerry, and pounded his hand on the table. "I am not responsible for 70 percent of the problems. No way! Bullshit!" He threw his hands into the air. "Bullshit! Bullshit!" Jeff was almost screaming. His face was the crimson of bad sunburn. The veins on his forehead stood out. Kevin sat quietly and studied the spreadsheets.

Jerry stared at Kevin, hoping for some kind of reaction. No help here. He turned back to Jeff.

"To be precise, your edicts, deviations from company policies, side deals, and clandestine research cost the company about one million, eight hundred thousand last year, or 73 percent of the two and one half million that has been pissed away. These are not my numbers. These are the numbers that the executives and managers estimated."

"I don't give a shit whose numbers they are, it's still bullshit. God damn, Kevin, you know it's bullshit."

Jerry and Jeff both looked at Kevin in anticipation of some response. Kevin continued to stare at the documents. Jeff walked back to his chair, picked up his copies of the spreadsheets, and threw them into the wastepaper basket next to Kevin's desk. He walked over to the window and looked out.

"I am so fucking angry, Jerry. We bust our asses for years and build the business and you come in here, not knowing anything about the current state of the market, and point your finger at me and say that I'm to blame for whatever is fucked up. You're unbelievable."

The crest of Jeff's anger had passed. Jerry waited a few minutes, and then, in the most non-judgmental voice he could muster, said, "You are not looking at the report in the proper spirit of the exercise. I'm not accusing you or anyone else. I'm just reporting what the managers stated to Kevin and me at the meeting. I'm only the messenger. If you don't like the message, don't pillory me. It will not solve the problem."

Jeff plugged his cigar back between his teeth, crossed his arms, and watched the view. Kevin continued to finger through the documents.

"Look, Jeff," said Jerry. "Whatever you and Kevin have done or failed to do in building this company is history. But we have a new calculus now. The company is fighting for survival. Let's sit down and calmly review these situations to see what we can do to improve things in the future and start chopping away at the two and one half million dollar problem." Jerry looked over to Kevin to see of he was paying attention. Kevin had placed the computer printouts on the table, picked up a pencil, and was doodling on a yellow tablet. Jeff turned away from the window and walked out of the room without saying anything.

The brothers sat at the table for several minutes. Jerry closed his eyes and listened to the sound of his breathing, the sound of his heart slowing down.

"Kevin, the company cannot go on like this. It will surely die. We must reign in Jeff."

"I know, I know. But I can't deal with it, with him." Kevin's eyes were unfocused.

"Then I'll deal with it, Kev. But you'll have to back me up. Understand?"

Long silence. Finally Kevin sighed. "Okay, but just let me know what you're going to do before you do it."

"Agreed." Jerry picked up his notebooks and files and started to walk out of the office.

"Jerry, please close the door."

Jerry looked over his shoulder. Kevin was sitting with his elbows on the table, holding his head in his hands.

"Right," he said. He walked through the doorway and then carefully closed the door behind him, leaving Kevin to battle his own demons.

As he opened his condo door, Chelsey greeted him with her big tail wagging. She let out a yip and planted her front paws on his chest. Finally, a friendly face. He crouched down and placed his hands on both sides of her head and allowed her to lick his chin.

"What would I do without you, girl?"

She ran over to the living room sofa, picked up the leash in her mouth, and brought it to him.

"Okay, girl, we'll go in a minute."

He walked through the living room to the balcony. It was large enough to accommodate the latrine he had set up—two layers of indoor-outdoor carpeting that he could rinse out and scrub as needed. Chelsey had pooped. He took a plastic shopping bag from the kitchen drawer, picked up the poop, and wrapped it tightly inside the bag. He clipped the leash on her collar and let her out the door, down the stairs and onto the grounds. He walked her around the back where the garbage bins were located and dropped the bag into the bin. The sun was close to the horizon and lit the furled sails of the boats tied up below. There was only about thirty minutes of daylight left. He decided to walk the mile or so to the convenience store and pick up a six-pack of Coronas—anything to get his mind off of the civil war.

He returned to the condo about eight. The sky was dark, but the lights from the boats and the boat slips illuminated the paths along the marina. As he opened the door, he was once again struck at how soulless the place was. He put two beers into the freezer and the remainder in the refrigerator.

The condominium consisted of a living area with a kitchen, living room, and half bath. There was a large master bedroom suite and a small second bedroom that Jerry was using as his office. He had moved in a desk, chairs, and file cabinets from National and it was already cluttered with papers and notebooks. The master bedroom and living room opened to the large balcony. The condo was furnished in blond oak with dark beige carpeting. The pictures on the wall were of landscapes, flowers, and boat scenes. The carpeting was new and smelled faintly of chemicals. The few pictures and photos that Jerry had brought from New York did not make a significant dent on the antiseptic Motel Six ambience. He made a mental note to call Helen.

He mixed six ounces of kibble and four ounces of canned dog food with warm water and placed it on the floor of the kitchen and called Chelsey over to eat. He took a beer out of the freezer, grabbed a yellow tablet from the desk, turned on CNN, and sat down on the sofa to watch TV and write the memo over which he'd been agonizing. After an hour and a half and two more beers, he had written three lines including the salutation. No matter how he edited it, he could not achieve the proper balance between the message that this was a new day at National and still honor the contributions of Jeff and Kevin. His muse had abandoned him in his hour of need. He put down the pen, grabbed the leash, and headed to the door with Chelsey for her pre-bedtime walk.

When he arrived at the office the next morning at ten, he approached Shirley, the longtime executive assistant. She was in her mid-thirties, attractive, and slightly overweight. She was divorced, had a daughter already in her teens, and made National the biggest part of her day. She had been with the company for over ten years and was a close confidante of his brothers. When she saw him, she smiled a bright, sincere good morning.

"Shirley, please draft the following memo for review by Kevin and Jeff. 'To all administrative and management personnel. Effective immediately, no deviations from company policies and procedures regarding product or service pricing, credit, etc. will be permitted unless prior approval is received in writing from Jerry Bascomb. Any manager or administrator who fails to adhere to written policies and procedures or who fails to obtain clarification of policies and procedures when they are ambiguous will be severely disciplined. Discipline may include termination. Set up signature lines for Kevin, Jeff, and myself."

Shirley finished typing and looked up at Jerry.

"Sounds pretty tough."

"It's meant to be. Please give it to Kevin when he comes in, and call me as soon as he acts on it."

Jerry turned away, walked across the hall and into his office, and shut the door. He sat down at his desk. He looked over at his inbox. Reports, memoranda, and mail created a pile over a foot high. He thumbed through the documents, pulled the top sheet off the pile, and began to read.

Ten minutes later, he realized that he had read the same paragraph several times. Jeff's passive-aggressive resistance was way beyond anything that he could have anticipated. No—he *did* anticipate it, but he had talked himself into believing that he could handle Jeff. He had even bragged to Shelia that his ability to deal with Jeff was one of the unique skills he brought to the table. He had been full of shit. He couldn't manage Jeff. Nobody could—other than his commanding officers in the military. The guy was a fucking loose cannon, Dimitri Fyodorovich redux.

Chased by frustration, he wandered down to the cafeteria, poured a cup of coffee, and sat for a few minutes reading the *L.A. Times*. He refilled his cup and headed back to the office, jittery and anxious, and still determined to focus on his inbox. He pulled the next document off the pile and began to read it. Ten minutes later, he was still reading the first paragraph. Even when he could sit still, his thoughts were being chased anywhere but to the work at hand. He tossed the document onto the pile, sat back in his chair, placed his feet on his desk, and closed his eyes.

The intercom buzzer startled him. Shirley announced, "Jerry, Howard needs to see you."

"I'm busy, Shirl. I need to plow through the junk in my in basket. Ask him if it can wait."

Shirley came back on the phone a few moments later and told Jerry that Howard would see him tomorrow morning. Jerry hated himself when he lied. But he felt too agitated to meet with anyone. He could not concentrate until this issue with Jeff was resolved. Dammit! How long did Kevin have to wallow in it? Jerry lifted himself out of his desk chair. He unbuckled his belt and straightened out his shirt, tightened his belt, zipped his fly, and checked his watch. It was close to noon. The waiting was driving him to every distraction in the book. He even dialed Helen, but got her answering machine.

He told Shirley that he was going home for lunch. He drove back to his condo, picked up Chelsey, and drove to the beach. He spent the next two and a half hours walking in the sand, enjoying the smells and sounds of the ocean and the sights of the bikini clad women. When Jerry returned to the office, he stopped at Shirley's desk. He noticed that Kevin's door was shut. "Shirl, is Kevin in?"

"Yes, but he's meeting with Jeff."

"Christ. Okay, tell him to call me when he's free."

A half hour later, Kevin was finally free. As Jerry passed her desk, he noticed that Shirley gave him a quizzical glance. Kevin was sitting at his desk holding his head in his hands. Jerry waited until the silence got awkward.

"Well?"

Kevin did not look up. "He won't sign the memo. He says it's a personal attack on him and a repudiation of his management style and he will not be a contributor to his own humiliation. He says that we can do anything we want and he'll cooperate."

Jerry was not surprised. In fact he was almost relieved—he felt the pressure in his mind lessen, knowing that his estimation of his brother was correct, as always. Jeff would continue to defy him every step of the way.

Jerry said, "So, now what?"

Kevin didn't respond.

"For God's sake, Kevin, we can't just sit on our hands. We have to address the problem or we will lose all credibility with the staff and ultimately with the bank. Jeff can't continue to run roughshod over the company's policies and procedures and piss the company's money away." Kevin still did not respond. "Kevin, I'm going to issue the memo over my signature. Will you co-sign it?" Kevin slowly raised his head from his hands. His eyes were red and wet. The weight that Jerry had felt pressing on his chest got heavier. Kevin was starting to buckle.

Finally he nodded. Jerry walked behind his desk, placed his hand on his shoulder, and bent down and kissed him on the cheek.

"I'm sorry, Kev. I know that this is tearing you apart."

Kevin placed his hand over Jerry's and nodded and started to cry. Again. Jerry stood next to him for a while, and then left the office, and closed the door behind him. He handed the memo to Shirley and said, "I'd like it distributed tomorrow before nine. Kevin and I will sign it."

Shirley looked up, surprised.

"Not Jeff?"

"No, he said. "Call Howard and tell him I'll see him now."

9

The Donatello's Jacuzzi was hot. Jeff had complained to the hotel staff earlier in the day, but they had not yet fixed the problem. Helen did not seem to mind. Neither did the other couple that was sharing the Jacuzzi with them.

"Don't you find it awfully hot?" said Jeff.

"About the same as last time," Helen replied.

"Seems a lot hotter to me."

He sat at the side of the Jacuzzi with his legs straddling her shoulders. "Live in the area?" asked the man.

"We're from LA. What about you?" Jeff replied.

"Vancouver."

"Washington or Canada?"

"Canada."

"Beautiful country." Jeff hated small talk, especially when he was horny. But he couldn't stand up to go to the restroom. "I vacationed in Victoria about three years ago. My wife loved the gardens and the scenery." Stupid, he thought. Don't mention your wife. "I mean my ex-wife. She loved the Butchart Gardens." Helen turned her head and flashed that ultra white seductive smile.

"Did you catch the latest news?" said the man.

"What news?"

"Saddam is accusing Kuwait of stealing his oil. Bush called up the reserves last week. Looks like trouble."

"Yeah," said Jeff. "I hope Bush follows through and shows the bastard we're serious."

"What do you mean by follow through?" said the man.

"I mean if they invade Kuwait, drive the bastards out for starters."

The man did not respond immediately. "You military?" he asked.

"Ex-military, 173rd Airborne."

"It figures." The man turned to his wife. "Honey, I'm waterlogged. I'm ready to go." The man's wife lifted herself over the side of the Jacuzzi. She was beet red. She disappeared into the women's dressing room, and the man walked up the steps of the Jacuzzi, nodding to Jeff and Helen. He was the color of boiled shrimp. His feet flapped on the tile as he rounded the corner into the dressing room.

"Thank God they're gone," said Jeff. "Loathsome people."

"Why did you ever quit the military? I remember you at the wedding, decked out in your uniform. You were so gung-ho."

"It's a long, complicated story."

"I remember asking Salli about it shortly after you quit, and she just brushed it off."

"I told her not to talk about it to anyone. Our story was that the opportunity Kevin was giving me was so enticing that I decided to take the plunge."

"So what was the real story?"

"When I was deployed in Vietnam in 1970, I commanded a platoon. During a patrol to set an ambush for the VC, one of my men, a guy named Rodrigues, panicked, started to yell, and ran. I ran after him, and in the course of attempting to get him under control, I accidentally killed him."

"You killed him? How?

"I stuffed a bandana in his mouth. He suffocated."

"Ugh. How horrible."

"Yeah. For all of us."

"What happened?"

"There was an investigation, and I was cleared. Rodrigues' death was ruled to be accidental. That was all very nice, but it left a pretty big mark on my record. Basically, the Army agreed that I wasn't a criminal, but I was still a klutz that killed one of his own soldiers."

"So, why did you leave the Army?"

"Around the time of the wedding, Sid learned that it was unlikely that I would ever be promoted beyond the rank of lieutenant colonel. I talked with Kevin and he offered me the National marketing job. I figured—correctly, as it turned out—that persuading general officers to support the projects that I promoted was a good foundation for selling National and its products. I took Kevin's offer and the rest is history."

"I'm so sorry, Jeff. The Army was your life."

"Yes, it was. And it was a great life while it lasted. Except for the tour in Vietnam. I was very, very lucky to get out of there alive, and with all my body parts intact—unlike several hundred thousand of other guys whose body parts are strewn all over the Vietnamese landscape. And speaking of body parts that are intact..." He slipped into the tub and pulled off his trunks and started to pull off Helen's bikini bottoms.

"You're crazy, Jeff, what if someone walks in?"

"They won't be able to see through the foam and the bubbles and I'll keep my trunks close, so that I can slip them on."

"Are you planning to fuck me in this Jacuzzi?"

"The thought crossed my mind."

Helen laughed and pushed him away. "Forget it. I don't like to live that dangerously. I'll keep my pants on. You'll just have to wait 'til we go downstairs."

"Okay, then fondle me." He pulled her down into the tub and he placed her hand on his erection.

"I can't believe you." She pulled her hand away. "You act as if you're celibate when you're not on a date with me."

"You're not helping me." He pulled his trunks back on. "Anyway, being married to your sister is about as close to celibacy as it gets."

"Don't bullshit me. I know you have sex with her. She tells me all the lurid details."

"She enjoys talking about it more than she does doing it. Everything has got to be perfect for Salli to screw. She can't be pissed off at me, her trust fund has got to show good earnings, the kids have to behave, and on and on. It's obvious that you two inherited your sex drives from your fathers." He put his arms around her back and tried to draw her closer. She didn't fight him off and they stood in the Jacuzzi with their arms around each other.

"You could have married me, Jeff, and never gone wanting."

"Don't think I haven't thought about it." He kissed her on the lips and pressed his body into hers. She felt the same to him as she'd felt the night he invited her to the embassy dinner as Salli's little sister, a chaste substitute while Salli was out of town. He was still only a fiancé then. That night she'd coaxed him into her apartment and fixed him a drink, and as she offered it to him, she smiled broadly, and with her other hand, quickly unzipped his fly, slipped her fingers under his briefs and gripped his already stiffening penis. Jeff looked at her in what was for him a unique state of mind—astonishment. Her eyes glistened and her white broad smile smiled at him in a way that he'd never seen in Salli. *I just wanted to see if you were as well-endowed as your reputation would have a girl believe.* Jeff was speechless. He had briefly considered removing her hand and chastising her for her behavior. But while he held on to his drink, Helen quickly pushed his pants aside and started kissing and licking. Within a very few minutes both of them had their clothes off and Jeff was fucking his future sister-in law.

Helen placed her foot behind his ankle and pushed him, and he tumbled backward into the water. When he surfaced, she was giggling, proud of her ability to best the warrior.

"Your sex drive may be strong, but your greed is, too. There is no way you would have passed up a five million dollar trust fund even if she never fucked you." Jeff smiled. He lunged at her and tried to pull down her bikini bottoms, but she pushed him away.

"Don't you worry about Salli finding out about us?"

"Don't you?" said Jeff.

"Hell, no. She couldn't possibly show me less affection than she has shown me for the past thirty years. And I don't have the income from a five million dollar trust fund at risk. But you—you have everything on the line. She'd probably cut you off, figuratively and literally. That would be a shame." She dove under the water and pulled down his suit. She came back up and pressed her body against him. "I think we better get you downstairs before we're raided." And she lifted herself out of the Jacuzzi, water streaming down her body.

Later that evening, they occupied a table at The Posteria, Wolfgang Puck's bistro located a half-block up Post Street from the Donatello. They both ordered glasses of Chardonnay, small salads, and angel hair pasta with sun-dried tomatoes and garlic. The discussion during most of the meal centered on National and its problems. But, as they were completing the meal, Helen put down her glass and folded her hands under the table, and took a long breath.

"What is it?" he said.

"Jeff, I've decided that I want to end our affair."

He felt that he had been hit in the gut, and he felt a sequel to the astonishment that had begun their relationship so many years before.

She didn't give him time to answer. "I don't want to see you anymore. I mean, see you sexually. I've enjoyed our relationship, but I've got to get on with my life."

He cleaned up the last few bits of food without tasting and without speaking.

She added, "I can't continue to rely on you to relieve my sexual frustrations and protect me from getting romantically involved."

He took a sip of wine to wash down the last few morsels, and wiped his lips.

"Why now?" His voice was gruff, but the wine was a good cover. He took another sip.

"Now is as good a time as any. I feel that I'm over my divorce. I'm ready to move on." Her wineglass was almost empty. She pointed to the glass, and said, "I'd like another."

"Don't you feel anything about me?"

He was whining, but Helen had come with a prepared speech. "Sure, I really like you," she said. "You've been the rock I could lean on these past six months. The sex has been fantastic. You're a phenomenal lover. I mean you can go on for hours. But you're my sister's husband and I've never thought that our relationship was more than a mutually convenient affair. It's been an escape valve for your miserable, near-celibate life with Salli, and it provided me with a safe source of companionship and sexual satisfaction. You know, like a halfway house between relationships. But I need to find someone stable, get married, have kids, and join the PTA." She laughed once, perhaps at herself. "Jeff, I need to get a life."

Jeff drained his glass and motioned for more wine. "Is there anyone else?"

"This is not about anyone else. It's about what I need for myself. But in the interest of full disclosure, I hope to develop a relationship with Jerry."

Jeff's face flushed. "I'm not surprised. I noticed that you were all taken up with him at Carolyn's dinner." He looked over his shoulder to see where his wine was. "Have you fucked him yet?"

"Come off of the victim role, Jeff. You know I'm serially monogamous. I've had one G-rated dinner with him and I've talked with him several times on the phone. And we've met for coffee twice. That's it. But I like him and I think he likes me."

"Why Jerry?"

"Why not? He's attractive, intelligent, makes a lot of money, has wide cultural interests, and if I'm really lucky, he'll have a sex drive like yours."

Jeff strained a laugh. "Don't count on it." The waitress appeared at the table with the glasses of wine. He sipped at it slowly, calculating whether Helen was really serious. Jerry. The traitor. The flatfoot's remark in the Jacuzzi lingered in Jeff's mind, and he thought of the time in Vietnam, on his leave, when his father had flown to Bangkok and they talked about Jerry's March for Peace in Stockholm. Once a traitor, always a traitor. Why should I be surprised that the little fucker did it again? he thought.

Helen must have believed that she could read his mind, and said, "Cheer up, Jeff. This isn't the first time we've broken it off." The clink of the silverware reminded him where he was. "Are you still here, Jeff?"

He focused on Helen's eyes. "Just daydreaming."

"What about?"

"The first time we made love."

"I was pretty aggressive, wasn't I?" She smiled at him. "It was crazy—we were crazy—sneaking off all the time to screw right up to the wedding."

"'Til the morning of the wedding when you told me you were feeling guilty and wanted to break up."

"Christ, you were marrying my sister. We had to stop sometime."

"You weren't too guilty to call me after you got to LA and offer to start up again. Did you leave all your scruples in Europe?" Jeff did not like the way his last sentence came out, thick with sarcasm and weakness.

Helen sat back, shaken. "Jeff, I'm not proud of the fact that I betrayed Salli. I excused my behavior before the wedding by telling myself I was a kid and this was recreational fucking and no one was really being hurt. Besides, I hated her and what better way to get back than to fuck her fiancé." She paused and closed her eyes for an instant. "This time was different. I never thought about Salli. I thought about myself and the fact that I needed a companion. I knew you were unhappy and you'd be available and, what was the most important thing to me, you'd be safe. You helped me, I helped you. But I don't want to go on any longer. Come on," she said, brightening. "Let's enjoy the rest of the evening."

He took another sip of his wine. He forced a smile that he didn't really feel and reached across the table, grasped her hand, and mouthed okay.

Jerry entered the spacious corner office of Sheila Crown, twenty-five floors above the Los Angeles freeway honeycomb. He carried a large briefcase stuffed with National financial reports and analyses, ready to deliver his first report to the bank. Sheila was dressed sharply in a forest green pants suit, matching green earrings, gold bangle bracelets, and green alligator heels. The dense green of her suit and earrings focused his attention on what she probably considered her best asset—her green eyes. She was attractive and apparently not above using her looks and presence at work.

"Hello, Jerry. It is so good to see you again. I've made arrangements for lunch at the bank's executive dining room. Is that okay with you?"

"That's fine."

She led the way to the elevator lobby, and they took the elevator to the top. The dining room might have been an extension of Kevin's den: hunting scenes, tapestries, dark paneling, and mahogany furniture. The ceilings were at least fourteen feet high. The room was windowed floor to ceiling, providing a panoramic bird's-eye view of the LA smog. Jerry ordered his typical Diet Coke and Sheila ordered an iced tea.

When the waiter went off for the drinks, Sheila said, "How are things going, Jerry? Any regrets?"

"Hectic, but no regrets."

"What have you been spending your time on these last few weeks?"

"Three weeks and two days to be exact." He laughed.

"You are precise."

"It's my engineering training. Most of my efforts have been devoted to trying to understand how the company operates and how money is spent. The company does not have any functional forecasting or budget system. So it was pretty difficult to do projections on a routine basis. I've added two analysts to Howard's finance department, and we should be able to have a forecasting and budgeting system functional in about two weeks."

"How's the order rate?"

"Good. Bookings are running above last year's rate and prices are steady. We should exceed last year's sales by at least 5 percent."

"How's the relationship going with you, Jeff, and Kevin?"

It seemed to Jerry that she was more interested in ticking off a list of questions than the content of the answers he was providing. The waiter arrived at the table with the drinks. They both ordered salmon filets and dinner salads. "There was a nineteenth-century French novelist by the name of Jean-Baptiste Alphonse Karr," Jerry said. "His comments about marriage and family are often quoted. The most famous one is, 'The more things change, the more they remain the same.' This pretty much sums up our family dynamics. We've settled into our traditional roles—Jeff wants to shoot the moon. I try to hold him back. Kevin plays the peacemaker and compromiser. Kevin and I have always had a good working relationship, and Jeff and I yell at each other a lot. But Jeff realizes that I'm the key to his survival, and although he may hate it, he is working with me."

Sheila appeared unaffected by his effort to respond honestly. "How have you progressed on the memorandum for lenders and investors?"

In an effort to slow the pace of the questions, Jerry dropped his knife on the floor. "I'm a klutz," he said. He leaned over and picked it up, wiped both sides of it with his napkin, and set it on the table. "I'm sorry, Sheila, I missed your question."

She smiled at him. "The memorandum for lenders and investors?"

"Right," he said. "We're making good progress. We've completed a draft of the text without the projections. I expect that we'll have a complete draft in three weeks and we'll start circulating the memorandum within the month." He let himself drone somewhat, offering a touch too much detail to every point he raised, smiling often in an attempt to relax Sheila away from her inquisition. She acted interested, but when their food arrived, she used the interruption to shut him down.

"That all sounds fine, Jerry. Any major problems?" Skepticism crept into her voice, implying she wouldn't believe news that was too good to be true.

"I've been pleasantly surprised. National is really a very good company—it's got good products and great customer relationships. Technical, marketing, and manufacturing personnel are strong. Of course financial management and controls were nonexistent. But in light of what happened, that's no surprise."

Sheila laughed. "No kidding. You know, the one thing about this deal that surprised me was how our bank could have gotten in so deep with a company whose financial capabilities appeared to predate the fifteenth century invention of double entry bookkeeping."

"*Touché*," said Jerry, smiling. He continued, "and it should come as no surprise that National has grown beyond the capability of top management to lead. Kevin was a terrific president when the company was small, under ten million in sales. And when Kevin ran out of steam, Jeff filled the void and grew the company to its current size. But outside of marketing, Jeff is not really trusted or respected. The engineers don't like him because he uses them as scapegoats for contracts he underbids, and he treats the manufacturing personnel as if they were automata, devoid of thinking and reasoning capacity. In my opinion, neither Kevin nor Jeff has the leadership ability to grow the company beyond its present level."

"Won't that affect your ability to refinance?"

He thought for a moment. He looked down at his plate and realized that he'd been so busy responding to Sheila's bandolier of questions that he had barely touched his food. He took a drink from his water glass. "I'm certainly not going to share my opinion with a new bank or an investor, and I hope that Jeff's line of bullshit will charm them out of their money."

Sheila took her napkin from her lap, wiped her lips, and placed the napkin on the table. She looked directly into Jerry's eyes. "What about you, Jerry?"

He wasn't sure what she meant. "Me?"

"Yes, you become CEO and lead the company."

Jerry chuckled. "No thanks. I've got a job that I love, and it pays well. Besides, having to work with Jeff over the long term would be purgatory for both of us. I just want to be the uncompensated workout manager in this deal. I don't have any other aspirations."

"You're certain?"

"Absolutely. But why do you ask?"

She sat back in her chair. "Well, the bank might reconsider its position with respect to National if it installed a CEO in whom we had confidence."

He was surprised. Sheila smiled. He waited a minute, so that he would choose just the right words to respond.

"Sheila," he said, "I appreciate the vote of confidence, but please don't make the offer. I meant what I said. I'm only in this deal until I can extricate my family from the financial mess. And then it's *adios, ciao, aufwederzehn, shalom*, or whatever. I have no interest in a permanent gig as National's CEO. I like my freedom."

Sheila held up her hand to stop him. "I understand, but I want you to know that it's an option. And..." she said, "And I certainly don't have to tell you that National needs all the options it can get."

Jerry took her meaning. In truth, there was no guarantee that National would be refinanced or sold within a time frame acceptable to the bank, and if it were not, he would have to scramble to find other options. The waiter came by with refills and more bread. Sheila was interested in the intricacies of the investment banking industry and Jerry was happy to talk about something that he knew and enjoyed. After lunch, they made their goodbyes, and Jerry agreed to call Sheila every week and brief her on developments.

As he rode down the elevator, he cautioned himself to keep in mind that regardless of how charming and ingratiating she appeared today, she was a tough banker, and as Birney had warned, could be ruthless. As the elevator car descended, he felt a kind of tension leaving his body—as if he had spent the last hour handling an adder, and finally released it back into its nest.

❖

The maitre-d' at Spago showed Helen and Jerry to a rear booth. Still more relaxed than usual since leaving the bank, Jerry ordered a bottle of Chardonnay, and they scanned the menu while they waited.

"What do you recommend?" he said.

"The mahi is terrific. I've also had the rack of lamb, which is their specialty."

Jerry nodded and kept his attention on the menu. He was feeling apprehensive about whether or not he could reestablish the rapport they had experienced at Kevin's house. He closed the menu and announced, "I'll go for the salmon. What about you?"

"I'm feeling carnivorous. The rack of lamb." He sensed that she was also nervous.

The waiter brought the wine. Jerry tasted it, and nodded with approval. The waiter filled their glasses and recited the evening specials. Helen ordered the lamb and Jerry changed his mind and decided on the mahi to show that he valued her opinion. They both ordered salads with dressing on the side.

"I see you watch your diet carefully," said Helen.

"Yeah, I'm concerned about cholesterol. Dad takes pills and Kevin's is over 250." He lifted the wineglass and reached across the table to squeeze Helen's hand. "To all the good times we're going to share."

"I'll certainly drink to that." They sipped their wine and smiled at each other through a long awkward silence. "How are things going, Jerry? Is National fixable?"

Jerry took a sip of wine while he pondered the question. "I'd prefer not to talk shop—for a couple of reasons. First, frankly after almost four weeks of twelve-hour days, seven days a week, I'm sick of it. My only dinner companions have been the guys at the office and Chelsey at home. I was hoping that we could enjoy a pleasant dinner *sans* National."

"And the second reason?"

"The second reason is that this deal is so incestuous, I'd prefer only making pronouncements and offering opinions in my official capacity. Salli's a major investor. I don't want to say something to you that might be misinterpreted when you talk with Salli—and I don't want to impose an obligation of silence on you. Do you see my point?"

"Certainly," said Helen. "I wasn't fishing for information. I was just making small talk. It's no big deal."

He set down his glass and wiped his lips with his napkin. "I'm sorry, I offended you."

Helen laughed. "You did not. It's just that you seem to be so obsessed."

"I'm always obsessed when I get into something new, something I don't understand. I can't rest or relax until I'm comfortable that I've got a handle on the situation and I see a path to a solution. It's a curse."

"Well, are you comfortable yet—if you can answer?" She laughed. She was teasing him.

Jerry laughed. "I'm happy to answer that question, and the answer is no!"

"Well, I'm certainly delighted you've come up for air long enough to take me to dinner."

He couldn't tell whether she was guilt-tripping him or making fun of him. "I've thought about you a great deal, Helen, but..."

"Work commitments come first? Right?" Her teasing smile lost a few watts.

"I don't like to put it that way. It's just that I have a hard time relaxing when I have a major project underway and I don't understand all the pieces. It's probably the reason I'm still single. No wife would ever put up with me." He picked up his glass, drained it, and refilled both their glasses.

"Speaking as a two-time ex-wife, I think you're being too hard on yourself. At least your wife would have a very successful husband." She smiled. "And at least you're honest about yourself. My problem in life is that I seem to find husbands who are excellent at deceiving themselves, and as a consequence, good at deceiving their wives."

The waiter brought their salads and conducted the ritual of dousing the salads with pepper from a two-foot high pepper mill. "When you're working like an animal, what do you do for social interaction?"

"You mean sex, don't you?"

"That, too." Helen smiled broadly. She seemed to realize its power, and Jerry wondered if she was flashing it for his sake or her own. He brought down his fork, which had been about to deliver his first bite of salad. He was intrigued by the power and flexibility of that smile, the way she used it to flirt, to provide cover for an overly candid remark, to question, and to disarm.

"I've got several girlfriends who like me enough to work around my schedule. When I'm not crazed, I lead a normal existence—dinner, movies, and weekends at resorts on the East Coast. It all works out."

"You've been in California almost four weeks. You haven't imported your New York lovers, or have you?" She took a sip of wine, sat back in her chair, and waited for his answer.

Jerry forced a laugh. "Did anyone ever tell you that you're very direct?"

"All the time."

"You would think less of me if I lied and told you that I can do without sex if necessary."

Helen placed her hand over Jerry's and squeezed it. "Poor baby, you *have* sacrificed a lot for the Bascomb clan." The waiter came with the entrées. Jerry ordered more bread. The waiter drained the wine bottle into their glasses and asked whether they wanted to order another bottle. Helen shook her head, so Jerry ordered a glass of Merlot. He used the few minutes while the waiter was getting the bread and wine to eat as much of his salad as he could before tackling the entrée. While he had been answering questions, Helen had cleaned her plate.

He was aware the mild irritation that he felt over Helen's persistent questioning was, much to his surprise, morphing into resentment. This was beginning to feel more like a job interview than a dinner date with a prospective lover. His wine came. As he lifted the glass, he said, "I don't get out much, so I'm giving myself permission to drink to excess tonight." He wondered why he was explaining himself to this woman.

"Have you ever had a serious relationship, Jerry?"

She's a fucking detective, he thought. "Two or three live-in deals that lasted a year or more."

"Did any of them ever get close to marriage?"

"One got to the point that we were talking about it, but that is as far as it got. We both graduated from law school. I wanted to go to Wall Street. She wanted to join the Peace Corps and go to Nepal. Neither of us was willing to put our relationship ahead of our careers."

"Any regrets?"

He shook his head. "Things probably worked out for the best." He squared his entrée in front of him and picked up his knife.

She took a sip of wine and placed her utensils on her half-eaten plate. "I'm getting stuffed already. It's delicious. You'll have to excuse me for a minute." She headed toward the restroom. Jerry was thankful for the respite. He sawed into his mahi and ate three quick mouthfuls, and washed them down with half of his wine. What happened to the old Helen, the one he'd met before the prospect of a relationship? This version was relentless. And transparent. And this was only their first serious dinner.

When she returned to the table, she picked up her napkin and settled into the same forward-leaning posture she'd held all through the meal. "Don't you want to have kids, Jerry?"

She seemed to be working from a list. Amazing. She wasn't even old enough to be desperate.

"Sure," he said. "But not so much that I'm willing to marry and play house with someone who isn't absolutely right. There are too many unhappy marriages out there. But I certainly don't have to tell you that."

"*Touché.*" She either did not perceive his growing discomfiture or chose to press on. "How will you be able to tell when a relationship is 'absolutely right?'"

There was a long silence. Finally Jerry said, "Can we talk about something else, you know, some subject that doesn't make me feel like I'm in a group therapy session?"

Helen laughed. "Boy, do you have a difficult time with intimacy." She sat back in her chair and pondered. "Okay, suggested topics for conversation: movies, politics, new cars, celebrities, religion..."

"I don't go to church."

"Neither do I. Not much to talk about there. What about childhood? Do you feel comfortable talking about your childhood?"

Jerry wondered how fake his smile looked. "I can handle that. I had a great childhood. What do you want to know?"

"What was it like growing up in the Bascomb house? What kind of relationship did you have with your brothers? What were your interests when you were a kid? All that stuff."

Jerry thought for a minute. He quickly processed many of the scenes from his childhood, selecting ones that he felt free to talk about and discarding the ones that Helen would over-examine. This dinner was proving to a hell of a lot more work than the dinner at Kevin's—and even his lunch with Sheila, for that matter.

"From my earliest memories, I remember our home being a central meeting place for the neighborhood. My mom and dad were both very outgoing. My dad was an army officer and had many friends in the military, and my mother was involved in United Way and other community organizations. They both made friends easily and always had bridge parties, barbecues, and football watching parties. Since Kevin is four years older than I am, I became kind of the mascot for his friends, boys and girls. Our house was like the canteen in a summer resort."

She was leaning forward, hanging on every word. "Sounds like fun."

He nodded. "It was like having an enormous extended family with aunts, uncles, and cousins of various ages. As I talk about it, I realize how much I miss it."

"How did you get along with your brothers when you were growing up?"

His smile may have become more genuine, because some of the glow of their former rapport returned. "Kevin was my idol and my hero," he said. "He looked after me, protected me, and taught me about baseball, football, basketball, pool, and swimming. One reason I excelled in a lot of sports when I was a kid was that I had Kevin as a private coach. Kevin even told me about sex. I would have done handstands on hot coals if Kevin asked me to. It was that way until he went away to college. God, did I cry when he left. I had lost a best friend."

"What about you and Jeff?"

The waiter took away the empty entrée plates and brought the dessert menus. Helen did not open her menu. Jerry looked at every item, using the time to organize his response.

"I asked about you and Jeff," she said.

God, why did she care? He did not have any clue as to how she felt about Jeff. He needed to be careful in everything he said. He definitely did not want to come off as a victim.

"Jeff and I were further apart in age—eight years—so he was more of an uncle than a brother. He was hypercritical of everything I did and his teasing was incessant. Once, when I was about sixteen, he got me so riled up that I threw a croquet mallet at him." He kept his voice light.

"What happened?"

"I missed."

"Did he beat you up?"

"Jeff was too smart to do that. He just told my mom who told my dad. My dad scolded me, forced me to apologize to Jeff, and grounded me for a month. My dad was so good that he had me convinced that my crime was so heinous that I deserved to be grounded for three months and it was out of compassion that he limited the punishment to one." He thought for a moment and then chuckled.

"What is it," she said.

"I just remembered that when I threw the mallet at him, I also called him Dimitri Fyodorovich. That pissed him off more than my throwing the mallet."

"Dimitri?"

"Yeah, after one of the main characters in *The Brothers Karamazov*. I loved the book. The over-the-top characters, the conflict between faith and doubt, the bizarre women, and the trial of Dimitri for the murder of his father." Jerry smiled. "When things didn't go the way I wanted, I'd refer to them by the Karamazov's first names. My father was Fyodor, Jeff was Dimitri, and Kevin was Ivan."

"And who were you?" she said.

Jerry smiled broadly. "I was Alyosha. The hero."

She leaned into the table closer, her chin resting on her arms. "How did they react," said Helen.

"Kevin went along with the game. He saw it made me happy, so he thought it was amusing. I think he was impressed by my being interested enough in a piece of literature that I actually took the time to understand it. But Jeff would get angry and tell me, 'Fuck off and don't give me any of that commie crap.'"

"And what about your father?" said Helen. "Was he amused?"

"He never knew about the game, let alone cared about novels. And I'd never refer to him as Fyodor Pavlovich to his face, anyway. It would have been an insult."

She seemed to have her bright, white Knudsen teeth dug into this one. She leaned even closer and asked. "Was there ever a time that you and Jeff were close?"

"We lived in the same house, shared the same parents, and were usually civil to each other. But he didn't like me very much, and therefore it was hard for me to like him." Case closed.

She raised her eyebrows and sat back in her chair, finally. "That sums up the relationship between Salli and me."

"You're kidding. I never would have guessed it." The tension in his neck and shoulders started to ebb. "I always thought that it was only brothers, and brothers and sisters that didn't get along. Most sisters that I know have always been real tight."

"Salli and I are only half-sisters, so your theory might still be valid."

This certainly piqued his interest. Maybe he had seemed equally interesting to her, and her interrogation was just innocent curiosity. "Why didn't you get along?" he asked.

"I never really understood it. I think it may have something to do with the fact that Mom and Charlie divorced when she was three, and I was born a year later and invaded her turf. She had been the little princess and the center of attention, and suddenly her father's gone and she has a rival for mother's attention. She probably felt that Mom had traded her father for me. She showed Mom how unhappy she was about the situation."

He shrugged. "Did she just ignore you when you were growing up?"

"No, it was worse than that. She constantly tried to—in fact she did—injure me several times." Helen's face flushed, but she continued. "My mom told me that when I was six months old, she tried to smother me by piling stuffed animals on my head when I was asleep. Fortunately, the maid came into the nursery. When I was three, she burned my arm with a Christmas candle. I remember that vividly—how much it hurt and going to the hospital."

She hid her red cheeks behind the last of her wine. He doubted this was something she spoke of often. It was uncomfortable, but he didn't know how to interrupt her without appearing callous. So she continued.

"And when I was six, we moved into a new neighborhood in Chicago. I was starting kindergarten and my mom gave Salli the job of walking me to and from school, so I would learn the way. Salli didn't want to do it. She wanted to walk with her friends and didn't want her stupid sister to tag along. But Mom insisted." Helen's eyes glittered—she was tearing up. "On the very first day, Salli intentionally lost me on the walk home. My mother was frantic. The police eventually found me wandering around in the dark and brought me home." Tears started to stream down her face. She opened her purse, retrieved a tissue, and dabbed her eyes. "It got worse as we grew older."

She reached for Jerry's half-filled glass of Merlot and took a drink. She dabbed her eyes again.

"What did your folks do?" said Jerry. He wasn't sure if he was supposed to take this in stride or be compassionate. "I mean it must have been a big problem for them with one daughter trying to kill the other."

"Not much. My father worked all the time and Mom was really afraid to talk to him about it for fear that he would insist that she pack Salli up and ship her back to her father. She'd yell at Salli and spank her. But it wouldn't do any good. Salli was absolutely intransigent. She was so defiant that every time an incident occurred, Mom had no choice but to defend her behavior—and she even had the gall to tell me to love Salli unconditionally, because maybe someday Salli would come around and love me in return."

Jerry was aware of his shock. "Did your mom ever get professional help?"

Helen returned the tissue to her purse. She was calm again. "My mom took Salli to several psychiatrists and child counselors. Mom told me that they all described our relationship issues as an extreme case of sibling rivalry and that she should keep Salli and me apart and maybe we would grow out of it. So they'd separate us in the summer and over Christmas. They either shipped Salli off to her father or shipped me to my grandparents, just so we'd be separated. I think the perpetual conflict between Salli and me drove my father away. He left when I was eight. Salli got the better part of the deal. I hardly ever saw my father much after that. He moved to Texas and remarried." She started to tear up again.

"That's unbelievable." It was, in fact, a saga of unrelenting child abuse. He took another drink of wine. She seemed comfortable in the moment's pause, glancing down the dessert menu again. He said, "How do you feel about Salli now?"

"I'm still working it out." She pushed the menu away. "I'm pissed that she deprived me of a normal childhood and a close sister-to-sister relationship. But on the other hand, we're not kids anymore and I realize, at least intellectually, that holding onto that anger will not do me any good." She wiped her eyes and took another sip from his wineglass. "Anyway, enough group therapy. Let's see if they have any high-calorie and high-fat desserts, so I can do something sinful with my mouth and my tongue— something that will be acceptable in a restaurant."

Helen leaned over to Jerry and gave him a long, gentle kiss on the lips. She sat upright in her chair close to the table and reached her right hand under the table and started to rub his thigh.

10

AUGUST 1, 1990

Jerry and Jeff were seated shoulder-to-shoulder on United Flight 8, the red eye to New York. In the morning, they would meet with Birney and some of Jerry's partners for their opinions—whether the company could be refinanced or restructured without raising new investment capital. Jerry knew refinancing was impossible, but kept his opinion quiet. For his brothers' sake, he wanted to make a sincere exploration of that option, even if it ended up being futile.

Because of the tensions that had developed between them in the office, Jerry had not been particularly enthusiastic about traveling to New York with Jeff. Kevin had planned to go, but he had not been feeling well and Carolyn wanted him to stay at home. So now Jeff was squished next to Jerry in the cheap seats. The plane was full. A mother and her crying toddler were seated across the aisle from Jerry. The takeoff roar subsided, and Jerry leaned closer to Jeff.

"What's the matter with Kevin?"

"Salli talked with Carolyn yesterday. He's been having angina pains. They keep him up at night. He feels sluggish and doesn't have much of an appetite." His voice held a note of concern.

"Kevin without an appetite? Has he seen a doctor?"

"Yeah. They don't know anything yet. Still doing tests. He's having the treadmill test today. It'll be the most exercise he's had since he played for UCLA, unless you count lifting a fork full of food from the plate to your mouth as exercise. Carolyn is worried."

"I don't blame her," said Jerry. "I'm worried, too. He's way overweight and he tells me he has high cholesterol."

"He's turned into a blob," said Jeff.

Jerry pulled out his calendar and made a note to ask Kevin out to dinner. It kept him occupied during the moment he would have otherwise liked to tell Jeff to lay off.

"So, Jeff, how are the girls?"

He folded up his newspaper and grinned. "They're bright, articulate, and very involved with school and friends. Michelle has a vocabulary that is incredible for a nine-year-old. It's better than mine, anyway." He laughed. "And Jessie's breasts have grown from lemons to oranges to small cantaloupes. She already looks eighteen. I'll have to hire a bodyguard next year."

Jerry chuckled. "No one is going to be able to protect your daughter from a teenager with raging hormones—like you were."

"Don't I know that?" said Jeff, grinning. "That's why I'm so damned worried."

"How's Salli?"

"Just as bitchy as ever."

"I don't see how you do it year after year," said Jerry. His view of Salli had soured considerably since dinner with Helen.

"It's easy. Kids. If you had any, you'd understand. I don't want to be a weekend father. And can you imagine divorce proceedings with Salli? She wrote the treatise on ball breaking." Jeff leaned back and reclined his seat. He picked up the *Wall Street Journal* and started to scan it. Small talk was over.

Jerry rummaged around in his briefcase until he found his collection of Kafka stories and found his place in "The Trial."

Ten minutes later, Jeff said, "Salli tells me that you're seeing Helen."

"We've met for coffee a few times and been out to dinner."

"Fuck her yet?"

Jerry let his book close. The first prickle of sweat jabbed at the back of his neck.

"Cat got your tongue, Jerry?"

"Jeff, I don't know how to answer you."

Jeff was grinning. "The question is: 'Did you fuck her yet?' Acceptable answers are yes or no."

Jerry's face had turned red. "I can't—I can't believe you, Jeff. We're not kids anymore. We don't compare scores like we used to. Why the hell is it important to you?"

"Simple. If you answered yes, I was going to ask you if she is real tight since I'm interested to see if it runs in the family. If you answered no I was going to ask 'Why not?' Why are you being such a choir boy?"

Jerry looked over to the lady with the toddler. She was staring at him with a frown. He quickly turned away. He really wanted to scream at Jeff. Despite his anger, he understood that Jeff had been able to pull his chain one more time. He clenched the armrests and clenched his teeth. "Jeff, I'm not going to talk about this. Period. You'll just have to wonder." He picked up his book and tried to find his place.

Jeff's grin turned into a smirk. "Okay, okay, don't be so defensive." He rattled the paper open—conversation over. Jerry's face was still flushed. *That son-of-a-bitch. He can still play me like a violin.* He took several deep breaths and turned his attention back to Kafka.

Jeff was telling Rodrigues to stay behind Corporal Smith in the column when a hand on his arm interrupted him. "Breakfast, sir?" The disorientation dissolved. He brought his head out from beneath the blanket and found a blond, perky stewardess above him. "It's six o'clock, sir. Would you care for breakfast?"

"Sure, you bet."

He glanced over at his brother. Jerry was already eating and appeared well rested.

"I told her to let you sleep as long as possible."

"Thanks, bro, I appreciate it."

The aircraft came to a stop just short of 6:30 a.m. Birney would be waiting somewhere around baggage claim. He followed the stream of passengers up the gate on stiff legs, warily following his brother. As they walked through the concourse, Jeff glanced at the television monitor. Wolf Blitzer was reporting some breaking news from the Middle East: Iraqi forces had invaded Kuwait the previous evening and were moving toward Kuwait City. The Emir of Kuwait had fled the country and set up an exile government in Saudi Arabia.

"Jerry," Jeff yelled. "Come here, CNN."

They craned their heads at the monitor. Wolf Blitzer said that the U.N. and the U.S. had both condemned the invasion and called for an immediate pullout and that the U.S. had frozen all Iraqi assets under its control.

"I sure hope we follow through with this deal," Jeff said. "We've got to stop letting these two-bit faggot dictators fuck us over just because they happen to be sitting on oil."

Jerry just stared at the monitor, his faced turning grim.

"Anything the matter, bro?" said Jeff.

"No. Let's go. Birney's waiting."

"Boychick," yelled a man's voice. The source of the yell was a short, swarthy, well-dressed businessman in a weightlifter's body, wearing a blue yarmulke. Jerry saw Birney and led Jeff over to where he was standing.

"Boychick, I've missed you." He enveloped Jerry in a bear hug, and said to Jeff, "Your brother left a hole in my office that's as big as a fucking battleship."

"Okay, Birney." Jerry tried to free himself. "You know how this embarrasses me."

"I know," said Birney, and then using his hands like a vise, he grabbed Jerry's face and planted a big kiss on Jerry's lips. "But I can't help it, I'm Jewish. There ya go."

Birney's exuberance was amusing, but Jeff couldn't help wondering how much of the display of feeling was sincere and how much was the New York investment banking shtick. Birney grabbed Jerry's tote bag and turned toward the terminal. "Come on, we're meeting the guys at Nate's for breakfast."

"We had breakfast on the plane, Birney," said Jeff.

"Airline crap! I wouldn't feed it to my dog if I had a dog. We've ordered a spread for two executives from California. Lox, bagels, sturgeon, whitefish. You'll love it."

The breakfast was raucous. Birney had invited the other five partners of Bricker and Weldon to join them for breakfast at Jerry's favorite Jewish deli. Jeff did not know any of Jerry's partners and could not understand nor participate in the investment banking gossip that dominated the conversation. The conversation was laced with so many Yiddish expressions—*schmuck, putz, dreck, nebbish, goy, kvetch, mensch, oy vey, shiksa, shmeer, yenta*—used so densely that Jeff could not discern the context and therefore could not fully comprehend the conversation. And, the partners did not talk; they yelled, and they did it with mouths stuffed with food. Jeff did not know when to smile, laugh, or nod knowingly.

His brother seemed to have taken on a New York Jewish personality like Woody Allen's Zelig. And the more he blended into the ethnic scene, the more uncomfortable Jeff felt. Jeff had made sure he sat next to Birney because he hoped to brief him on the company's situation and prospects. But the clamor in the restaurant and Birney's lack of interest in anything but gossip and stuffing his face was appalling. Not wanting to be rude to his host, he abandoned his culinary restraint and overate with the natives.

It was ten thirty before Birney and the senior partners, Jerry, and Jeff assembled in the Bricker and Weldon conference room. In front of each occupied chair, Jeff meticulously placed a binder, containing National's brochure, recent promotional and PR material, and a summary of the financial performance over the past five years. He had also included several product brochures, including those describing their monitoring systems, both their Mil-Spec Iris Scanner and their Commercial Iris Scanner, and their Mil-Spec Retina Scanner and their Commercial Retina Scanner.

Birney called the meeting to order, stating his assumption that the partners had reviewed the material that Jerry had sent by FedEx the previous day. Therefore, they would first listen to Jeff and Jerry's presentation, and then brainstorm about refinancing, seeking an option that would keep Jeff and Kevin at the helm. Jeff and Jerry were to focus on clarifying the issues that the partners raised and ensure that they conveyed what Birney called the schmaltz of the deal. The whole morning had been set aside for the National discussion. They planned to adjourn by two o'clock, so that Jeff and Jerry could make the four-thirty out of Kennedy.

"It's your show, boychick," Birney said. "I've gotta relax and digest that breakfast before lunch gets here."

Jerry laughed and stood up at the head of the table. "Jeff and I are very appreciative of the hospitality you've shown us and the time you've set aside to hear our story. I certainly know how busy you guys are and how this must have screwed up your calendar. And I know that once I'm back here, you will all make sure that I pay dearly for it." There was general laughter. One partner, Bill Goldman, shouted, "I'm already planning it, Jerry."

"I'm going to turn the presentation over to Jeff in a minute. He's been the driving force behind National's rapid growth, and is far more knowledgeable than I. But before I do, I want to make one point. National is an excellent company. It is a leading player in the access control systems market. Its technology and engineering staff are outstanding and far superior to those of its competitors. Jeff has done a remarkable job of establishing National as a premier player in the market. Unfortunately, it's in a precarious situation. Whether the problem can be resolved without having to give up control is what we hope to discern. You guys are the best in the business, and if it is doable, I know that you can and will be able to do it. My family and I thank you for your efforts."

There was a long silence. Jerry nodded and gave the seat at the head of the table to Jeff.

During Jerry's introduction, Jeff's guts were cramping. He was angry with himself over his lack of control and distracted by the possibility of losing an escalating battle with his GI tract during the meeting. He forced a smile and accepted the lead seat from his brother.

"Access control systems were created to protect property from unauthorized access or vandalism, and to protect individuals by keeping them away from places that are hazardous to their health—such as nuclear power plants, medical labs, and airport tarmacs. ACS systems are supposed to let the good guys in and keep the bad guys out and be one hundred percent successful at their task."

Jeff described the security industry's five broad technologies: keypad based, for tennis courts and the like; audio based, for apartments; TV based, for convenience store surveillance; card based, which was essentially an ATM system; and biometrics based, used in secure government and industrial facilities. He stated that the keypad and audio systems market were very competitive and did not provide much opportunity for innovation, so National had focused on card, TV, and biometrics-based systems. The relative market sizes of these technologies compared to the total ACS market were about 75 percent, 10 percent, and 5 percent, respectively.

"Last year, National's sales were just above fifty million, giving us about a 20 percent market share," he said. National ranked third behind ADT and Continental Industries. He cited research conducted by Frost and Sullivan that predicted overall growth in ACS market of about 4 percent per year, and while the market share of both card and TV systems would decline over the next decade, the market for biometrics systems would increase by about a 150 percent. "That's why we're putting so much of our energy into this area," said Jeff.

Bill Goldman interrupted. "In reviewing your financials for the past five years, it appears that margins have declined significantly—about 20 percent. What's the explanation and what are you doing to reverse the trend?"

Jeff sipped some water. His guts were still roiling. "I'm glad you pointed that out, Bill. Except for the biometrics systems, the ACS technology has matured to a point that differentiating among products is difficult and commodity pricing has set in." He looked to Jerry. Their eyes met. Jerry nodded. He turned back to Bill. "There has been a shakeout in the industry, and many of the smaller companies that were driving down prices in order to survive have folded. We believe that we'll be seeing improved margins during the next few years. I'll speak to that issue shortly."

Goldman nodded.

"So explain to us why you think that the future is so bright for access control," said Birney.

Jeff smiled at him. "Birney, I thought you'd never ask."

"You'll have to forgive me, Jeff. I'm a little slow this morning—too much gefilte fish."

Jeff went over to the whiteboard, picked up a blue marker, and wrote on the board as he spoke. "We see growth opportunities in three major areas: monitoring, service, and biometrics. We're investing heavily in all three areas." Out of the corner of his eye, Jeff noticed Jerry wince. Jeff realized that "investing heavily" was somewhat of an overstatement. He hoped that the partners would not notice Jerry's wince. "As systems have become more complex, monitoring and maintenance have become more of a challenge. We've embarked on a plan to develop monitoring and service capability throughout the entire country. The third major investment area is in biometrics systems since they offer the opportunity for the highest level of security, and the potential for greater differentiation and higher margins." He put the marker down and returned to his seat at the head of the table.

"But being able to provide service and monitoring is a requirement for being able to sell to the end user, isn't it?" said another of the partners. "It's like being an auto dealer. In order to hold a franchise to sell cars, you have to be able to offer parts and service. Also service and monitoring are labor-intensive. It's going to be very difficult to wring big margins from those areas—don't you agree?"

Jeff's face started to flush. He put on his steeliest face and glared at the questioner, whose name he had forgotten. "I don't agree. If you have strong capabilities in service and can cast a wide net for monitoring, you will be able to sell your systems at a higher price than your competitors. It's as simple as that."

Jerry shifted around in his seat, but kept his eyes riveted on Jeff.

"Okay," said Birney. "Tell us about the biometrics stuff."

Jeff turned off the steel and brightened. "Probably the best way to get an understanding of the motivating force behind the push for biometrics systems is to look at the limitation of ATM card systems. The magnetic stripe on a card contains information about both the owner of the card and the property to be accessed. The user is provided with a personal identification number that must be used in conjunction with the card to validate that the card is actually being used by the designated owner. But as you well know, there have been literally hundreds of cases where an individual's life has been threatened in order to obtain their PIN. Once in possession of the card and a victim's PIN, a bad guy can access any property controlled by the card.

"In the case of a biometrics system, the card is replaced by some physical characteristic of an individual that cannot be stolen or separated from the individual who has access to certain property. Examples include the characteristics of a person's retina or iris, his handprint, his voice, his signature, fingerprint, vein structure, all of which are unique. The combination of a physical attribute with a PIN provides access control security that is orders of magnitude greater than that which can be achieved with card systems." Jeff paused, looked around the room, and indicated his willingness to accept questions. He was back at the head of the charge.

"So what biometrics technologies are you focusing on?" said Goldman.

"We believe that the iris and retina systems offer the most promise and we've concentrated our R and D in this area."

"Why?" said Birney.

"Two factors. First you get lower rates of false positives and false negatives with iris, retina, and fingerprint systems than the others, making the system less dependent on a PIN for backup."

"So why not systems based on fingerprints?" said Goldman.

He looked around the room. He loved this part of it. He smiled at Goldman. "It's relatively easy for a committed bad guy to cut off a finger and use it to gain access. Plucking out an eye and not destroying it in the process is somewhat more difficult."

"Ugh," said Birney. "Disgusting."

Unfazed, Goldman continued. "Have you delivered any biometrics systems?"

"We have three systems in beta test at customer installations. If they perform to the customer's satisfaction, they will buy them. Also we're working with Japanese Bank on a proposal to equip all of its ATMs with iris scanners."

"So who is currently buying biometrics systems?" said Birney.

"You mean now?" said Jeff.

"Yeah, now."

"Industrial and commercial customers account for 5 percent of the market and government agencies comprise 95 percent of the market."

"And the future?" pressed Birney.

Jeff hesitated. He knew where Birney was going. Here it comes, he thought, the Achilles heel of the whole deal. Jeff cleared his throat and looked through his notes. "During the next ten years, industrial and commercial will grow to about 8 percent of the market. Government agencies will account for the balance."

"Let me understand this," said Birney. "As of now, government agencies purchase 95 percent of biometrics systems and ten years from now, they will only be purchasing 92 percent of the systems. Doesn't that fact make National a government contractor? I mean those bureaucrats are in a position to really put the screws on a company and clamp down on their profit margins."

Jeff licked his lips. His face had begun to redden again. It was the same argument that Jerry had made when they discussed the prospects for new financing. Namely, the largest part of the ACS market was mature, lacked opportunities for differentiation, and was experiencing significant margin decline. The hot new thing in access control, biometrics systems, was currently dominated by government agency purchases, and forecasters, such as Frost and Sullivan, were predicting that the industrial-government mix would not change significantly over the next decade—barring a calamity that would expand the government's purse. Conclusion: National is not a very attractive prospect for financing.

Jeff looked over to Jerry. He thought he detected a hint of a smirk on his face. He faced Birney. "We don't agree," said Jeff, his voicing rising in volume.

"Why not?" said Birney.

"Two reasons," said Jeff. "First, much of the technology we use in our everyday lives owes its origin and development to government agencies. The Internet was originally an intra-government communication vehicle. Then there is Velcro, every skier's favorite fastener—the original major users were NASA and the military. And what about GPS? Created by the government and developed by the government, and now look at the expanding commercial applications. The installations of biometric access control systems will expand over the next several years, too, and the prices of the systems will come down as the applications expand, and the demand will expand even more."

Birney's expression was inscrutable, but he appeared to be listening carefully. As for Jerry, the smirk was gone; his expression revealed pure admiration. Jeff smiled to himself. The little fucker. He thinks that he's the only one who does his homework.

"I get it," said Birney. "What's your second point?"

"The Frost and Sullivan forecasts are not reliable," said Jeff. "No one answering the Frost and Sullivan survey can judge what their security world will be like and what options they will choose, based upon the current embryonic size, technology, and investment in biometrics systems. As an example, go back and look at the Frost and Sullivan reports for the PC market in 1980 and see how the predictions for the market in 1990 compare with current reality. The individuals responding to the survey do not have an adequate frame of reference to respond to the questions. because they don't know what the pricing and features will look like, nor can they imagine all the applications that will be created over a ten-year time period."

Jeff looked over to Jerry and caught his eye. Jerry kept a straight face, but nodded back. Jeff's heart pounded, but he felt good, in command.

"What about that, Phil?" said Birney, addressing another of Jerry's partners.

"My recollection is that the majority of the forecasters underestimated the PC market by orders of magnitude. Jeff's point is very valid."

"But we would have to deal with the Frost and Sullivan forecast in any offering memorandum, wouldn't we?" said Birney.

"Absolutely."

Birney looked through the documents that Jeff had provided. "Is the Frost and Sullivan report in...Here it is." He held up the report and looked around the table at the partners. "We should all read this tonight. It will pose a big hurdle." He turned back to Jeff. "Who are your major competitors in the biometrics area?"

"The only four that we currently worry about are Identix, Fingermatrix, Eye Dentity, and International Electronics. Their market shares combined with ours account for 80 percent of the current biometrics systems market," said Jeff.

Jerry had leaned back in his chair and his eyes were closed.

"Boychick," said Birney. "Don't fall asleep on us. We need you to outline your ideas as to how this deal could be structured to meet the owners' objectives and lure investors."

Jerry looked around the room sheepishly. "I think the jet lag is catching up with me." Jeff grinned, relishing Jerry's embarrassment. He took his seat.

Jerry went to the front of the room and began his presentation, summarizing the financial history of National and its prospects for future performance. Jeff was still savoring his recent intellectual triumph and only half-listened to the colloquy among Jerry, Birney, and his partners. Lunch was brought in and the discussion continued. Jeff was high on it. Jerry's financial presentation was convincing and Birney and several of his partners appeared genuinely interested in pursuing the deal. So far, so good.

At about 1:30 p.m., Birney stood up and looked around the room. "It's getting late," he said. "And Jeff and Jerry need to catch a plane out of JFK. Anyone have any questions?" There was no response. "I think we have the schmaltz," said Birney. "You've given us a lot of stuff to digest, and we'll call if we have any questions. We'll let you know by the end of the week if we think we can be of help. Okay, boychick?"

"That's fine," replied Jerry. The conference room emptied quickly. The tension that had filled the room drained through the door with the departing partners. The space metamorphosed from a battlefield to a mere room. Birney soon excused himself and said that his secretary would get a car to take them to the airport.

When they were alone, Jerry turned to Jeff, grabbed his hand, and shook it vigorously. "You were great, Jeff. An exceptional performance."

"You seem surprised." Jeff kept his poker face.

"Frankly, I was."

Jeff bristled. "Well you shouldn't be, Jerry. Just because we fucked up in the financial management of the company doesn't imply that we're incompetent. We do understand our markets and our competition, and we have a viable vision for our role in the industry. We just need the opportunity to see it through. That's where you come in."

Jerry held his hands out in front of him and spread his fingers. "I understand my role, Jeff."

"I know you understand it, Jerry. I just hope that you'll be successful at it."

❖

Jerry tried to draw Jeff out during the cab ride to the airport, but his brother just stared between the front seats, out the windshield. Kafka proved to be a more interesting travel companion, as well as Dostoevsky, who occupied Jerry on the plane and during the several hours' delay due to crappy weather.

The LA morning welcomed him back with sunshine and vivid patches of light and shadow. He woke up early and drove to the kennel to get Chelsey, called in to National to take the day off, and treated himself to a morning of propping his feet up on the coffee table and watching CNN over bowls of cold cereal.

In addition to the unpleasantness that had been caused by the flight delays, Jeff's demeanor had set a new low for surliness. Jerry had hoped that by exposing Jeff to the piercing no-holds interrogation, typical of a presentation to investment bankers, that Jeff would gain some understanding of the difficulty of National's situation. The meeting had unintended consequences. Jeff took every thrust and parry from Jerry's partners as a personal attack on his capability, his management style, and his accomplishments. The leave-taking had been strained and stilted, with Jeff making no attempt to hide his surly mood from Jerry's partners. The smile that he pasted on his face as he shook hands with Birney would have done Count Dracula proud.

He glanced at his watch to see whether it was too early to drink. Ten forty-five, close enough. He went into the kitchen, set up the blender and mixed himself a margarita. He poured tortilla chips into a large bowl, sprinkled salsa over them, and carried his drink, the bowl of chips, and the current issue of *The New Yorker* toward the balcony. He sprawled out on the lounge chair, slipped off his briefs, and allowed the ninety-five degree sunshine to blanket his nude body.

The ringing of his phone woke him. He checked his watch. He had been asleep for a few hours. He jumped out of the lounge chair and headed to the living room to answer the phone.

"Boychick. Shirley told me you were playing hooky. How was the trip home?" The loud voice was out of place in the quiet condo.

"Hi, Birney. It was long. The plane was delayed five hours. We didn't get in until after midnight."

"I presume your brother told you jokes to pass the time."

"You're not funny, Birney." He was uncomfortable and needed to pee.

"Christ, is he defensive. We didn't treat him any differently than any other principal who comes to us for financing. That's what you said you wanted."

"I know. It wasn't you or the guys. Shit, in the old days he would have picked up the gauntlet and enjoyed every minute of it." He paused. "Birney, can I call you back in about fifteen minutes?"

"Sure. I'm still at the office. Call my private line."

Jerry headed for the bathroom to relieve himself and then jumped into the shower. He quickly toweled himself dry, pulled on a pair of jeans and a T-shirt, went into the spare bedroom, and sat down at his desk with a yellow pad. He dialed Birney's number.

Birney said, "I hope that we haven't made your task more difficult."

"I'm not sure that's possible." He pushed away a pile of notebooks, so that he'd have some room to write. "Have you had an opportunity to discuss our deal?"

"Yeah, we met at eleven. Morgan did the research yesterday after you guys left and was able to talk with several analysts this morning. I'm faxing you his report."

"And?" Jerry tensed up waiting for the answer he knew was coming and that he didn't want to hear.

"His report is mixed. The good news was that the market for access control is strong and growing. The bad news is that the sexy part, the biometrics stuff, is forecasted to be dominated by the government for some time and will depress margins. The analysts Morgan talked with see the opportunity in ACS as a consolidation play. The market is very fragmented and is ripe for a Blockbuster type of rollup—but that isn't National's strategy."

Jerry shifted the phone to his other ear. "Sounds as though the analysts are just parroting the Frost and Sullivan report."

"Probably. What the fuck would you expect from an analyst? They're just a bunch of whores. Problem is, Jerry, I don't see how we get any traction in this deal. National hasn't made the case for a compelling market opportunity."

"You mean Jeff hasn't made the case."

"Whatever."

Jerry had been taking notes during the conversation. He quickly reviewed them. "How much of Morgan's opinion is influenced by National's current financial problems and the events that caused them?"

"Nada, zip, it's irrelevant. You should talk to Morgan yourself. He's gone into the details."

"Anything else?" said Jerry, even though he knew nothing else really mattered.

"Yeah. This Iraq deal is going to chill the money sources. The word is all over the street. There is going to be a general battening down of the hatches until the situation gets sorted out over there."

"I'm not surprised," said Jerry. "My heart fell into my gut when I saw the news yesterday. Raising money for this deal is going to be tough, maybe impossible."

"I'm sorry, boychick. I truly am."

"I know you are, Birney. It's a damn shame. The timing is awful." He leaned back in his chair and put his feet on the desk. "So your recommendation is that we sell."

"I don't see any other shop giving you a different assessment."

There was a long silence. Jerry was trying to think of some other questions, but he knew, and he knew that Birney knew, that all further discussion was pointless. Morgan was smart. Jerry would speak personally to him to complete the process, but nothing would change. National's future as an independent company was dim.

"Boychick?"

"Sorry, Birney, I was ruminating. Any suggestions?"

"Yeah. I think you should go with Blanchard and Co. They're based in San Francisco and they have excellent contacts in the Silicon Valley high-tech area and venture community. If anybody can sell National for you, they can. The guy you'll work with is Ethan Wilson. He's an Aussie. You'll like him. I'll call him this afternoon to see whether he has any conflicts and if he's interested in doing it. I'll call you back after I speak with him. Okay?"

Jerry started to chuckle.

"What is it, boychick?"

"Nothing." If anyone had conflicts it was himself. "Sounds good. I really appreciate your help."

"Don't mention it. I just wish I could have given you a recommendation that your family would like."

Jerry sat quietly at his desk, reviewing the entire National situation. Chelsey strolled in from the balcony and put her paw on his thigh. "Okay, girl, I'll take you out." He located the leash and led Chelsey out the door.

When he returned to the condo, he called Morgan, who gave him a reprise of Birney's comments, except he wasn't as diplomatic. He called Shirley next. "I need to arrange a meeting with Jeff, Kevin, Richard Krimble, and Howard as soon as we can all get together."

"Kevin's at a doctor's appointment and he's not going to be back today. I'll call Richard Krimble and determine his availability. Jeff didn't come in today either, and I haven't talked with him."

"It's almost five. Don't worry about it tonight. I'll call Jeff at home." Jerry wondered whether Jeff was at home licking his wounded ego.

Moments after he hung up the phone, Birney called to say that he'd talked with Ethan Wilson and determined that there were no conflicts. He provided Ethan Wilson's business and home numbers and wished him good luck. Jerry called Wilson immediately. Wilson's accent and use of Aussie slang shocked him into full attention. He was going to have to learn a new language. Birney had already briefed Wilson on the most significant aspects of the project, so they agreed that Jerry would come to San Francisco to meet with Ethan and the other senior partners. They scheduled the meeting for the following Friday, August 10. Jerry said he would overnight several National profile packages to Ethan, so that he and his partners could bone up on National and the ACS industry.

He pushed himself out of the desk chair and went into the kitchen to mix another margarita. He walked out onto the balcony and watched the boats maneuver in their slips.

He walked back into the living room, sat down on the couch, and dialed Helen's work number. She answered after two rings. "It's Jerry. How's your day going?"

Jerry could feel the electric charge of exuberance originate at Helen's end of the line, or else it was coming from his own gut.

"Fantastic, what about yours?"

"Not fantastic yet. The reason I called is that I will likely have to go to San Francisco for a meeting next Friday. Could you come along? We could spend the weekend, take in a show, and gorge ourselves at the Mozart Café and Ernie's."

"I'd love to. It's about time we spent some quality time together to see if we really like each other."

Jerry laughed. "I'll make reservations at the Donatello. Jeff tells me it's a great hotel for a romantic weekend."

"The Donatello?"

Jerry detected what sounded like a combination of surprise and hesitancy. "Is there a problem?"

"No, not really, but, but..." She sounded confused. "I've stayed there before and had an unpleasant experience. A maintenance man barged into my room without showing any identification and really frightened me. I complained to the management and they were not that sympathetic." Helen said the last sentence as if she were just discovering an elusive excuse.

Jerry saw no point in pushing the issue. "No problem. What about the Cliff Hotel? It's about two blocks from Union Square at Gary and Taylor."

"That will be fine." Her voice brightened again. "I'm really excited about this, Jerry. I know we'll have a great time."

"No doubt about it. I'll make the reservations for the hotel and get the plane tickets. I'll call you later to give you the details." As Jerry hung up the phone, he was aware of a wisp of doubt about Helen's behavior. But the issue seemed so trivial that he decided not to give it any further thought.

When Jerry arrived in the National conference room on Monday morning, Shirley was busy serving coffee to Jeff, Kevin, and Howard. "Richard is in Kevin's office making a call," she said. "He'll be in shortly."

Howard had a big smile on his face. "Here, boss," he said, as he shoved a document over to Jerry. "This should put a smile on your face." Kevin looked happy for the first time in two months. Jerry nodded at Jeff and quickly scanned the document. National was reporting a profit that would exceed projections. He was more relieved than elated. Finally, some good news.

"I heard you had a great trip," said Kevin. "Jeff said that they sounded real interested."

Jerry gaped. He wondered whether he and Jeff had been at the same meeting. There was no way that Jeff could have misread the skepticism of his partners.

"While we're waiting on Richard, I'd like you all to read the report that Morgan prepared on National along with a memorandum, relating to my conversations with Ethan Wilson. Wilson is an investment banker in San Francisco. It will only take a few minutes." Jerry handed out the report and memo, and held one up for Richard Krimble, who'd just settled his stalk of a frame at the table. Richard opened his briefcase, took out his laptop, typed for a few moments, and then turned his attention to the document.

Jerry took his place at the table and reviewed some internal memos. He calculated that they would be able to absorb the major elements of the report in about five minutes. He knew all too well that this meeting would be difficult—it offered Jeff another opportunity to undermine his efforts. He also knew that it was his burden to be dispassionate, to lay out the facts like Sergeant Friday in the *Dragnet* television series, and let his brothers discern the implications of Morgan's report. He sat back in his chair and waited.

After about four minutes, Jeff tossed the report on the table and said, "No surprises here. They implied as much during the meeting in New York."

Howard laid his copy on the table. Richard put the report to the side of his computer and began to type. Kevin stared at the report. The happiness trembled and slipped away. Jerry's face heated—he was afraid Kevin would start to cry. But he merely placed the report down on the conference table and said, "I think I understand the gist, Jerry. Why don't you give me your interpretation?"

All eyes turned toward Jerry.

"Whenever a bank invites a customer to take its business elsewhere, that customer has only three options. One: Refinance the loan. That is, find another bank that will fall in love with the company and pay off the existing bank, and extend additional credit. If that effort is successful, business goes on as before and there is little disruption in the company's activities. Two: Sell the company. A buyer brings his own financing package to the equation and the old bank is paid off as part of the sale process. Three: Liquidate the loan by converting all the assets that are securing the loan to cash and pay them over to the bank. If the sale of assets generates a surplus of cash, the unsecured creditors get paid a percentage of what they're owed, and in those very rare cases where the liquidation is adequate to cover the secured and all the unsecured creditors, the owners can pocket the overage. If the sale of assets is insufficient to cover the outstanding loan, the guarantors, who are usually the owners, are supposed to dig deep in their pockets and come up with the difference. You all know this, and I haven't delivered this speech as part of a pedagogical exercise. But I want us all to be clear about the limited options we have."

"Make your point, Jerry, before we're overtaken by boredom," said Jeff.

Jerry ignored the comment and stayed with Kevin. "Do you understand, Kev?"

He nodded. Richard and Howard were silent.

"The message of Morgan's report is that the company cannot be refinanced, because the business strategy that National formulated and pursued is not consistent with the way the investment community views the marketplace. Therefore, the probability of achieving a private placement through an investment bank or sub-debt group in an amount to pay off the bank is considered, by Morgan and the Bricker and Weldon partners, to be highly unlikely. Furthermore, since the company's collateral is inadequate to support a secured loan with an asset-based lender, the refinancing option is not available.

"Which leaves a sale or liquidation as the available options," said Howard.

"Liquidation is not an option," said Jerry. "Because the shortfall in the value of the collateral compared to the size of the loan to the bank will wipe out Jeff and Kevin. They will both have to file Chapter 7 bankruptcy petitions. Right, Richard?"

"Unfortunately, you are correct," he responded. "I am confident that the bank will sue Jeff and Kevin for the shortfall, and they would have to seek court protection to preserve a few assets and put the National matter behind them. It is not a pretty picture."

"Kevin, Jeff," said Jerry as he looked from one to the other. "You have only one option and that is to sell the company while we still have a company to sell. There is no other strategy that makes any sense to me."

"Or to me," said Richard. "I think we need to face reality and do so quickly. I just got off the phone with Bill Bromfield. The bank has asked for an all-hands meeting some time within the next three weeks. They've given me a detailed agenda. In substance, they want a report on what progress the company has made pursuant to taking them out. We cannot afford to appear unfocused at that meeting."

"What are the specifics of their agenda?" asked Jerry.

"There are three main subjects. They want a complete financial review of operations, gross margins, inventory analysis, operating profit year to date, et cetera. Second, they want a thorough analysis of progress we've made in resolving the inventory deficit and an estimate as to when we expect to have completed digging ourselves out of the hole that Johnson and Potter created. And finally, they want a presentation on the status of our efforts to refinance or sell the company and get them paid off. Our current deal with the bank expires on September 30—which gives us seven weeks to work out a new deal. In light of the discussion we've just had, it seems futile to talk about any scenario other than a sale."

Jeff was silent. Kevin said, "I certainly don't see any other option. I can't speak for Jeff, but I'm worn out by the stress. I'm not opposed to fighting with the bank if there was a reasonable prospect of success. But it doesn't appear to be the case. I'll cast my vote for the sale option and suggest we all get behind the effort."

Jerry's eyes widened. He was astonished. He would not have bet a single dollar on this reaction. Kevin had accepted the devastating news that National, his creation, the baby he had nurtured to adolescence, was going to be sold out from under him.

Kevin turned and faced Jeff. "What do you think, Jeff? You're 50 percent of this deal."

Jeff looked at Morgan's memo and scribbled a few notes. He spoke with deliberation. "This is the way I see it," he said. "Jerry's analysis of the options is based on the opinion of one firm. I'm not saying they did not do a competent job in analyzing our situation. I just feel that we should not let the future of this company, and the future of Kevin and myself and our families, be dictated by one firm's opinion. I think we need more input and some other opinions."

Jeff was giving Jerry the steely-eyed stare he'd given Birney's partners. Of course he would be critical of the work that Jerry's firm had done as long as he could still appear objective and professional to Kevin, Richard, and Howard. It was all Jerry could do to contain his anger. His mouth was dry. He ran his tongue across his lips.

"Of course," Jerry said. He reminded himself about how he had let Jeff get to him during the trip to New York, and made his breath reach deeper, so that he didn't sound so strangled. "And how do you propose we search out these other opinions?"

Jeff smiled. "Beats me, bro, that's your business. You're the investment banker in the family. I'm just the marketing drudge."

"Jeff's got a point," said Kevin. "Maybe there are other options." Jerry's palms were wet and the constriction in his throat tightened. But he kept telling himself that Jeff was operating in good faith and that his ignorance of corporate finance and the investment banking process was certainly understandable.

He spoke as slowly and helpfully as he could. "Jeff, you're absolutely correct. This is a game of probabilities. Morgan's paper should be viewed as a report of the consensus of the investment bankers that Morgan contacted. They say the company is not a viable candidate for financing. But there is the universe of investment bankers and sub-debt investors that Morgan has either not spoken with or doesn't know. I presume that there are those within that universe that would fund the deal. But the problem is how do you identify them and arouse their interest, while the bank is holding a gun to your head and demanding that you make a deal that pays them off." Jerry pulled his voice back a notch. "I don't have a solution to that problem, and I'll bet no one else does, either. We do not have the luxury of time and management capacity to effect a shotgun approach and go off in one hundred different directions looking for Japanese money, Arab money or whatever. The bank would cut our balls off..."

Kevin was shaking his head and pounded his fist on the table. "This stuff is too deep for me, okay? Can't we stop arguing and come to some decision. Richard?"

Richard sat up in his chair, straight as if there was a steel rod supporting his spine. He seemed to understand the importance of his reply. Jeff and Kevin's display of frustration must have been a common sight to him: Lawyers and investment bankers make it their jobs to comb through every nuance, every uncertainty, and every potential unintended consequence of a deal like this, and emotion does not get a seat at their table. But to the client they are hired to help, they seem insensitive to the fact that he and his family have poured years of hard work, deprivation, savings, cancelled family vacations, nights, weekends, and failed marriages into their baby, their pride and joy, the vehicle that provided them their social position, stoked their ego, and gave them a great lifestyle. So, even a fair price often looked like a pittance in comparison to so much emotional currency.

Richard stopped typing and spread his fingers wide on the table. "Here's what I think we should do. Jerry should meet with Wilson this Friday. We should enter into a contract to sell the company. The contract should contain a clause that allows the company to cancel at any time by paying a cancellation fee to Blanchard and Co. Jerry commits to fully support the sales effort, which will satisfy the bank. The bank will hopefully give us another six months to create a market for the company and get the deal into escrow. In the meantime, the company can, on its own, continue to contact financing prospects until there is an offer on the table. If the company doesn't have a financing plan that will take out the bank before there is an offer on the table that is acceptable to the bank, it will be difficult to reject the offer. The bank would go ballistic. On the other hand, if the company can locate funds to take the bank out, it can refinance, pay the cancellation fee, and pay off the bank. The company needs time to find prospective investors. The only way the bank will give us time is if we convince them that we're doing our best to pay them off, which means putting the company on the block. Would that approach satisfy you, Jeff?"

"Who's going to search for the financing?"

"We all will," said Richard.

"What about hiring a money finder?"

"No way," said Jerry. "No way." He shook his head. "You can't have two guys on the street selling the same deal. No one will get serious, because they're not sure who controls the deal and they don't want to waste their time. Besides, the bank won't approve two retainers."

"What about you, Jerry?" said Kevin. "Will you continue the search for refinancing?"

"Sure, I like Richard's plan." Jerry saw that the conflict was abating. He made a note to also remember Richard in his will. "I'll certainly do everything I can to look for financing."

"Then it's settled," said Kevin. "Right, Jeff?"

After an uncomfortable pause, Jeff said, "I agree."

"Good," said Richard, as he closed his laptop. "Now, let's set the date for the bank meeting."

Jerry eased back in his chair and let Richard guide Jeff and Kevin toward a date eighteen days out. Part of him stepped back from the scene around the table, and observed what was forming beneath the flipping of Day-Timer pages and tapping of computer keys. These men were engaged to the full extent of their training in the creation of an intangible thing—future financing, money in one of its most abstract forms. The men's work was already growing and stretching into a plan, also intangible. Yet this was also Jerry's family. His brothers and his parents were depending on these filament-fine threads for the quality of the rest of their lives.

There was no objection to the next meeting date, and the meeting around them now broke. Kevin worked his way around the table and put an arm over Richard's shoulder. "Thanks," he said. He, Richard, and Howard left the conference room.

Jerry remained seated and made no attempt to gather his things. As Jeff neared the door, Jerry said, "Could you stay for a few minutes? I'd like to chat." The words felt oddly flat in his throat, and he realized as Jeff sat down that he was exhausted. He could say anything he wanted without a hint of emotion, because his well was, for the moment, dried up.

He said, "The tension between us is affecting Kevin, the management staff, everyone. It's hurting the company. You and I need to come to some understanding. We need to declare a truce."

Jeff did not respond.

"What do I have to do to get through to you?" said Jerry.

Jeff closed his eyes for a moment, then leaned forward and looked at Jerry. His eyes were watery. "Words aren't going to change anything. You have your agenda. I see your logic. You're doing the best you can to implement your agenda. I understand your rationale, and there is a part of me that agrees with you and wants to support you. But there is another part of me that recognizes that if you succeed, my dreams and my life go into the toilet. So why would you expect me to be enthusiastic about what you're doing?"

"There is no alternative. If you push this thing too far with the bank, they will foreclose. Not only will you get nothing for the company, but you'll be in bankruptcy court. I can't believe either you or Salli is enamored with that prospect."

Jeff shook his head. "Right now, I'm not enamored with any prospect."

The self-pitying comment put a hook in him and snagged the last few drops of real anger. "I'm working my ass off for you, Kevin, and the family," he said. "That's all I can do. Cut me some slack."

"Does the 'working your ass off' include nuzzling Helen's pussy?"

"What in the fuck does my seeing Helen have to do with anything?"

"It doesn't just as long as you keep your priorities straight. I know how addictive and distracting a sweet smelling pussy can be."

Jerry tried to respond, but the words would not come out. Jeff's stare was intense. He had to look away. He suspected that the last remark was not made in an entirely generic context. He did not respond. It needed no response. He stood up and left his brother sitting there.

11

FRIDAY EVENING, AUGUST 10, 1990

Salli turned over on her side. "God, I needed that!"

Jeff was on his back. "I could tell. You were pumping like a locomotive on a full head of steam. All I had to do was hang on to your butt and wait for the explosion."

"It's been a while, Jeff. You know how I am when I get really horny."

He tried to remember when the last time was. He had to be careful not to mistakenly include the times that he had been with Helen. It'd been two weeks, no three weeks since he and Helen were in San Francisco, and it had been at least a week or more before then. He decided to be conservative.

"I think it's been about a month." He reached over and stroked her face.

"It's been exactly thirty five days, Jeff. I checked my diary this morning."

"You're right, it has been a while. Why do we do this to ourselves?" He turned over on his side and pressed against her. She didn't answer, so he added, "A purely rhetorical question, Salli, purely rhetorical."

"Good." She turned toward him and ran her hand slowly over his chest and stomach and down between his legs and fondled his testicles. "Let's not destroy the moment. I'd like this to last for a while. I'm just getting started."

Jeff pulled her close, so that he could feel the pressure of her breasts and thighs. Every time he screwed Salli, he marveled over the incredible shape she'd gotten herself back into. The two hours a day at the gym and the personal trainer three times a week had given her a body even a Baywatch actress would die for. She was kissing and stroking him now, and he ran his fingers through her hair and massaged her neck and shoulders. She rolled onto her back, pushing his head down toward her navel.

"Now you work on me a while," she said. She turned on the television and brought up the sound.

"Aren't you going to give me your undivided attention?" he said.

Salli laughed. "I'm planning to do some screaming and I don't want the kids to hear us. Go back to work."

An hour later, they were lying in bed, reading. Michelle had returned from the movies, said goodnight, and went to her room. Jessie was at a girlfriend's sleepover. Salli intermittently turned on the television and channel surfed, and when she did, Jeff let himself drift on the tide of commercials, news, and snippets of TV movies. He looked at her in the flickering artificial light, and she was as beautiful as when they first married. Yet, for the last several years, their lovemaking had been perfunctory, antiseptic. The object had been to relieve their sexual frustrations. Nothing more. Sexual encounters were brief and devoid of foreplay, after-play, kissing, caressing or cuddling. It had been more like sex with a prostitute than sex with a lover. She shut the TV off again, turned on her night-light, leaned against him, and opened her book. The last three hours were every bit as exciting, exhilarating, and enjoyable as any evening with Helen he could remember. Salli had been animated, and even, he hesitated to even think the word—loveable. He chuckled silently and opened his magazine. He wondered whether this evening was a portent of a change in Salli's attitude or an aberration brought on by almost five weeks of abstinence.

She was reading the latest Jane Smiley. Her expression was one of serene contentment—like Ingrid Bergman in *For Whom the Bell Tolls* after she felt the earth move.

He ran the back of his hand over her cheek. "How do you feel?" he asked.

She smiled. "Satisfied, very well satisfied," she said, and continued reading.

"We'll have to do that again, sometime soon," he said.

"I hope so."

He threw the magazine on the floor, turned over on his side, and in less than a minute was asleep.

❖

The next morning, Salli, Michelle, and Jessie were seated at the breakfast table. Salli was reading the paper and sipping her coffee. The girls were working on crossword puzzles. Jeff had donned an apron and was assembling the necessary utensils and food to cook.

"What are you making, Daddy?" asked Michelle.

"Blueberry pancakes. Unless you'd prefer a ham and cheese omelet." He had forgotten how much he enjoyed cooking breakfast for the family.

"Blueberry pancakes would be cool."

"There goes my diet for the day," said Jessie. "Are you at least going to use skim milk?"

"Of course, honey."

"That will save me fifteen calories and one and a half grams of fat per pancake," said Jessie. "I'll have two—no, make it three. I just won't eat lunch."

"How many for you, lamb chop?"

"Four," said Michelle. "I don't have to starve myself for boys like you-know-who."

"Shut up," said Jessie. She turned to her sister and stuck out her tongue.

"Girls, please be civil. This is a very special occasion," said Salli. "We rarely get your father into an apron. Go ahead and have your juice."

Jeff could not remember when he had felt better. He and Salli had made love at six in the morning and then stayed in bed and read the paper, drank coffee, and giggled. He sensed that something was different, but he was afraid to think about it too intensely for fear the moment might suddenly evaporate. He located his favorite large stainless steel bowl and measured out sufficient pancake mix for fifteen—eight for Michelle and Jessie, two for Salli, and five for himself. He added twice as many eggs as the recipe called for—his way of making sure the girls got their protein—poured in the skim milk, and used the big whisk to whip up the batter. He doused the skillet with an ample quantity of Pam, and turned up the burner to a medium flame. He poured out enough batter to form three pancakes and announced in his most commanding drill sergeant voice, "Girls, grub in three minutes."

The pancakes were a hit. He had underestimated. The girls ate five each, so he wound up with three. Jessie recounted the sleepover at Kristen's house and how a group of boys from the church choir came over to serenade them, and how Kristen's parents invited the boys in to have the ice cream and cake that were left over from Kristen's party. Since the girls were all in their pajamas, which were too revealing for a soirée with boys, they all got dressed again, which created an overload situation for the bathrooms. Jessie had Salli and Jeff laughing uncontrollably, as she mimicked and imitated Kristen's parents and several of her friends. Jeff felt as though he had been miraculously transported into a television sitcom. Was it just he who sensed a change? What about the kids? They hadn't shared a breakfast with this level of good spirits for—God knows how long. And what about Salli? What does she feel? But he knew he wouldn't ask because asking might break the spell, like when Wile E. Coyote runs off a cliff and is fine until he looks down and sees that he's been running on air.

After breakfast, Michelle left for soccer practice and Kristen and her mother came by to take Jessie to the mall to meet their friends. The kitchen was a shambles. Dirty dishes were stacked in the sink. Jeff could still hear the echo of his daughters' voices laughing and shouting their approval of his culinary skills. He stacked the dishes in the dishwasher and picked up the skillet and began to scrub it.

Salli was reading the morning paper and drinking her third cup of coffee. She looked up and asked, "How are things going at National?" This was the first time that Salli had asked a direct question about National since the first bank meeting.

He continued to scrub. "Not bad, but not good either."

"What do you mean?"

"The company is doing well. We're beating our projections. But Jerry doesn't see any way to refinance it. We had a long meeting yesterday to figure out what we're going to do. It looks as though we'll have to sell. There aren't enough options." Jeff put the last dish into the dishwasher, added soap, and started the cycle. The noise of the dishwasher droned through his last statement

"How do you feel about that?" she said.

"Depressed, angry, frightened."

She dumped the contents of her coffee cup in the sink, tore off some paper towels, and wiped down the kitchen table. She threw the paper towels into the trash.

"I understand the depression and anger—but why the fear?" There's the old Salli. How could she not understand the fear? Be calm, he told himself. Be calm. He placed the gleaming skillet on the counter and started working on the large bowl that had held the batter. "Because, when the company is sold, I'm out. The buyer will probably retain Kevin in some capacity, but it's likely I'll be gone. And I don't have any idea as to what I'm going to do or how the hell I'll make a living."

Eggshells, all over again—but Salli laughed. "You're acting as if a catastrophe were looming, Jeff. You're smart, energetic and good-looking. You'll figure something out. I'm not worried."

"Thanks for the compliment. But I'm also forty-eight years old. That's pretty old for a marketing executive to be looking for a job." He hoped he did not sound as caustic as he felt.

She took a dishtowel from the drawer, dried the skillet, and stored it in the drawer under the stove. Jeff handed her the bowl.

"How's Mr. Goody-Two-Shoes doing?"

Jeff laughed. "Mr. Goody-Two-Shoes. You certainly have him pegged, Salli." He put down the scrub brush and leaned on the counter. "Jerry's working real hard and making things happen. And I'm being a real pain in the ass. I seem to go out of my way to make things hard for him. It's stupid."

"Why do you do it," she asked. She poured herself a fresh cup of coffee. "Do you want a cup?"

He shook his head. "Frankly I don't know. It's like a reaction. He says white, I say black. We're reliving the same battles we fought growing up and at National when Jerry was chief engineer." He held out his palms and sighed. "I probably should see a shrink about this, but I can't devote any energy to it now."

"Have you talked to Charlie about National? Maybe he can come up with something." She sat down at the kitchen table.

He sat down facing her. "I didn't really want to get your father involved in our dirty laundry."

She put her cup down and stared into his eyes. She was engaged in his—their—problem. "You're being hypersensitive, Jeff. Don't be an ass. In the position you're in—that we're in—you've got to take advantage of every contact. And my father is probably the best contact you have. He likes to feel needed." She looked up at the kitchen clock. "You're playing golf with him today, aren't you?"

"Yeah, at 1:30."

"Talk to him. Stop acting like a victim. The Jeff I married was never depressed. I'd like to see that Jeff again."

Jeff looked at Salli and tried to conceal the wonder he felt. I can't believe it, he thought. She actually gives a shit.

❖

As he drove to the golf course, Jeff was planning how he would describe the National situation to Charlie. Fortunately, he and Charlie were so close that he did not have to tiptoe around the issue—nor his continuing conflict with Jerry. The relationship with Charlie was a relief, compared to Jeff's relationship with his own father; no matter what, his father was "the General" and Jeff was the junior officer. One of the unexpected perks of his marrying Salli was that he got Charlie as both a father-in-law and a buddy. Not only did they frequently play local golf, but Charlie took him on some very expensive golf outings with his well-heeled friends—in Scotland, Hawaii, Augusta, and Pebble Beach. And Charlie paid for everything. Jeff often wondered whether or not their relationship would survive a split with Salli.

Charlie missed his putt when the ball veered off to the left just before it should have dropped, and now, Jeff crouched behind the ball and sighted twenty-five feet to the cup. He lined up his putt a half-cup's width to the right and stroked it, remembering to follow through. The ball rolled along his line and landed with a rattle.

"Son-of-a-bitch, he made it," said Charlie. He picked up the flag, shook his head, and walked over to the cup. He reached down and retrieved Jeff's ball, tossed it to him, and then jammed the flag into the cup.

Jeff looked over at Charlie, smiled broadly and said, "I guess you go down to defeat again."

"I don't see how you can keep pulling those twenty-five foot putts out of your ass. God dammit! This was my round."

"You know, you might consider retiring those golf shoes. It might help your game."

"It's not my fifteen-year-old shoes, Jeff. It's your incredible luck." He shook his head again. He looked up to the sky. "God, why won't you let me beat him, just once?"

Jeff reviewed the scorecard and said, "I won ten holes, you won three, we tied five, so you owe me seventy bucks to add to your misery."

"All right, all right. Enjoy your moment in the sun. Come on, you can at least buy me a drink." He rammed his putter into his bag. They got into the cart and drove over to the lounge.

The lounge in the Wilshire Country Club was almost empty. There were just a few golfers having drinks and watching television. They took a seat near the window overlooking the eighteenth green. Jeff ordered Vodka Absolut and Charlie ordered a gin and tonic.

"You sure play above your level when the pressure's on," Charlie said.

"It's the story of my life." He took off his baseball cap and placed it on the chair next to him. He took a handful of nuts from the dish and tossed them into his mouth.

"Marrying my daughter ensured that you would always be under pressure."

"I know. I can't say you didn't warn me."

"How's the relationship?" The waiter brought their order and they both took long drinks. Half of Charlie's drink was gone when he set it down. Losing always seemed to put him in the mood to drink. Jeff took another handful of nuts.

"Status quo." He and Charlie had talked often about his dysfunctional marriage, so there was no need to gild the lily. He had long ago gotten past any qualms about complaining to the man about his own daughter—Charlie even enjoyed their mutual gripes about women, marriage, and sex. "She nags incessantly," Jeff said. "I eventually react. We fight. We don't speak. She eventually gets frustrated and needs to fuck. We fuck. We make nice-nice for a while and after a week or two the cycle begins all over again." He took a drink. "The last three days have been great. I'm holding my breath."

Charlie's eyes sparkled. "You didn't mention that you get frustrated," he said. Jeff just grinned. "So you got something else going? I don't blame you. When I was married to Salli's mother, I got sex whenever and wherever I could. It kept me from crawling up the walls. How are my grandchildren?"

"They are fine. Jessie's bust is growing at warp speed. We can't keep her in bras. She's spends a good percentage of her waking hours in front of a mirror assessing every aspect of her appearance."

"That was Salli," said Charlie. "And Michelle?"

"Busy with everything. School, soccer, dancing. You name it, and she's involved. Salli spends two hours a day shuttling her between activities."

"They are great kids. You and Salli have done a super job raising them. I hope you guys can last until Michelle's in high school." He tossed back the rest of his drink, and there was a lull in the conversation.

Jeff took a long sip of his. "I need to talk to you about National."

"Okay. But you'll have to buy me another drink." He motioned to the waiter and ordered another round. "Shoot!"

Jeff moved his chair closer to the table. He drained his glass and leaned into the table. "I guess the last time we talked, I told you that my brother, Jerry, was coming to lead the turnaround. Well, we went back to see Jerry's partners to explore whether the deal could be restructured using secured debt exclusively, and their verdict was negative."

Charlie appeared to be distracted, anxious for his drink to arrive. "What firm is that?" he said.

"Bricker and Weldon."

Charlie grimaced. He was no longer distracted. "Jews, niggers, and spic cunts!"

Jeff laughed, "No, Charlie, its Jews and African-Americans, and Hispanic women. Let's focus on the reputation. I understand it's great."

"Bullshit."

"Charlie, can you put your white sheet away for a minute, so we can talk about my problem?"

The waiter arrived and placed the drinks on the table. Charlie grabbed his, tossed his head back and nearly drained it. "It just pisses me off to see niggers in the banking business. They should be sweeping the fucking floor of the Exchange instead of trading on it."

"Okay, Charlie, okay." Jeff shook his head and took a breath. "Now assuming that Birney—Birney's the managing partner—assuming he is right, we're left with two options. One, a sale. It's likely that Kevin and I won't receive much and I will certainly lose my job. Or two, a major investment by a sub-debt player who will let us stay in control and grow the company to the point that we can take it public."

"What about a white knight? A company in the industry who likes your products."

"Too risky. The guys would come in with their own management team and Kevin and I would be squeezed out. If that was the only alternative, I would just a soon see the damn thing sold, and then I could go do something else with my life."

Charlie lifted his glass and saw that it was almost empty. "Jeff, this conversation is going to cost you." He motioned to the waiter and he ordered another round. "You're probably right. You certainly wouldn't be running your own show afterwards." The waiter arrived with the third round. Charlie took a short sip. He sat back in his chair and closed his eyes. Jeff wondered whether he was going to doze off then and there. Suddenly, Charlie opened his eyes. The sparkle was back. He grabbed some more nuts, tossed them into his mouth and said, "We should be able to attract someone. I know that Warren likes the industry, for one. He's got a small investment through Berkshire in one of your competitors—a company with a name starting with an E or an I…"

"Eye Dentity or Identix?"

"That's it, Identix. We might be able to key off of that. Do you have any information on Identix and how it compares to National?"

"Plenty. We go up against them all the time. I'd have to gather it from the marketing and technical guys."

Charlie's face was red and he was talking faster. "Put a package together for me on National and compare National to the competition with particular attention to Identix. What's National's debt now?"

Jeff explained National's financial condition. National owed the bank thirteen million and needed at least an additional five million to pay down accounts payable, to rebuild the units that had been borrowed from customers and pay off Jerry's line of credit—two million dollars by October.

Charlie took a scoring pencil out of his shirt pocket, turned over the cocktail napkin, and started to write. "What will the asset-based lenders give you?"

"Eleven to twelve, depending on the appraisal."

"Let's assume eleven and one half. What's your conservative estimate of the next three years' average earnings before taxes?"

"Four to five."

"That's conservative?"

"Yeah."

"Let's assume four," said Charlie. "What about depreciation and projected capital investments?" He reached for the napkin in front of Jeff and continued to write.

"Depreciation is running at the rate of two hundred thousand a year," said Jeff. "And we're projecting capital equipment purchases of about one fifty."

Charlie turned the second napkin over and chewed on the back of the pencil. Jeff held the glass in his hand and watched Charlie think. He had never talked serious business with his father-in-law and didn't know what to expect. Charlie put the pencil down and studied the second napkin. Finally he said, "I think this could work. Your pre-tax earnings plus depreciation minus average capital expenditures is about four million fifty. Since you're growing by about ten percent a year, a mezzanine financier will value the company at four to five times the four million. We'll be optimistic and assume five times. That's about twenty million two fifty. We'll give one third of the deal to the investors, so you and Kevin can each keep a third. One third is worth six million, seven hundred and fifty. Can you sell anything to raise some cash?"

"Not really."

"Any tax refunds?"

Jeff shook his head.

Charlie wrote some more numbers on the napkin. "How about another drink? It gets my creative juices flowing. I'll buy this round."

"Christ, Charlie, that's four. They'll have to carry us out."

After Charlie ordered another round, he turned back to his napkin and checked some figures. "Here is the deal. We sell one-third to the investors for six million seven fifty. The current note holders will have to subordinate to the new investment. Assume the eleven and one half from the asset-based lenders, Foothill, Congress, or whoever. That gets us to eighteen million. Figure one million for legal fees, accounting fees, and loan fees and we're at seventeen."

"That's not enough," said Jeff, trying to keep up.

"Indulge me for a minute," said Charlie. "The bank takes a one-and-one-half-million-dollar haircut and reduces their loan to eleven plus. We pay off the bank and Jerry and you've got about four million in cash to take care of your other problems. Tight, but doable. Build it up over the next three years and do a public offering, and you'll be as rich as your wife. By the way, is the trade current?"

"We've stretched them from thirty days to forty-five."

"Not too bad. If you need more cash, you'll be able to stretch them a bit more."

Jeff picked up the napkin and looked over the numbers. "It's been a long time since Finance 101, but I think I follow." He was feeling woozy and finding it difficult to stay up with Charlie. He took a small sip, determined not to drink much of the fourth round. "What do you get out of this, Charlie?"

"I'll take fifty thousand plus some warrants. Peanuts."

Jeff leaned back in his chair. He looked at the napkin again. He was beginning to believe. "How confident are you of being able to get an investor group to bite?"

"Depends how National compares to Identix," said Charlie. "Warren's sprinkled the holy water on Identix. If National shows good numbers in market share, market growth rate, margins…I'd expect to create a lot of interest."

"What about the bank's haircut? Sheila already said no way."

"Of course she did. She hasn't been presented with a real deal. You were talking hypothetically. She's not going to negotiate against a phantom. When we get the loan commitments and have the deal ready to go, we'll meet with her and show her the eleven million. She'll take it. Like the guy who sells suits on television says, 'I guarantee it.'"

Jeff wanted to jump up and yell he was so happy, but he concealed his buoyancy for now. "I ought to discuss this with Kevin."

"I don't think that's a good idea. Kevin will feel obligated to tell Jerry and in light of Jerry's role as the bank's surrogate, he will be loath to pursue a deal that requires the bank to discount their note when the bank has already taken the position that they will not do it. You're going to have to sit on this, and do it yourself until we have the commitments."

"I see," said Jeff. "But I hate to have secrets from Kevin."

"Can't be helped. How do we get access to the books without tipping off Kevin and Jerry?" He folded both napkins and put them in his shirt pocket along with the pencil.

"We'll get the stuff through Howard. He's loyal to me. He'll keep quiet if I ask him to."

They sat in silence. The reddish tint of the setting sun drifted over the silent lounge. They both sipped their drinks. Charlie took the napkins out of his pocket again, carefully examined them, and returned them to his pocket. Jeff stared through the window and watched the flag for the eighteenth green, as it gently fluttered in the late afternoon breeze. Jeff reached over and grasped Charlie's hand and squeezed once, firmly.

"Okay, let's do it." He started to laugh. "Let's do it!"

Charlie was matter-of-fact. "No problem, kid. Anything for the father of my grandchildren."

They stood up, shook hands, and then hugged each other.

What incredibly bad luck, thought Jerry. We find ourselves with almost perfect conditions to ensure that a deal will not get done or get done at a bargain basement price. The hill up which he had to move the boulder had gotten a lot steeper during the past two weeks: The economy had been stagnant for several months before the invasion. The growth stock index had eroded and there was rampant speculation about the possibility of a recession. Now the Chicken Littles were in full voice, expressing concerns about the rise in oil prices, increased military expenditures, looming budget deficits, and higher unemployment rates. He felt sick every time he picked up a *Wall Street Journal.*

On TV, Iraq dominated the airways. CNN was reporting that on Saddam's orders, American and British citizens were reporting to specified hotels, apparently to serve as "designated hostages." As he and Birney had expected, the invasion of Kuwait had thrown the economic markets into turmoil.

His intercom buzzed. "It's Ethan Wilson of Blanchard and Co."

A moment later, Wilson clicked on.

"G'day, how's it going?"

Jerry clicked off the TV. "Fine. Have you seen the news?"

"Yeah, it's iffy. This is going to be one bodgy market over the next few months."

"I agree," said Jerry. "The timing for our deal could not be worse. Anyway, I'm looking forward to our meeting tomorrow."

"That's why I called. I have to be in LA for a meeting this evening. So I'm planning to spend the night and we can get together tomorrow morning. Will that work for you?"

Jerry hesitated. His first inclination was to tell Wilson that he had other business in San Francisco—which in one sense was true. But the disappointment of not taking Helen on a trip was quickly crowded out by his drilled-in professionalism.

"That's fine. It will save me a trip."

"Ace," said Ethan. "Ten a.m."

Jerry hung up and dialed Helen. She said she was a little frantic because she had a major collector on the verge of a ten thousand dollar purchase.

"Good for you!" said Jerry. "I'll be quick, then. The guy I was going to meet in San Francisco will be in LA on Friday and we'll be meeting here. Unfortunately, that means you and I will not be going to San Francisco." He tried to express his real disappointment over the change in plans.

"Oh, no! I was so looking forward to it."

"Me too," said Jerry. "We'll go in a couple of weeks, after the bank meeting. Is that okay?"

"Then at least come to dinner Saturday night."

Jerry didn't hesitate. "Sure! Yes, I'd love to. Thanks."

"Seven p.m. Bring red wine and your appetite." Her voice stirred and a smile entered it. "And plan to stay a while."

For the past two weeks, Jerry had focused the bulk of his time writing, producing, and directing the performance that he needed to stage for the bank. He felt like a regular Woody Allen. National needed time to find a buyer and put a deal together, and Sheila had life and death power over whether an adequate extension of the bank agreement would be granted. It was his job to ensure that the National story was presented in a cogent, gripping, and persuasive manner.

The National team would include the starring five: Kevin, Jeff, Howard, Richard Krimble, and himself. He decided that he needed the presence of the key experts to tell their stories personally to Sheila. He arranged for Ethan Wilson to be present. He called on Birney to lend Tom Morgan out for the bank meeting to give an independent evaluation of National's market position. Birney agreed to provide Tom for the cost of travel expenses. He wanted to make certain that when Sheila left the meeting she was humming the main tunes and would sing the company's praises to the bank's senior management.

When the show time arrived, the bank's main conference room was full of dark-suited bankers, lawyers, and executives about to lay bare an accurate picture of National's financial condition and prospects. Sheila Crown was there, along with Bill Bromfield, Jerry, and the rest of the National cast. After coffee, rolls, and juice, Bill Bromfield announced that he would serve as chairman of the meeting. He distributed a tall stack of agendas. And so it begins, Jerry thought, the key performance in the magic show of creating a future for my family.

Bill said, "Before we get into the meat of today's business, I want to make a few remarks to set forth the bank's position so there are no misunderstandings in the future. This credit has received a great deal of attention by senior management. First, because it is a large credit for this bank and second because of the, shall I say, unique circumstances that created the problem. The current arrangement with the company expires on September 30, approximately five weeks from today. If the bank is not fully repaid on that date and no other agreement has been worked out between the company and the bank, our office has instructions to institute foreclosure proceedings. The purpose of this meeting is for the company to bring the bank up to speed on its progress toward getting the bank repaid and to persuade the bank to either extend or enter a new agreement. Is that your understanding, Richard?"

"That's our understanding," said Krimble, looking up from his laptop. "The company's ownership understands that the bank is serious and is determined to be repaid, and those facts are guiding their efforts."

"Good," said Bill. He turned to Jerry. "This is your show. Proceed."

Jerry nodded at Bill and stood. "In light of the problems National has caused the bank and the amount of senior management time that has been consumed by our problems, the bank is extremely gracious to provide breakfast." There was a general snickering. Jerry held Sheila's gaze. "I know that you personally went to bat for us to persuade the bank's senior management to give the company an opportunity to control its own destiny. That took a lot of courage and faith. I am sure that by the time this meeting concludes, you will feel that your confidence in us was justified. This is our program."

Howard went first. He summarized National's financial position at the time of the discovery of the Johnson-Potter scheme and compared it to the current position. The gist of his presentation was that the company had generated a pre-tax operating profit of about three hundred thousand dollars. Gross margins and G-and-A rates had returned to their 1989 values. Jerry invested a lot of time coaching and preparing Howard for his presentation and was as proud as a father watching his six year old perform in a Christmas pageant.

Howard then presented an analysis of the inventory deficit. He showed production schedules indicating that the deficit had been approximately halved during the past two months and was predicted to be zero within the next three months. After answering some perfunctory questions from Sheila, Howard sat down.

Jeff spoke next about the company's sales and marketing situation. His presentation emphasized the efforts to calm irate customers who were complaining about the length of time it was taking to perform warranty repairs on their units. As part of his presentation, he showed letters that were sent to various customers, and described several customer meetings in which he personally participated. Jeff completed his presentation using charts showing the company's order rate during the current year and comparing it to previous years. He emphasized that the company was on course to show an improvement of approximately 15 percent in the order rate. Jeff's presentation went well. He was enthusiastic, positive, and in command—the very opposite of his demeanor during the New York meeting. Jerry felt his anger toward Jeff subsiding.

Tom Morgan went next and presented his report on the analysis of the access control industry, emphasizing National's strength in biometrics. Sheila and Bill followed the presentation closely and asked Tom several questions, most of which focused on the reliability of the data underlying the analysis.

Jerry then called on Ethan Wilson. At six foot two, with the build of a basketball player and rust colored hair, he cut an imposing figure as he walked to the front of the room. First he described the history and background of Blanchard and Co. and the qualifications of the senior partners. He also discussed their most recent merger deals in the high-tech industry, and concluded with an action plan for marketing National, along with time estimates for completing each of the key phases of the sales effort and his cost projections.

He said, "To summarize, we think there are a lot of blokes who'll be stoked to look at National." As he returned to his seat, he said, "Incidentally, I delivered our contract and an invoice for the retainer to Howard and he's been told that Bill is reviewing it. I want everyone to understand that we've got Buckley's chance of meeting the schedule unless we get our retainer by the end of this week."

Jerry smiled. "We know the drill, Ethan. I'm in the same business."

Sheila and Bill appeared very pleased. She said, "Jerry, I want to thank you and your team for the excellent presentation. You covered all the bases." And to Krimble, she said, "Does National have a proposal?"

Richard stopped typing on his laptop and set it to one side. "As you can see from the material that was presented today, the company has been stabilized and is profitable. The customer base is solid and sales are increasing. Based on the information that Ethan presented, it should be a very attractive asset for a number of firms. Ethan needs time to create a market for the company and hopefully attract two or more buyers, so that the price is maximized. That's in the best interest of both the bank and the Bascombs. The company needs a six-month extension of the current arrangement to achieve that objective."

"How do you feel about this, Jerry?" said Sheila.

"We have over a month left on the current deal. A six-month extension to March 31 should be adequate."

"Give us a few minutes to talk." Sheila and Bill left the conference room. As the door closed, Kevin, who had remained silent through the entire meeting, asked Krimble, "Do you think they'll buy it?"

Richard smiled. "I try never predicting what a bank will do, but I think yes."

"How do you feel about this, Jeff?" said Kevin.

Jeff was in the process of stuffing his presentation and notes back into his briefcase. He glanced at Kevin, looking sour. "Shit, I don't know. I can't see that it matters that much. I don't think that another six months, nine months, or a year is going to put any more money in our pockets. No matter how you slice it, this is a forced sale, and we are going to be fucked. I guarantee it."

Jerry saw no point in commenting. Jeff was right. It was a forced sale and maybe by some miracle, if two or more buyers got interested, they could create an auction and generate a price that would get some substantial money to the Bascombs, but in his heart, he knew the probability was low.

After about five minutes, Sheila and Bill returned to the conference room and resumed their seats. Sheila said to Krimble, "We are very pleased with the company's progress. We believe your request is reasonable and we are prepared to grant it. We will extend the present agreement for six months. The bank will require an extension fee of one hundred thousand dollars, payable upon signing. Bill will draft the extension and send it over to Richard." She looked around the room. "Anything else?"

Ethan spoke up. "Does the bank expect to approve our contract and authorize the retainer?"

"I'm in the process of reviewing it," said Bill. "I don't see any problems yet. I will get back to the company with any comments by tomorrow evening. I expect that we will be able to meet your time table."

Sheila said, "Bill and I are running behind today. Are we done?"

Krimble made a check of his side of the table and shrugged. "I think that does it. We appreciate the effort you have both put into this deal. The company is committed to bringing this matter to a satisfactory conclusion."

"Amen," said Jerry under his breath.

12

TUESDAY, AUGUST 28, 1990

Howard was ebullient. The installation of the new MIS system was completed, all the test reports had run without a glitch, and the meeting with Jerry to review his ninety-day performance evaluation had been super. The guy could not have been more complimentary—and in fact, there were times during the meeting that he felt maybe, just maybe, Jerry's effusive remarks were a manifestation of his surprise that a black chief financial officer could be competent. Or it might be that Jerry felt that he, being black, needed an extra dose of laudatory comments to build his self-esteem. Well, frankly, he didn't care what the story was. Compliments were nice, and Jerry told him he was giving him a ten-thousand-dollar-a-year raise. That ten thousand brought him back to what he was pulling two years ago. When he called his wife right after the meeting to tell her, her scream damn near punctured his eardrum.

He was on a roll. There was the little nagging concern about National's future, though—seven to eight months down the line, Jerry, his mentor and advocate, would be gone, the company sold, and he might have to look for a job again. Not a pleasant thought. The last time he was laid off, it took him six months to find one. But, he thought, then is then and now is now, and I'll be damned if I'm going to spoil this glorious day by dwelling on negatives.

Howard walked through the parking lot toward his car. He had forgotten his reading glasses and needed them in order to get through a stack of computer spreadsheets. He was always losing them or breaking them, and maybe he should get contacts and finally escape the glasses bullshit. It would be a treat to himself for getting the raise. Just then, a large truck pulled out of the delivery gate. The company's name, Technology Recyclers, was stenciled on the driver's door.

Howard hadn't seen the truck before and he wasn't familiar with the name of the company, not from either the accounts receivable list or the accounts payable list. Howard prided himself on being familiar with every customer and every vendor, and it irritated him that he didn't recognize the name. He made a mental note to follow up on the name when he got back to his office.

He reached his car and looked into the glove compartment for his glasses. Not there. He looked in the front and back seats, on the dashboard, under the seats with the same result. He slammed the door in frustration and headed back upstairs.

While he sifted through his desk, still looking for the damn glasses, he called Angie, his bookkeeper, and asked her whether Technology Recyclers was a customer or a vendor. About an hour later, she called him on the intercom and reported that Technology Recyclers was neither a customer nor a vendor and had not been either for at least five years.

"Thanks," said Howard. "Probably a guy looking for directions." He had located a magnifying glass to help him cope with the small type of the printouts and was engrossed in reviewing them.

Ever since the Potter-Johnson blow-up and his promotion to CFO, he had been clocking fourteen-hour days. Some evenings he'd return home so tired that he'd go to bed without eating or undressing and fall immediately asleep. This was a big job, the biggest he'd ever had, and he was determined to do it well. He was therefore surprised that the image of that damn truck would not go away. What made it stand out was the fact that it was a beat-up relic, a wreck that you would see in the hood, not in the back parking lot of a fifty-million-a year high-tech company. And there were no offices in the back of the building other than shipping and receiving. The image of the truck continued to nag at him.

Two days later, he was eating lunch in the company cafeteria when Enrico, the shipping and receiving supervisor, sat down at the end of his table. He finished his meal, picked up his coffee cup and moved down opposite from Enrico.

"Got a minute to talk?" he asked.

"I always have a minute for the guy who signs my paycheck. What's up?"

"Are you familiar with a company called Technology Recyclers?"

Enrico thought for a minute and said, "No, don't know them. Why?"

Howard told him about seeing the truck and not being able to find the name in the accounts receivable or accounts payable listings. "Sorry, I can't help, man. Incidentally, how's business? Should I update my résumé?"

"The company's doing very well. I think we're over the hump." He gave Enrico a sideways look; the guy was one of the best first-level supervisors in the company. "You're not serious are you?"

Enrico laughed. "Just kidding, man. Just kidding. Look, I've got to go. Sorry I couldn't help."

Later that afternoon, while Howard was squinting over the computer printouts again, Enrico called. "Hey, I checked with my guys about Technology Recyclers. The reason I didn't recognize the name is that the guy who owns the business operates under a number of different names. Guy's name is Bob Simone. He buys obsolete computers and peripherals and scavenges them for the components and precious metals. We've been dealing with him for a long time."

"Under what names would he be listed?" asked Howard.

"Beats me. He takes all of our old stuff. Works right off of a price list. I've got one if you'd like to see it."

"I'll be right over." Howard hung up the phone and rushed out of the accounting department. When he reached the shipping and receiving department, he peered through the office door's glass window and saw that Enrico was alone. He walked in and sat down in the chair in front of the desk. Enrico shoved the price list over to him. Howard held the paper about eight inches from his face and attempted to read it.

"What's wrong, man, can't you see?"

"Lost my reading glasses."

The document showed the prices that Technology Recyclers offered for various electronic parts, assemblies, printed circuit boards, printers, and chassis. The prices were specified in terms of so much a pound for metal and mechanisms, and so much a square inch for printed circuit boards. There were various handwritten notations on the sheet, which Howard could barely make out. Enrico read the notes out loud.

"Do you know this guy well?" said Howard.

"Yeah. Been doing business with him since I came here."

"When was that?"

"Christ, ten years."

"Then, why isn't he on any list?"

"Shit, I don't know, man. All I do is make an inventory of what we're selling him, estimate the value using this here price list, and arrange for the shipment. When he comes in to pick it up, he makes us an offer, we dicker, and then he pays me cash for the amount we agree on. That's it."

Howard felt his heart start to beat a trifle faster. "Cash?"

"Yeah, cash. Dead presidents. It's the way he wants to deal. Fine with me."

Howard tried to remember whether Angie had ever mentioned receiving significant cash deposits.

"How much cash are we talking about, Enrico?"

"We usually get between five grand and ten grand for a shipment. Sometimes more, sometimes less. The shipments at the end of the year bring twelve to fifteen."

Howard felt his heart beat increase and a film of sweat start to form on his hands. "How many shipments per month?"

Enrico's tone started to mirror the intensity of his own. He knew he was getting grilled. "Usually one, sometimes two. It varies. Say, why the hell are you asking me? You're supposed to be the money man." Despite the small hint of irritation in Enrico's voice, he was still smiling. Howard also smiled. He definitely did not want Enrico to dwell on his escalating concern that the accounting department was not receiving five to fifteen thousand dollars once or twice a month from Technology Recyclers or anyone else.

"You know, I'm new. I'm still trying to figure out how things work around here." Howard took a deep breath. He didn't want to ask the next question because he knew that there was going to be no good answer. "Exactly what is the procedure in your department for handling the cash that you receive from Simone?"

"Not rocket science. I get Simone to sign a copy of the shipper and I put the shipper and the cash in an envelope. I seal it and I deliver it personally to Mr. Bascomb. Oh, and I keep a file of the shippers in that file over there." He pointed to a four-drawer vertical file across the office. Howard took another deep breath and it felt a little like a gasp. His efforts to look inscrutable weren't paying dividends. He smiled and thanked Enrico for helping him understand the procedures National was using to deal with salvage. He shook Enrico's hand and realized he had made a mistake; his hand was drenched in sweat. As he left, he mentioned in as nonchalant manner as he could muster that he would be back in about an hour to take a look at the files.

❖

Jerry took Howard's call shortly after 6:00 p.m. and agreed to meet that evening at the condo. When he asked about the issues that Howard wanted to discuss, Howard replied that they were sensitive and he didn't want to talk on the phone.

Footsteps banged on Jerry's walk shortly after 8:00 p.m., and he went to the door and opened it, so that Howard didn't have to juggle the files to reach the doorbell. Howard was out of breath and perspiring, having lugged a banker's box stuffed with documents from a parking place two blocks away. Jerry offered him a drink and Howard opted for a Diet Coke. He was agitated and paced around the living room. When Jerry handed him the drink, Howard apologized for barging in.

Jerry headed back to the kitchen and got his drink, a bowl of pretzels, and some napkins for the dining area and suggested that they sit at the table. He wanted Howard to be comfortable for whatever he had come to say.

Howard described his chance sighting of the Technical Recycling truck, Angie's failure to find references to it in the company's records, and his meetings with Enrico. He handed Jerry a number of spreadsheets and explained how he had prepared them. He went over the various entries on the spreadsheets, taking pains to ensure that Jerry completely understood the sources of the entries and the manner in which any calculations were performed.

Jerry listened to the recitation of events. When Howard got to the part about Enrico's receiving cash, he realized that Howard had uncovered embezzlement and his mind wandered as he thought about how he might deal with the problem, depending upon who the suspected embezzlers were and how much money was involved.

Jerry was startled out of his channel of thoughts when Howard said, "As you can see, Jerry, during the time period covered by these shippers—about eight years—Enrico collected and turned over $659,000 in cash to Kevin, and there is no record of any of these transactions in the company's books."

Jerry's mind went blank. He reached for his drink and took a long sip, using the time to figure out how he was going to respond, but the only thing that flashed into his mind was sitting around the campfire drinking Jack Daniels with Kevin and Jeff. He was aware that Howard was observing every nuance in his expression and demeanor. His hand began to shake and he quickly put down the glass.

"Kevin?" he said.

Howard nodded.

He appreciated that Howard could drop his easy friendliness for a dry, businesslike demeanor as he related what he knew to be devastating facts, facts that would have serious consequences for the company and the principals. Before he could ask any other question, Howard abruptly stood, and like the TV detective who tells the victim's mother that he's sorry for her loss and quickly departs, said that he had another engagement.

At the door, Jerry made a feeble smile and extended his hand. "Great piece of detective work, Howard. I'm sickened by your result, but I'm proud of you."

Howard took his hand and shook it. "Thanks, boss," he said and attempted a weak smile back.

The pendulum wall clock chimed once. Jerry awoke and realized he had dozed off. He was still clutching a highball glass full of melted ice and Jack Daniels, for old time's sake. Chelsey was lying by the side of the couch breathing deeply. CNN Headline News flashed on mute. He'd been out maybe two hours. He slowly raised himself from the sofa and walked stiffly to the kitchen. He looked at the pile of documents on the dining room table and remembered that he'd dreamed of spreadsheets and numbers. Eight ounces of liquor and he was neither sick nor drunk and still felt awful.

He passed the table without stopping to look at the documents and entered the kitchen. There he dumped the contents of the glass down the drain and fixed a fresh one over ice. The phone on the counter blinked. He punched the button—three from Helen, the most recent at eleven thirty, and one from Kevin.

He vaguely remembered reviewing the spreadsheets that showed the dates and amounts of the cash transfers. But after Howard dropped the bomb, he was in a fog. He listened, he heard, but it was as if some news commentator was describing events in Turkey or Tibet. There was only this evening to pass through the five stages of grief and get back to functioning again. He figured that he had emerged from denial at about 9:30 p.m. and was well into anger when he dozed off. He had probably worked through his anger in his sleep, because when we awoke, he wasn't angry with Kevin anymore. Sure, he had called Kevin every name he could conjure up between 9:30 p.m. and 11:00 p.m. He had been loud and ecumenical. He had even used the few Yiddish terms of contempt that he had learned from his partners. It had been therapeutic. There was no one to hear him but Chelsey.

But now he was just depressed—horribly depressed with no one to talk to. He couldn't risk it with Helen, his parents, or his partners. Sure, he'd talk to Jeff in the morning, but that would be business. And the more he realized how alone and isolated he was, the more alone, isolated, and depressed he felt.

What exacerbated his despair was that he felt like a fool. His words to Shelia coursed through his brain—*The key to this deal is being able to manage and control Kevin and Jeff. I certainly know my brothers better than anyone on this planet...* "I don't know shit!" he shouted. "I can't manage or control either of them, and that will soon be clear to the bank. "Shit! Shit! Shit!"

Chelsey awoke, lifted her head, and looked at him. Jerry felt an icy cold fear envelop his body. Coming in the wake of the Potter-Johnson fraud, Kevin's embezzlement would give Sheila ample evidence to conclude that he was a blowhard, and that they were all a bunch of crooks. In order to save her job, she just might play Pontius Pilot, wash her hands of the whole mess, declare a default, foreclose, and liquidate. He could see the headlines in the *Wall Street Journal*: Jerry Bascomb, noted investment banker, leads National into bankruptcy. The street would suck it up with glee. Every asshole that he had ever bested in a deal would be dancing around the funeral pyre of his reputation. The bank would have to report this to the regulators and they'd indict Kevin for bank fraud, tax fraud, and God knew what else. They'd be flushed—Kevin, Jeff, National, Mom, Dad, and him.

Jerry could not remember when he had been so frightened. A physics final? The bar exam? The time his ex-girlfriend coaxed him to screw her in the living room while her mom and dad watched television in the den twenty feet away? No, he remembered when. It was when he was thrown out of the raft in a Class 5 rapid and damn near drowned. He was terrified and he had reason to be.

"Chelsey?"

Her ear twitched, but she had gone back to sleep. His throat felt tight. He had trouble swallowing. He did not have the luxury of wallowing past seven. He would have to start taking action at first light to contain the damage. There was no alternative. As chief financial officer, Howard had an obligation to keep the company's financials accurate, and the failure to record the proceeds from the sales to Simone made them inaccurate. He would have to advise the bank in a timely manner.

He went into the kitchen and pitched the contents of the glass down the sink and poured the half bottle of Jack Daniels down after it. He tossed the used coffee grinds and filters into the trash compactor and set up the coffee maker to make eight cups of Starbuck's European Blend.

He checked his watch. Two thirty-five. It's good that I'm scared, he thought—anxiety has overtaken depression, and fear is the number one motivator. He walked over to the small desk and found a yellow pad and pen. He lowered himself onto the sofa and started to write his plan. His only regret at the moment was that he could not think of any appropriate prayer. But he hoped that the deities would look with favor upon his efforts. He needed help from every corner.

At 7:30 a.m., he called Kevin. The phone rang several times. Carolyn came on the line. "Sorry to get you up so early," Jerry said. "I need to speak with Kevin. Is he still home?"

"Yeah, I think so. We went to a late movie. I'll go see if he's in the kitchen." The scuff-scuff of Carolyn's slippers on the hardwood floors came through the phone. A few minutes later, Kevin picked up the phone.

"Hi Jerry, what's up?"

"Could you come over to my apartment this morning? I need to go over some things with you without being interrupted by the National chaos."

"Sure, my schedule's clear. What are we talking about? I can start thinking about it on my way over."

Jerry was prepared. He used the same parry that Howard had used on him twelve hours before. "It's pretty sensitive stuff, Kevin. I'd prefer not to talk about it over the phone. We'll have plenty of time to hash it around when you get here." Before Kevin could respond, he said, "See you about eight-thirty, okay?"

"Yeah, okay," said Kevin, sounding flummoxed.

An hour later, he was at the door. They hugged and Jerry motioned Kevin over to the sofa. "How about some lox, bagels, and cream cheese?"

"Terrific," said Kevin. "Do you have any coffee? I left the house in such a hurry, I didn't get a chance to charge my batteries."

Jerry brought out the two trays he had prepared and set them down on the coffee table. He went back to the kitchen for the coffee. "So, what did you see last night?"

"Some art film. French with subtitles."

"Any good?"

"Didn't follow it too well. I kept dozing off."

"What was it about?"

"It was about this respectable woman who is married to a wealthy guy, but she has the urge to be a hooker. It was very confusing. One of her lovers eventually shoots her husband and winds up paralyzed in a wheelchair."

"*Belle de Jour*. It's a classic."

"What do I know? I go to these things for Carolyn." He took a large bite from the lox and bagel sandwich and sipped his coffee. "Anyway, what do you want to talk about? You sounded very mysterious."

Jerry had sorted Howard's spreadsheets on the dining room table, and now he went through them again to make sure they were in order. Kevin finished his sandwich, gulped down the remaining coffee in his mug, and wiped off his hands. He handed the spreadsheets to Kevin, sat down on the chair opposite the sofa, and waited. Kevin pulled his reading glasses out of his breast pocket, adjusted them, and turned his attention to the spreadsheets.

All the blood seemed to drain out of his face. He looked through the pages for another few minutes. His hands trembled and beads of sweat formed on his forehead. He folded the spreadsheets carefully and handed them back to Jerry. There were tears in his eyes. They were unfocused and not directed toward Jerry, but seemed to be searching for something out in the marina.

"How did you find out?"

"Howard saw the truck leaving and investigated. Enrico filled in the details and provided the shippers. Enrico believes that the money he gave you was reported to accounting. Howard didn't volunteer that Enrico was misinformed."

"I see," said Kevin. He put his head in his hands and looked at the floor.

"I've got to ask you whether Jeff knows and whether he got any of the money."

"No, no one knows, including Carolyn," he said.

"I assume that includes the IRS."

Kevin raised his head, looked at Jerry, and smiled sheepishly. "Of course not, that's why I did it."

"Did you have any plans to tell Jeff or me?"

Kevin stood up and headed for the kitchen. "I need some more coffee." When he returned, he remained standing, drinking his coffee and looking out at the boats. His speech was flat. "This started a long time ago when I was the sole shareholder. When Jeff came into the business, I didn't see any way to tell him without his being compromised and my being exposed. It was too risky to start turning the money into accounting since somebody in the department would eventually ask why there were no records of funds being turned in for the sale of recycled parts. So, I just let the deal go on. I kept hoping that I'd figure out a way to end it without creating unintended consequences. Obviously, I never did." Tears streamed down Kevin's face. He wiped them away with his hand. "I'm terribly sorry, Jerry. I know I've let you down, big time. I'm sorry."

"Where's the money?" said Jerry.

"What I haven't spent is in a safe deposit box at the Bank of America."

"How much?"

"Somewhere between $350,000 and $400,000. I haven't counted it for a while.

I spent the rest on travel, furniture, and the kids' education, whatever. It's gone."

Jerry was quiet for a few moments, on purpose. Kevin sat down in the chair facing the sofa and leaned back. Jerry glared at him.

"Kevin, I want you to really listen to what I say. In the next two hours, I'm going to have to take certain actions that could irrevocably change the course of our lives. I'm sure I don't have to tell you that the potential consequences of your actions, once disclosed, are enormous. There are liability issues and criminal issues that you will have to deal with. You will need your own attorney. I'm not sure what the bank's position will be when we tell them, but I'm expecting the worst. I've got a call in to Richard. I plan to meet with him and Howard to plan our strategy. Someone will have to tell Carolyn, Jeff, and Salli, since they are all inside shareholders. That person should be you." Kevin was silent. He buried his head in his hands. He looked up, and Jerry saw the fear and dejection in his face. He seemed to have aged five years in fifteen minutes.

"Isn't there any other way?"

Jerry stood up and walked around the room, talking as he went. "I've been wrestling with the problem since nine o'clock last night. I'd give everything that I have or will ever have not to be in this position. There's no other way. Howard is the CFO. He's given the bank a financial statement he knows to be false. He will be personally at risk if he does not inform the bank in a timely manner. There are no alternatives to full disclosure. I'm as sorry as I can be, Kevin."

Kevin held his head in his hands and sobbed quietly. Jerry thought about going over to Kevin and putting his arms around him to comfort him—but he could not bring himself to do it. Kevin was still his big brother. He had to leave him some dignity. Kevin looked up and wiped his eyes with his hands, and said, "I see. All right. I'll tell Carolyn, Jeff, and Salli."

"When?"

"When do you want me to?"

"Immediately, this morning."

"All right."

Jerry could not bring himself to look at Kevin, so he stared at the two insipid Motel Six – quality landscapes hanging on the wall over the sofa. Kevin sat with his eyes closed. Chelsey whined as she needed to go out.

"I better get started," Kevin said, and headed for the door where Chelsey was waiting.

Jerry jumped up and grabbed the leash. "I'll walk down with you."

They walked down the stairs and onto the lush greenery of the complex that sparkled in the Southern California summer. Before Kevin turned away, Jerry dropped the leash and threw his arms around Kevin. "I love you. I can't stand to see you hurt. We'll get through this. I promise."

Kevin didn't respond. He squeezed Jerry, then released him, turned away, and headed down the path.

Later that day, Jerry and Howard met Richard at the Bicycle Shoppe, a bistro on Wilshire Boulevard near Richard's office. The section of the Wilshire corridor between Westwood and the ocean had been gentrified in the eighties, and a number of condominium complexes and office skyscrapers, including the one that contained Richard's office, now stood along the route and seemed to observe Jerry with their attractive, blank façades.

After they were seated around a table of iced teas, Diet Cokes, and coffees, Jerry asked Richard about the status of the revised bank agreement and loan extension. Richard replied that he had completed the draft of all the documents several days before, and they were in Sheila and Bill's hands. He went on to describe the bank's attitude as being the most optimistic and enthusiastic that he had ever seen in a workout. He went on to compliment Jerry again for orchestrating an absolutely outstanding meeting with the bank.

"Well," said Jerry, "I'm afraid we have some information which will dampen that ebullience."

Richard froze, the glass of iced tea suspended midway between the table and his mouth. He stared at Jerry. "And what's that?"

Howard told Richard in as much detail as he could remember how he had discovered the embezzlement. He was just finishing when the food arrived—a feast, including blackened salmon, coleslaw, and French string beans, which they ate silently without tasting. Finally, Richard placed his knife and fork down, carefully wiped his lips with the linen napkin, and said, "I'm sure I don't have to tell either of you how unfortunate this is and how difficult a situation it has created for all of us. Does Kevin appreciate the depth of the pit we're in?"

"I'm not sure," replied Jerry. "Right now, he's embarrassed and frightened, two emotions I'm sure we all share. As we speak, he's breaking the news to Carolyn, Salli, and Jeff. I'm confident that discussion will be quite sobering."

"Jerry," said Richard. "You have twelve hours' head start on me. Any ideas?"

"If you deduct the time I've spent drinking, crying, and sleeping, I'm only about eight hours ahead of you. But I do have some ideas. Do you have time?"

"I've got a court appearance at two. That gives me about a half-hour. We can get together after four if necessary."

Jerry pulled two sheets out of his briefcase and gave them to Howard and Richard and waited while they read the memo. Richard made a few notes. He looked up, and there was a flicker of a smile on his face.

"It just might work, Jerry. It's brassy enough, so it might just work."

"No, Richard, it will work. It has to. If it doesn't, we're toast."

"We'll do our best." Richard turned to Howard. "Incidentally, since we're all now working in a world with a high degree of uncertainty and none of us can predict what the bank will do, would you mind paying me up to date and sending me an additional twenty-five thousand to cover the next two weeks?"

Jerry laughed. "Howard, you have just seen how an attorney displays confidence in his client."

Richard started to say something, but Jerry touched him on the shoulder and held up his hand. "Sure, Richard, we'll get the check out this afternoon. There's no reason why my brother's stupid greed should put you at risk. Just get me a list of prospective attorneys by four. Kevin will need to retain someone by Monday."

When Jerry got back to the office, he called Helen to apologize for not returning her calls. She sounded pouty. "Any other woman would start suspecting you of seeing someone else," she said. Jerry explained that he had worked until the wee hours and presently felt like a zombie, and he had to go home and get some sleep.

"How about I come over about eight?" she said. "I'll cook up some pasta for dinner and bring it over."

Jerry mulled over the suggestion and rationalized that he deserved some personal time.

"Sure, see you at eight."

He went back to his condo and took Chelsey for a short walk around the marina. When he returned to the condo, he stripped down to his shorts, set the alarm for 4:30 p.m. and quickly fell asleep.

When he was thirteen, he and his brothers went whitewater rafting on the Green River. The Green River winds through Utah and Nevada and has a collection of Class 4 and Class 5 rapids, with Class 6 being the max. Kevin was in his prime—he had more muscle than Jeff and Jerry combined, and his mountaineering buddies called him "Daniel Bunyan," a cross that embraced his outdoor skills and shooting ability, and his ability to bench press his brothers simultaneously. And for once, he didn't invite any of the other friends who usually cluttered their excursions.

Their second day inbound, the brothers arrived at the most difficult section of the trip. The river was high that year. They beached the raft and walked along the bank to get a better look at the rapid and to figure out a strategy for running it. Jerry had little whitewater experience. Jeff was an experienced guide, but not as good as Kevin. As the two older brothers weighed alternatives, Jerry tried to hide his fear by paying very close attention to everything they said and nodding seriously at every observation. The rapid contained two big holes that were separated by about thirty feet. The big problem was how to get by the upstream rapid without going right into the middle of the downstream one. Falling into either of the holes guaranteed a capsize. His brothers agreed on a plan that required them to head directly for a large boulder after they passed the upstream hole, bounce off the bolder as if they were a billiard ball, and slide past the downstream hole. Jerry's assignment was to row like hell when Kevin gave the order.

They climbed in the raft and tightened up their vests. A twig and wet leaves had caught in the strap of Jerry's vest, And while Jeff had climbed into the raft, Jerry plucked out the twig, dropped it in the water, and watched it swirl and bounce on the glittering surface. He told himself he wasn't scared anymore.

They passed by the upstream hole. Jerry rowed with every bit of energy his arms could muster, right into the boulder, as Kevin shouted and cheered him on. The raft scuffed it and bounced off, but not far enough. It fell into the second hole, capsized, and Jerry was full of the sensation of flying, then total, cold submersion in a battering current. Although he was a good swimmer, the currents overwhelmed him. He got his head above water, gasped, and picked out the yellow blob in his vision. Try as he might, he was not able to get to the raft. Jeff and Kevin were clinging to the sides and trying to right it. Jerry wasn't tired enough to call out for help yet. He continued to struggle and tried to get to the raft, but was pulled further downstream. He treaded water. Kevin yelled to him, asking whether he was all right, and he yelled back that he was. He knew if he asked for help, Kevin would be there.

He drifted and treaded water until Jeff and Kevin had righted the raft and rowed over to pick him up. Jeff complimented him on his initiation into the ranks of the Class 5 river runners, and Kevin grasped his forearm in a strong, wet grip and tugged him out of the water. That evening, they sat around the fire, drying their clothes on a branch, and Kevin gave him his first shot of Jack Daniels.

❖

The alarm went off. It took him almost a minute to shut it off.

"Fuck!" Jerry sat on the edge of the bed, teary eyed, knowing that some things were gone, dead, over. He picked up the handset and called Richard, and pulled his yellow tablet onto the comforter. While Richard dictated, he scribbled a list of names—several criminal attorneys—and a few notes on each one. After he got off the phone, he made a pot of fresh coffee, poured a cup, and carried it over to the sofa. He called Kevin at home. Carolyn answered.

"Jerry, my world has collapsed."

"I know, Carolyn. So has mine. How's Kevin?"

"Not good. He's been in the den for the past three hours, drinking and crying. Frankly, I'm so damn mad at him that I can't bring myself to console him. He's not the man I thought I married and raised three kids with. I still can't believe he's done what he's told me he's done."

"Did he speak with Jeff and Salli?"

"Salli was out for the day. He had lunch with Jeff."

"Did he say anything about his conversation with Jeff?"

"I haven't spoken with him since he came back. He went right into the den, carrying an unopened fifth of Jack Daniels."

"I need to speak to him, Carolyn. Please ask him to come to the phone."

Several minutes later, Kevin uttered a slurred hello.

"Kevin, it's Jerry. Now listen to me. You need to sober up. You can't afford the time to wallow." He wanted to come across as firm, but he didn't want Kevin to feel bossed around. He wasn't sure he was being successful. "Get a pencil and paper and write down the following names and phone numbers. These are the attorneys Richard recommends. You need to call them and decide whom you want to retain. Do you hear me?"

"Yeah, I hear you. Wait a minute. I've got to find something to write with. Okay. Shoot." Jerry read the three names, phone numbers, and backgrounds of each attorney.

"Does Richard have a favorite?"

"Richard says they're all very good. Your choice. After you retain one, have them call Richard." Chelsey put her paw on Jerry's bare thigh. He reached down and scratched her behind the ears. "How did your lunch with Jeff go?"

Kevin did not answer immediately. A glass clinked in the background. "He just listened."

"I see. How do you feel?"

"Like a very small piece of shit."

"I can understand that, but you've got to pull yourself out of this. We just don't have the time for you to grieve. Get sober and make the calls. Right?"

"Sure. So long." Kevin hung up.

It was just short of five o'clock. Jerry called Shirley to pick up his messages and asked to speak with Jeff. He arranged a breakfast for the next morning at Dinah's Restaurant on the corner of Sepulveda and Centinella. Then, he set the alarm for 7:00 p.m. and went back to sleep.

13

SATURDAY, SEPTEMBER 1, 1990

The next morning, Jerry awoke a half-hour before the alarm was to go off. Helen was still sleeping. She was on her side; the comforter covered the lower part of her body. She seemed to be smiling. Jerry pulled on a sweat suit, grabbed the leash and the whistle, and took Chelsey out to his car. He drove the several blocks to a middle school that had a large fenced park. He let Chelsey out of the car and allowed her to run free.

One night with Helen, and he almost was able to convince himself that life was good and everything would work out for the best. A line from *Candide* kept coursing through his mind: "All is for the best in this best of all possible worlds." Unfortunately, the noise of the garbage truck emptying the dumpster brought the euphoria to an abrupt end and he was again thinking about Kevin, Carolyn, Jeff, Salli, and himself and how awful everyone must feel. He had not allowed himself to think about the effect that this whole sorry matter would have on his mom and dad. He was hopeful that if his plan worked out, they would never know that their middle son was a thief.

He returned to the condo slightly before 7:00 a.m. Helen was up and making coffee.

"Chelsey have a good run?"

"Ask her. I walked. How are you feeling?"

"Couldn't feel better. Want to have another go at it?" She put her arms around him and pressed her body against him.

It was Pavlovian. As soon as his body touched her, he was hard. "Can we make it a quickie? I've got a meeting at eight."

Helen looked over her shoulder at him and smiled. "After last night, how can I deny you anything? Want any breakfast?"

"Just coffee. Meet you in the bedroom in five minutes."

He stripped off his clothes as he walked off to the bathroom.

Shortly after eight, showered, shaved, and rejuvenated, Jerry entered the restaurant. Jeff was already at a table.

"Hi, Jeff."

Jeff nodded, but did not respond. Bags shadowed his eyes.

"Do you want to talk about it?"

"That's what we're here for, isn't it?"

"We're here to deal with the business aspects of the problem, Jeff. We'll do that. But what I want to know is do you want to talk about the emotional part of this? You know, brother to brother. How you feel. How I feel. How Kevin feels. How Salli and Carolyn feel. The effect of this on our family life. How best to keep it from Mom and Dad. How we're going to deal with it during the rest of our lives."

Jeff didn't respond. Instead, he picked up the menu and scanned it. The waitress came by and took their orders. When she left the table, Jerry said, "Are you going to answer me?"

"I'm not trying to be difficult, Jerry." His voice revealed his exhaustion. He took a drink of orange juice. "But I'd prefer to pass on the emotional part of the discussion. Maybe another time. It's too fresh, too complicated. I don't have my thoughts together. I'm not sure how I feel about anything just now."

Jerry had expected sarcasm to show, but it didn't. "I understand," he said. "It's probably too soon. But we have a pressing, serious problem. When I meet with the bank and tell them the whole story, Kevin immediately becomes a dead player. The bank will not have anything further to do with him. And somehow, we—you and I—have to use our best efforts to limit the damage to the bank's opinion of the Bascombs. Do you have any thoughts about this?"

Jeff rubbed his eyes and shook his head. "I'm afraid I don't. I guess the only insight I can offer comes from my experience in Vietnam. When you're in a firefight and the platoon leader is shot, you do what you can for him, but the leadership immediately goes to the next in command, the master sergeant; and if he gets shot, the senior squad leader takes over. The rest of the platoon needs to press forward without looking back, or else the entire mission is jeopardized. I know this may sound insensitive, but you and I simply have to move forward and do the best we can. There is no time to agonize over the fallout from Kevin's stupidity."

Jerry sat quietly for a minute, digesting the reason in Jeff's advice despite a pang of rejection. He was here for his family, but somehow, had to keep his emotions out of it. Finally, he nodded. "I understand, we'll stick to business." He dug around in his briefcase and pulled out his notes.

❖

The following Thursday at precisely 8:00 a.m., Jerry and Richard were ushered into the main conference room of the bank. The sky was overcast and no one had thought to turn on the lights.

"How are you doing?" asked Richard, as he set up his laptop and organized his notes. Richard was dressed in a dark blue suit, a blue shirt, and a blue and red striped tie. The light from his laptop made the red look purple and cold.

"Better than I expected," said Jerry. "What's the occasion? You're normally the sport jacket and slacks guy."

Jerry located the light switch and turned it on. Unfortunately, the addition of light did not lift either the coldness of the room or his own spirits.

"I've got a hearing today on a big case. My wife thought I should pull out all the stops." He sat down at his computer and typed a few strokes. "So, how's Kevin?"

"Not good. Very depressed and drinking heavily. Carolyn took him to see a psychiatrist. He's been taking antidepressants, so he really shouldn't drink. Carolyn tells me that he won't talk to her. He just sits in his den, drinks, and cries."

"I'm sorry, Jerry. You certainly didn't sign on for this kind of duty."

"Don't worry about me. When this deal is over, I'll go back to my previous life in New York. But I worry about Kevin getting over this. He's not handling the stress well at all."

The door to the conference room door opened, and Sheila and Bill came in. Jerry and Richard stood up and greeted them.

"What a surprise," said Sheila as she greeted them. "I did not expect to see you so soon." Both Sheila and Bill wore broad smiles. They all shook hands.

"Nor did we," said Richard.

"I'll bet you can't resist the great food we serve."

"You're so right, Bill. I'm still trying to work off the lunch of two weeks ago."

"Incidentally, we've just completed our review of the extension agreement. I plan to get it back to you tomorrow with the few comments we have. There's nothing of substance," said Bill.

They took seats at the conference table, Sheila and Bill on one side, Jerry and Richard on the other, banker facing banker, and lawyer facing lawyer. Richard pushed his computer to the side, leaned forward in his chair, took a deep breath, and fanned out his fingers on the table.

"Bill, Sheila, the reason we called the meeting on such short notice is related to the extension agreement."

Sheila's smile faded every so slightly. "In what way? You don't want to change the deal, do you?"

"It's not what we want to do, Sheila," said Richard. "Let's say that circumstances compel us to change the deal. The company has recently discovered that the financial statements that it provided to the bank are inaccurate in certain respects. While the effect of these discoveries will turn out to be beneficial to the bank, we need to disclose the source and substance of the inaccuracies."

Sheila's face colored, and she glowered at Richard. Bill sensed Sheila's growing unease and said, "Richard, this all sounds very mysterious. Tell us what you have on your mind in plain English."

Richard was trying to muster his most serious look. "Indulge me. I'm sure you will get the picture in a few minutes. This matter is sufficiently sensitive that I have to be very careful in what I say and how I say it. Please."

Sheila's mood had turned sour. She opened her purse and pulled out a pack of cigarettes and a lighter. She pulled a cigarette from the pack, lit it, and took a long drag. She spoke through her clenched teeth. "Go on," she said.

"The company discovered that the proceeds of the sale of certain salvage parts were not accounted for using generally accepted accounting procedures. The amount in question is six hundred and seventy-five thousand dollars. The correction has been reflected in the financial statement we are now providing." He handed Sheila and Bill copies of a new financial statement for the period ending the past month. "Three hundred and sixty-seven thousand dollars of the six hundred and seventy-five thousand dollar error is reflected in the cash account. The balance is in the form of an 8 percent five-year note made by Kevin Bascomb that is secured by his personal residence. We've had an appraisal of the residence, and there is in excess of one half million of equity available. The net effect of this correction is to increase the company's net worth by six hundred and seventy-five thousand dollars."

Sheila and Bill exchanged worried glances. Sheila looked over to Jerry, who noticed out of the corner of his eye, but kept his attention focused on Richard. Richard continued, "I also want to advise you that for reasons of health, Kevin has resigned from his positions as an officer and director of the company and voluntarily placed all of his common stock in a voting trust, the trustees of which are Jeff and Salli Bascomb."

Bill's face was beet red. "Dammit, Richard, just what are you saying? I mean, what is this all about?" His voice was rising and his face was almost purple. "You can't just..."

"Calm down, Bill," said Sheila, placing her hand on his arm. She stood up. The color had left her face, and the scowl had been replaced by a faint smile. "I think I get the picture. Please give us a few minutes to talk." She turned to Bill and said, "Why don't we go over to my office?" As she was walking out the conference door, she turned to Richard. "I'll have the receptionist bring in some fresh coffee and some cookies."

Jerry and Richard sat silently. After several minutes, Jerry couldn't take it anymore. "What do you think, Richard?"

He grinned. "I think you've done one hell of a job of damage control. They'll go along after some posturing."

Ten minutes later, Sheila and Bill returned. Jerry noted that Sheila's smile was gone and she was wearing her serious, no-bullshit face. She spoke calmly without any trace of the irritation he knew she was feeling.

"I've got three questions. First. Who discovered the fact that the transactions weren't properly recorded?"

Jerry answered, "Howard."

"Second question. When?"

"Six days ago, last Thursday."

"Third question, when can we send in our auditors to meet with Howard and review this?" She raised the new financial statement from the table, and allowed it to drop.

"As soon as you like."

"Fine. We will contact Coopers, and see what their schedule is, and call you. After we review the auditor's report and discuss the situation with senior management, we will advise you how we want to proceed. Any questions, gentlemen?"

Jerry and Richard both shook their heads. Everyone stood up and shook hands. As Sheila was shaking Jerry's hand, she looked into his eyes and said, "I know how difficult this must be for you. Good luck." Jerry did not answer. He forced a smile and turned away before Sheila could notice the tears that had welled up in his eyes.

Shortly after ten o'clock on Saturday morning, Jerry awoke amid bedding and clothes that looked to have been organized by a cyclone. He and Helen had flown to San Francisco the previous afternoon, checked into the Cliff Hotel on Geary Street. After unpacking, they headed to the Mozart Café on Bush Street.

His head ached. He remembered that he and Helen had consumed two bottles of wine during the dinner at the Mozart Café and one bottle during the following four hours of sexual athletics. She was insatiable and he loved it. He even let himself forget about the embezzlement during the peak of his drunkenness.

A perfect evening—and yet.

There was the gnawing uncomfortable feeling that something was not, as Birney would say, kosher. Despite her smiley exuberance, the warmth she lavished on him, the tenderness, and the constant compliments, he could not shake the feeling that she wasn't authentic. The lame excuse she had offered for not wanting to stay at the Donatello was one thing. But there was something else, something more than just his hair-trigger distrust.

Jeff's admonishment that he should take care and not be distracted by "sweet-smelling pussy" had rattled around in his mind for weeks. At first, he had thought that Jeff was just making a point in as crude and offensive manner as possible. But the comment had been accompanied by an expression that could be interpreted as a leer. And the comment plus the leer were persuading him that Jeff was not referring to "sweet-smelling pussies" in a generic sense, but to a specific sweet-smelling pussy, namely Helen's. He was now almost convinced that Jeff was sending him a message, i.e., that he, Jeff, knew all about Helen's pussy and that it could be very distracting.

He turned over in the bed to face Helen. He placed his right hand on the back of her left knee and slowly, slowly ran his hand up the back of her thigh, over her buttocks, and gently rubbed her back.

"Umm, feels good."

"I wanted to make sure you were still breathing. I was concerned about you dying from exhaustion."

She laughed. "Wine and sex are my drugs of choice. The more I get, the more I want."

"Don't I know it?" He leaned over and kissed her on the forehead.

"Hey, I know you can do better than that."

She threw her arms around him, kissed him on the lips, rubbed herself against him, and soon they were at it again.

"How about some breakfast? I'm not used to so much physical labor," said Jerry.

Helen smiled. "Both of our batteries probably need to be charged. Take me somewhere where they serve lox and eggs. I feel like eating Jewish today."

"We'll eat at David's, right across the street, okay?"

"Terrific. I'll throw on some sweats."

She pulled out a brand new Nike tank from her suitcase, cut off the tags, and put it on over her bare torso. She grabbed some other clothes and disappeared into the bathroom. She emerged a few minutes later, looking as though she had walked out of the pages of *Sports Illustrated*.

They crossed Geary Street and threaded their way through the phalanx of homeless people, jangling their change in Styrofoam cups. The restaurant was crowded, typical for a late Saturday morning. When they were finally seated, Jerry grasped Helen's hand.

"Happy?" he said.

"Ecstatic."

While they were eating breakfast, they began to exchange childhood memories and anecdotes. Jerry told Helen how Kevin had been much more of a father figure to him than his father.

"You were lucky," said Helen. "You had two fathers looking out for you, protecting you from Jeff."

Once again, the incessant conflict with Salli. He tried to listen carefully to the story, but he was distracted by a lingering concern that the description of her lonely childhood was in some way contrived to manipulate his feelings for her.

"Weren't there any times in your childhood that you and Salli got along? I mean, there had to be some pleasant moments. There certainly were with Jeff and me."

Helen poked away at the food on her plate and drank some coffee. She appeared to be struggling to come up with an appropriate answer. "Well, yes, there were a few good times. The ones I remember vividly are the times that I went with Salli to stay with her father."

"You mean Charlie."

"Yes, do you know him?"

"I haven't met him, but I know his reputation."

"What kind of reputation does he have?"

"Tough, driving, intelligent, big ego, a risk taker."

"That's Charlie. He treated me very well, much to Salli's displeasure. He had this large ranch outside of Santa Barbara with horses, a private lake, and a few hundred acres. It was like a camp. Salli would stay there for the entire summer and I'd visit for about two to three weeks. He had all sorts of servants fawning over us. I loved it. I looked forward to going and hated to leave. Now that I think about it, the time I spent at Charlie's was among the few times when Salli and I got along well."

"How many years did you go there?" said Jerry. He motioned to the waitress for more coffee.

"'Til I was in high school. I think the summer before the tenth grade was the last time I went. You know, at that age boys and your girlfriends are very important. I hated to leave them even for two weeks. And there were a few things that made me uncomfortable."

"Like what?" said Jerry. "It sounds as though you had a really sweet deal."

Helen hesitated and seemed to be rehearsing in her mind what she planned to say.

"Charlie treated me very well. He was always gracious and charming. He went out of his way to make me feel at home, that his house was my house. But he was a real bigot, I mean, with a capital B. When you're young, you don't notice those things. But as I got older, I started to pick up on the contempt and disdain he had for anyone who wasn't a WASP. He'd refer to Jews as kikes, hebes, or hymies, blacks as niggers or spades, and Hispanics as spics. I didn't personally know any minorities until I started high school. But in ninth grade, I became real close with a black girl, Shawna Johnson. We did homework together, were in the drama club together, and slept over at each other's houses, that kind of thing. When I went to Charlie's that summer, his comments about blacks really hit me. They seemed so outrageous, so shocking. I was really uncomfortable."

"Did you ever say anything to Charlie about being offended? Or to Salli?"

"I was a guest and I didn't want to rock the boat. I appreciated all Charlie had done for me and I wouldn't say or do anything that would upset him. Besides, it was time to move on." She smiled broadly, pushing the conversation back into shallower waters. "There were some happy times, for sure."

As Jerry asked for the check, he realized that he had learned two important things about Helen—that she wasn't a bigot and she wouldn't tolerate a situation that offended her moral sense, no matter how comfortable it was. It was reassuring to learn that they shared some values. He was glad for a reason to brush away his suspicions about her.

They left the restaurant and walked across the street to the Cliff Hotel. When they got up to their room, the message light was blinking. Jerry called the concierge and learned that Jeff had left an urgent message about an hour earlier. Jerry sat down on the bed and dialed his number. The phone rang eight times and Salli answered.

"Salli, this is Jerry. Jeff left a message to call."

"Jerry, I'm on another call. Jeff's not here. Give me your number and I'll call you back." Jerry thought that Salli's voice sounded strained. He gave her the number of the hotel. "Got it. Call you back in a few minutes." She hung up. Jerry sat on the edge of the bed, staring at the receiver.

"Anything wrong," asked Helen.

"I don't know. Salli said she'd call back. Why don't you take your shower first and I'll wait for the call."

Fifteen minutes later, the phone rang again. Salli's voice was more composed than before. "I have bad news. Kevin passed out at breakfast this morning. An ambulance took him to UCLA."

Jerry's ears started to ring, and Salli seemed to be speaking from a great distance, explaining that she had been on the phone with Carolyn. Carolyn told her that the diagnosis was not final, but they suspected a heart attack. They were going to perform some more tests and they hoped to have a final diagnosis in a few hours.

"Where's Jeff?" he managed to ask.

"He's at the UCLA hospital with Carolyn. Your folks are there also. Your mother is very upset. Jeff said that she's been crying hysterically."

Jerry glanced at his watch. He told Salli that he could probably get to the hospital by four and asked her to call Jeff to tell him that he was on his way.

He slowly hung up the phone. His face felt hot and his throat filled up with a sob. Helen came out of the bathroom toweling herself and stopped. She walked over to the bed and placed her hand on his shoulder. The touch broke the last membrane holding back his tears. He looked up at her and between sobs managed to tell her that Kevin was in the hospital and they had to leave.

Jerry would remember the flight from San Francisco to Los Angeles as the longest one-hour plane ride of his life. At thirty thousand feet, time expanded. He and Helen barely exchanged five words, but she held his hand in hers and squeezed it every once in a while. He sat straight up with his eyes closed and watched the panoply of scenes on the movie screen inside his mind. All the scenes were of Kevin and himself—Kevin teaching him to ski, Kevin teaching him to fly fish, he and Kevin playing basketball in the schoolyard, and Kevin's wet hand reaching over the slick yellow raft, reaching out for him. Their meeting at his apartment was to discuss Kevin's surreptitious business. As the time frame of the images moved from the past to the present, his feeling changed from nostalgia and warmth to guilt and depression. He noted and put words to it all, and that seemed to help him.

Ever since he got the call from Salli, he had been wrestling with the reality that he had been screwing Helen, while Kevin was being rushed to the hospital. He argued with himself. He told himself that he was being foolish and that his making love to Helen had no relevance to Kevin's illness. He could have been working, skiing, playing golf, eating, sleeping, shopping—and Kevin would still have had his attack. Yet there was something unclean, something smutty about his having experienced the apex of ecstasy while Kevin was experiencing shortness of breath and chest pains.

Or maybe the manner in which he confronted Kevin over the embezzlement had given Kevin the attack. He went over and over every word he had said and everything he had done, searching for something that he could identify as a flaw, a harsh statement, or an insensitive gesture. But he could no longer remember the conversations exactly, and he realized that it was impossible for him to judge whether Kevin regarded a remark as harsh or a gesture as insensitive. Jerry knew enough psychology to know that all the mental gymnastics would not change anything and that he was punishing himself because of an outcome that probably had little to do with anything he had said or done. But at least, his mind was occupied.

They retrieved Jerry's car from the airport parking lot. Helen offered to drive to the UCLA medical center, and something in her voice hinted that maybe Jerry shouldn't be behind the wheel. When they arrived at the hospital, they were told that Kevin had been moved out of emergency and into the cardiac intensive care unit. After some difficulty, they located the department in which Kevin was being treated. His parents and Salli were seated in the lobby adjacent the double green doors that led to the rooms where the patients were treated. His mother was crying quietly, and her eyes were so swollen that her face had become unfamiliar. His dad was sitting by her side. She was leaning her head on his shoulder. Jerry hugged her and tried to comfort her, but she was inconsolable. The pale green walls, cheap furniture, shiny checkerboard tiles, and bright lights created an oppressive ambience that deepened his gloom.

His father was thumbing through an old *People*. He glanced up from his magazine, acknowledged Helen and Jerry, and then turned to look at his wife. "She's been like that all day," he said. "She just can't seem to stop crying. This thing is such a shock. Kevin was always so healthy, so athletic." He shrugged and went back to his magazine.

For a moment, Jerry wanted to grab the magazine from his hands and send it fluttering across the room. He wiped his palms on his pants and instead sat down next to his mother and took her hand. He knew that his mother was very fragile and was concerned that Kevin's sudden illness could push her toward a mental breakdown. He turned to Salli, "What's the word from the doctors?"

"Jeff and Carolyn are meeting with them now. We should get a report within the next few minutes."

"And Carolyn?"

"Her usual steadfast self," said Salli. "She's saying all the right things to persuade us that she is in control, but I'm not sure she believes them. She's going to stay with us for a few days until this is sorted out. I want to be able to watch her."

"Good idea. Dad," he said, speaking softly, so that his mother did not hear. "Does Mom have anything she can take to calm her down?"

He answered in a normal voice, which could be heard across the waiting room. "She took a tranquilizer about a half hour ago. I'm hoping it kicks in soon."

"Mom, how are you feeling?" said Jerry. He placed his hand on her back and gently stroked her. She didn't respond, but then shook her head and buried it in her husband's chest. He gently rubbed her back and her neck.

Jerry would never understand them. During the next twenty minutes, he sat next to them, silent and ruminating on the pleasure he'd felt with Helen while Kevin suffered this catastrophic collapse of his health. Now, she and Salli chatted quietly. Jerry glanced at them, noting that the mutual disdain Helen had described was not evident. Quite the contrary. They were acting as if they enjoyed each other's company.

The green double door opened and Jeff emerged, grim-faced. He entered the lobby area and greeted Jerry and Helen and sat down heavily in one of the empty chairs. The atmosphere in the lobby matched Jeff's expression.

"The report is mixed," said Jeff. "Some good news and some bad news. The good news is that he's out of danger and his pulse, blood pressure, and temperature are stable. He will recover." Jeff hesitated. He pulled a tissue from his jacket and wiped his nose. "The bad news is that there was some damage to the heart muscle. They don't know how much and to what extent it may affect his future activity. There's also a major blockage on two of the arteries, which will have to be dealt with down the line. He's going to be on a strict diet from now on and the doctors recommend that he organize his life to minimize stress. They said that Kevin was a heart attack waiting to happen. It's pretty clear that the pressure he's been under recently pushed him over the edge." He held Jerry's gaze for a moment too long.

"Can we see him?" said Jerry.

"Not until tomorrow," said Jeff. "They're only going to let Carolyn see him tonight. She's going to sit with him for another hour and then we're going to take her home with us."

"Is there anything I can do?"

Jeff looked at him with contempt—as in, you've done enough, asshole. "Why don't you see that Mom and Dad get something to eat and take them home? I'd just as soon they not drive."

Jeff's naked coldness had rekindled the feelings of guilt that he had been wrestling with all evening. He could only manage a feeble, "Okay."

They went to an Italian Bistro in Westwood that Helen suggested. Their mother had finally stopped sobbing and was able to participate in the dinner conversation, which focused on Kevin's illness and the myriad ramifications that it would have on all of their lives. Jerry kept his mouth shut during dinner. His contribution to the conversation consisted primarily of monosyllabic acknowledgments, nods of agreement, and smiles to indicate comprehension of what was being said. He was grateful that Helen acted as hostess and allowed him to coast. There were a few times that she squeezed his hand or jostled him in order to pull him out of a reverie. His mind was too busy reliving everything that had happened since Kevin first called him in June, and attempting to ascertain, at least to his satisfaction, whether his actions and decisions with respect to the bank, Kevin, Jeff, and Helen had brought on the trouble.

He was also in the process of convincing himself that the relationship between Helen and Jeff was something more than in-laws. Of course, he didn't have proof and he wouldn't have it unless he confronted Helen. He and Helen were sufficiently involved, so maybe she wouldn't lie to him. However, he wasn't sure he wanted the truth or if he got it, that he could handle it. But the uncertainty about Helen's relationship with Jeff created one more layer of trouble. The lawyer and engineer in him wanted to confront the problem head on, deal with it, and cross it off his list of problems. The lover in him was hesitant to do anything to jeopardize the warmth and potential for a long-term, stable home life.

When she suddenly pulled her hand away, he realized that he had been squeezing it too hard.

He felt clear enough to drive his parents to their home in North Hollywood, and Helen followed in Jerry's car. Then he drove her to her apartment. When they arrived, she invited him to spend the night and he agreed. She poured two glasses of white wine, handed one to him, and sat down next to him on the sofa.

"You've been very pensive, honey. Penny for your thoughts."

"They're not worth that much."

"I don't mind overpaying. That way, I'm assured of good service."

Jerry took a deep breath. He hadn't planned to raise this now, but he was feeling so alienated from everyone and felt so depressed that it suddenly seemed like a great idea.

"I've come to suspect that you and Jeff have a relationship that goes beyond the normal in-law thing. I don't like having these suspicions because

I've fallen in love with you and they threaten to contaminate what could be a beautiful relationship. I need to know the truth."

The smile faded from Helen's face. Her lips turned into a slit. She adjusted herself in the sofa and placed her wineglass on the coffee table. She picked off some dead leaves from the flowers in the vase in the middle of the coffee table.

"Well, I certainly wasn't expecting that." She paused. He waited patiently. "I knew that if we got serious, I was going to have to deal with that problem. If I weren't in love with you, I'd deny that I had any relationship with Jeff, because it would be none of your business. I don't tell everyone I fuck who my other lovers were or are. But we're getting in deep and you have a right to know about Jeff and me." She ran her hand through her hair, and took a sip of wine. She looked directly into his eyes. "Your suspicions are right on. Jeff and I have been lovers."

Jerry swallowed hard.

"How long?" His throat was very dry. He took a sip of wine.

"We started the affair when I returned from Europe. I ended it shortly after you arrived in California."

"Does Salli know?"

"I don't think so, but I'm sure that if she did, she would never admit it to me."

She shrugged like it was no big deal. "Salli and I, as you know, have never been close, and Salli and Jeff have been at loggerheads for years. According to Jeff, they have sex rarely and only for medicinal purposes."

"Were you—are you in love with him?"

Helen laughed. "It was purely recreational, very superficial. I needed a source of sexual satisfaction that would not put pressure on me. He needed the same thing. It was a business deal."

Jerry took a sip of wine and used the cocktail napkin to wipe his mouth. "The hostility that Jeff has heaped upon me since you and I started seeing each other would seem to indicate otherwise."

"Look," said Helen, her voice rising, "I'm the one who ended the affair. I did it because I was interested in you. I'm sequentially monogamous. Jeff doesn't like to lose and he can't handle rejection. If he was in love with me, he certainly never indicated it."

"Helen, didn't it bother you, on some level, that by fucking Jeff, you were deceiving your own sister? You're so cavalier about it. I mean, for Christ's sake, you were fucking your sister's husband on a regular basis." No sooner were the words out of his mouth that Jerry knew he had gone too far. Helen's eyes flashed. Her lower lip pushed out, showing her white bottom teeth, now suddenly fierce.

"You don't have any right to judge me, Jerry Bascomb. You don't know shit about my life or my needs. You asked me about my relationship with Jeff and I told you what you wanted to know. You didn't ask, and you don't have any right to ask, what psychological rationale, if any, I had concocted in order to justify betraying my sister. And I have no intention of telling you if I have one. You're not my judge, minister, rabbi, or therapist. You're the guy I'm in love with. So far, I've given you my time, my affection, and my body. I'm not prepared to offer you my soul."

Jerry did not respond. He tried to think of something to say, but nothing came to mind. He decided that saying anything would probably make the situation worse. Kevin's sudden illness, Jeff's scorn, and Helen's attack had eviscerated his defenses. He sat quietly and sipped his wine.

Helen stood up. "Look, it's been a rough day. We're both tired. This is not a good time for a spat. Why don't you go home and we'll talk tomorrow."

Jerry continued to sit and sip his wine. He felt a stubborn need not to be rushed. But Helen was right. He was overwrought and much too tired to continue the conversation. He stood up, placed his half-finished glass on the coffee table, and said, "You're right, let's call it a night." He put a perfunctory kiss on her tight, dry lips, turned away, and walked out the door.

14

THURSDAY, SEPTEMBER 27, 1990

Jerry waited in Krimble's office. It was appropriate for the meeting at hand—functional, modest, even stark. There was no valuable artwork on the walls, only framed diplomas and certificates evidencing Richard's education, skills, and experience. Unfortunately, none said he was certified in working miracles.

Jerry was waiting on Jeff, Ethan, and Brad Simon, the criminal lawyer Kevin had hired. He was steeling himself for his first meeting with Jeff since learning that Helen had been his lover. The fact that he was no longer having to agonize over his suspicions had somewhat mitigated the anger and disappointment—now, he just had to deal with the person who caused them. He looked up from the paper when he heard Jeff's voice.

"Hi, Jeff! Glad you could make it on such short notice."

"No problem. It's been a slow week." He sat down in the chair opposite Jerry.

"What are you hearing from your military friends about this Iraq deal?"

"About the same as you see in the papers," said Jeff. "They're gearing up for an invasion. You can bet a duffle bag drag and a bowl of cornflakes that they're looking forward to it." He smiled.

"Looking forward to it?"

"Sure. They want the opportunity to prove that the military can fight and win. They feel they need to set things right after Vietnam, Iran, and Lebanon. They are itching for it. I wish I were with them. It would be a hell of a lot more meaningful than the bullshit I'm involved with here."

"You're not thinking about going back in, or are you?" said Jerry, allowing a smirk to show in his voice, if not on his face.

Jeff shook his head and chuckled. "Don't worry, Jerry. As much as I want to, I can't. I've got to see this deal through—even though I hate it." He grimaced as if he were preparing for his own execution. He shook his head again and brightened. "Anyway, what's up?"

"Ethan Wilson is in town. He wants to get together with us to talk about Kevin and how his condition might affect the marketing of the company. Krimble thought we should all meet. He's asked Brad Simon, Kevin's criminal attorney, to join us."

Twenty minutes later, they had all gathered in Krimble's conference room on the second floor of the suite. When Brad Simon entered the office, it was all Jerry could do to conceal his surprise. He didn't look anything like what Jerry expected a lawyer to look like, let alone a lawyer that Krimble would have recommended. He was huge. Jerry estimated six foot four and three hundred pounds. He seemed to have consumed whatever empty space there had been in the office. He wore his long white hair in a ponytail. His bushy beard was also white and unkempt. His voice was deep and gruff. He was the very archetype for Hollywood's image of a mafia enforcer.

"Brad is on a very tight schedule," said Krimble. "He's got a court appearance at three, so we better get started."

Jerry pulled some papers from his briefcase and slid them across the table. "We've got three items to cover. One, the identity, level of interest, and status of the prospective buyers; two, the effect of Kevin's illness on the selling process; three, a report by Brad on a number of personal matters involving Kevin. Ethan, why don't you start?"

Ethan Wilson passed around copies of a two-page memorandum. "We've identified about twenty prospects for the company. All but five have been contacted. We'll get the rest by the end of the week. Of the fifteen we've talked with, ten expressed some level of interest. We're collecting non-disclosure agreements and mailing the prospectus. All the prospects will have the memorandum in hand within a week."

"Any discussions of substance yet?" asked Krimble.

"Two. Continental and Burle Industries."

"No surprise," said Jeff. "These guys have been trying to steal our stuff for years. We're going to save them a lot of grief by just giving it to them."

Jerry winced, but decided to ignore the remark. "Any discussion about price?"

"We're telling them our asking price."

"How do you feel about the response you're getting?" asked Jeff.

"Great," said Ethan. "National's technology is tops, not to mention it's got a bloody good reputation. People are listening."

"And the timetable?" asked Krimble.

"We still hope to close a transaction by March 31." Ethan looked around the table. "Any questions?" There was none. "Right," he said. "Bring me up to speed on the Kevin situation and what we're going to tell the buyers when the issue comes up."

Jerry turned to Krimble. Krimble pulled a sheet from his briefcase and read from it. "Kevin has had a heart attack. He is under doctor's orders to minimize the stress in his life and adhere to a strict regimen of diet and exercise. He will not be able to work at the company on a day-to-day basis. However, within about three months, we expect him to be well enough to participate in activities that are concerned with formulating the marketing and technology strategy of the company." Krimble looked over to Ethan. "That is the party line. Are you comfortable with it?"

Ethan nodded.

"How will that play with the buyers?" said Jerry.

"We'll have to give it a burl. I've never been in a situation where the creative genius behind the product line of the company in play is not able to give one hundred and ten percent. I won't bring it up until there is a level of interest to initiate due diligence. We'll disclose it at that time—unless of course someone asks."

"Do you think it will chill the price of the transaction?" said Jerry.

"There's no way to tell," said Ethan. "As the process unfolds, Kevin's situation will clarify and we'll have more certainty."

"Fair enough," said Jerry. "Jeff, do you have any questions?"

Jeff shook his head.

"I guess you're done with me." Ethan got up and closed his briefcase. "I guess I'll leave the field."

After he was gone, Krimble said to Simon, "I spoke with the bank this morning and I've set a tentative meeting with Bromfield for tomorrow to submit our written proposal for resolving the 'accounting error,' as we're calling it. Have you had an opportunity to talk to your client about the matter, and is he competent to deal with it?"

"I've met with Kevin and Carolyn twice," said Simon. "He seems rational, although it's apparent that he's very depressed. I think he's competent, but then I don't know him." He looked over to the brothers. "What do you guys think?"

Simon's gruff voice had interrupted Jerry's reverie. He had been attempting to visualize how Simon would look in front of a jury. Commanding presence would certainly be an understatement. "I saw him last night," said Jerry. "We walked all around the hospital floor. If he wasn't wearing a hospital gown and carrying a bag of urine, you wouldn't know there was anything wrong with him."

"I stopped by this morning," said Jeff. "He looks fine. They are going to discharge him tomorrow. I think you can assume that he's competent to make business decisions."

Simon nodded into his great beard. "I advised Kevin as to the exposures and potential liabilities he has to the bank, the bank regulators, the IRS, and the Franchise Tax Board. He and Carolyn are fully informed that even if they go along with the company's proposal for resolving the problem with the bank, they will still face substantial taxes and penalties and potential criminal prosecutions. They don't see any alternative to Jerry's plan. They're prepared to go along with it, subject to my reviewing, and approving the documents."

"Good," said Krimble. "I'll go ahead with my meeting with Bromfield. I'll fax you my drafts of the various documents."

Jeff, Simon, and Krimble left the conference room, while Jerry fumbled with his papers, trying to fit them into his overstuffed briefcase. Simon's remarks had caught him up short. Although he had used the same kind of emotion-laden words like *potential criminal prosecution*, they seemed much more ominous coming so easily from the mouth of an experienced criminal attorney. They were horrible words, foreign words—words that he had never expected would need to become part of the vocabulary he employed to discuss his family.

The ambience of the restaurant was stereotypical romance. It was located on the main channel of the marina. Their table provided a front row seat to the dancing reflections of lights along the harbor, the parade of festooned yachts, and the strollers and sightseers who moved past the window. The management offered a special weekend dinner package that included a twenty-ounce prime rib for two, a bottle of wine, a fifteen-minute fireworks display, and no-hassle occupancy of the table.

Helen chose the restaurant as the place she wanted to celebrate the three-month anniversary of their relationship. Jerry barely remembered to celebrate Christmas, New Year's, and Thanksgiving, and then only did so because his family, friends, and co-workers expected it. Labor Day, President's Day, and the Fourth of July were, as far as he was concerned, working days. He often forgot Mother's and Father's Days and depended on Kevin or Jeff to remind him, so that he could get a card in the mail on time. He hated Valentine's Day because its arrival meant that he had to choose which girlfriend to celebrate with, and make up lies about having to work to placate the others. Having never been married, he had not been trained by a wife to remember and make special plans for birthdays and anniversaries.

When Helen mentioned the looming three-month milestone, his reaction was to feel a glimmer of surprise—that their relationship had been in progress for such a long period. He was not feeling much like a lover, and moreover, his passion had cooled. Even so, he had made a point of talking with her every day, and they had seen each other for dinners, movies, and sex. He launched the campaign in part because he felt guilty for having insulted Helen during their argument. Now, her desire for a romantic dinner at the marina certainly indicated that the relationship was, from her perspective, back to its pre-argument status. That would of course make it more difficult for him to do what he felt he had to do.

She was as lovely, coifed, and elegantly dressed as ever. She had on a simple beige dress that was sufficiently low cut and sheer enough to be interesting. He couldn't decide whether or not she was wearing a bra. He decided to purge his mind of thoughts about the engineering of Helen's undergarments and enjoy the vision of one of the most beautiful women he had ever been with. By eight forty, they had finished dinner and two bottles of chardonnay. Jerry ordered cappuccinos. The fireworks display was scheduled to start at nine. He moved from the chair opposite her to the seat beside her in the booth, so they would both be looking out the large windows.

"I like that better," said Helen. "I like you close." She moved her right hand under the table and placed it on his thigh. Then, as she sipped her wine and chatted, she slowly moved it upward. Jerry leaned over to her and whispered in her ear.

"Helen, I don't think that is a good idea." Helen smiled broadly, showing her whitey-white smile. By now his body had a mind of its own, but he placed his hand on hers and gently pushed her away.

"I just wanted to test your equipment. I'm happy to say it's working perfectly."

"Has it ever failed you?"

"Never, but I enjoy the testing process."

As the waiter brought the cappuccinos, the maître-d' announced the last call for drinks. Once the show started, the lights in the restaurant would be turned down and there would be no drink service.

"Let's have some cognac," said Helen.

"Christ, I'm woozy now. Who's going to drive?"

"I'll drive. Don't worry. I'm very cautious when I'm transporting precious cargo."

She moved her right hand over to his crotch again and gently squeezed it. "Ha," she said, "good."

At nine o'clock, the lights in the restaurant went out and the explosion of the fireworks display lit up the western sky. During the next quarter hour, the restaurant was filed with ooohs and ahhhs of approval—of both the display and the eerie flashes that bounced off the restaurant's mirrored walls. Helen was one of the most exuberant, screeching, throwing up her arms, and generally behaving like a child.

Jerry was for the most part quiet. Periodically he said "great" or "terrific" just so he would feel part of the festivities. He avoided drinking the cognac, because after having observed Helen during the last half-hour, it was clear, he would be the one driving.

After the fireworks were over, he moved back to his original seat. Helen looked at him quizzically. Jerry bought time with a drink of water.

"Helen, we have to talk. I know this is not the right time or the right place to be serious, but I have to discuss a few things with you."

Helen took a sip of cognac. She leaned back in her seat. "Go on, you have my attention."

"Helen, during the past week, since Kevin's attack, I've done a lot of thinking about—well, about a lot of things. I've been down, really dejected. It's been hard for me to get going in the morning. The combination of Kevin's illness and learning about your relationship with Jeff has really fucked me up. I'm real unhappy, Helen. I'm used to being in control. You know, having my handle on the levers. Being able to calculate and predict how things will turn out..."

Helen grasped his hand. "It's normal. You're still grieving. You're grieving about Kevin and you're grieving about losing the idealistic image you had of me. You'll get over it. It's normal."

He expected this to be hard. It was worse than hard. He wasn't at all certain that he should even continue. He took another drink of water.

"It's more than that, Helen. I don't think I was unrealistic about who I thought you were. I assumed you were a straight shooter, what my partners would refer to as a mensch. I tend to think that about any friend, especially the women with whom I fall in love. In fact, I have to feel that way in order to fall in love."

"And I disappointed you?"

"Worse, you crushed my illusion. I was brought up to value family relationships above everything else. Lying to, stealing from, or betraying a sibling or a parent or a cousin or an aunt was the ultimate sin. I don't know how—I can't cope with the reality, that is, specifically what you've done." He reached for his previously untouched glass of cognac and drank most of it. He suddenly felt warm, stifled.

Helen made an attempt to smile. "You sound like a priest, Jerry. Aren't you being overly dramatic?"

Jerry shook his head. "No, I don't think so. It's very important. It will affect our life together—assuming we will have one. I'm trying to sort out my feelings."

Helen's smiled faded. "That sounds ominous."

"Let me tell you a little story that will give you some insight into why this is so important to me. Are you up to hearing a story?"

"Sure, tell me your story, I'm all ears, " said Helen. There was a trace of sarcasm in her tone, but she seemed to be listening.

Jerry leaned into the table. The noise in the restaurant had subsided. "When I was working for National in the engineering department, I met a woman at one of the National functions—Lynn Colten. She was the office manager of the public relations firm that represented us. I was infatuated from the first time I saw her. She was sexy, smart, and newly divorced. I went home with her. We screwed like rabbits for three days, and then I moved in with her.

"Two weeks later, her ex-husband was in a scuba diving accident. The paramedics discovered her name and address in his wallet and called her just as she was leaving for an EST training weekend. They said that they were taking him to USC Medical Center. We rushed over there. We were sitting around in the lobby waiting to see the doctor. Lynn located a telephone and proceeded to spend the next hour negotiating with an EST administrator how to recover her deposit and when she could reschedule the training. I mean the fact that her ex-husband was in a near-death situation did not factor heavily in her personal calculus. As I watched this drama, my first reaction was horror over how indifferent she appeared. Then, I decided that I was being too critical. After all, this was an ex whom she didn't really like, Who was I to judge? You know, I wasn't walking in her moccasins. So I suppressed the reaction that was based on my own ethical system and embraced a 'judge not lest ye be judged' philosophy.

"The doctor eventually emerged to tell us that many of his critical systems were gone and that he would survive for a few months as a vegetable—he couldn't communicate and it was doubtful that he could understand. As soon as he was stabilized, they would move him to a nursing home where he would get decent care and where he would die of pneumonia within six months. Lynn shed a few tears. We thanked the doctor and left. On the way home, she explained to me the arrangements that she had worked out to take the EST training.

"During the next year, we continued to live together. She went to graduate school. We had a great social life and a fabulous sex life. We were beginning to talk wedding bells. Then, Jeff came into National and took over marketing, and he and I took up our conflicts where we had left off when he went to college. I was under a tremendous amount of stress at work and took it home. Lynn and I argued a few times. Then, one day, I came home and she had packed my bags. She told me that she would no longer tolerate the stress that I had brought into her house and that she felt the relationship had run its course. She loved me, but not enough to put up with my anxiety and depression. Time to move on. Goodbye."

They both were quiet for several minutes.

"Interesting story," Helen said, "But what's the point?"

"I don't see how you could miss it," said Jerry.

"I'm not as subtle as you are. Humor me."

"Lynn's throwing me out when I was undergoing a crisis in the office was totally consistent with her indifference toward her ex-husband's accident. No matter what the circumstances, Lynn was the most important character in her life's drama and her needs and wants demanded and deserved immediate gratification. During the incident at the hospital, she had revealed her character, but the lover in me denied the information that would have prevented me from wasting a year of my life on a self-centered bitch."

"So?" said Helen. Her eyes had filled with tears.

"So, I can't afford to overlook behavior that is abhorrent to everything that forms the foundation of my being, who I am and what I stand for. That's the point of the story."

She dug into her handbag, found a tissue, and dabbed her eyes. She drained what was left in her glass of cognac. "So, I'm the new self-centered bitch on the block. I can't blame you for being wary, but I don't know what to say. You're putting me on trial."

"That wasn't my intent. I certainly don't want to hurt you, but I'm obsessed. I think about it all the time. I love you and I think we could make something of our relationship. But I'm very disturbed by what you did to your sister."

"Jerry," she said. The tears were back, and the corners of her mouth were tight. She was about to really cry. "I'm sorry you feel that way, but there is nothing I can do about the past. Moreover, I don't view my affair with Jeff as having been despicable or immoral. And I'm not going to pander to your sense of outrage by apologizing or..."

Jerry interrupted her. "I don't expect you to. It's my problem. I need to work it out. Unfortunately, I don't have the time and energy to invest. I need to focus all my energies on resolving National's financial situation. I can't afford to let anything distract me and, well, this problem..."

"Spit it out, Jerry. You want to break up. Is that it?"

"I want to put our relationship on hold for a while. It's not fair to either of us to go on as long as I have these unresolved conflicts. I need some quality time by myself to deal with them, time that I presently don't have." He paused, took a sip of the Courvoisier, and repositioned himself in his seat—anything to slow down the torrent of distress he felt radiating from Helen. "And look, it's clear to me that a lot of Jeff's animosity is due to his feeling that I stole his girl. My relationship with him has always been strained. My involvement with you has moved it to the breaking point and it may affect my efforts to save National. If it comes down to the line. I need everything I can get from him."

Tears were running down Helen's cheeks. She reached for her bag and pulled out another tissue. She blew her nose.

"I think we should leave," she said. "Please take me home."

❖

Bill Bromfield's office was expensive. It was at a corner of the building and approximately four hundred square feet, and had a one-hundred-and-eighty-degree view of Santa Monica, Brentwood, and Beverly Hills. The short view was of the rolling fairways of the Rancho Country Club. Bill's desk looked like an eighteenth-century country kitchen table and the two bergère chairs in front of his desk were upholstered in fabric that matched the drapes. The walls held several oil paintings that were in the style of Millet and Daumier.

"Your office is exquisite," said Jerry. "A pleasant change from the monastic quarters of Counselor Krimble."

"Thank you," said Bromfield. "I spend so much of my life between these four walls I decided to be very kind to myself. Besides, my wife loves to decorate."

"He has ten associates busting their asses ten hours a day, six days a week to support a partner's lifestyle—a benefit I don't enjoy," said Krimble.

"You could," said Bromfield.

"I prefer to practice law rather than practice babysitting." He smiled without animosity. "Just kidding. But I do enjoy the solitary life, devoid of office politics. Have you reviewed the drafts of the documents with Sheila?"

Bill escorted Jerry, Richard, and Bill to the small round table in the corner of the office, and made sure they had cups of the surprisingly adequate office coffee. "Yes. She'll be here in a few minutes. She called me from her car. Traffic on the freeway is terrible this morning. I'll need to meet with her brief—oh, here she is."

They all stood as Sheila walked into the office. She was dressed in a yellow tailored suit and green scarf that emphasized her small waist and green eyes. She certainly knew how to command attention.

"Sorry I'm late. I took Wilshire to avoid the freeway traffic, but it didn't move at all." She extended her hand to Jerry and then to Richard. "I hope you haven't been waiting long."

"No, we just got here," said Jerry. "We were admiring the decorating."

"It's the reason I try to set meetings at Bill's office." She turned around slowly and gestured at the paintings. Then, she placed her hand over her heart and raised her eyes. "I want to experience what it's like to be rich, so that I have something to look forward to." She took her hand off of her heart and pointed her finger at Jerry and said, "If you think this is nice, you should see his house. Every time I visit, I feel sure I'm going to run into Robin Leach." She smiled broadly. Jerry was very happy to see her in such a good mood.

"Sheila, we need a word," said Bill.

"Fine," said Sheila. "Richard, you and Jerry make yourselves comfortable. We shouldn't be long."

Jerry got up from the armchair and walked over to the leather club chair that was situated in front of the TV. He plopped into the chair, propped his feet on the leather ottoman, and closed his eyes.

"Tired?" asked Richard.

"Stressed."

"I don't wonder. Did you have a pleasant weekend?"

"Not really. Woman problems. Helen and I broke up."

"Sorry to hear that. She seems very nice."

"She is very nice. But she takes more maintenance than I have the time and energy for. I had to cut back on my emotional involvement. If it's meant to be, we'll get back together."

Jerry yawned. He had thought that breaking up with Helen would free his mind and energy and give him some peace, but now he was totally absorbed with thoughts of her and feelings of remorse over having hurt her. He had only slept three hours the previous night, and now, Bill's chair seemed more capable than his own bed of sending him into a quiet doze.

"Your client seems relaxed."

Jerry awoke when he heard Bromfield's voice.

"I was meditating," he said.

"Good for you," said Sheila. "I meditate frequently. It's the only way I can keep this crazy job from driving me over the edge. I dropped my blood pressure and ten pounds through meditation."

"Well, let's get started," said Bill. "We've reviewed the documents you prepared, Richard. Coopers has debriefed us on their investigation of the cash sales and we've reviewed the appraisal of Kevin's house. We have some proposed changes to the agreement, but they're not substantial. Before we get into the details, Sheila wants to make a comment. Right, Sheila?"

Sheila's smile took in both Jerry and Richard.

"I don't want to bore you with the details of my meetings with senior management. They were animated and surprisingly contentious. There are several members of the committee who were prepared to declare a default and start foreclosure actions. They distrust the management," She hesitated. "That of course doesn't include you, Jerry. Senior management holds you in the highest regard. Your integrity is not in question. Your bringing Kevin's cash sales to the attention of the bank required a level of courage that we rarely see. However, senior management has no confidence in your brothers. I have used the limit of my influence to espouse management's position and keep the plan on course. The committee agreed to accept management's proposal to cure the default. However, you need to know that I cannot go back to the well again. Senior management insists that the loan be paid by March 31 of next year. If it is not, the bank will foreclose. Moreover," she looked directly into Jerry's eyes, "if this deal has another blip, I will not be able to dissuade senior management from shutting down the company. You understand, Jerry."

Jerry nodded. He was elated; however he maintained an inscrutable expression. "Perfectly. The company appreciates your support, Sheila. I know you've gone out on a very long limb for us. I don't intend to let you down."

Sheila laughed. "I hope not, Jerry. My kids are counting on my bonus for their spring ski vacation."

15

FRIDAY, OCTOBER 5, 1990

Jeff dropped the girls off at their school early and was still stewing about Jessie having conveniently forgotten the lunch he'd packed for her, which contained gruyere and therefore probably too much fat. He tossed it on the back seat. The irritation dissolved, however, as soon as he caught sight of Helen. She was waiting on the sidewalk outside her condominium with her luggage, wearing a black trench coat and silk scarf. It was no contest. She'd be the most attractive woman on that plane. He got out of the car and opened the trunk. They exchanged an embrace, got her bags loaded, and drove off.

"What time is it, Jeff?"

He took his eyes off the road and glanced at his watch.

"It's 7:30. Your plane isn't until 9:30, right?"

"I think so. Let me check the ticket."

Helen rummaged around in her purse and peered into a white envelope. "United Airlines, Flight 1121, 9:38."

"We've got plenty of time. Nervous?"

"Very nervous. In fact, I think I'm having an anxiety attack."

Jeff turned off of Century Boulevard onto the departure roadway of the Los Angeles Airport. Traffic had been light and they reached the airport a half hour early. "You'll feel better when you're on the plane with a glass of wine in your hand."

"I hope you're right," she said. "God, I feel like shit. I'm probably out of my mind to go back to Paris. Tell me that I'm not crazy, Jeff." She'd placed her hand on his shoulder.

He felt a twinge of nostalgia for the good times he had enjoyed with her, but he kept his eyes straight ahead as he maneuvered through the airport traffic. "I had a human resources professor once tell me that when you're in an emotional snarl and you can't seem to get any kind of resolution, leaving the scene can be a solution, at least temporarily. You'll distance yourself from the problem, get your career going again, and contact old friends. In a few months, you may be able to see things from a different perspective."

"I've got to get my life started, you know—a real life—kids, dogs, a house with a patio, a barbecue, and a picket fence. I'm going to be thirty-seven in April. I'm too old to play Holly Golightly."

Jeff turned into a parking space in front of the United Terminal. He set the brake and turned off the motor. He turned to Helen. "I wish I could help you, Helen."

"The hints about our relationship that you dropped to Jerry certainly didn't help my situation." As soon as she said the words, she immediately lowered her eyes.

Her embarrassment was evident. Jeff placed his finger under her chin and lifted her head so that she would look directly into his eyes. "Listen, I'm not very proud of what I did. It was childish and thoughtless. I was distraught, hostile, and angry. I saw Jerry as a threat both to my professional life and my personal life. I was lashing out at him. I'm very sorry. What more can I say?"

"You can't." Tears started to stream down her face. The svelte, sophisticated, and composed woman he picked up a half-hour ago was gone.

He took her hand in his. "In any event, if the two of you were going to talk wedding bells, I would have insisted that you tell Jerry about our relationship. There is no way that I would allow my brother to start a marriage without knowing the real score."

"Like you did to Salli?"

"Like we did to Salli. That deception is just one more problem that I've had to deal with. Because of our relationship, I've never been able to be completely honest with Salli and I'm sure, in some way, she senses it. Who knows? Maybe that's why it's not such an Ozzie and Harriet marriage." He took out his handkerchief and wiped the tears from her face. "You were going to have to deal with the problem anyway, Helen."

She took his handkerchief and dabbed at her eyes. "But at least I would have had the opportunity to deal with it rather than have Jerry figure the thing out like a detective."

"You're absolutely right, Helen. I make no excuses." He shook his head. "I was a jerk and an asshole. I'll send you a voodoo doll in my image and some pins, so you can put a curse on me."

"Fuck you, Jeff. Fuck you in hearts and spades."

They were both quiet. Helen was crying. Jeff reached over to put his hand on her shoulder. She pulled away. "Don't."

"Christ, Helen, where is your sense of humor? Lighten up. Put that sexy smile back on your face—the one that can make a guy hard at a thousand yards. Your life isn't a tragedy. You're going to France to work in a fancy gallery and hobnob with the upper, upper class of Europe. You're beautiful. You have the body of a Venus. Ninety-nine percent of the women in this country would give up a tit to be in your spot. You're going to be fine. Take it one day at a time."

Helen pulled down the visor mirror and checked her makeup. Then, she turned and glared at him. "I am not a tart. I'm an educated, mature woman who can do more than just fuck well. I would have hoped that you would have learned that through these many months of our relationship. It's apparent that you haven't." She started to open the door to get out of the car. "Thanks for the lift," she said.

Jeff reached over and pulled her hand back and turned her toward him. She looked perplexed. He hesitated, uncomfortable with what he needed to tell her. "Listen, don't write Jerry off, Helen. He is under a tremendous amount of pressure and he is operating on overload. He can't afford to put a lot of thought into complex romantic and family problems when he's spending every waking minute trying to dig us out of a financial mess. Jerry would make a good husband. Just cut him some slack."

Her eyes widened. Her anger had evaporated. "I'm surprised to hear you say that. I didn't think you liked him very much."

An airport security officer tapped on Jeff's window and motioned that he needed to move the car. Jeff rolled down the window and said that they would unload and be gone in three minutes. The security officer held up three fingers and nodded.

He turned back to Helen. "We've been at odds for so many years I'm not sure how I feel about Jerry. But I certainly respect him. He'd be one hell of a provider. He's sincere, and I know if you're interested in him, he must be an excellent lover."

Helen laughed. "He is, but don't ask me how he compares to you, because I'll never tell."

He and Helen got out of the car. Jeff removed her baggage from the trunk and carried it over to the porter. Helen handed her tickets to him along with a five-dollar bill.

"Thanks again for the lift, Jeff. I really appreciate it."

Jeff put his arms around her and kissed her on the cheek.

"I want you to be happy, Helen. I care about you. You can always call on me."

"I know, Jeff. I know." She kissed him lightly on his lips, turned, and walked into the terminal, pulling her carry-on bag.

Jerry awoke at 6:21 a.m. on Saturday to the realization that (a) he was alone, and (b) he had absolutely nothing to do. At first, he rejected both thoughts as crazy. But slowly he began to accept that his insight was valid.

Chelsey's tongue was warm and slick on his hand, and the anxiety began to subside. I'm not alone, he thought. Harry Truman once said, "If you need a friend in Washington, get a dog." All right, that was a start.

Helen had been gone for a week. There was no candlelight dinner, no tearful goodbye, and no sex—just a telephone call to give him a heads-up that she was going to Paris to look into a business opportunity and she'd call him when she returned. She expected to be away for at least two weeks.

Jerry called Chelsey up on the bed, rolled her over on her back, and moved his hand over her chest and stomach. He never tired of observing that beatific grin on Chelsey's face when her belly was being stroked.

It was a quarter after seven in the morning. What the hell was he going to do today? Or tomorrow? Or on Halloween or Thanksgiving or Christmas or New Year's? For the first time since the breakup, he realized that his rejecting Helen without having a replacement in the wings was tantamount to shooting himself in the foot. He hit his forehead with the palm of his hand.

"Schmuck!"

Chelsey rolled over and stared at him. He patted her head. "Good girl. Daddy's sorry."

He made himself a breakfast of oatmeal, fruit, and coffee and then read the morning paper until eight. Then, he punched the speakerphone button and called Kevin. He answered on the second ring.

"Kevin?"

"Yeah?"

He took a sip from his coffee cup and stared at a woman in a bikini, scrubbing a boat. "How are you doing?"

"Okay, I guess. Saw the doc yesterday, and he says I'm on the mend. He was convincing to the point that I asked the minister to return the retainer for my funeral."

"Not funny." Jerry went over to the sofa and began to fluff up the pillows.

"I'll get better. I'm still working on my gallows humor."

"Christ, Kevin, you must have more exciting things to do with your time." Chelsey jumped up on the sofa and Jerry shooed her off.

Kevin's voice was flat. "Not really, Jerry. I'm afraid I have very little to do."

Jerry tossed the tennis ball across the room, and Chelsey bounded after it. Mustering his most enthusiastic voice, he said, "I've got a great idea, Kev. Why don't you and I jump into the car and drive to Vegas, check into a fancy hotel, and hang out for a few days. We'll swim, gamble, ogle the waitresses, avoid the whores, and fantasize what it would be like to fuck the showgirls. What about it?"

"You're kidding?"

Jerry ratcheted his enthusiasm up a notch. "No, I'm serious. Look at it as part of your medical treatment. Come on. *Carpe diem*! It will do us both a hell of a lot of good. Carolyn can live without you for a few days, can't she?"

"No problem there," said Kevin, with a touch of sarcasm. Jerry ignored it.

"I'm going to call Shirley and tell her I won't be in Monday. I've got to make arrangements to board Chelsey. I should be able to pick you up by ten. Just bring your gambling money. The rest of the expense is on me. Okay? Be ready at one." He hung up the phone before Kevin could respond.

Jerry pulled into Kevin's driveway and honked his horn. He noticed Kevin's rollaway bag on the front step. He smiled. Until that moment, he wasn't absolutely sure that Kevin would go. Kevin emerged from the front doorway carrying a small satchel. He placed the satchel on the step. He picked up the paper, opened the door, and tossed it inside. He reached into his pocket, took out a key, and locked the door. He walked over to Jerry's car with his rollaway. As he opened the car door, Jerry said, "Where's Carolyn? I wanted to reassure her that I'll keep you out of trouble."

"She's been gone since early this morning." He slid into his seat and pulled the car door shut. "I've left her a note. Let's go."

Strange, thought Jerry. He moved Kevin's bag to the trunk and got back into the car. Kevin put on his mirrored sunglasses and gave Jerry a huge grin. "Okay, Scotty, beam me to Las Vegas. I want to party."

They arrived in Las Vegas shortly after four. Jerry had made reservations for two rooms at the Mirage. He had originally planned to share a room in order to maximize togetherness, but he modified his plan just in case he was successful in attracting female companionship. This action was evidence of the panic he had been experiencing over the prospect of celibacy. Juggling several relationships, his typical social challenge had in hindsight been a hell of a lot easier, and a lot more fun than scrounging for one-night-stands.

Jerry made reservations for the Siegfried and Roy dinner show and the Allen and Rossi comedy late show at Bob Stupak's Vegas World. Jerry thoroughly enjoyed the Siegfried and Roy show. The pair cavorted on the stage with white tigers, causing them to periodically appear and disappear. Jerry occasionally turned to Kevin to comment on the incredible acts of prestidigitation. Kevin was smiling, but appeared to be unimpressed.

When the show was over, they both ensconced themselves at a blackjack table. Jerry pulled out his wallet and placed ten crisp $100 bills on the felt. The dealer picked them up one by one, quickly inspected them, and deposited each bill into his safe. He counted out $1,000 in chips and pushed the pile over to Jerry. Kevin reached for his wallet. Jerry touched him on the arm and pushed one half of his chips over to Kevin.

"I'm staking you for $500. I get one half of your winnings. Okay?"

"No dice," said Kevin and he pushed the stack of chips back to Jerry. "I plan to keep all my winnings." Kevin pulled out his wallet and laid a $1,000 bill on the felt. Jerry stared at the bill and looked at Kevin as if to say, "Where the fuck did you get a $1,000 bill on a Saturday morning?" Kevin merely smiled at him. The dealer motioned to the pit boss, who came over to inspect the bill. The pit boss gave the bill back to the dealer, who put it in his safe and gave Kevin $1,000 worth of chips.

By ten thirty, Jerry had grown his stack of chips by a factor of three, and Kevin was down to two $25 chips. Kevin was showing the results of the three drinks he had consumed. He slumped in his seat. His hair was disheveled and beads of sweat stood out on his forehead.

"We'd better go, Kevin. The show starts in an hour."

"One more hand," said Kevin, and he placed his remaining chips on the betting line. Jerry swept all of his chips into a big cup. As they fell into the cup, they made the clicking sound of chips cascading on each other. He could not help feeling smug over his success, which he estimated at a full 300 percent return on his initial stake. As he was finishing the process, Kevin was losing with a twenty against the dealer's twenty-one.

"Shit, the story of my life."

Jerry winced. "Let's go Kevin. You're just warming up. I'm sure the show will be great." He was right. Marty Allen and Steve Rossi delivered seventy minutes of rapid-fire jokes that kept them in hysterics. Jerry glanced at Kevin intermittently and was pleased that a smile remained plastered on his face throughout the show. He even passed up the second of the two drinks, the minimum that were included in the admission charge. Jerry was relieved. When they returned to the hotel, he suggested a nightcap. They located a quiet bar and ordered cognacs from a very smiley waitress.

"Thanks for suggesting this trip, Jerry. I haven't had this much fun for many, many months. Many months."

"Every once in a while, I do get a good idea." He pulled out his wallet and searched for the credit card he used for personal expenses and set it on the table.

Kevin laughed. "That's your problem, Jerry, you're much too humble."

The waitress brought their drinks, a gin and tonic for Kevin and a Jack Daniels and water for Jerry, and picked up the credit card. They sipped them in silence. Jerry got to the bottom of his glass and said, "Boy, this is weak." He motioned to the waitress for another round. "How are things at home, Kevin?"

Kevin looked up from the empty glass he'd been staring into and said, "Now why would you ask me that?"

"Because I think things are not great and I want you to talk about it."

Kevin leaned back in his chair. He looked around the room. "Where is that damn waitress? I need another drink." He remained silent, turning the empty glass around and around. Finally, he said, "How could you possibly know? Carolyn and I have done a pretty good job of keeping our dirty laundry in the hamper."

"Lots of little things, Kevin. Carolyn doesn't seem to be as concerned about your present situation as I would have expected. She's made no attempt to arrange the family gatherings that have been her *sin qua non*. You invariably answer the phone—which means that she's out a lot without you. The fact that she wasn't there this morning when we left and you wrote her a note tells me that you didn't know where she was at ten in the morning and were not able to call her. Smells like Trouble in River City, brother."

The waitress returned with their drinks. Kevin took his from her hand, thanked her, and immediately drained the glass. As he placed the glass on the table, he smacked his lips and said, "You'd make a good detective, Jerry. Carolyn and I have been, been—how do you say it?" He groped for the right word. "Estranged. We've been estranged for almost two years."

The fact of the estrangement was not a surprise. The two years was. "Do Mom and Dad know?"

"I think so, although we've never talked about it."

"What about Jeff and Salli?"

"Yeah."

Jerry struggled to avoid showing his irritation. He spoke in a calm and non-confrontational voice, attempting to expunge any hint of the indignation he was feeling. "Why haven't you leveled with me, Kevin? Don't you think that I had both a need and a right to know?" Jerry felt his face heating up. He closed his eyes, took another sip of his drink, and took his handkerchief out and wiped his forehead. "Sorry, Kevin. I'm out of line."

Kevin looked down into his glass. He glanced up and said, "No problem. Don't worry about it. I didn't intend to hide it from you. With all that's been going on, there just wasn't a good opportunity to talk about it."

Jerry put his handkerchief away and leaned forward. "What happened, Kevin? You two always seemed to have the quintessential marriage. I mean your relationship with Carolyn and your kids, the trips, the barbecues—it all seemed so perfect."

Kevin looked into his whiskey. "I really don't know why it all went to pieces. Probably a number of things. I'm not as good as I used to be—in bed I mean. It's the medication I take for depression and cholesterol. Then, about two years ago, Carolyn decided to finally get control over her weight. She went on Weight Watchers, joined a gym, and lost about six dress sizes."

"She is in great shape," said Jerry.

"She made some new friends through the gym, some of whom were divorced, and she started going out with them occasionally, then frequently, and now five times a week."

"Where do they go?"

"They dress up in tight jeans, boots, fancy shirts, and cowboy hats and go line dancing at cowboy bars."

"What does she tell you? Do you talk about it? Do you argue? What about sex?" Jerry realized he was starting to come on too strong, but he could no longer control his frustration over Kevin's apparent detachment from events that were central to his life.

"What's sex? With whom?"

"Kevin, don't bullshit me!"

Kevin answered as if he were delivering a technical paper at an engineering convention. "She moved into one of the kid's bedrooms shortly after she lost the weight, and we haven't slept together since."

"Is she seeing someone?"

Kevin laughed. "Don't be so naïve, Jerry." He used his fingers to enumerate the facts. "One," he held up his index finger, "She's a forty-five year old woman who looks thirty-five. Two, she dresses in outfits that are so tight that you can almost make out the crack in her vagina. Three, she goes out five nights a week and often doesn't come home until noon the next day." He pulled his fingers back into a fist and slammed it on the table, causing the glasses to rattle. Raising his voice, he said, "What in the fuck do you think she's doing?"

Jerry was quiet. He felt that he was down in a very deep pit—Kevin's pit, and it was frightening. He didn't respond for several minutes. They both sat, sipping their drinks. He thought about asking Kevin whether his kids knew about their parents' problems, but he decided that there was no point.

"Kevin, I'm so sorry. Is there any way I can help? Is there anything I can do for you?" He tried to keep his voice from sounding desperate. Kevin shook his head.

"I don't think so, Jerry. No. I've come to realize that I'm beyond help. Anyway, thanks for asking." They sat in the bar for several more minutes. Then, Kevin got up.

"Let's go to bed, Jerry. It's been a very long day."

❖

Jerry pulled up to Kevin's house at five thirty on Monday evening. Kevin had slept during most of the trip. After he turned off the engine, he touched Kevin on the shoulder and said, "Time to go, big fella."

Kevin grunted and opened his eyes. He opened the car door and, using the door jamb for support, pulled himself out of the car. He stretched his arms into the air and yawned.

Jerry removed his bags from the trunk and set them down on the curb. He threw his arms around Kevin and kissed him on the cheek.

"I had a great time, Jerry. Thanks for putting this together."

Jerry loosened his grip. "So did I. It was good to spend some quality time with you." He picked up the tote bag and handed it to him. "Are you coming in tomorrow?"

Kevin smiled. "I'll come in if there's something for me to do. I'll call you. Thanks again." He picked up his suitcase and walked to the door. Jerry stood on the sidewalk, watching him, and Kevin opened the door and waved, as if trying to assure his little brother from afar that everything was fine. Jerry's throat tightened and he turned away, thinking that those days were far away indeed.

Kevin closed the front door and yelled up the stairs, "Carolyn, I'm home." He waited for a response. When he didn't hear one, he walked in the direction of the kitchen, calling, "Carolyn, hello?" He opened the refrigerator and removed a Corona, opened it, and took a long drink. Carrying the beer, he walked back toward the entrance and started to climb the stairs when he heard her respond. "I'll be down in a minute."

"I'll be in the family room," he yelled. He walked back into the family room, sat down in his barker lounge chair, kicked off his shoes, and started to scan the newspaper. Moments later, he heard the clop, clop, clop sounds as Carolyn descended the staircase in her cowboy boots. As she walked into the family room, Kevin knew she was not planning to spend a quiet evening at home hearing about his exploits in Las Vegas. She was dressed to the nines in her regalia: denim shorts that were in the style of hot pants, an embroidered suede belt, pink snakeskin boots, and a matching cowboy hat. Her cotton blouse was open sufficiently to show her ample breasts and a horn necklace with rhinestones.

She sat down on the sofa facing him. "Did you have a good time?"

He folded the paper and placed it on the coffee table. "Yeah, real good. The shows were terrific and the food was great. Jerry paid for everything— uh, that is, everything but the thousand bucks I lost at the blackjack table."

He paused. "Incidentally, I borrowed the money from you. I took it from your stash. I knew you wouldn't mind."

Her visage darkened slightly and she sat upright. "Well, you could have asked me."

He took a drink from his bottle of Corona. "I had to leave at ten on Saturday. You weren't home. If you were, I would have asked." He took another drink.

Her eyes darted around the room as if she were looking for a clue that would remind her where she was on Saturday morning. "Just be sure to pay me back, Okay?"

"You really don't have to worry about that." He paused. "I see you're going out."

She looked at her watch. "Yes, and I'm late—I'm meeting Jody and Chris for dinner and then we're going dancing at the Buckeroo. I'll be home after twelve." She started to walk toward the door.

He laughed, sarcastically.

She stopped. "And what the hell is that supposed to mean?"

He took a drink, emptying the bottle, and sat silently looking at the label.

"I said," she said raising her voice, "what the hell is that supposed to mean?"

"It means, mother of my children, we both know that come the witching hour, you'll be fornicating with some yokel that you picked up. That's what it means." He put the empty bottle on the coffee table.

"You bastard." Furious, she grabbed the bottle and cocked her arm and was about the throw it at him when he jumped out of the chair and caught her right arm and pried the bottle from her fingers. As he was doing so, she hit him in the nose with her left hand, causing an explosion of pain that sent him falling back onto the sofa.

She stood over him as he writhed in agony. "You don't know squat about what I do when I'm out and that's the way I'm going to keep it. I'm still young and attractive, and I'm not going to waste away in this mausoleum with a guy who can't get it up anymore." She walked through the door and slammed it behind her.

Kevin lay on the sofa and used his handkerchief to keep the blood from staining the new upholstery. Finally, he pulled himself up and staggered to the kitchen. He stuffed a plastic sandwich bag with ice, wrapped a dishtowel around it, and held it on his nose. With his free hand, he filled an eight-ounce glass with ice and Jack Daniels, went back to his lounge chair, and turned on the television to watch the evening news.

16

SATURDAY, OCTOBER 20, 1990

"Mom, Dad, it's Grandpa."

Jessie opened the door and threw her arms around her Grandpa Charlie. He put his arms around her waist, lifted her off the ground, and twirled her around. Charlie wore white trousers. His white collared shirt was open at the neck. A thick gold rope chain hung from his neck.

"Damn, you're getting big. I'm going to have to start lifting weights." He set her down carefully, stood back, and admired her. "New dress?"

Jessie pushed her hips forward and her shoulders back. "Like it? I bought it this morning. It cost an entire month's clothes' allowance."

"I love it. And the dress is lucky to have you to decorate it."

Jessie took Charlie's hand and led him into the family room. Jeff and Salli were seated on the sofa, close together, drinking coffee. They were smiling as if they had just finished laughing over a joke. Salli walked over to her father and kissed him on the cheek. Jeff shook his father-in-law's hand theatrically. "Looks like you're on the way to Palm Springs."

"As a matter of fact, I am. Got any beer on ice?"

"Bud Light, Amstel Light, or Beck's." Jeff already knew the answer, so he pulled three Amstels out of the refrigerator and opened them all. He got himself situated on the sofa with Salli and her dad, and they toasted their bottles.

"How's Kevin?" said Charlie.

"Better," said Salli. "But the damage to the heart was greater than the doctors initially thought. He's looking at a long recovery and a major lifestyle change."

"I hate to be crass or insensitive, but..."

"But," interrupted Jeff, "You want to know how Kevin's being sidelined will affect the business. Right?"

"I know how inappropriate the question must seem," said Charlie. "But I'm going way out on a limb on this deal and..."

Jeff held up his hand. "We understand, Charlie. You don't have to explain. Kevin's health, availability, and survival are important issues. We've talked extensively among ourselves—Jerry, Howard, Allen, the chief engineer, Richard. The plain fact is that Kevin's main non-management activity during the past five years has been in the product development area. I've handled the marketing with little involvement on his part. We fully expect that within three months, Kevin will be in a position to participate in research and development work. He just will not be able to do it on a full-time basis. In the deal we're talking about, Kevin will not be involved in executive management or finance—the activities that contributed to his stress. We're confident that with Kevin available part time and with me assuming executive control over operations, the business will not be impacted."

Charlie thought for a moment. "You really believe that, Jeff? You wouldn't hype your dear old father-in-law, would you?" He forced a laugh.

"Dad," exclaimed Salli. "Don't be an ass! You know Jeff wouldn't do anything that would risk embarrassing you."

"I couldn't have said it better, Charlie," said Jeff. "The company will not be impacted by Kevin's having to cut back his time."

"Okay," said Charlie. "Let's move on. Here is the way the deal will be structured."

He handed Jeff and Salli several sheets of paper. He described the structure of the investment, the backgrounds, and proposed stake of each of the investors, the timetable to close the investment, the composition of the board, and Jeff and Kevin's compensation. Jeff and Salli read the papers. Jeff made several notes.

"In essence," said Charlie. "My investment group is going to buy 40 percent of the company for nine million. We have a commitment from Foothill to provide twelve million secured by receivables, inventory, and capital equipment. That will give us twenty–one million in cash. We'll pay off Jerry's line of credit, Foxx's breakup fee, and give ten million to the bank, which will give them a 78 percent recovery. The existing sub-debt becomes subordinate to our investment. The capitalization table shows that if all shares are converted, our investment group will own 34 percent, the sub-debt will own 10 percent, Jeff and Kevin will each own

25.5, and the management, excluding Kevin and Jeff, would potentially own 5 percent. Legal, accounting, and consulting costs will run about eight hundred fifty thousand. I know I'm throwing a lot of numbers at you, but what they mean is that you will have almost seven million for additional working capital. I'll be chairman, Jeff will be CEO, Kevin will be vice president of R and D. Jeff, and Kevin will each get five-year contracts at two hundred thousand dollars a year. We will formulate a cash bonus program that will include Jeff, Kevin, and key management." He peered at his notes through his bifocals and then looked up at Salli and Jeff. "I think that does it. Any questions?"

Jeff asked, "When can we close?"

"We're going to use Arthur Anderson to do the accounting and due diligence and Gibson Dunn to do the legal work. I've already met with the responsible partners at both firms and they say if your financials are up to date, we could close in sixty days."

"What do we do about Kevin and Jerry?" said Jeff.

"I don't think you can tell them until all my investors are committed," said Charlie. "We have to keep them in the dark."

Salli raised her eyebrows. "You're not serious?"

Charlie's lips pressed into a slit and he shook his head.

"You are serious," she said.

"Jerry is in the bank's lap," said Charlie. "He's committed himself to selling the company to pay the bank off in full. If Jeff told him I had a deal in the works that would give the bank a substantial haircut, he'd be placed in a terrible position. He'd feel obligated to tell the bank, and Jeff would take the position that his telling the bank was revealing confidential information. And I don't want the bank to have much time to think about this deal once my investor's money is committed." He gazed at Salli a moment longer than what was conversational."

Jeff put his arms around Salli. "Your father's right, hon. I don't like it either, but it's the only way."

Salli extracted herself from Jeff's arms and flipped through the TV channels with the sound off. Charlie and Jeff continued their conversation, feeling that indeed the rest of the world was muted for their conspiracy.

Salli watched them over her shoulder for a long while and sighed. It was loud enough to make them pause. She looked Jeff squarely in the eye. "I'm not surprised that Dad would do this, but I am surprised that you'd screw your brothers like this. I regret ever suggesting that you approach

Dad with this witch's brew." She turned on her heel and turned the TV, so that she could watch it from the other side of the room.

Jeff made no response. Charlie shrugged. "Jeff, are you sure our consultants and accountant can have access to the key managers at National without anything leaking to Jerry?"

"No problem. Once the managers realize that my deal is the only way to keep the company from being sold, with all the uncertainties for their careers and incomes, they'll do anything I ask. Just make sure all the professionals interface with me personally—not my secretary. They probably should contact me using the home number. We have voicemail and I'll make sure I check for messages frequently. They can also send documents to our house fax. Keeping Jerry in the dark is the least of our problems. Besides, he's too busy fucking Helen to notice."

Salli turned her attention away from the TV. "That's what I love about you, Jeff," she called. "You're so subtle." She began fidgeting with the papers Charlie had brought. Charlie let out a slow whistle.

"I didn't know they were an item," said Charlie. "He's got good taste." Salli lost interest in the conversation as soon as Helen's name was mentioned and was about to stand up when Charlie waved at her to settle down.

"There's one other issue I need to cover with you. It's somewhat sensitive, but I'm sure you'll be able to handle it."

"Shoot."

"The nigger's got to go."

"The what?" said Jeff. Salli rolled her eyes and shook her head.

"Howard, the black guy, the CFO," said Charlie. "After the deal is closed, I want you to replace him. I'm not going to be chairman of any company that depends on a spade for its numbers. Is that a problem?"

Jeff started to feel the rush of anger moving through his stiffening neck through his cheeks to his forehead. Beads of perspiration formed on his hands and upper lip.

"Oh, Dad, you can't be serious," said Salli. She abandoned the TV and drifted to Jeff's side. "What you're asking Jeff to do is illegal. There are laws against it."

Charlie was very calm and matter-of-fact. He had thought this through. "I'm well aware of the law. But I know that there are ways around the problem—putting a little pressure on Howard at the right time, letting the word out that he's unhappy, setting tough goals that will frustrate him. I'm not suggesting that Jeff fire him. I just want Jeff's commitment that he'll get rid of him, discreetly."

Jeff stood up and walked over to the bar. "How about another beer, Charlie?"

"Sure, I'm ready."

"This is a mistake, Dad," said Salli, her voice rising. "We're in the nineteen nineties, not the eighteen nineties."

"You're entitled to your opinion, honey, but at this point in my life, I don't want to have to start working with and depending on niggers, and that's that."

Jeff came back to the sofa with three bottles of Amstel. He passed them out and then fell back down into the couch. The anger that initially overcame him had subsided. He took a long swallow, placed the bottle on the coffee table, and smiled broadly.

"If this deal goes down, Charlie, you and I will be in a new relationship. I think it's important that we both understand each other's perceptions of the relationship and the postulates that will govern our interaction. Postulate number one: You will be an investor, the chairman of the board of directors and a very influential member of the management. Postulate number two: I am my own man and neither you nor anyone else is going to have any fucking say as to who I hire, including where they come from or what color they are. As long as I'm CEO, that is my prerogative. Postulate number three: If you get involved in National as contemplated, you are going to keep your bigotry to yourself. I will not allow your prejudice to infect the social fabric of the company and the working relationships among our employees that has taken years to develop."

Charlie raised his hand. "Now Jeff..."

"Let me finish, Charlie." Jeff took a sip of beer and reached over to grasp Salli's hand. "I want this deal to happen. It's all I think about. I will be devastated if we have to sell the company. But if you're telling me that my agreeing to chop Howard is a deal point, then I am prepared to let the deal die." He drained the bottle and firmly set the empty bottle down on the coffee table, so that the sound of the beer bottle meeting the glass punctuated what he said.

There was a dense quiet in the room. Salli's eyes were riveted on Charlie's face. Jeff continued to smile and look directly into Charlie's eyes.

Charlie re-crossed his legs. "You don't mince words, Jeff."

"You know that I'm pretty direct, Charlie, especially when I feel strongly about an issue."

"You're asking a lot of me. I'm very uncomfortable around those people."

"I know. But you'll have to learn to be more comfortable if you want to complete this deal."

Charlie and Salli sat quietly, drinking their beers. Charlie drained his bottle, placed it on the table quietly, and stood. "At least I'm putting my money on someone who has the courage of his convictions, even if he is a nigger-lover." Charlie smiled his most ingratiating smile, showing all of his unblemished teeth. He extended his hand to Jeff. "We've got a deal."

Salli hugged her father, kissed his cheek, and saw him to the door. When she returned to the family room, Jeff was still sitting on the couch, sipping a third beer. She sat down next to him and snuggled under his arm.

"Did you really intend to blow the deal if Charlie hadn't backed off?"

"I have no intention of playing Pinocchio to your father's Geppetto. I'm happy that he threw me such a clear-cut issue to make a stand over. It's nice to be on the side of the angels for once."

Salli leaned over and kissed him, then stood up and pulled his hand. "Watching that last act has made me incredibly excited. Jessie's gone to the movies, so what do you say..."

Howard had just decided to head for the cafeteria to get another cup of coffee when Shirley called and asked him to meet with Jeff. Howard glanced at his watch and noticed that he only had forty-five minutes before the First Chicago contingent arrived, and he had not completed the materials. He told Shirley that he was really pressed for time and asked whether Jeff could wait until the afternoon. Shirley said that Jeff was not flexible and asked him to come immediately.

Talk about anxiety. In the more than six months that he had been with National, Jeff had never met with him one-on-one. So why the hell would he want to meet now? He wasn't even his boss. Anxiety morphed into fear. He couldn't think of anything that he had said or done that would cause Jeff to call him on the carpet like he was obviously doing. Goddammit. He wished he had gotten that second cup of coffee. No time now. He started to reach for the phone to call Shirley and ask her what he should bring, but he second-guessed himself. She had been pretty curt.

He pushed himself out of his chair, picked up a pad and pen from the desk, and headed out the door. He walked briskly down the hall toward the executive offices. It was still early, and he didn't encounter anyone who'd expect him to make small talk. He pasted a smile on his face to perk himself up, but it did little to compensate for the lump in his throat.

When he arrived at Shirley's desk, she motioned to the door to Jeff's office, which was closed, and told him to go right in. Jeff was seated at his desk reviewing spreadsheets.

He looked up and said, "Hi, Howard, thanks for being so prompt. Please sit down."

Howard sat in the chair in front of Jeff's desk. Jeff got up from his chair, came around to the front of the desk, and sat down opposite Howard.

Jeff crossed his legs, put his fingers together in a steeple, and looked directly at Howard without speaking. After thirty seconds, Howard was feeling very uncomfortable, and at one minute, he started to perspire. Finally, he could stand it no longer and blurted out, "Jeff, the First Chicago meeting is in a half hour and I don't have all the packages put together. I really need to..."

"Calm down, Howard, this won't take long." He was silent for a few moments more and finally he said, "Howard, do you like it here? I mean, do you enjoy working at National?"

How the hell do I keep from pissing in my pants? he wondered. Wasn't this the kind of discussion that Jerry was supposed to handle? He had been a participant in these types of conversations before, the kind that started with, "Do you enjoy working here?" and went to, "Good, I'm happy to hear it. So why are you fucking up so much? If you don't stop fucking up, your enjoyment will come to an end because, you pissant, you won't be working here anymore."

Howard cleared his throat, pasted a smile on his face, and looked directly at Jeff. "I love working here. It's the best damn job I've had since I graduated. I feel that I'm making major contributions to this company."

"I'm happy to hear it," said Jeff. Howard braced himself. Jeff leaned forward and spoke very softly. "I need to confide in you, Howard, but I'm not sure I can trust you. Can I trust you, Howard?"

Howard's fear subsided slightly.

"I don't understand, Jeff. Trust me about what?"

"I need your help, Howard, and I need you to keep the conversation we are having absolutely confidential. I mean you can't tell anyone. Not Kevin, not Jerry, not your wife. If you can't or won't respect my need for confidentiality, this conversation has just terminated."

Howard's hand had steadied and he pulled out a handkerchief and mopped his brow. "But Jerry's my boss."

"Right, but I vote all the stock," said Jeff, "And ownership always trumps management. Don't you agree?"

Suddenly, as if by magic, the anxiety was gone, along with the perspiration. Howard got the picture. The power in the company was shifting from Jerry to Jeff. Jeff was in fact "the boss," the guy who would determine his future at National. He leaned forward in his chair until his head was about a foot from Jeff's.

"You can count one me, Jeff. What is it you want me to do?"

Shortly after they arrived, the bankers from the venture capital group of First Chicago were ushered into the main conference room where Jerry, Jeff, Kevin, and Howard were waiting. Shirley entered with an overloaded tray of coffee mugs, coffeepots, and cinnamon rolls.

"The rolls are from Bodacious Buns in Century City," she said. "I arranged for one of the guys to pick them up on his way to work. They contain about one thousand calories and twenty grams of fat, but they are scrumptious. You can't have any Kevin. I brought you a plate of fruit."

"You're not much fun, Shirley," said Kevin. "You ought to be my wife."

"I'll take that as a compliment," said Shirley.

As everyone fed on cinnamon rolls and drank coffee, Ethan Wilson guided the conversation, so that the bank group and the National group could explore and share their common areas of professional experience, education, sports team preferences, and the like.

Jerry admired the way Ethan controlled the conversation without any hint of being in control. He was feeling better than he had in weeks. First Chicago had a track record of a 35 percent cash on cash return since they started up in the late seventies.

Even Kevin was in excellent spirits, and his conversation was animated and enthusiastic. First Chicago was very interested in National's technical position, and Kevin was a better salesman of National's prowess than anyone at the company.

Jeff was quiet during their meeting. He mostly listened and nodded. Jerry wasn't surprised or particularly concerned. Jeff had made it very clear that he was not happy about selling the company, and he could sulk all that he wished. By nine thirty, most of the rolls were gone and the conversation started to wane.

"I think we should get started," said Ethan. "We've got a lot of ground to cover." He looked around the table and smiled at everyone. "I've already spoken with the National people about First Chicago's level of interest. I think you can assume these blokes are very serious just based on the amount they spent on airline tickets to bring everyone here today. I've advised First Chicago that there is a lot of investor interest in National. I am in touch with a number of potential buyers and am being bombarded for information. I've known Larry and Eric for many years and have sold them a number of companies. I know that when they are interested, they are able to move quickly to close. They've prepared a detailed list of what they want to cover today. Why don't I just pass it around and then we'll figure out how best to get through it."

Larry scanned the agenda and said, "Before we get into the plan, I'd appreciate it if Kevin would give us some historical background—how the company got started, major accomplishments, major setbacks, you know the drill."

Kevin brightened immediately. For him, talking about the history of National was a bigger turn-on than sex. Another good omen. As he had done so many times before, Kevin told how he had started National in his garage, developed the first product with the help of a few engineers who moonlighted for him, and carried the prototype in a briefcase when he called on purchasing agents and engineers. He told the story of the first time a customer insisted upon visiting his "plant." He had spruced up the three-car garage, so that it looked presentable, but he realized that he had no employees to show, because everyone who worked for him moonlighted. So, he enlisted Carolyn and some of her friends to be "employees." And in order to make them look legitimate, he bought some white coats, sewed on National logos, and spent an evening training them on how to look engaged. Amazingly, the "plant inspection" went well and he received the first substantial order for National's initial product.

The bankers appeared to enjoy Kevin's animated storytelling, but Jeff was fidgety. "Okay, Kevin," he said. "They asked for a brief history. We don't really have time for a pageant. How about speeding things up a bit? As Ethan said, we've got a lot of ground to cover."

There was shifting around the table. Jerry sent a back-off glace at Jeff. Kevin looked over to Ethan, eyes pleading for support and permission to continue. Then, he dropped his chin and aimlessly shuffled the papers in front of him.

"Please go on, Kevin," said Ethan, recovering. "We've got plenty of time."

Larry joined in. "I'm fascinated by your story. Please continue."

Jeff shrugged and slumped down in his chair.

Kevin quickly recovered his stride and told several anecdotes on the theme of how he repeatedly overcame tremendous odds to build the company to its position of market leadership. He avoided any mention of the Johnson-Potter debacle, assuming that those events, which led to their present circumstances, had been well chronicled.

At about ten-thirty, Kevin finished up and Larry asked Jerry to summarize the salient points of the business plan and to describe the most critical assumptions and management's identification of the primary risk areas. Jerry opened the large black notebook that contained the business plan that he and other key members of management had spent several agonizing months creating. He launched into a well-rehearsed discussion of the company's strengths and weaknesses, the key success factors for the industry and the company's future prospects. He summarized the major financial objectives for the next fiscal year, specifically sales, operating profit, capital investment, and net profits before taxes. As Jerry was about to begin discussing management's rationale for selecting these objectives, Jeff interrupted.

"Jerry and I don't necessarily agree on the sales forecast. I'm convinced that we can grow at a much faster rate and hope to move the company in that direction."

The quality of silence in the room changed and grew awkward. Ethan glanced over to Jerry, puzzled. Jerry smiled wanly. Jeff then went into a long tirade on "how the people who wrote this plan don't have any fucking idea what the company can do" and "how I'm going to show my managers what's possible as soon as I get that fucking bank off my back."

Jerry suddenly realized what Jeff was doing. He was intentionally sabotaging this meeting. This was not the emotional Jeff playing his normal Attila the Hun role. This was a cold, calculating Jeff that was trying to scuttle a deal before it could get off the ground. Jerry realized that there was nothing he could do to control Jeff at this point. They were all on center stage. His only hope was to minimize damages. Gone were the ebullient feelings of two hours ago.

Jerry tried to restart his presentation, but was again interrupted.

"Howard, did you complete the analysis of the anticipated production costs on the upgraded design of the 986 model?" said Jeff.

Jerry was struggling to contain his anger. Ethan Wilson realized that this meeting was now out of control and suggested that they immediately break into the smaller groups. Jerry left his binder open on the table, assuming that he would pick up where he had been interrupted when the breakout meeting convened. He looked over at Jeff, who was busy talking with Howard. Jerry swallowed hard and left the conference room for a trip to the restroom.

During the breakout meeting with Larry, Eric, and Ethan, Jerry reviewed the business plan in detail, discussed the assumptions underlying the projections, and explained the basis for the sales forecasts and capital investments. Jerry enjoyed this aspect of the meeting. He was dealing with peers. The roles each of them played were dictated by circumstance. He normally played Ethan's role, the investment banker; but he had represented investors like Larry and Eric and was very familiar with their thought process, risk analysis techniques, and so forth. They had all learned their trade from the same books. They all had MBAs. They were all professionals. They knew that even though he was representing his family's interests, he wouldn't bullshit them. They knew his reputation for integrity and he was sure that Ethan told them that his word was golden.

They asked about Kevin's situation and he told them what he knew. Kevin was on a very restricted work regimen. The future was uncertain. He would probably be available for limited service, consulting on technology and strategy issues. It was unlikely that he would ever be able to work a normal workweek again.

They adjourned at twelve-thirty, and Jerry went back to his office to pick up his messages. When he got back to the conference room, the table was set with sandwiches, salads, and soft drinks, all untouched. Mary and Darryl, First Chicago's marketing consultant and computer consultant respectively, were the only people in the room, They were seated at the table, engrossed in a serious conversation. As Jerry walked in, Mary looked up with her face flushed. Darryl quickly stood, grabbed Jerry's arm, and led him just outside the door.

"Things got a little animated in there. It seems that Mary asked Jeff a few questions about the lack of consistency in bookings and he got very defensive. He said that the performance of his sales organization was being hampered because he had to spend so much time on the reorganization reports for the bank. I guess the more penetrating the questions, the angrier he got. When she asked him to explain the differences between the written business plan and the plan Jeff talked about during the meeting, she said that he made some statements that didn't make any sense to her. When she tried to probe further, he got very abusive, yelled at her, and said that she obviously doesn't understand the industry. The meeting went downhill from there."

"Where's Jeff?" said Jerry.

"He had to run an errand. He said he'd be back in an hour. I've been trying to calm her down. She's very embarrassed at not being able to deal with him."

Lunch proceeded. Kevin chatted about his current view of the access control industry and where it was headed. He discussed each of National's competitors, reviewed their strengths and weaknesses, and offered an assessment as to which ones would survive in the market over the long term. Jerry let him run. Kevin had a gift—he shined with it, with his ability to understand complex technology issues and then explain them in a clear and entertaining manner.

Next up was a plant tour, and Kevin told Jerry that he was feeling tired. After confirming that the bankers had no further questions for Kevin, he complimented Kevin on his outstanding performance and suggested that he call it a day. Kevin said his goodbyes to the bankers and Ethan and went home.

Jeff returned at two and conducted the plant tour. He had metamorphosed into his normal upbeat salesman style. He was enthusiastic, knowledgeable, witty, and gracious. He was very solicitous of Mary and made every effort to ensure that she saw everything she wanted to see and had every question answered. The bankers appeared to be very impressed with the automatic subsystem test stations and engaged Jeff in a long conversation regarding their operation, cost effectiveness, and reliability. All hints of the irritating, self-centered egomaniac were gone.

The bankers wanted to meet among themselves prior to getting together for the wrap-up. Jerry showed them to the small conference room adjacent to his office and then went to the main conference room where Ethan and Jeff were waiting.

"What's your feeling, Ethan?" said Jerry.

"They're very interested. I expect that they will make an offer."

"Have they talked with you about the price?"

"No. That's not their style. They'll figure out what its worth to them and they'll send us a letter. They don't dicker."

"Anything new with any of the guys in the wings?" said Jeff.

"As a matter of fact there is. During lunch, I returned a call to Jim Sykes of Alex Brown. He represents ADT in all their acquisition deals. I also talked with Phil Borgue. He represents Foxx Enterprises. They both want to talk. What do your calendars look like next week?"

"I'm okay," said Jerry. He looked over to Jeff.

"I'll have to check and I need to touch base with Kevin. I'll call you in the morning."

"Fine," said Ethan. If he was confused about Jeff's behavior, he hid it.

The First Chicago contingent came into the conference room and arranged themselves around the table. Shirley brought coffeepots, coffee mugs, and soft drinks. After several minutes of shuffling cans, pots, and mugs around the table, Larry spoke, "I think we've done it. Eric and Howard have come to an agreement as to what financial documents we'll need. It's been a good meeting." He looked over to Jerry and Jeff. "I guess Ethan has told you that we are very interested. I expect that we'll be drafting a Letter of Intent during the next two weeks, assuming of course that we get the financial stuff within the next week."

"We'll see that you get it," said Jerry, and feeling almost as bright as he did that morning, exchanged handshakes all around.

It was just past the plant closing time, and most of the employees who worked in the executive office area had left. Shirley was still at her desk. Jerry nodded to her, as he walked into Jeff's office. He closed the door and sat down on the chair in front of the desk. He waited for Jeff to look up from the pages of a book that he held in front of his face.

"What the fuck were you trying to do this morning, Jeff?"

"What do you mean, Jerry?" A sheepish smile slowly emerged.

"You know very well what I mean. You were intentionally trying to piss off the bankers. What the hell were you thinking?"

"I can see why you're upset. But you're wrong about motivation. There was nothing insidious. I really was out of control. I realized it during my meeting with Mary when I totally lost it. That's why I left the plant. I went over to the beach for an hour, sat on the sand, and looked at the waves. When I calmed down, I came back. I'm really sorry."

Jerry was caught short. "So, what happened to you? Why did you blow?"

"I guess it finally hit me that this party was coming to a close. You know. National was really going to be sold and I would be out—and I was participating in a meeting whose purpose was to bring that future event to fruition. I was fashioning the noose for my own hanging. I've always been the provider for the employees, in my own way, and now that that's getting taken away, I got scared and angry. It wasn't very professional."

"I think I understand how you feel but... "

Jeff pitched the book on the floor. "You can't possibly know how I feel. I'm forty-eight years old. I've got a lousy marriage, no significant investment in a retirement plan, and no future. National has been the vehicle that gave me status. I felt good about myself and proud that I had accomplished something worthwhile. Without it, I'm just another middle-aged unemployed peddler. What if next I can't get a decent job and support my family? The Forty Plus offices are chock full of guys my age with résumés that are as good or better, and who have been out of work for years. No, Jerry, there's no way you can appreciate what I'm going through. The feeling is worse—it's as sickening as betrayal."

"Jeff, Jeff," said Jerry. "You're making this out to be worse than it is. You have lots of talent. You'll get something out of the National sale, and maybe you can use it as a stake to start something new."

"If I get anything out of National, it will have to support me until I can get another job. That's if Salli doesn't divorce me and take half of it." Jeff walked over to the door and made sure it was shut. "I remember attending a seminar once. I was with Salli and we were trying to put our marriage back together for the zillionth time. The speaker was some pop psychologist. Maybe Wayne Dyer. Or was it Dennis Waitley? I forget. Anyway, during the questions and answers, someone asked him whether he had a formula for achieving happiness. I'll never forget his answer. He said that based on his thirty years of clinical experience, all the people who described themselves as being happy and at peace with the world had three foundations in their lives. They all had someone to love, physically, something to do that was enjoyable and gave them a feeling of mastery, and they had something to look forward to." He paused and wiped his nose with the back of his hand. His eyes were watery. "The realization that soon I will have none of them is gut-wrenching. I haven't experienced this level of fear since I left Vietnam."

"Come on, Jeff. Let's not have a pity party. When I left National, I had to start all over. I went back to school and…"

WHAM! Jeff's fist came down on the desk. "Christ, Jerry. You were a kid. How old? Twenty-five?"

"Twenty-six."

Jeff's arm trembled. He was still driving his fist against the desk. "You didn't have kids, you didn't have responsibilities. You were light years away from my current situation. And I also resent you're insulting comment about my having a pity party." He opened his hand, lifted it off the desk, and leaned back in his chair. "You asked me why I was out of control and I told you. Let's not talk about it anymore. I'm in touch with the problem. I won't embarrass you again."

Jerry didn't answer. Jeff was right. He was being flippant, sophomoric, and insensitive. He would never have talked with a client like that. What the hell was wrong with him? He needed to back off and stop acting like a galley slave driver.

"I've checked my calendar," said Jeff. "I talked with Kevin. Any day next week except Thursday will be fine for the meeting with Phil Bourge, Foxx's guy. Will you call Ethan?"

"Yes," said Jerry.

"Then I think I'll go to my happy hearth. I may get lucky tonight. Salli and I had sex on Saturday. I'm hoping that she may want to make it a habit." He rose from his chair and headed to the door of his office, grinning. Jerry stood up quickly, knocking over the chair, and intercepted him. He placed his left hand on Jeff's shoulder and extended his right hand.

"Are we still friends?" said Jerry.

Jeff turned and grabbed Jerry's hand. "Sure—and brothers."

"It's Helen," said Shirley.

Jerry put down his tablet. Helen ought to have still been in France. He picked up the phone.

"That was fast. I didn't expect you back so soon."

"It didn't take as long as I expected."

"Was the trip successful?"

"They made me an offer. A really good offer. It's nice to feel needed."

He laughed. Her voice sounded distant and more controlled than he had remembered it. But after all, they had not parted on the best of terms. "Am I supposed to read something significant into that remark?"

"Come on, Jerry. Let's not play games. That remark had nothing to do with us."

"Okay, okay. I'm sorry."

"Apology accepted," she said. "I'll get to the point. I was very disappointed with the way I acted when we celebrated our anniversary. I've thought about that evening a lot. I'd like to talk to you about it—about us. I think we both need some closure."

Her voice sounded somewhat softer. Warm excitement and anticipation cascaded through his body. "I agree," he said, getting aroused. "I was not very happy with my performance either."

"Come to dinner tomorrow. Six-thirty or so."

"Fine. Can I bring anything?"

"Get a bottle of a good Merlot. I'm cooking lamb."

Jerry's body was bursting. He was addicted to her. He looked at his watch. Twenty-eight hours until Helen time.

He appeared at Helen's apartment the following evening at exactly six-thirty. He rang the bell. Helen opened the door immediately, wearing a two-piece Hawaiian dress with a halter-top that revealed much more than it concealed. The long skirt was made of a silk material that clung to her body, and she was wearing a lavender lei around her neck.

"Welcome to the islands," she said, and threw her arms around him and kissed him. "God, I missed you." She held him tightly. "I tried not to, but I wasn't very good at it."

"I missed you, too," he said. They were all the words he could muster. All of his energy was consumed in taking in her smell, tasting her lips and neck, and burying his body in hers.

They stood in the open doorway, holding each other for several minutes until Helen squirmed out of his arms and said, "I've got to check the lamb. You like it medium rare, right?"

"Right. I'll open the wine and let it breathe."

She swiped the front of his pants and said, "You're going to have to put that fella on ice for a couple of hours. We've got some serious eating to do."

Helen had prepared a gourmet dinner. The first course consisted of sliced Bartlett pears over mixed greens with citrus dressing, garnished with bleu cheese crumbles and candied walnuts. The cool sweetness of the pears stimulated his appetite. The entrée was a peppered rack of lamb served with chutney-flavored mint jelly, boiled new potatoes, and French string beans. The lamb was medium rare, perfect. Helen cut him off five chops from the rack. When Jerry protested that he couldn't possibly eat that much, she merely smiled and said, "We'll see."

The aroma of the lamb combined with the three glasses of Merlot and the vision of Helen, smiling and chatting, pulled him out of his body, as if he was floating over the table, watching himself eat. The table was beautiful. The candles glittered in the wine bottle and on the glistening food, the perfect balance of salt and spice, with the curl of an extinguished candle's smoke around the window. Helen rose and replaced it, and struck the match. The smell of sulfur returned him to his senses, a little.

For dessert, she had prepared chocolate soufflés.

Their conversation concerned her trip to Paris, and merely touched on her job interviews, the search for an apartment, and the relative prices of groceries. There simply wasn't much room between bites to discuss anything heavier than the food they were consuming. They both scrupulously avoided talking about their relationship and the fact that she could soon go back to Paris to start her new job.

Jerry was bloated. He had parked his self control at the doorway to her condo. Helen was such a fantastic cook; he simply couldn't resist stuffing himself. As she cleared off the dessert dishes, she suggested that he make himself comfortable in the living room while she prepared espressos.

"I found these fabulous white chocolate macadamia cookies. I'll serve them with the espresso."

He stood up and loosened his belt. "I'm going to have to spend four hours at the gym tomorrow to work off this feast." His voice was slow and thick.

"Indulge me, Jerry. I don't get to cook very often and I don't expect I'll have much opportunity to show off my culinary skills in France." She seemed unaffected by the meal.

Jerry walked into the living room. He looked through Helen's collection of CDs, selected the Jupiter Symphony, and inserted it in the CD player. He adjusted the volume to keep the music in the background and sat down on the sofa, unbuckled his belt, laid his head back, and closed his eyes. Shapes moved on the insides of his eyelids. Ten minutes later,

Helen walked into the living room, carrying a tray containing two cups of espresso, two brandy snifters, and a plate of cookies.

"Are you going to flake out on me?" she said.

Jerry sat up. He had dozed off. "No, just resting my eyes, and gearing up my strength for the next course."

Helen placed the tray on the coffee table, handed him his espresso, took one herself, and sat down next to him. They were silent as they drank the espressos, sipped their brandies, and decimated the cookies. Jerry kept turning his head to look at her. He could not keep his eyes off of her. He was anxious to have the dinner over, so that he could again experience the ecstasy of her naked body. But he did not want to seem too anxious. Finally, after he had consumed two cups of espresso and a snifter of brandy, his head spinning, he reached over to Helen and tried to draw her closer. He was surprised when she wiggled out of his grasp, stood up, and said, "We need to talk first, okay?"

Jerry tried to appear nonchalant, but suddenly the quiet music seemed a trifle too loud, and the cognac had a strong aftertaste. He looked up at her and said, "Sure, shoot."

"I really need you to pay attention to what I'm about to say. It's important to me. Are you too tired? Would you like to take a nap before we talk?"

"I'm fine, Helen. A little full, but I'm okay. Give me a restroom break and I'll be bright eyed and bushy tailed." He stood up and headed for the bathroom.

"Okay, then I'll get the dishes started."

Jerry hunkered over the sink and buried his face in a handful of cold water. He rinsed out his mouth, checked his teeth, and took several deep breaths. He splashed his face one more time for good measure and scrubbed the towel hard on his skin and over his eyes. When he returned from the bathroom, he noted Helen had refilled the brandy snifters and espresso cups. She was sitting on the sofa and motioned for him to sit next to her.

"I took the liberty of refreshing your drinks. So, let's get started."

She turned her body, so that she was looking directly into his eyes. "When I was in Paris, I had the opportunity to do a lot of thinking about my life and my various relationships. I tried to be analytical about what I'd like my life to be and to evaluate how well or poorly I'm achieving my vision. It was the first time in a very long time that I've tried to get perspective on my life." Her cheeks were gaining color. She took a sip from the brandy snifter.

"I've led most of my life like a typical sixties brat. You know, drugs, sex, and rock 'n' roll. I did what made me feel good. And I am good at justifying those things to myself. I usually did not give a fuck about anyone who either criticized me, or was hurt by my actions." She paused and ran her hand through her hair. "When I was in Paris, I had an epiphany. I recognized that my self-centered view of the world is what has prevented me from getting what I want most in life, namely a devoted husband, children and a warm, loving home." She reached over to him and took his hand and held it firmly. "I also realized that I love you more than I've ever loved anyone else and I want to marry you and have you be the father of my children..." The last word was strangled, and tears welled up in her eyes. She took a hard breath and held his gaze. "And I was, and am devastated because you don't trust me—but I can't say that I blame you. My affair with Jeff was indefensible. I used Jeff and I betrayed my sister. I have not shown much integrity in the area of personal relationships."

Jerry did not quite know where Helen was going, but he made himself hold eye contact. He changed his position on the sofa carefully, so as not to interfere with her train of thought or her holding of his hand.

"Jerry, if you and I are ever to have a relationship that includes the possibility of marriage, you need to be able to trust me and not wonder whether some event or fact from my past might surface to again undermine your opinion of me. I need the same thing. I need to know that you and I have no secrets. I have been keeping secrets all my life—from Salli, from my mother, from my lovers, and from my husbands. And from you."

She dropped his hand and took another sip of cognac. Then, she reached over and took a tissue from the box on the table next to the sofa and touched each eyelid once, gently. Her makeup smeared anyway. She turned and looked at him again.

"Keeping secrets has not gotten me closer to my goal. In fact, it's made the goal more elusive. I'm through with secrets. I've decided to implement a new policy: absolute honesty. Tonight you are going to learn every sordid thing about my past, especially my sexual history. You will know more about me than any other human being. You may not like what you learn, but if you choose not to continue or restart a relationship with me because of my past, then so be it. Fuck it. It's who I was."

He grasped her hand. "Honey, calm down. It's okay."

She started to cry. "Dammit, it's not okay. It will be okay when you and I don't have any more secrets." She got up from the sofa and went to the bookcase. She pulled out a clean, slender, legal-sized manila file folder and presented it to him.

"I put this together when I was overseas. Look it over while I finish doing the dishes. Then, we'll discuss it." She went into the kitchen, leaving him holding the folder.

Inside were four spreadsheets titled, "Helen's Intimate Relationships." The spreadsheets came as a surprise. He would never have associated Helen with spreadsheets. Spreadsheets were one of the basic tools of his trade. He spent many hours of each week creating and analyzing spreadsheets in the course of evaluating companies and deals. This seemed like a cruel joke or a bad dream, being presented with spreadsheets, in order to analyze and evaluate a lover's sexual history.

The combination of the overeating and the cognac made it difficult for him to focus on the tiny lines. He blinked several times and held the spreadsheets farther from his face.

The column headings of the first spreadsheet were: Name of Lover, Time and Duration of Relationship, Gender (Male/Female), Degree of Sexual Satisfaction Achieved (scale one to ten), Level of Intimacy Achieved (scale of one to ten), Positive Aspects of the Relationship, Negative Aspects of the Relationship, and Reason for Termination.

There were a total of twenty-seven entries, five of which were female. All but one of the female relationships occurred prior to Helen's college graduation. The last relationship with a female occurred within the past fifteen months. Her sexual experiences with men started when she was fourteen and consisted of oral sex with a sixteen-year-old neighbor. She rated the sexual experience a four and the level of intimacy a one. It appeared that in the five years between her graduating college and her first marriage, she had a total of fifteen lovers. At times she had up to three simultaneously.

Entries in the Positive Aspects column included, "Taught me how to masturbate," "Taught me how to ski," "First time I had an orgasm via clitoral licking," and, "Introduced me to pot." In the Negative Aspects column, "Gave me a bad case of the crabs," "Insisted that I have an abortion," "Came as soon as he stuck it in," "Terrible body odor."

Helen returned to the living room. "Any questions yet?"

Jerry looked up from the spreadsheets into the whiteness of Helen's glistening smile. It boggled him—and proved either that the smile exhibited a masterful defense mechanism or the genuine relief of confession.

"You put a lot of work into this," he stammered. "How did you remember all the names and dates?"

"A lot of it came from just thinking about my history. I set up the spreadsheets on my computer during my free time. When I got back to town, I went through boxes of old calendars and diaries to fill in the blanks. It wasn't that hard. The hard part was getting up the motivation to do it and the courage to show it to you. Come on, now, fess up! There must be a few entries that pique your curiosity."

Jerry looked back at the spreadsheet. "Well, there are a few. I'm assuming that your three female lovers prior to college were, well, let's say, for sexual experimentation. Right?"

"Yes. The normal summer camp stuff."

"What about Beth Decatur? It shows that you had a two, no, a three year relationship with her when you were at Middlebury College."

"Beth was my first serious love affair. We met during freshmen orientation and we were attracted to each other instantly. We had similar interests—art, music, and literature. We both took French and used it as our language. We exulted in each other's company, and we satisfied each other sexually."

"Weren't you attracted to guys at all?"

"Most of the guys that I met in college were obnoxious and disgusting. They spent their time drinking huge quantities of beer, farting, picking their pimples, and scheming to get laid. The ones who were sensitive and delicate and had intellectual interests didn't excite me. By my senior year, I was convinced that I was gay."

"How did the relationship end? Why did you two split up?"

"It's right there, Jerry. On the spreadsheet. I'm surprised you missed it."

Jerry looked back at the row with the entry for Beth Decatur and traced it across to the Reason for Termination column. He stared at the entry: "To pursue my affair with Jeff."

Jerry was confused. Helen was hovering over him, studying his every reaction. "Did you have an affair with Jeff while you were in college? Wasn't he engaged to Salli?"

Helen sat down next to him and clasped his hand. "I can understand your confusion. The answers are yes to both questions. I had met Jeff several times when he was dating Salli and of course I got to know him during the engagement period and the huge engagement party that Charlie gave her. Jeff needed an escort for some function and Salli was not available. She suggested that he take me and he agreed. Up until that time, I was just the kid sister. After the dinner party, I invited him back to my apartment and seduced him. It was my first really satisfying heterosexual experience. We screwed all night. It was wonderful. The irony was exquisite. It was poetic justice. I was fucking Jeff and Salli at the same time. That night, I decided I was not a lesbian, and the next day I spoke with Beth, explained the situation, and we agreed to end our romantic relationship."

Jerry had previously noted that Jeff, like himself and her two ex-husbands, rated a 10 in the Quality of Sexual Experience category.

"How long did this go on? I mean with Jeff."

"For a year and a half, until two hours before the wedding ceremony. The sex was wonderful. And I was exhilarated. Jeff was a mature, caring lover. He made sure I came every time we made love. And the knowledge that I was screwing Salli's fiancé made the orgasms that much more excruciating. You know, it was ancient justice. The harassed kid sister who has been treated like Cinderella finally gets even. I was the last person he fucked before he said 'I do.' We did it in the back of his car dressed in our wedding clothes."

Jerry tried but couldn't conceal his surprise. His voice came out louder than he intended. "And Jeff? What was Jeff thinking during this affair?"

"I can't really remember. All I know was that he was always horny and Salli wasn't that available. She was traveling a lot. I was available and convenient. I wasn't asking questions. I enjoyed the experience."

"If he was that attracted to you, why didn't he marry you?"

Helen laughed. "I can give you five million reasons. Salli's trust fund. I was never in the running for the prize of Jeff, assuming I was interested."

"What happened after the wedding? Did you continue to see him?"

"The sex in his car before the wedding was the last time we made love until I returned from Europe. When we saw each other at family functions, we treated each other like in-laws. We were both very discreet."

"And after you returned from Europe?"

"My situation had changed. Jeff's situation had changed. We worked out an accommodation. But we've talked about that already."

Jerry looked back at the spreadsheets and pulled his hand away, ostensibly to turn the pages. He was doing his utmost not to appear judgmental. He understood what Helen was doing. All her dirty linen was being thrown on the table for one huge laundry load, and she wanted him to inspect each and every sheet, towel, and pillowcase to make sure he understood how it got dirty and if he didn't understand, to ask her.

Finally, she put her hands on his shoulders and turned his body, so that she was looking at him. "Jerry, I know what you're thinking. There is no justification for what I did to Salli. I don't believe she knows about Jeff and me. And of course, my revenge couldn't be complete unless she did know. The funny thing is that now I'd like her to know, so that I could get rid of the burden of carrying the secret, but I don't want her to be hurt, and I don't want to add gasoline to a marriage that's already incinerating. Chalk it up to my immaturity, naiveté, and insensitivity. I was turned on by sex. Your brother was a terrific lover. It had been the best sexual experience of my life, and I wasn't prepared to give it up." She dropped her hands from his shoulders and said, "I'll get us some fresh coffee."

She stood up, picked up the cups from the coffee table, and went into the kitchen.

Jerry stood up and walked around the living room. He was feeling very disoriented and wanted nothing more than to go back to his apartment and go to sleep. It was too much. He could see half of Helen past the kitchen doorway, working, filling the two coffee cups from the coffee in the pot. She threw the filter with the coffee grounds into the trash compactor and set up the coffee maker to make a fresh pot. As she turned to go into the living room, the expression on her face was dire, as if she were daring herself to jump off of a cliff. As she passed the doorway, she tucked the expression out of sight and replaced it with a more neutral one. Jerry said nothing.

She came in and placed the two cups on the coffee table. She said, "You need to focus on another entry in my spreadsheet. It's the entry just below Jeff." She sat down on the couch next to him and studied his face.

"The entry following Jeff is 'GSB,'" said Jerry. "He became your lover after Jeff got married and the affair continued for three years until you became engaged to Pierre. So who is GSB? Should I know him?"

Helen's eyes grew wet. She held his hand as tight as she could and said, "It's your father."

Jerry stared at the spreadsheet as in a catatonic trance. General Sid Bascomb. He read the entries carefully, mouthing them to himself, so as to distract himself from the enormity of the revelation. Duration three years, two months, sixteen days. Level of sexual satisfaction, ten. Positive aspects of the relationship: the highest ranking officer I ever fucked. He made me feel important. Negative aspects of the relationship: too many seedy motels. Level of intimacy: five. He dropped the spreadsheet on the coffee table. He kept shaking his head and was having trouble swallowing. Finally, he managed, "How did it start?"

"While I was dancing with him at Salli's wedding, he slipped his card into my hand and asked me to call him. I was shocked and elated. A good-looking guy in uniform always turned me on. And here was a four-star general who was interested in me, a newly minted college graduate. I literally died and went to heaven. The sadness that I was experiencing over having to end my affair with Jeff did not last through the reception. It was extinguished by the prospect of a much greater conquest, a four-star general. I called him the following Monday and we arranged to meet for drinks. We wound up in bed in a rented room and screwed all through the night. He became a very big part of my life."

Jerry remained silent. The enormity of what Helen had revealed had completely drained him. He picked up the spreadsheet and stared at it.

"Does Jeff know?" he said.

"No. There was no reason to tell him." Helen seemed to steel herself for rejection and leaned over and caressed his face. He didn't push her away, so she went on, "I'm so sorry, Jerry. I'm sorry that I told you and I'm sorry that I had to tell you. I knew you'd be shocked and mortified. But there was just no way to sugar-coat it." She sat back and took a sip of brandy. "Do you want to stop for a while? I know I'm putting a lot of pressure on you, asking you to sort through my baggage. Maybe we should call it quits for now, to give you some time to absorb it."

He saw that she was hurting, and talking to cover it up. If he could detach himself from his own emotions, he could enjoy the irony of the situation. Helen had fucked three quarters of the Bascomb men over a fifteen-year time span. Only poor Kevin had been left out. And as for his father, Fyodor Pavolvich Karamazov, he was finally able to get his Grushenka into his bed. Bravo, Fyodor! Bravo!

He sat silently for several minutes, his eyes closed, trying to grasp the enormity of her disclosure. He dozed off and actually slept for a half hour. He was aware of her presence in the chair opposite him. He awakened suddenly, refreshed. She was smiling at him.

"You fell asleep."

"Yeah, but I feel a lot better. Let's press on. You did the right thing, Helen. You had to tell me sometime. Better now, better now." He leaned over and kissed her.

"I'm sorry," she said. "I'm not as cool and detached as I'd thought I'd be."

Helen returned to the kitchen to get more coffee and brandy, though her cup was barely touched. And she was gone long enough that by the time she returned, he had written out questions in the margins of the spreadsheets. "You know, Helen, you have the raw material for a great novel."

"It's been done, Jerry. *Fanny Hill*, by John Cleland, 1749. Promiscuous women are nothing special." She gave him one of the brandy snifters, took the other for herself, and sat down next to him on the sofa.

He called forth the last of his focus, propped the folder on his leg, and pointed at one of the columns. "I just have a few questions. Tell me about your scoring systems for Level of Sexual Satisfaction and Degree of Intimacy."

"Pretty rudimentary. For Level of Sexual Satisfaction, I scored nine to ten for the lovers who brought me to orgasm on the average of two or more times a night, seven to eight for the lovers who did it on the average of more than once, five to six for those who did it at least once, and one to four for those who either never or occasionally did it. I'm sure you've already noticed who the tens are."

"And the Level of Intimacy? I notice that none of your lovers, including me, scored over seven."

"Seven is the top score so far because I have had secrets with all my lovers including you. You, my two ex-husbands, and Beth Decatur are the top scorers. Casual and recreational sex affairs got a one to two, live-in lovers got a three to five. I gave your father a five and your brother a six. That column was a real wake up call—when I realized that I've had two marriages and twenty-plus affairs, and couldn't assign any of them a ten."

"I see." He looked down at the spreadsheets. "Who are Myra and Maurice? The dates indicate affairs with them sporadically over a fifteen-month period starting last year."

"I met them shortly after Jeff and I restarted our affair. They're a couple that Jeff knew from the days he was in the military. They're very eclectic in their sexual tastes."

Helen got up from the sofa and walked over to her bookcase. She pulled out a photo album and brought it over to the coffee table. She opened the album and thumbed through the pages, stopping at a page labeled "Black's Beach, March 13, 1990." There were approximately ten nude photos of Jeff, Helen, and a six-two very well endowed black guy with rippling abs and well-defined biceps, and a tall, athletic, small-busted black woman.

Jerry studied the pictures carefully, looking for the clue that would explain the spreadsheet entries. The pictures were explicit in that all four of the subjects flaunted their sexual attributes, but no more than typical "play in the sun" nudist publications.

He looked quizzically at Helen. "So, what's the relationship between you and Maurice and Myra?"

Helen smiled at Jerry. "Well, let's just say that Jeff and I would party with them from time to time."

"Party, as in *ménage á trois* and *un quatour*?"

"Yup," said Helen. "Precisely. Very sexy!" She closed the photo album and took the spreadsheets from his hand. "You've worked long enough. How about some fun?"

She zipped open his fly and pulled his pants and briefs off and climbed up on the sofa, straddled his hips and rubbed his penis against herself. "I sort of figured we'd wind up like this, so I dispensed with the undergarments. Did you notice?"

Jerry couldn't respond. He felt on some level that his body was betraying him, or that it knew something about love that he did not—and it and Helen had happily let the conversation evolve into the warm murmurs of sex. He shut his eyes and tried to linger in the safety of his mind.

Helen shifted her position and held on to his shoulders with an urgent grip. Jerry squeezed his eyes shut and reminded himself that he needed time to think about all that he'd learned, but he could no longer resist the irresistible call of her pleasure.

Once again, he let himself be seduced.

Ethan Wilson was reporting that the National sale was creating a buzz in the ACS community. A deal was likely, even though the ultimate selling price was still anybody's guess. Larry Wolf of First Chicago had told Wilson that they were working on a letter of Intent. Ethan expected to receive it within the week, and he'd already brought out three additional buyers as backup. The routines had been similar to the First Chicago visit. Jerry's weight increased two pounds, primarily as a result of the Bodacious Buns. He was feeling good. Jeff had held up his end of the deal and there were no more scenes. His behavior could not have been better. It seemed he had resigned himself to the inevitable and was trying to make the best of what was for him a really bad deal.

Jerry found that he could reduce his hours at National from the twelve-hour, six-days-a-week schedule to an eight-hour, five-days-a-week schedule, allowing him to spend a lot more time with Helen.

He had slept over at her condo the night of the spreadsheets. In the morning, he asked her to postpone her decision to return to Paris to give him time to sort things out. She agreed to call her perspective employer and arrange to delay her decision until the end of November. He realized that if he was not able to make the big commitment during the next few weeks, she was off to Paris. The commitment was, of course, Helen moving in with him when he returned to New York, and wedding plans.

He went into the office to review with Howard the previous month's financial report, and around noon, told Shirley he was taking the rest of the day off. He returned to his condo, took Chelsey for a brief walk, fixed himself a sandwich, opened a bottle of Corona, and went out to his patio to look at the boats and think.

He was still trying to get his mind around the information dump that Helen had laid on him. Unlike the relationship with Jeff, the revelation of Helen's three-year affair with his father was a shocker. Christ, she was in her early twenties and he was in his mid-fifties. And then again, why should he have been shocked? It reminded him of that famous line from *Casablanca* when Claude Rains turns to Humphrey Bogart, the owner of Rick's Café, feigning surprise and indignation, and says, "I'm shocked that gambling is going on here," just prior to receiving his winnings.

From the time I was sixteen, he thought, I knew that Dad played around. Jeff, Kevin, and I talked about it all the time. Jeff's take was that it wasn't any big deal. If the Kennedys could do it, Sid could do it. Although, as a masturbating teenager, he had experienced sexual pleasure, he had no appreciation for the obsessive passion that the sexual attraction between a man and a woman could trigger, nor that his father, the General, would succumb to that obsession. Yet in retrospect, his father's behavior was what one would expect from Fyodor Karamazov redux.

And that business with Maurice and Maya—what did that mean? Nothing, other than that Helen had very few sexual inhibitions and was game to try anything. He had to admit that there was a part of him that envied her willingness to explore.

He went back into the condo and opened another Corona. He opened the pantry door, located a large bag of chips, ripped open the bag, and poured the chips into a bowl. He returned to the patio, dropped into the lounge chair and closed his eyes.

It had taken a great deal of discipline and courage for Helen to have created and then presented the spreadsheets. She certainly didn't have to tell him about her relationship with his father. That took guts. Jerry wondered how long she agonized before she inserted the "GSB" entry. She could have easily avoided it and he would have been none the wiser. There is a lot of perfectionist in her, he realized—once she set her mind on something, she followed through. This surprised him vaguely, but only because he had not gotten such a sweeping view of Helen's inner workings until now; his lack of curiosity was uncharacteristic, but he chalked it up to the National affair. Now, with time to think, he found himself impressed by his lover.

In her defense, the affair with his father only *looked* like an enormous event because Jerry loved her. At the time, it was probably no big deal. Christ, it was in 1975. Before aids, during the divorce epidemic. Everybody had been fucking everybody else.

He took a long drink of the Corona, closed his eyes, and peacefully slept.

He awoke around 5:30 a.m., showered, and dressed in shorts and a t-shirt. He put the leash on Chelsey and took her for a long walk all around the marina, all the while ruminating about Helen.

When he got back to the condo, he called Helen and asked her if she was available to spend two nights at the Hotel Coronado Resort in San Diego.

"What's the occasion?"

"Nothing particular. I just thought that it was time for us to spend some quality time talking about our mutual dreams and hopes for the future and the issues that we need to deal with if we are serious about getting married. That's all. You'll love the hotel. It's Victorian and right on the beach."

She didn't respond immediately and his anxiety kicked in. After about fifteen seconds of silence he said, "Are you still there, Helen?"

"Sorry, I was looking at my schedule to see how I can arrange to take the time off. I'll have to get back to you. But I think that's a terrific idea."

Jerry's anxiety evaporated. "Great," he said.

She called back in an hour and said that she was good to go.

"Good. I'll pick you up around ten a.m."

After dropping off Chelsey at the kennel, Jerry picked up Helen at her condo. She was wearing white cutoff shorts and a blue halter top. Her hair was tied in a bun, and her smile took on a different quality—it was just as beautiful, but somehow more genuine.

On the drive down Highway 405 and then Highway 5, they talked about current events. She shared her nieces' recent scholastic and athletic achievements. And for the first time, Jerry talked about the progress of the National financing and his hopes for an early resolution. The weather was Southern California gorgeous—bright sunshine, clear blue sky, and seventy-five degrees. They arrived at the Del Coronado shortly after noon, checked into their rooms, and immediately undressed and jumped into bed. An hour later, they donned their swimsuits and gathered up the pool and beach paraphernalia. Helen wore a white bikini, a Mexican-motif cover-up, and a broad brimmed straw hat. She seemed unconscious of her beauty, for once, which only served to amplify it—it radiated from her like light around a pearl, leaving its center concealed. Jerry thought he detected a pensiveness in her manner, but he might have been projecting his own nervousness onto her smooth, deflecting surface.

They sat at a table adjacent to the pool and ordered turkey sandwiches and Coronas. Helen took off her hat and pointed her face toward the sun.

"This is great, Jerry. Thank you."

"I thought that a change of scenery would help us address some of the big picture aspects of our relationship." He took a long drink of his Corona. "Tell me about your time in France and your previous marriages."

She laughed. "Thinking back on it, I'm surprised there is so little that's worth remembering or telling—but I'll do my best. I went to France shortly after your father and I broke up. I was looking for adventure and had always been fascinated by French history, art, and the language. I accepted a position as an *au pair* for two doctors and took care of their two young sons. I learned two things in that job: how to speak fluent Parisian French, and that I had a very strong maternal instinct. I loved those kids and they loved me. Separating from them when I got married was difficult."

She took a drink of her Corona. "I better put on some lotion or I'll turn beet red." She rummaged around in her purse and found her suntan lotion. She spread gobs of it on her face, arms, chest, belly, and thighs. As Jerry spread lotion on her neck and back, he realized that the process was acting as an aphrodisiac. He immediately finished up and sat down. He made a mental note that he should keep his hands off of her bare skin when they were in public.

"I met *numero un*, Pierre, at a singles bar. He was handsome, charming, sexy, and unemployed. He had not gone to college, had no trade skills, and would not accept jobs that he considered to be beneath him. I married him anyway. My salary from the gallery I worked at was our sole means of support except for his occasional part-time and temporary jobs."

She paused, smiled, and then laughed. "I almost forgot. He was always concocting get-rich-quick schemes with his friends, which repeatedly consumed what small savings we could accumulate. We'd walk all over Paris, looking into the shop windows, fantasizing what it would really be like to actually buy something from a shop on the Champs Elysées. We never found out. After five years, I called it quits."

"And your second husband," said Jerry.

"Anton was *numero deux*. Pretty much the same guy, but in a slightly different package. He did have a job, which was an improvement on Pierre. But he'd go out drinking with his buddies two to three nights a week and would often saunter in after one in the morning. I didn't see any future for myself, so I left. And there you have it."

"Unfortunate," said Jerry.

She leaned over, clutched his hand, and looked directly into his eyes. "I don't have a very good record at selecting husbands. I hope to improve on it the next time I get up to the plate."

He signed the check, pushed his chair back, and stood. "Let's go sit by the pool. I'd like to swim a few laps."

"Good idea." They picked out two lounge chairs that would catch the sun for the next few hours. Helen produced a paperback from her purse and began to read. Jerry walked to the end of the pool, dove in, and began swimming laps. He pulled hard and concentrated on form—he was concerned with efficiency, even now. His pace through the water accelerated, but his arms were not accustomed to the effort of swimming, and after ten minutes he was tired. He flipped over onto his back and tried the backstroke.

The cool water and the exertion provided a welcome respite. So far so good, he thought. But now comes the hard part. He knew that he needed to be careful in his speech and avoid triggering an emotional response from Helen. What he was going to discuss with her was too damn important.

He emerged fifteen minutes later and collapsed in the chair. "That was great," he said.

"How many did you do?

"Ten or fifteen, I lost track."

"I'm impressed."

"Don't be. It isn't that great." He toweled himself off. "Want a beer, or anything else?"

"Another Corona would be fine." She went back to her book.

He looked at the title and smiled. "You're reading *The Brothers Karamazov?*"

She looked up at him, a smirk on her face. "Why are you so surprised? I'm just doing some research on the Bascomb family. Besides, it's a really interesting story."

"Well, it will certainly give us a lot to talk about." He walked over to the bar and returned with two Coronas and a large bowl of chips. He handed her a beer. "Can I interrupt? I'd like to talk."

"Sure. " She marked her place and put the book on the table beside her. "Shoot."

He turned on his right side, so that he could look directly at her as he talked. "Helen, I've been in an emotional and mental snarl since we had words after Kevin's heart attack brought us back from San Francisco."

"Don't remind me. You really said some hurtful things. I was shocked."

"I understand. Anyway, ever since that time, I've really tried to get a handle on how I feel about our relationship, and specifically, why I've been so reluctant to consider marriage. What's most bizarre is that my passion for you exceeds anything that I've experienced since I was demonstrating in Sweden in 1970. I felt passion then and I feel it now, and I haven't experienced anything similar for twenty years."

She turned her body slightly, stroked his cheek, and ran her hand through his hair. "Honey, I know you've been in turmoil."

"So," he continued, "Why won't I commit? Why, as they say in poker, won't I go all in?" Without giving her the chance to comment, he went on. "The spreadsheet dump of your sexual history helped me focus and I figured it out. There are two issues that I need to deal with, and unfortunately, you can't help me with either one."

"Just wait one second," she said. "I need to fortify myself for this." She picked up the bottle of Corona that was three-fourths full and drained it. "Reminds me of my college days. Okay, I'm ready."

"The first issue is that I'm scared to death that our marriage could wind up like the other three Bascomb marriages. So far, my family is zero for three in the marriage department."

"That's not true," she said. "Kevin and Carolyn have a great marriage, don't they?"

"Your information is outdated. When you were in France, Kevin and I went to Vegas and he told me that their marriage has been on the rocks for several years. They're just going through the motions until they can get some money out of National to allow them to go their separate ways. Our family *is* zero for three."

"I'm really surprised about Kevin and Carolyn. I had no idea." She shook her head.

"And I don't need to tell you that your track record is not a positive indicator.

So, if we were to marry, we'd both be betting on the hope that we can change the pattern."

The sky had become overcast and the breeze had cooled. She put on her cover-up and sat up on the lounge chair facing him. "Is there something else? You started with *first*."

"Yes. I've been running my own life for twenty years. I've been fortunate in my career that I can pretty much do anything I want, when I want it, and how I want it. No one tells me what I can or cannot do. Getting married will have to change that if there is to be any hope of building a successful marriage. I just have to decide that I'm ready to do that. That's it. Now you know."

She gave him a smile of a sort he had not seen before. It was small and enigmatic, and somehow more intense than the whitey-white, magazine-cover Knudson grin. It was personal, and for him alone. "I'm really proud of you," she said. "But what do we do now?"

"Let's talk about that later. I'd like to go up to the room. How about room service for an early dinner and some time just for us? That smile excites me."

❖

A week after the night of the spreadsheets, Helen's dining room table was covered with newspapers, maps, and brochures. She saw the pained look on his face and said, "Please don't be hurt, Jerry. I'm simply planning for the slim possibility that you can't commit." She shrugged one shoulder. "I'm sure you finance guys know all about hedging your bets."

"Hedge away, by all means."

She turned a sharper eye on him. "And besides," she added. "If you ultimately decide that you don't need this warm and tender body next to yours, you wouldn't want to feel guilty over my having lost the opportunity of a lifetime. But let's not focus on that eventuality..."

She grabbed his hand and led him in the direction of the bedroom.

Later, when he was inside her, he was distracted by the fantasy of Helen sucking Maurice's very large organ. The fantasy reminded him that Helen was her own woman, matured by a lifetime of making her own decisions, and that he was only one in a very long line of her lovers. And with this thought, he realized that he had gone soft. He pulled out of her and turned over onto his back.

"I'm sorry, honey, I can't," he said.

She leaned over and kissed him. "That's okay, sweetie, you're probably tired. We'll try again in the morning."

As he lay there, frustrated over not being able to perform, he conjured up Dionysian images of Helen having sex with Jeff, with his father, with Maurice, and with Maya. He eventually fell asleep and relived the images in his dreams. When he went into work the next day, those same images popped up. They occurred when he was in a meeting, when he was reading a report, when he was having lunch with Howard. He wished he could take his brain out of his skull and wash it clean.

Helen was not pressing him. When they talked about marriage, houses, and kids, the conversations were still abstract, no dates, and no arrangements. Helen knew, and he knew, and Helen knew that he knew, that by giving him the spreadsheets and showing him the Black's Beach photos, the problem had become his. She was at peace and willing to see him work it out at his own pace.

But time was not on his side. The gallery expected an answer from her by Thanksgiving and wanted her to start work at the beginning of the year. He thought it unlikely that he would be ready to make a commitment by then.

Shirley buzzed Jerry to tell him that the management meeting was scheduled for the large conference room. He asked her to dig out the most recent budget file, so he could take it with him. Jerry put away the reports he had been reading and rearranged the top of his desk. He took the file from Shirley and scanned the contents as he walked over to the main conference room. He was not in any hurry. The meeting was to address some routine administrative and organizational issues. He did not expect any controversy.

Everyone had assembled by the time Jerry got to the conference room. Jeff and Howard were poring over a report. Allen, the engineering manager, was calmly drinking a can of Diet Pepsi. As Jerry came into the conference room, Allen handed him a copy of the report. Jerry sat down at the conference table and quickly read it. When he was finished, he frowned at Howard.

"I thought this was supposed to be a budget meeting," he said.

"It is," replied Howard. "Look at this."

Howard handed him a form titled, "Proposed Capital Equipment/R and D Expenditure." Jerry scanned the one-page document and whistled. "Those are some big numbers," he said.

"Very big," responded Howard. "If we approve the expenditures called for in the memo, we've blown our budget through the roof. I'm not even sure the bank agreement would allow us to do it."

"He's right, Jeff," said Jerry. "These proposed expenditures are off the chart. The bank will have a hemorrhage."

"You don't have any choice," said Allen. "Not if you want to stay competitive. If we can't go forward with this plan, we're making a decision to exit the biometrics market. It's that simple. The technology will move on, and by next year, we will no longer be contenders."

A few drops of adrenaline entered Jerry's bloodstream. He woke up to the reality of the other men, the room, and the sharp white paper next to his coffee mug. Not a routine meeting. "Come on," he said. "We've got the number one technical position in the iris market, thanks to you guys. It's not going to evaporate over the next few months, is it? Allen, you know our situation with the bank. They want us to conserve capital and sell the company. We can't afford the risk."

"What risk?" said Jeff.

Jerry moved his voice up a notch. "The risk of pissing off Sheila to the point that she won't cut us any slack if we don't meet our plan numbers, or we can't close by the deadline, or we screw up somehow and find ourselves in technical default. She is the only one at the bank who gives a shit about this company and I don't want to do anything that will embarrass her." He stood up and started pacing around the conference room. He stopped across from Jeff's chair and said, "Christ, Jeff, you know all this. Why do we have to keep going over old ground?"

"Because," said Jeff, "According to Allen and the other technical gurus, if we don't begin investing in this new technology, we will probably not have anything of value to sell. That's your position, Allen, isn't it?"

"You bet it is."

"Jerry," said Jeff, speaking very calmly and businesslike. "Put on your old engineering hat for a minute. This isn't a tough decision. You're the guy who used to pound the table and yell 'invest or die.' The technology is even moving faster now. We've got to move with it or we'll be out of the game. If we don't begin now, we will place the company in jeopardy—which will be one hell of a lot worse than exceeding the budget."

Jeff was pushing one of Jerry's most sensitive buttons. Jeff knew how he had valued his reputation as a top-flight engineer and was appealing to that engineer in him to look at the issue. But Jerry resolved that he wouldn't fall into the trap. Every engineer will spend every dime at his disposal to stay up on technology. That is the essence of their being. It's what drives them. Jerry noticed that the room had gotten very quiet. Jeff, Allen, and Howard were all looking at him, waiting for his response. He was perspiring, so he loosened his collar, sat down, and tried to collect his thoughts.

"Allen has made an excellent argument for pushing ahead. I read the report. I'm certain that if I were in his position, I'd feel the same way. But I'm not. My responsibility is to resolve the financial problems of this company. In order to do that, I need the bank's continued support. I can't support this level of expenditure." He paused and looked over to Allen. "I'm sorry."

"I guess I'll have to overrule you, Jerry," said Jeff putting on his game face. "This is a policy matter that comes under the jurisdiction of the board of directors. Therefore, it's my call. I'm going to approve the authorization and direct Allen and Howard to implement the plan. I'd appreciate it if you would meet with Sheila and brief her. I think that about does it."

Jeff started gathering up his papers. Allen and Howard pushed back their chairs and stood up. Jerry remained seated. He felt his face flush and was aware of his increased heartbeat. He couldn't move. Jeff had cut his legs off in front of his own staff. He had done it intentionally. He realized that Jeff had planned the entire meeting to humiliate him. No question about it. The humiliation of Jerry was Jeff's prime objective. He expected that a report of the drama that had just taken place in the conference room would propagate through the halls of the company during the next five minutes.

Allen and Howard left the room. Jeff was about to go through the doorway. Jerry was still sitting at the conference table, alone.

"Jeff," he said. Jeff stopped and turned. Jerry saw a hint of the supercilious smile of triumph on Jeff's face. "Let's talk for a minute."

Jeff did not move.

"What's there to talk about?"

"Don't give me that shit," Jerry said, ending up at a yell. "You know fucking well what we have to talk about!"

Jeff walked back into the conference room and shut the door.

"You can't do this," said Jerry. "I won't be a party to it."

"It's not your call, Jerry. I've talked with Richard about it. I can call a meeting of the board and go through the motions of presenting Allen's report to the board. Since I vote all the stock, I'm the board. Allen will make his argument that failure to go forward will put the corporation at grave risk. I will listen to your argument for staying on budget and currying the favor of the bank. I will then ask for a resolution to accept Allen's plan and go forward, recognizing that we are exceeding the budget that has been presented to the bank. I will call for the vote. I will vote for the resolution. Case closed! Call Richard if you like. We can do it together."

Jeff came back to the conference table, pulled over the phone, pushed the speaker button, and dialed Richard Krimble's office.

The receptionist answered. "Law offices."

"Hi Beth, Jeff Bascomb. Is Richard in? Jerry and I need to speak with him for a minute."

"I'll ring," she said. A few moments passed, and Richard Krimble's voice came through the speaker.

"Hello, Jeff, Jerry. What's up?"

"Richard," said Jeff. "Jerry wants your input regarding the discussion we had on the issue of implementing Allen's plan, recognizing that we will be exceeding the budget we presented to the bank."

"Exceeding is a euphemism," said Jerry. "How about 'ignoring,' or 'blowing,' or..." He knew there was a better word. "Or showing the bank our middle fingers. This is crazy. I told Jeff I couldn't approve it and he has replied with a 'fuck you, it's not your call.' If we go ahead with this, it will destroy all the good will that we've laboriously built up with the bank. This is idiotic."

"As you can see, Richard, Jerry feels very strongly about this. I explained to him that if we fail to implement Allen's plan, we would be placing the company in jeopardy. Therefore, the decision of whether to accept the plan is up to the board, and since I vote all the stock, it's my decision. Am I correct?"

"Yes," said Richard. "You have properly summarized the substance of our discussion."

"That's the case even if, by busting the budget, we are deliberately deviating from the plan we presented the bank?" said Jeff.

"That's true. The bank has its remedies. After they are told or discover what National is doing, they can send us a letter stating that we're in default of the bank agreement and demanding that we cure the default. That will undoubtedly give rise to another series of discussions and negotiations. However, I'm fairly certain that if we are involved in serious negotiations with one or more buyers, they will not take a very aggressive position. They don't care whether National stays on budget. They want the company sold and their money paid back. But Jerry, you are right. The bank could certainly create a lot of grief."

"But at this stage, it's the board's decision," said Jeff.

"That's correct," replied Richard. "And you are the board."

"Any more questions, Jerry?" asked Jeff.

"No," said Jerry.

"Speak up," said Jeff. "I'm not sure Richard heard you."

"*No*," said Jerry. He was about to explode.

"Thanks, Richard," said Jeff, "We won't keep you any longer."

"So long," Richard said and hung up. The speakerphone emitted the buzz of the dial tone.

"I've got an appointment," said Jeff. "You will talk to Sheila, won't you? Take Allen along if you think it will help."

"Sure," said Jerry. "I'll call her today." He spit the words out. He was exhausted. He was a schmuck to have put Jeff into the catbird seat in order to deal with Kevin's embezzlement. He wanted to scream and rant—but most of all, he was angry with himself for not anticipating how Jeff might exploit his position as sole voting shareholder to manipulate the situation, to undermine Jerry's efforts. He should have known better. But he needed to mitigate the damage of Kevin's embezzlement, and he had been under incredible time pressure. He didn't have the time to think through all the nuances and potential unintended consequences of giving Jeff voting control. He was worried about the bank killing the company—but not Jeff, not his own damn brother.

The following Monday, Jerry telephoned Sheila to set up a meeting at the bank to bring her up to date. The agenda he prepared was upbeat, and he hoped that it would make an impression that would ameliorate the budget's negative one. He decided that the only way to deal with the fact that Jeff had overruled him on the budget matter was to be candid about his disagreement with Jeff, but also provide Sheila the essence of Allen's argument. Jerry's attitude about the budget controversy had modified to the point that he was almost ambivalent. Ethan Wilson had briefed him daily about inquires from investment bankers and interest among the buyers they represented. No letter of intent to purchase had been received, but Ethan had assured Jerry that one or more was on the way. The discussions with Ethan had imbued Jerry with sufficient confidence that he was prepared to pass the information to Sheila.

They met in the bank's executive restaurant, and Sheila was already at the table when Jerry arrived. She rose and extended her hand, saying, "It's so good to see you." She had changed her hairstyle. It was short and tousled and made her look younger. They sat down and ordered coffee. Jerry handed Sheila a sheaf of documents that contained the quarterly financials, the Allen report along with the revised budget, and a chart listing all the prospective buyers, their current level of interest, the status of their due diligence, and their estimated decision dates. Jerry realized that his equanimity was in no small part due to the fact that the potential buyer list contained at least five prospects with the comment "serious" in the level of interest column.

Jerry had expected Sheila to be harried because of her tight schedule, but she appeared to be relaxed and under no particular time pressure. She placed the documents on the table.

"So, how are you feeling about all this, Jerry?"

"Pretty good. I think we're finally on the downhill slope with the wind to our back."

"That's terrific, Jerry. I know how hard you've worked on this and the stress that you've been under—with all the family issues compounding and exacerbating the business problems. I really feel for you."

Jerry appreciated her expressions of warmth and empathy, and especially the confidence she had in him. That confidence, he believed, was the reason for her relaxed manner. His anxiety over the budget issue was diminishing. Between bites of chicken salad and sips of the executive dining room's pedestrian coffee, he reviewed all the buyer activity that had occurred during the last two months. Sheila had made it clear that she wanted every intimate detail of every interaction between National and prospective buyers, including those who had initially expressed interest and withdrew. She was preparing a report for senior management, and the status of the company's sales efforts was going to be its primary focus. Jerry searched through the papers, located the chart that Ethan Wilson had prepared, and gave it back to her. Using the chart as a prop, Jerry spent the next forty-five minutes describing the background of every prospect, all the communications and meetings that had occurred, and the basis of Ethan Wilson's opinion as to the prospective buyer's level of interest. Sheila questioned Jerry carefully, showing both her overall experience and her specific knowledge of the National situation. She asked about issues that he had not previously considered, and there were several times that he had to struggle to offer a rational and coherent response. But by the time he had finished the briefing, she was absolutely ebullient.

"You've done an outstanding job, Jerry. The situation looks very positive. Don't you agree? I mean this is your business, right?"

Jerry smiled. "Yes, I am feeling very positive. I think we'll have at least one letter of intent by the end of next week. And I think a few others will follow."

Sheila nodded. "Are you anticipating any problems in closing a deal?"

Jerry was not surprised by the question. "Like what?" he asked.

"Like Jeff or Kevin. Do you think that when the day comes, they will actually agree to sell the company? I know I'm putting you on the spot, but I sure as hell don't want a big surprise."

Jerry filled his and Sheila's coffee cups from the carafe. He opened a packet of sweetener and poured it into his cup, and he took a sip from the cup. Sheila stared at him, waiting for him to finish hedging.

"I doubt it," he said. "Of course, I can't give you any guarantee, but I'm convinced that Kevin will go along with any reasonable deal. I don't really see that either his health or financial situation gives him any alternative to a sale."

"What about Jeff?"

"Jeff's more unpredictable," said Jerry. He smiled. "After all, I'm only his brother."

"I know. That's why I'm so paranoid. I certainly hope you can keep him from screwing this deal up."

"I'll do my best."

"Your best may not be good enough, Jerry. I want you to do more than your best. I'm counting on you to shepherd this deal through to completion. If you don't, everything that you and I have accomplished during the past five months will be for naught. You need to know that senior management will not tolerate anyone screwing this deal up. If this loan is not paid off by March 31 per the extension agreement, they will order Bill to initiate foreclosure actions."

Jerry was incredulous. "My God, Sheila, that would be draconian." He took a drink of water and let it open up his throat again. "It doesn't seem reasonable that the bank would shut down the company if it had a transaction in progress. I just can't believe they would do it."

"I'm very serious, Jerry. I told you a couple months ago that I had my last time at bat. It will be taken out of my hands." She looked at her watch and then gathered up the papers Jerry gave her, stood up, and thrust out her hand. Jerry quickly stood up and caught her hand.

"I didn't realize you were so pushed for time. I needed to go over a budget issue with you. We're going to exceed our budget forecast over the next..."

"Send me a memo about it. Budget issues are not a real concern now. We're focused on the sale. Get us out of this deal, Jerry. I'm counting on you. Now, stay a while and finish your coffee. No need to run. Order dessert if you'd like. See you."

She turned and walked away from the table. Jerry stood for a few minutes watching her leave. He sat down, drank his coffee, and contemplated Sheila's parting threat.

He did not return to National until after 5:00 p.m. By that time, most of the employees had left for the day and the executive offices were dark. He made his way to his office and before he turned on the overhead light, he noticed that the red message light on his phone was flashing. It was from Ethan Wilson. Jerry dialed him on his night line.

"G'day, mate." His voice was cool and clear, and there was no background noise. "I received a letter of intent from Jim Foxx's group, the guys that Phil Borgue represents. I'll fax it to you. When you get it, call me back and we'll go over it."

"How does it look?"

"Let's say it's a basis for discussion."

The fax arrived a few minutes later. He scanned it quickly and then dialed Richard's number again.

"Okay, I've got it in my hand. It looks pretty thin."

"I know. It's just their opening salvo. That's the way these guys play the game."

"What about First Chicago?"

"I talked with Larry. They're still working on it."

"I'm going to have to get the family together along with Richard Krimble and yourself to discuss it in detail. What's your schedule like?"

"I'm flexible. We have to respond within seven days."

"I have to track down Jeff. He's out of town. I'll shoot for seven p.m. on Wednesday at Kevin's."

After they signed off, Jerry reread the letter of intent. It was marginal, and he knew it would piss Jeff off. He needed to distance himself from the emotional potential of the offer and analyze it in the context of the Bascombs' financial and legal challenges. The best course of action was to prepare a comprehensive memorandum on the offer and vet it with Richard prior to presenting it to his family. That would allow him to maintain some level of objectivity and independence, while everyone else became mired in the inevitable emotional snarl.

He called Helen and told her that he had to work late and would not be coming over. "Anything serious?" A little of the life had gone out of her voice.

"Not really," he replied. He tried to sound nonchalant. "I have to prepare a report for the bank and I'm on a tight timetable. I hope to be clear by tomorrow. Will that work?"

"Sure," she said. "I'll just continue to take cold showers."

Jerry laughed and said goodbye. He called Richard Krimble's office and left a message that he wanted to meet tomorrow afternoon. He gathered up all the documents and files he would need to work on the report at home. He was ready to tackle the project. He smiled to himself as he walked out of his office lugging the overstuffed briefcase. He was back in his element—squeezing clarity out of chaos. There simply was no one better than he.

❖

Carolyn had prepared appetizers, and the coffee table was packed: a bottle of wine, cocktail glasses, coffee cups, and cans of soft drinks. The room was warm. Jerry, Jeff, Salli, Kevin, Carolyn, Richard Krimble, and Ethan Wilson, and the senior Bascombs were all present and seated uncomfortably close around the coffee table. Jerry stood up and clinked a wineglass. The din in the room slowly subsided.

"I think we better get started. We've got a lot to cover tonight, and Ethan Wilson has a ten-thirty flight to San Francisco in the morning." He paused. "I believe that every one except Carolyn and Salli have previously met Ethan. But you all know that he was retained by the company, on the advice of my partner, to manage the sale of National in accordance with our agreement with the bank. Ethan and his people have worked on this project for about two months, and we're starting to see results. We received a letter of intent from the Jim Foxx group. We need to respond by next Thursday. The purpose of this meeting is for Ethan and me to explain the offer, provide an evaluation of it from the perspective of the shareholders, and offer a recommendation as to how the company should proceed. Ethan will also bring you up to date on other buyer activity and offer an opinion as to what we can expect on that front."

As he sat down, he looked over to his father, who was smiling and attentive. Jerry was surprised that he did not feel any different at all about the man, even knowing about the long-ago affair with Helen. Sid was still the father he knew two weeks ago with the same attitudes, personality, and neuroses. And he was still the father he hoped to have for many more years. Jerry was relieved—even impressed with himself—that he harbored no ill will about the past.

Ethan rose and walked outside of the tight seating area and stood in front of the entertainment unit. His red hair, tall frame, ruddy complexion, and wide smile made the overcrowding feel like part of one big, amusing joke. The atmosphere lightened. "G'day, mates. I'm very happy to have the opportunity to meet the rest of the players in this drama I'm going to distribute a number of documents to you that I hope will clarify the things we're going to talk about."

He walked around the room, handing out colorful, half-inch thick spiral binders that contained several tabs.

"The binders contain all the documents and analyses that we'll be talking about tonight. Tab 1 contains the letter of intent. Tab 2 summarizes all of the key aspects of the offer and includes further elucidation of the letter that was provided by Foxx during the last few days. Tab 3 provides Jerry's analysis of the offer from the perspective of all National's stakeholders, the bank, the shareholders, the creditors, the employees, et cetera. Tab 4 compares the offer to the market values for other related industry and company deals that closed during the last year. Tab 5 is our up-to-the-minute scorecard on other buyer interest."

"What about your recommendation, Ethan?" asked Jeff. "Are you prepared to provide one?"

"I haven't written it up, but I'll provide it before we quit for the night. I don't think it will mean much until we get through the binder. Is that all right with everyone?"

"Fine with me," said Jeff. Everyone nodded in assent.

"Good," said Jerry. "Why don't you continue, Ethan?"

During the next two hours, with only a fifteen-minute bathroom break, Ethan covered all the material in Tabs 1 through 3 of the binder. Jerry was impressed at how well prepared Ethan was and how familiar he was with the details of the deal.

Foxx was offering to purchase National for twenty-two million in an all-cash transaction and operate it as a wholly owned subsidiary of one of his other companies. Ethan walked them through his analysis of the deal. Foxx would assume all of the existing obligations of National with the exception of the obligations to the bank, and the holders of the sub-debt, and any professional fees incurred by the company to complete the transaction. All employees of the corporation other than Jeff would be retained and any obligations to them, including accrued vacation, accrued sick leave, and so forth, would also be assumed by Foxx. Kevin would be offered the position of senior technical advisor with a five-year contract at two hundred thousand a year plus some stock options. Jeff would be given a six-month consulting contract for one hundred thousand dollars to help in the transition. Ethan said that Foxx did not have a position for Jeff. Ethan explained that two million of the consideration being offered by Foxx was allocated to five-year agreements not to compete for Kevin and Jeff—that is, during the next five years, they would not be able to work for anyone else in the access control industry.

Ethan estimated that after paying off the bank, Jerry's line of credit, Salli, their parents, and the other sub-debt holders, and paying his firm's fee plus the legal, consulting, and accounting fees to complete the transaction. Kevin and Jeff would each retain about one million dollars. He added that Kevin's personal note in the amount of $308,000 would be forgiven. He also pointed out that he had not analyzed the tax implications for Kevin and Jeff and that they would have to consult with their own CPAs.

"It goes without saying," said Ethan. "All of the personal guarantees that the shareholders have with the bank would be extinguished once the bank was paid."

"What is this breakup fee all about," said Jeff.

"Oh," said Ethan. "I forgot to mention it. The break-up fee is the amount of money Foxx will receive in the event we elect not to close the deal. For example, if another offer comes in that is more attractive than Foxx's and we elect to cancel the contract, so that we could go with the new suitor, we'll have to pay Foxx the break-up fee. It's like liquidated damages."

"They are asking for a million dollars," said Jeff. "Isn't that pretty rich for this deal?"

"Yes. it is," said Ethan. "If we decide to move forward, we can negotiate it. They're entitled to something because by being the first to sign up and to start the process, they will incur legal and accounting costs."

"Any new buyer would have to beat the Foxx deal by at least a million dollars for us to consider it," said Jerry.

Ethan sat down in the leather chair and took a sip of the glass of white wine. Krimble was aimlessly turning the pages of the binder. Jeff, who had been taking extensive notes, continued to scribble. Kevin and Carolyn were engrossed in a whispered conversation. Salli sat quietly, her hands folded in her lap, with a look of unconcern on her face that was appropriate for someone who had more than five million dollars in the bank and whose future wellbeing was mostly unaffected by the issues being discussed. Sid and Mrs. Bascomb had both listened intently to Ethan's presentation, but now stood and busied themselves by clearing away the dirty dishes and glasses.

Jerry sat back, testing the atmosphere for any hint of a spark. He was surprised that the mood was so docile; he had expected Jeff to explode when he saw just how chintzy Foxx's offer was. Something didn't feel right, but his suspicion was so tempered by relief that he started to believe that the Foxx deal might work out.

After several minutes, Krimble spoke up. "I assume you're going to give us your opinion as to the fairness of the offer?"

"Sure," replied Ethan. "But I wanted to give everyone an opportunity to absorb the proposed deal."

"Setting fairness aside for a moment," said Krimble. "The offer does provide a solution to the family's financial problems. It pays off National's debt to the bank and Jerry's line of credit, releases the family's guarantees, forgives Kevin's note to pay to the company, pays off investments made by Mr. and Mrs. Bascomb, Salli, and the other sub-debt investors, provides some return to the common shareholders, and gives Kevin a source of income for the next five years. Don't you agree, Jerry?"

Jerry glanced at Jeff and Kevin. Kevin was smiling. Jeff continued to write.

"It does solve the family's financial problems," said Jerry. He saw little point in committing himself to cheerleading the deal until he had heard from his brothers. "What do you think, Kevin?" he said.

"I had hoped that we'd come out with more cash. One million before taxes is not much to show for fifteen years of work. But we're not in very good bargaining position, are we? I'll have to think about it a while, but my first reaction is that Carolyn and I could live with it. I want to see Mom and Dad and Salli get their money out of National and the bank paid off, and the guarantees released. Anything more than that is gravy. What do you think, Jeff?"

Jerry noted that Jeff had finally stopped writing, and did not look pleased. He said, "It looks to me that they made us the stingiest offer they could contrive that would preclude us from being able to ignore the offer as not being serious. I think it sucks. They're offering us a deal that values National at five and one half times EBIT. Right, Ethan?" Ethan nodded. "Isn't that way below the price of the other deals you discuss in here?" He pointed to the binder on his lap.

"That's correct," said Ethan. "Since you raised the issue, let's take a few minutes to discuss the comps and our opinion regarding the fairness of the offer. Will everyone please turn to Tab 4?"

Ethan described how his staff had analyzed five transactions involving companies operating in National's industry. All of the deals had closed during the previous twenty-four months and therefore reflected the current market price. Three of the sales involved public companies, so the details of the transactions were accessible in various public documents.

Two of the sales involved companies that were privately owned. Ethan's firm had represented the buyers and therefore had access to the numbers.

He said, "The measure of viability and value of a business is its historical and projected earnings before interest and taxes, commonly referred to as EBIT. The prices paid for these five companies ranged from 5.7 EBIT to 11 EBIT. The average for the seven transactions was 7.5 EBIT and the standard deviation was 1.3 EBIT. A realistic value for a company like National would be in the range of about 6.2 EBIT to 8.8 EBIT."

"According to my calculations, even an offer at the low end of your range would mean another three million to National and about one and one half million additional to each of us. Isn't that right?" said Jeff.

"That's correct," said Ethan. "Before your taxes."

"So, what should we assume for taxes?" said Jeff.

"Use combined federal and state tax rate of forty percent," Jerry said. "That's close enough."

Jeff punched the buttons on his calculator and stared at the result. "That's a difference of nine hundred thousand after taxes. That is a hell of a lot of money for each of us to leave on the table, isn't it?"

Jerry smiled to himself. He knew what was coming. He'd been in Ethan's position many times.

"You're not leaving anything on the table, Jeff," said Ethan. "It's not on the table. The range we calculated is purely theoretical. It provides us with an indication of what we'd expect a willing buyer to pay a willing seller in an arm's length transaction where neither party is under any external pressure to act. That..." he paused to emphasize his point. "Is a far cry from National's current situation. None of the companies in our analysis was under any external pressure. No bank, investor, trade creditor, or government agency was threatening a suit that could bring the company to its knees. It is likely that the potential buyers know that National is being pressured by its bank to sell. It's part of our reality, and that's why Foxx's offer is below my range."

"Do you think their offer is fair?" asked Salli.

"You mean if there was no pressure from the bank?"

"Yes."

"I do not," said Ethan. "Absent the pressure from the bank I'd value National closer to the midpoint of the range or even slightly above, maybe 7.0 EBIT to 8.0 EBIT."

"I see," said Salli. "So the bank's pressure is depressing our value in the marketplace by almost ten million dollars?"

"It's the same thing you'd experience if you had to sell anything under duress," said Ethan. "When the Jews were being forced out of their homes in Germany in the 1930s, they were forced to sell on very short notice. Most wound up selling their houses, household possessions, and businesses for pennies on the dollar. It's an unfortunate fact of life. Selling anything under duress depresses value."

"I'm not interested in your fucking homilies, Ethan," snapped Jeff. "It's not a theoretical deal. Kevin and I have worked our asses off for years." He slammed the binder on the floor in front of him. "Their offer is a joke. They're trying to steal the company like we all knew they would."

"That won't help anything, Jeff," said Richard. "The buyers are not responsible for National's plight. They'd be stupid not to take advantage of our distress. Let's calm down, so that we can review our options."

"Just what are our options," said Kevin, to no one in particular.

"Maybe before we talk about the options for this deal, I should bring you up to date on other buyer interest."

Before Ethan could continue, Mrs. Bascomb suggested that they take a short break, so that she and Sid could serve coffee and the pastries she prepared.

"That's the best idea I've heard all night, Mom," said Jerry. "I'll take decaf."

After everyone had gotten their coffee and picked over the pastry tray, Ethan began the review of the fifth tab. He explained that they had contacted a total of twenty strategic buyers, domestic and international, all of which could benefit by acquiring National's technology and marketing organization. Of those, fifteen expressed some interest, signed the non-disclosure agreement, and were sent a copy of the National confidential memorandum that his office had prepared. Six returned the book, leaving a total of nine potential buyers with what he termed moderate to serious interest. "Of these nine, four have visited the facility and are analyzing the purchase. Foxx submitted an offer. First Chicago is working on an offer. I haven't been able to determine the status of ADT and Continental. I plan to call them both in the morning to see if they're interested."

"So, at this point, there are several other players who have what you would consider a serious level of interest in National," said Jeff.

"That's correct. And anticipating your next question, I think that they will all shake out within the next thirty days."

"Well, why the rush to consider this crappy offer from Foxx?" asked Jeff. "Isn't it in our best interest to bring everyone who's interested to the table and get them to bid up the price? I don't understand the urgency of this meeting." The volume of his voice rose with each succeeding sentence. "Damn, damn—this pisses me off."

Salli placed her hand on Jeff's shoulder. "Come on, Jeff, calm down."

"I'm not going to calm down until I get an explanation as to what the fuck is going on. Why are we even considering an offer from these pricks?"

Ethan looked at Jerry, pleading. It wasn't necessary. Richard Krimble spoke up. "The workout agreement with the bank requires us to notify the bank when we get an offer and to consider and respond to any legitimate one that will get the bank paid. We don't have any choice, Jeff. It would be a major breach of the agreement to either ignore their offer or not respond in a timely manner. We don't have the luxury to be able to wait until all the players decide to come to the table."

"It's even more serious than that," said Jerry. He told them about his conversation with Sheila. "In substance, we have to close a deal by March 31 or the bank will shut National down," said Jerry.

"How do you know she's not bluffing?" said Jeff. "I can't believe that the bank would flush this entire company and the whole family for another sixty or ninety days. Do you?"

"I don't think Sheila's lying to me. We have developed a good working relationship. If she tells me the bank will foreclose, I believe she's been so advised by the bank's senior management. Do you want to bet your net worth, Kevin and Carolyn's net worth, and Mom and Dad's net worth on the assumption that Sheila is lying? Do you, Jeff?"

The color suddenly drained from Jeff's face. He slumped down in the sofa. The room grew silent.

"Jerry, you, Richard, and Ethan are the professionals," said Kevin. "This is your business. I'm an engineer with a heart condition and my brother is a peddler—a good one—but still a peddler. Trying to figure out this puzzle is above our pay grade. What is your recommendation, the three of you? What do you guys think we should do?"

Kevin and his parents were fading, and Jeff was sulking. Jerry looked at his watch. It was ten p.m., and neither the hour nor the environment for making decisions that would affect everyone's financial future.

"It's getting late," said Jerry. "I'm sure we're all tired. I suggest we break up for the night. Ethan, Richard, and I will talk for a while. The three of us will hash out a strategy and we'll discuss it with you in a conference call tomorrow afternoon. How does that sound?"

"Great idea," said Kevin, relief written all over his face. "Is that okay with you," Jeff?"

"Yeah, that will be fine," said Jeff. His lack of interest was apparent.

"We'll use your living room for a while, Kevin, and when we're through, we'll let ourselves out. No need to wait up. You guys can go to bed."

The next afternoon, Jerry asked Shirley to gather up Ethan, Richard, and Kevin for a conference call and to tell Jeff that it would be hosted in his office. When Jerry arrived, Jeff was already seated in front of the speakerphone paring his fingernails.

"How'd you sleep?" said Jerry.

"I was still reading at three-thirty. Too much stress."

Jerry pulled out a chair next to his brother and sank down into it. "I can't blame you. You and Kevin have put your life's blood in this thing. I know it's tearing you apart. I wish there was an alternative, Jeff. I really do."

Jeff didn't respond. Shirley came on the intercom to tell him that the operator had everybody on the line. The operator did a roll call and excused herself.

"How is everyone this afternoon?" Jerry asked, trying to force some sunshine into his voice.

"Harassed," said Krimble. "I need to leave for a hearing in thirty minutes. Will that give us enough time?"

"I think so," said Ethan. "Let's get started. Jerry, Richard, and I met for almost an hour last night. I think we've come up with a plan that will give you a shot at improving the deal without undue risk to Kevin, Jeff, and National. The latest close date for a deal is March 31, the day the loan is due. That's about one hundred and forty days from today. I am confident that all the accounting, legal, and environmental due diligence can be done in seventy-five days from a dead start. That means we've got at the outside about two months to bring in another buyer, assuming one is interested. Our recommendation is that Jerry and I meet with Foxx tomorrow or Saturday and try to improve the deal as best we can, but sign it before the Monday deadline. That way Jerry can inform the bank that you have accepted the deal and you'll be in compliance. We will start the due diligence process with Foxx on the basis of a one-hundred-and-twenty-day schedule to close. That way we'll move ahead, but not too fast to preclude another buyer getting involved. During that time, I'll try to stimulate the other prospects and see if we can bring another offer to the table. I guess that summarizes it. Did I leave anything out, Jerry? Richard?"

"You might go over the objectives of our negotiation," said Jerry.

"Right. We've got three objectives. Improve their offer by at least three million dollars to twenty-five million. That will get us to a sale price of about 6.25 times EBIT and get each of you another one and a half million. Bump up Kevin's consulting contract to two hundred fifty thousand a year guaranteed for five years no matter what."

"No matter what?" asked Kevin.

"No matter whether you work or don't work," said Jerry.

There was a pause and Jerry heard Kevin laugh. "And no matter whether I live or die. Right?"

There was a pause with no answer and Ethan continued. "And we're going to ask that Jeff also be given a five-year consulting contract for two hundred and fifty thousand dollars a year. That's it."

"Do you think they'll agree to all that?" asked Jeff.

"Don't know," replied Ethan. "We'll just do the best we can."

"What about the breakup fee?" said Jeff.

"We've decided not to touch that," said Jerry. "We want them to think that we're very serious about their deal and are committed to making it work. They know we're not going to sit on our hands until the close, but we don't want to flaunt the fact that we're actively looking for another buyer."

"We're probably going to have to argue against their wanting to raise it as a trade – off against the other things we're asking for," said Ethan. "That's probably where the battle will be. This will not be an easy negotiation. We really don't have any leverage."

"Nothing but fairy dust," said Jerry.

"Any comments?" asked Ethan.

"Sounds great to me," said Kevin. "Go for it. What do you think, Jeff?"

"It will certainly make the deal more palatable to me if you guys are successful." His voice was anything but enthusiastic.

He's given up, thought Jerry.

"All right then," said Ethan. "I'll call and try to set something up. I'll be in touch with you, Jerry. Keep both tomorrow and Saturday free. Okay?"

"Right," said Jerry. Kevin, Ethan, and Richard hung up.

Jerry turned off the speakerphone. He and Jeff looked at each other. Jeff stood up and extended his hand to Jerry. "Good luck in your meeting." He smiled faintly and left the conference room.

❖

Momentum is critical. The self-fulfilling prophecy law takes over. When everyone working on a deal believes it's going to happen, has the motivation to do the things to make it happen, feels as if it's going to happen, acts as if it's going to happen, then other potentially interested parties are often discouraged because of the effort they need to mount a freewheeling train. The other arrow they had in their quiver was the commitment of the owners to do a deal. Foxx would not have to contend with the vacillations and indecisiveness of a reluctant bride. National wanted a deal, needed a deal, and Foxx would be spared the endless rounds of the negotiation dance that it often takes to snag an unmotivated seller. He'd be able to quickly add the National prize to his list of technology companies.

Jerry and Ethan were seasoned investment bankers, and they knew their negotiating position was weak. The only thing they had to offer Foxx was that by signing now they would be the front-runner in the deal and start to build the momentum for a close.

The following morning, Jerry boarded a plane for Salt Lake City. Ethan had arranged to meet with Jim Foxx and his investment banker, Phil Borgue, at the Foxx headquarters. Foxx was leaving for Europe the following Monday and would be gone for ten days. The plan was for Phil Borgue to fly in from New York City, and Ethan from San Francisco. Jerry would meet them at the Salt Lake City Airport and the three of them would drive to Foxx's campus. Ethan had agreed to make arrangements with Hertz for a car.

Jerry's plane arrived just after 11:00 a.m. He walked over to the gate where Ethan's flight was to arrive in twenty minutes and sat down with a newspaper. Ethan emerged from the jet way.

"Good morning! How was your flight?" said Jerry.

"Okay," said Ethan. He opened his briefcase and pulled out a sheaf of papers. "Let's sit down for a minute. You need to read this before we meet Borgue. It's a letter from Larry at First Chicago." He handed the papers to Jerry. As Jerry read the first paragraph of the four-page fax, he felt himself deflate.

"Oh shit! Why?"

"It's the issue that Morgan and Birney identified at the get-go. The major customers for National's cutting edge technology in biometrics will be government agencies—at least for the foreseeable future. Therefore, they don't see the rate of growth that will justify the market capitalization rates that we're looking for."

"Damn!" Jerry quickly read through the rest of the fax and handed it back to Ethan. "We're fucked."

He put his hand on Jerry's shoulder. "It can still come good, mate. Foxx doesn't know that Larry was in the game. It won't affect what we want to get done today. It just changes the probability estimates on being able to get a better deal in the door before the hammer comes down."

"Have you heard anything from the others?

"No. I've placed calls. I'll check with my office later in the day."

As Jerry was recalculating the probabilities, his attention was distracted by a strange group who passed by. Four middle-aged women and approximately fifteen children, two of whom were being carried by the women, followed an elderly man dressed in overalls, boots, and a wide brimmed hat. The women and the girls wore long, patterned dresses. The boys all wore long pants and white shirts. He was mesmerized as he tried to comprehend the group's structure.

"Polygamists," said Ethan. "I've seen them in Australia. There's a bunch of them in Utah."

"Jeez," said Jerry. "I've heard about them, but I've never seen them up close."

"The men are mongrels. They use their religion to justify carnal relations with children. Disgusting."

Jerry watched them as they moved down the corridor. He picked up his briefcase and said, "Where are we going to meet Phil?"

"At the baggage claim. If his plane was on time, he should be there now. Let's go." Ethan grabbed his arm.

"Let him wait a few minutes. I want to talk to you about Foxx." He noticed a coffee kiosk down the corridor. He steered Ethan to the kiosk. They both got cappuccinos and sat down at a small round table. "I stopped at the library last night," said Jerry. "I picked up some magazine and newspaper articles on him. The articles paint him to be a workaholic egomaniac who treats people like shit—including his wife and kids. You've worked with him before. What's your opinion?"

Ethan took a drink from his coffee mug and wiped the foam from his lips. "I worked with him on the sale of Western Vision. I represented the selling shareholders and creditors. I'm not sure my personal experience is that helpful because Western was in bankruptcy and we were selling it as part of a plan of reorganization. I met him several times during the negotiation. He is a tough, crude bottom-feeder. But he's all business. He won't play games. And I think he's honest. Once he makes a deal, he'll stand by it. That part is refreshing."

"What do you mean by crude?" said Jerry.

Ethan laughed. "You don't want to eat lunch or dinner with him. He slurps his food, he talks with his mouth full and spits food all over himself and everyone else at the table, and he picks his nose a lot. Does that suffice?"

"Ugh," replied Jerry. "Thanks. How did he get his empire going?"

"Let's go over to the baggage area," said Ethan. "I'll give you the background as we walk."

Foxx was a high school dropout. He worked at a number of jobs, and when he was twenty-seven, he became the production manager of a large precision sheet metal company named Utah Metals. The company wound up in bankruptcy because the owner had pulled out money for his other business ventures. The owner was in poor health and tired of it all and did not have any interest in rehabilitating the company. The company had great long-term contracts with a number of aircraft companies like Lockheed, Boeing, and Northrop, so sales were guaranteed. The creditors needed someone to operate the business. They got to know Jim through the bankruptcy process and asked him to run the company. Since Utah Metals had plenty of business, his main job was to run the manufacturing operations and deliver quality parts on schedule and control costs, the things that Foxx had demonstrated he could do. He and a few key employees got all of the stock as part of the reorganization, and he became president. As Boeing grew, he built the company to over seventy-five million in annual sales with profits in excess of ten million. He took it public in 1983, and started acquiring companies using his stock as the legal tender. He had made about fifteen acquisitions in the last eight years, primarily in technology, broadcasting, and waste disposal.

"How did he get into technology? I mean, he had no background," said Jerry.

"Don't really know. He bought his first high-tech company five years ago and saw its sales grow five-fold in two years. I don't think he's in love with technology. He is in love with making money."

They had reached the crowded baggage claim area. Richard looked around and suddenly raised his hand and shouted.

"Phil, Phil, over here." Jerry noted a tall, thin, partially bald man with glasses wave back and start to move toward them. "Do you know Phil?" asked Ethan.

"Not well," replied Jerry. "I met him at a local conference about five years ago."

"He's a good guy," said Ethan. "You'll enjoy working with him."

Phil greeted Ethan and Jerry. "Did you guys bring bags?"

"No," said Ethan. "We're optimistic. We hope to get out of here tonight."

Phil's laugh was grating. "Amen."

Jerry and Phil chatted while Ethan filled out paperwork for the rental. Phil was fifty years old. He had been a commercial banker with Bank of America and learned the investment banking businesses when he moved into a management position in the bank's investment division. He earned a bachelor's degree at Princeton and graduated from the Harvard Business School. Jerry was pleased to discover that they had several friends in common.

They got a beige Ford Taurus. Ethan asked Phil to drive, since he knew where they were going. When they were on the road, Phil asked Ethan if he had a meeting agenda.

"Yes, it's fairly short. Three items. The price, Kevin's contract, and Jeff's contract. That's all."

Phil laughed, emitting the same grating sound, but louder. "What else is there?"

"Your letter was three pages long and listed fifteen terms. We only want to talk about three."

"You guys really should have brought a change of clothes. This is not going to be a short meeting. Jim feels as if he's already overpaying."

"Phil, Phil, this is me, Ethan. I know this market. Your offer is about thirty-five to fifty percent below the market. You know it. Don't bullshit me."

Phil didn't respond immediately. "Well, you're going to get the chance to persuade us."

After they had traveled thirty miles, Jerry announced that he needed to use a restroom and asked Phil to stop at the next gas station. Shortly thereafter, Phil pulled into a dirty, decrepit Texaco. Jerry was about to ask Phil to keep driving, but the airport cappuccino had caught up with him and the drive was another twenty minutes. As he got out of the car and headed to the building, he passed a large number of motorcycles parked under the canopy. The bathroom was free. And no wonder—it was filthy. He resolved not to breathe and tried to avoid looking at the human detritus that littered the room. When he emerged, he was so intent on getting to the car that he crashed into a corpulent biker who was relieving himself against the corner of the outhouse building. A can of beer was in the grass and Jerry knocked it over, and some of it spilled on Jerry's shoe.

The biker laughed heartily. "Don't be in such a rush, little feller." He zipped up and pointed to the letters "FTW" emblazoned on his t-shirt. "Fuck The World," he said.

Jerry was transfixed, immobile. He stared into the biker's smiling face. Soon the other bikers in the store were looking at Jerry and laughing. Finally Jerry was able to mutter, "Sorry, excuse me," and quickly returned to the parking lot and the car. His heart was pounding. He took out a handkerchief and wiped his shoe.

"Anything wrong, mate?" said Ethan.

"No," said Jerry. "I just bumped into a guy on the way out. No problem."

An hour later, Phil stopped at the gatehouse of the Foxx complex and flashed his identification. The guard made a telephone call and waved them through. Phil started to drive down a long road lined with cypress trees.

"How big is this place?" asked Jerry. They could be headed toward Dracula's castle, he thought.

"About fifty acres," said Phil. "There are a total of five buildings that house all the corporate administrative offices, the international operations, and the research labs. There are about six hundred and fifty people who work here. That's not many for this amount of space, but Jim expects to grow this business far beyond its current size." He pulled into a parking space in front of a three-story office building. "We're going to meet in his office."

They entered a two-story edifice built out of glass and green marble. Even Jerry, who was used to seeing sumptuous offices of egomaniacal executives, was overwhelmed. The reception area looked like a gallery at the MOMA. As he walked down the long corridor that led to Foxx's office, he was able to identify some of the artists. Jerry whistled to himself. There were several million dollars of artwork in the front of the first story alone.

Waiting at the door was Jim Foxx. He was a lot shorter and stockier than Jerry's expectations, the ones he'd formed from the articles. Jim Foxx had a round face, a shaved head, and a broad, exuberant smile. He wore a long sleeve blue shirt with a button-down collar, and dark grey slacks held up by a pair of garish blue and red suspenders.

"Hi Phil, good to see you. And Ethan. So good of you to come out here on such short notice. I really appreciate it."

Jerry extended his hand. "Jerry Bascomb, Jim. I've read a lot about you. It's good to meet you."

Foxx's clasp was firm. His perfect teeth seemed to belie Richard's description of his crude habits. "Don't believe most of it. When you try to play the press, you often can't predict how they spin what you tell them." He moved them forward into his office. "Anyway, come on in, make yourself comfortable. There are various types of sandwiches and soft drinks."

Jerry took a seat at the conference table in front of Jim Foxx's desk. The office walls were high and broad, festooned with another few million dollars in artwork. The thought crossed his mind that Jim Foxx had done pretty well for a high school dropout and that Jerry Bascomb had probably spent too many years getting an education and not enough years street fighting. He tried to purge his mind of envy.

Two other Foxx executives soon joined them. "I hope you don't mind the fact that we outnumber you," said Foxx. "We know what sharpies you California guys are, and we're just a bunch of dumb Mormons. We need more of us to keep up."

Ethan and Jerry both laughed appropriately and exchanged cards with Foxx and the other executives. As they consumed their sandwiches and soft drinks, Jerry noted that contrary to Ethan's description, Jim Foxx was very meticulous in his table manners. He might have upgraded with an etiquette course. He also spoke non-stop about his most recent acquisition, a radio station in Montana, and the difficulties he'd experienced in integrating it with his portfolio companies.

"I was probably stupid to buy it. But the leverage on radio stations is phenomenal and I couldn't pass it up. It's my major weakness. I'm a sucker for a good deal."

"Like National, Jim," said Ethan. "Is that what attracts you? The prospect of stealing it?" Ethan smiled when he said the word stealing. Jerry looked carefully at Jim. Foxx's grin vanished. He looked startled. Good tactic, thought Jerry.

"We're not stealing National," said Phil. "We've analyzed the deal and we've offered what it's worth to us." He turned to Jerry with a patronizing smile on his face. "I can understand your sensitivity, National being your family's business."

Jerry's face reddened and Ethan grasped Jerry's shoulder and laughed. "We're not being sensitive, mate." His face was blanketed in a warm, friendly smile. "You blokes are being greedy." He quickly turned to Jim Foxx. "But let's move away from the name-calling. Jim, I have the permission of National to share with you the market analysis we performed in order to back up our 'fairness opinion.' It will give you a perspective as to our view of National's value and the basis for the counteroffer we plan to make." Without waiting for Jim to respond, Ethan distributed the "Analysis of Recent Transactions" tab from the memo that he had presented to the Bascombs. He then strode over to the whiteboard at the end of the conference table and delivered a flawless twenty-minute summary of the report. Jerry noticed that Ethan's attention was focused on Jim Foxx as if he was his only audience. He ignored Phil and the two stuffed shirts beside him.

Jerry's gaze was fixed on Jim Foxx, too. He tried to follow every change in facial expression; there were very few. Foxx was an excellent poker player. He appeared to be absorbed by Ethan's presentation, but showed no response to indicate whether or not he was buying the argument or its conclusions. Ethan finished his presentation and asked if there were any questions. When there were none, he glanced at Jerry and sat down.

"I appreciate the information you presented, Ethan," said Jim. "I think our team needs to caucus. Give us about half an hour. We'll move to another office. You and Jerry make yourselves comfortable. Use my phone if you need to make any calls. Dial nine to get an outside line." He stood up and headed for the door. Phil and the executives followed him.

When they were alone, Jerry turned to Ethan. "Well, what do you think? Did we make any headway?"

"I haven't got a clue. We'll have to see what they come back with. I need to make some calls." He sat down at Foxx's desk, which was perfectly bare, and picked up the receiver.

"Go ahead," said Jerry. "I'll amuse myself by trying to estimate how many dollars Foxx has nailed to his walls."

Jerry was uncomfortable and intimidated, sitting aimlessly in the large office, staring at so much expensive artwork. The day had been so surreal. The encounter with the polygamists, the run-in with the biker. And now having to stare at the expensive trophies accumulated by a high school dropout, while a bunch of vultures decided his family's fate—his confidence was ebbing.

Jim Foxx and his entourage returned less than a half hour later. When everyone was seated, Phil said, "We've had an extensive discussion about the material you presented. You've done a through job. I'm not surprised. I've seen your work on previous deals, Ethan. Frankly, we can't find any fault with your analysis." He had a smug expression and his manner was condescending. "Oh, there might be a few points that we could contest—but the effect on the overall results would be insignificant. We can't see any reason to increase our offer, so there's no point in your submitting a counter. I'm sorry that you had to make the trip with nothing to show for your efforts. But that's our decision."

Ethan had nothing to come back with. Jerry clenched his fists under the table. His throat was very dry. He could not believe that they had stiffed him, insulted him. He took a few deep breaths. The bastards knew more than they're letting on, he thought. They're acting too coy.

Ethan began putting his papers in the briefcase, preparing to leave. Jerry continued to sit at the table, looking at Phil, who averted his eyes.

Jim Foxx put on his most ingratiating smile, looked at Jerry, and said, "You fellas have done one hell of a job turning National around. We're excited to have you join our family of companies. My guys are looking forward to working with you, Jeff, and Kevin in the transition."

The executives nodded in agreement. Jerry sat quietly and did not move. Finally, he stood and glared at Foxx. His face was distorted with anger. "You cocksucking troglodyte." He couldn't feel his lips moving. He didn't recognize his own voice. "You'll get National over my dead body." Jerry moved down the table to where a very frightened Phil Borgue was sitting, catatonic. "I know a setup when I see one," he said. He pushed his face within five inches of Phil's. "You've got a line to the bank—don't you?" He snarled at him. "Don't you? Someone's been whispering in your fucking ear. They've been whispering in your ear. I thought you were a professional." His hand started to shake and turned into a fist, which he kept to his side. "You're a professional asshole!"

Phil's face turned beet red under a film of sweat. He opened his mouth but all that came out was high-pitched guttural sounds. Jerry kept his face right up to Phil's. Then, he grabbed him by the tie and yanked him from side to side. Phil was paralyzed with fear. His eyes bulged and spittle dripped from his opened mouth. His upper torso was rigid like a crash dummy.

"I'm so fucking mad I could strangle you, you miserable excuse for a banker!" Foxx and the executives did not make any move at rescue. They were transfixed, immobile. Finally, Ethan rushed over to Jerry, grabbed his arm, and pried his fingers from Phil's tie. Jerry pushed Phil away and walked back to his seat, pulled his papers together, stuffed them in his briefcase in a haphazard manner, and then turned and walked to the door. His knees were weak.

"Come on, Ethan. We've got a lot of legal work to do. I intend to make the bank and these asshole co-conspirators rue the day they first thought about fucking us. Let's go. Now!"

Ethan completed packing his briefcase, nodded to Phil and Jim Foxx and joined Jerry at the doorway. "I'm sorry it turned out this way, gentlemen, but..."

"They're not gentlemen, Ethan. They're a pack of thieves. Let's go." Jerry turned the knob and opened the door to the hallway.

"Please, wait a minute."

Jerry turned to see Jim Foxx rise grim-faced from his seat.

"Please give us a few minutes to talk," said Foxx. "I know you're upset and you have every reason not to trust us." He spread his hands, pleading. "Give me a few minutes to talk to my people. Jerry, you're here anyway. It won't make any difference in the scheme of things if you leave now or fifteen minutes from now." Foxx was doing his best to smile. Jerry could tell it was strained.

"Okay," said Jerry. "You've got fifteen minutes."

"Good," said Jim. "You guys stay here and we'll go to another office."

"Fifteen minutes," said Jerry. "Or we're out of here."

Foxx, his executives, and a much-shaken Phil Borgue filed out of the office. When the door closed behind them, Ethan said, "How the hell did you know that they were talking with the bank?"

Jerry showed no expression. His jaw was still clenched. His elevated heartbeat was approaching its resting rate. "I didn't. I guessed. Phil was so fucking smug. They didn't want to give us a dime, even for face-saving." He sat down, loosened his tie, and leaned back in the chair, exhausted and disoriented by his own loss of control. "I'm sorry, Ethan, I absolutely lost it. It was so clear to me what had happened, that Phil had a back channel to the bank. I'm just fortunate I didn't have a gun or I would have killed the son-of-a-bitch. I never do that. I'm sorry. It certainly wasn't professional." He closed his eyes.

"Don't be. I'm in awe of your performance." Ethan assumed a military posture and gave Jerry a salute.

"Hold your sense of awe in check until we see what they plan to do."

Fourteen minutes and eleven seconds passed. Jim Foxx with his executives in tow entered the room. Phil was absent. They sat down at the conference table. Jim turned to Jerry and said, "I want to make two statements. I hope you'll accept them as being sincere. First, I want to express my apology for what Phil did. I assure you that neither I nor any member of our staff knew that Phil was having those types of communications with your bank. What he did was wrong and I'm furious that he placed my company and me in this position. If I were in your position, I would be just as pissed off as you are. I'm sorry. I hope you'll accept my apology.

"Second, I am sincere in my interest in buying National. It's a good fit with some of my other projects. I think it's got great potential. I'd like to work out a deal with you that you and your brothers think is fair. I don't want to overpay. But I'll pay a fair price. Now what do you think? Can we put this shit behind us and move on?"

Jerry glanced briefly at Ethan. He sat quietly for a minute, not wanting to appear too eager to give up the moral indignation that had apparently gotten Phil sacked. Then, he leaned across the table and extended his hand to Foxx.

"I accept your apology, Jim. And I want to apologize to you for the outburst and the name-calling. That's not my style. My emotions just, well..."

"Forget it," said Foxx. He was now smiling broadly. "If I had been in your position. I would have broken some windows and torn the place apart. Now let's talk. What do you need to make a deal?"

Jerry looked down at the yellow pad in front of him. He shoved the pad along the table to Ethan. The room was silent except for the swish of the pad sliding on the table. Ethan looked at the pad. He took out his calculator, made a few entries, and compared the results with Jerry's calculations. He jotted some notes on the pad and slid it back to Jerry. Swish. Jerry read Ethan's notes and added some additional marks. He looked up and faced Foxx. He was calm and confident.

"I appreciate your candor, Jim. I'm prepared to be equally candid. I need you to be more flexible in three aspects of your offer. If you can see your way clear to meeting our objectives on these terms, I'm willing to support a deal and tell Ethan to shut down his marketing operation. In order to achieve that objective, National has to be sold for thirty million, which is about 85 percent of Ethan's estimate of its market value. In addition,

Kevin needs a five-year guaranteed salary of two hundred and fifty thousand a year, for which he will sign a covenant not to compete. And Jeff also needs two hundred and fifty thousand a year for five years to sign a covenant not to compete. If you can pay that price, I will recommend that Kevin and Jeff sign a term sheet, and we can put this puppy to bed."

One of the executives had been taking notes and punching on his calculator while Jerry spoke. He looked up and said, "Give me a couple of minutes to summarize this for Jim."

"Sure," said Jerry. He turned to Ethan and they talked in whispers, reviewing the notes on the yellow pad. Jim Foxx stood up and conferred with his staff at the back of the conference room. They huddled for ten minutes, and then Foxx turned toward the conference table and said, "I understand your position, and we need to caucus. We'll need about a half an hour." He headed to the door.

"Well, what do you think," said Jerry.

"I don't know," said Ethan. "Foxx likes to buy cheap. When you add in the two and one-half million for Kevin and Jeff, our offer is over 90 percent of market value. Ninety percent of market value for distressed goods is not cheap. It depends on how badly he wants it."

Foxx and his entourage returned in less than ten minutes.

"We're prepared to accept your numbers," said Foxx. "Let's go over the term sheet in the letter agreement, incorporate your proposed changes, and get you the hell out of here while I still have some money left." He laughed and extended his hand to shake.

The bright morning light filtered through the partially drawn blinds and drenched Jerry's eyelids with its intensity. He was barely awake. He had been lying in bed for over an hour not wanting to interrupt his lazy sleep despite the strong urge to urinate. He turned to look at the alarm clock. It was covered with the t-shirt that he had ripped off during the night. He threw the shirt on the floor and turned the clock, so he could read it. Ten thirty-five. He fell back on the bed, stretched, and smiled. He hadn't slept this late for months. I drank too fucking much, he thought. But that was a helluva party. He sighed, stretched again, swung his legs over the side of the bed, and headed for the bathroom.

Helen was in the kitchen making breakfast. "I'm happy to see you're alive. I was about to call 911."

"I think I have a hangover," he said. "I haven't drunk that much since I was in college."

She turned away from the sink and allowed her robe to drop from her shoulders. She pressed her body against him and gave him a kiss. The only sounds in the room were the eggs sizzling in the frying pan. "You were incredible last night. We have to arrange to have these big deals more often. I bet your level of testosterone was off the charts."

He chuckled and picked her up and carried her back into the bedroom.

Jerry had made the victory call to Kevin from the Salt Lake airport.

"You're a fucking miracle worker! You're a genius. I can't believe it."

Jerry asked him to assemble Jeff, Salli, and his parents, so that he and Ethan Wilson, who was flying back to LA with him, could go over the deal. He explained that he had promised Foxx that he would fax the acceptance of the letter agreement by Monday.

During the flight, Jerry and Ethan each consumed three drinks, toasting each other's accomplishments, intelligence, perseverance, and other character features. By the time the plane landed, they were both feeling warm and serene. They took a cab to Kevin's house. When they arrived, they found all the lights on and a raucous party in full swing.

As Jerry walked through the door, a very flushed-faced Kevin rushed over and wrapped him in a bear hug, lifted him off the ground, and kissed him full force on the mouth. He returned Jerry to the floor and turned to the fifty or so guests and yelled, "Let's have three cheers for Jerry and Ethan, our conquering heroes. Hip-hip hooray, hip-hip..."

Every one started clapping and yelling. Jerry and Ethan stood awkwardly near the front door, nodding, smiling, and accepting congratulations. Jerry's parents pushed through the crowd and each took turns shaking Ethan's hand and hugging Jerry. Carolyn followed. As she hugged Jerry, she whispered, "You've saved his life, Jerry." Then, she kissed him.

As Jerry got more used to the throng around him, he started recognizing people—National's executives and their spouses: Howard and his wife and Allen and his wife. He looked for Shirley, but couldn't find her. Jeff and Salli were paired in the alcove, ostensibly waiting to congratulate Ethan and him, but clearly engaged in a serious conversation. As Jerry's eyes caught Jeff's, Jeff grabbed Salli's hand and pushed through the throng around Jerry.

"A spectacular job, Jerry. I've got to hand it to you, little brother. You did us proud." He shook Ethan's hand. "You're every bit as good as Jerry said you were. Thanks."

Salli held Jerry's hand, while she gave him a peck on the cheek. As she pushed away from him, he noted that she averted her eyes. But just then Howard, bleary eyed and grinning, grabbed his right hand and almost crushed it. "You guys cleaned their clock. Fantastic job, Jerry. We're all happy for you and the rest of the Bascombs."

"Thanks, Howard. Things went a lot better than we expected. Now we have to close it. I hope you've warned Kris that you'll be working your ass off for the next ninety to one hundred and twenty days."

"Not a problem, boss. I can't wait to get started. How the hell did you get them to buy that price? Jim Foxx is a bottom fisher. Paying retail is against his religion."

Jerry smiled. "Let's just say that I made him an offer he could not refuse."

Howard roared. "That's good, that's really good. You're a fucking Godfather."

By midnight, Jeff, Salli, and all the guests had left. Carolyn and Mrs. Bascomb cleaned up the kitchen while Kevin, Jerry, and Sid sat in the den smoking cigars, drinking brandy, and telling dirty jokes. At half-past midnight, Jerry got up from the soft lounge chair he'd been buried in. "I'm going to call for a cab. I'm drunk and beat."

"Why don't you stay here?" said Kevin. "Mom and Dad are taking the guest room, but we can fix up a bed for you on the sofa."

"Thanks, but no thanks. Helen's waiting for me. Where did I leave the letter agreement?"

"It's on the piano," said Sid. Jerry walked over to the piano, picked up a manila folder, opened it, and studied the letter inside. "We pulled off an incredible coup," he said. "I need to pinch myself periodically to make sure I'm not dreaming."

"You're not dreaming," said Kevin. "Unless Dad and I are dreaming in sync with you. Are we, Dad?"

Sid was in the process of dozing off. "I'm too drunk to dream, Kevin. It's got to be real."

Jerry got out of bed, shaved, showered, and dressed in his casual, play-golf type clothes. Helen was still sleeping. He stopped in the bedroom to kiss her. She turned over and smiled at him. "You're not leaving?"

"Just taking Chelsey out. I'll be back in an hour."

"No lazy morning in bed?"

He laughed. "Hold on to that thought. I'll see you later."

Jerry strolled into his office at ten a.m. the following Monday.

"Congratulations, Jerry," said Shirley. "I'm sorry I missed the party—I couldn't get a sitter on short notice. I hear it was a blast."

"It was a mega blast. I'm still feeling the effects. Do you have any aspirin?" He handed her the agreement and two cover letters. "Please fax these to Foxx and Sheila. I need them to go out right away."

She looked at the cover letter that Jerry had prepared on his computer at home.

"You do good work, Jerry. You're going to make me obsolete."

An hour later, he called Sheila Crown on her direct line. She answered on the second ring. "Sheila, Jerry. Hi."

"Good to hear from you, Jerry. I just finished reading the agreement. You guys negotiated an incredible deal for your brothers. I hope they appreciate it."

"Kevin does. I'm not sure that Jeff would like any deal that doesn't leave him in control of the company. If it comes down to a choice between his ego and his money, he'll always choose his ego."

"Will he follow through with the deal?" said Sheila. Jerry detected a twinge of doubt in her voice.

"He'd be a fool not to."

"Don't give me such a good opening, Jerry. We both know your brother is often irrational."

"I can't conceive of any set of circumstances that would induce him to blow this deal. Even if he were personally inclined to self-destruct, there is no way that he could jeopardize our parents' financial security or Kevin's financial security. He may be crazy, but he isn't a sociopath."

"I hope you're right. What's the game plan?"

"We expect to have the definitive agreement signed in three weeks and to close in ninety to one hundred and twenty days."

"Do you anticipate any problem in meeting those dates?"

Jerry hesitated. "Well, I did, but we've solved it. Jeff is leaving for Hawaii on Friday. He'll be there over Thanksgiving and is coming back on Monday the twenty-sixth. I convinced him to take a fax machine and his computer, so that he can work on the deal."

"You're kidding me."

"Unfortunately, I'm not. I tried to get him to defer it until after the close, but he said he couldn't because their plans involve another couple, and besides, Salli would have none of it." He paused. "He's just wired differently."

"He's got more chutzpa than brains," said Sheila. "Don't let him fuck this deal up, Jerry. My ass is hanging out in left field on this one. I'm counting on you."

"I know," said Jerry. "I'll do my best."

"You have to do better than your best. You need to make it happen."

17

Jeff adjusted the screen of his laptop computer to get it out of the bright sunlight. He took a sip from the bottle of Amstel light, looked at the marked-up document to his side, and began typing. From the lanai of the condo at the Kanipalli Alii, he could see the broad expanse of Kanipalli beach and the bright blue ocean beyond. To his right, behind the sliding glass door, was the dining room that he had converted into an office. There were two Hewlett Packard fax machines, two telephones, a Canon bubble jet printer, a desktop Minolta copier, and a half dozen banker boxes stuffed with files. Piles of paper covered the dining room table.

Behind the table were two artist's easels, each holding a large flip-chart pad. On the left-hand pad was printed FOXX DEAL. On the right-hand one was MY DEAL. On each chart he had listed with red Magic Marker the dates of the month, and beside each date, written in black, were the tasks that needed to be done or events that were supposed to occur.

The phone rang. He picked up the receiver from the cradle at his feet.

"Howard? You got the fax?"

"Yes."

"Are the changes clear?"

"Perfectly. I'll incorporate them into Charlie's draft and fax the revised agreement to both of you tonight."

"Good. What else is happening?"

"We're compiling the schedules that we need for Charlie's agreement. Fortunately Foxx asked for some of the same schedules, so I can use my staff to prepare them without creating a problem."

"Is anyone suspicious?" He'd been anxious about a possible slip-up that would draw the questions that could unravel his plan. However, each call from Howard slightly ameliorated his fear. Howard knew how to hold things together.

"Naw. Shirley and I are controlling the faxes, the source documents, and all the drafts."

"You're certain that Jerry doesn't have a whiff of what we're doing?"

"No chance. Relax. Jerry's still on a high over the deal he cut with Foxx. Shirley says he spends most of the day bullshitting with his New York cronies and accepting their kudos. He's only coming into the office a few hours a day. And I talk with him about the Foxx deal at least a half dozen times while he's here. If he were the least bit suspicious, I'd know it."

"What's he saying about the Foxx agreement?"

"I told him that you got the package yesterday and that you planned to review it and have your suggestions to me by the weekend. He was satisfied with the schedule."

"You're going to have to drag your feet preparing some of the exhibits. We need to get the completed deal back to Charlie by Friday. That will give us two weeks to sew it up before our time runs out with Foxx. The very last thing I want to happen is for the Foxx purchase agreement to be ready for a signature before we get Charlie's deal signed and have Charlie's investors committed." He took another sip of beer. "Christ," he said, under his breath. "I feel like I'm running a CIA operation."

"What was that?" said Howard.

"Nothing. I'm just ruminating."

"Well, stop. We have the schedule of the Foxx deal under control. Foxx's lawyers asked for a number of schedules that aren't on Charlie's list. Like they want a history of the land from the time of the dinosaurs until today. Because Foxx knows the garbage business, he's real worried about any hazardous waste on the property. You won't believe the detail. It's like they want the social security number of every person who ever pissed on the dirt. We've got the environmental consultants coming out tomorrow to do their initial assessment."

"That's terrific," said Jeff, brightening. "That should slow things down."

"And another thing," said Howard. "They want us to document every product that we've ever shipped during the history of the company. Foxx wants to make sure he's not acquiring some latent product liability claim."

"What did Jerry say when you told him?"

"He shook his head and said that Foxx is the eight-hundred-pound go-rilla and for thirty-two and one-half million dollars, he could have 'every fucking document he wanted and any way he wanted it.' He's authorized me to have my staff work whatever overtime hours it will take."

Salli walked onto the lanai. She was wearing a turquoise string bikini and carrying two frothy margaritas. He looked up at her and covered the mouthpiece. "Hi, honey, I'm talking with Howard."

"Tell Howard hello and then get off the phone. I bribed Jessie to keep herself, Michelle, and the other girls away from the condo for two hours, so that we can do you know what." She pumped her hips back and forth. "We're on a tight, hopefully exquisitely tight, schedule."

Jeff laughed. "Okay, I'll shut 'er down." He removed his hand from the mouthpiece. "Howard, Salli says hi. Incidentally, have you seen Kevin?"

"Kevin hasn't been to the office since you left for Hawaii. When I need something from him, I call him. He's cool."

"I think we've covered it for now," said Jeff. "I'll look for the fax tonight and call you in the morning." He placed the receiver back in the cradle and took his margarita from Salli's hand. "I hope you're not planning to go out in public in that."

"Would I embarrass you? He who walks up and down the beach in a Speedo that leaves little to the imagination?"

"I wouldn't be embarrassed. You look incredible. I just don't want you to get any ideas when those twenty-year-old Samoan and Hawaiian studs start to hit on you."

He put his hand on Salli's buttocks and pulled her down on his lap. She set her drink on the table along side the computer, kissed him, and with her free hand started to caress the back of his head. He pulled her close and kissed her.

"How about we move to the bedroom. I'd feel guilty if the guy with the binoculars in the condo across from us had a heart attack."

"Deal," said Jeff. "Bring a pitcher of margaritas."

An hour later, Jeff and Salli were sipping their drinks in bed. She gripped his hand. "You have better stamina than when we were first married."

"It's the turquoise bikini. It provides inspiration for the geriatric set."

"I like you like this, honey."

He leaned over and kissed her. "So do I."

She ran her fingers through his hair and down the back of his neck and kneaded the muscles with a firm but gentle pressure.

"Feel good?" she said.

"You're spoiling me," he said.

She was quiet as she continued to message his neck. She took a deep breath and said, "Jeff, would you mind if I changed the subject?"

"I wasn't aware that we were on a subject."

"I'd like to be serious. That's if you feel comfortable being serious."

He turned to her, surprised. "Sure, I'm as relaxed as I'm going to be. Shoot."

She removed her hand from the back of his neck and reached for her drink. She took a sip and replaced it on the nightstand. "I'm growing increasingly uncomfortable about the deception we're involved in. It's really starting to grate on me. Deceptions, betrayal, evasion, dissembling—they are not my strong skills. As we've gotten deeper into this thing, I'm aware of how engulfing it is." She took another drink and covered herself with the sheet. "I'm lying and obfuscating to my closest friend, Carolyn, and to your parents, and your brothers. I mean this is a script out of a James Bond movie."

Jeff watched her eyes, and absorbed each word as she formed it. He hadn't given much thought to some of the issues she was raising. But he saw her point.

"But what disturbs me the most is the extent to which you are betraying Jerry. When this comes to a head and he realizes what you've done, he may walk out of your life and never look back. Lord knows, I would. And as insensitive as you are, darling..."—she smiled when she said *darling*—"you will eventually experience a terrible guilt, a horrible excruciating guilt."

Jeff sighed. He took a sip from his margarita, placed the glass on the nightstand, leaned over, and stroked her face. "Why didn't you say anything before? I mean, after our meeting with Charlie?"

"I already said that I thought it was a bad idea. But you were so committed, so focused that I didn't see any point in bringing it up again. But it has really troubled me, especially after the victory party. Remember when we walked over to greet Jerry? I had the epiphany while I walked the twenty or so steps to where he was standing. I mean like KAPOW." She hit her forehead with the heel of her right hand. "It hit me. Here was your brother, my brother-in-law, returning home after negotiating a truly incredible deal for us, and we were up to our armpits hatching a plot that would play him for a fool. Shit, Jeff, I couldn't look him in the eyes. I've been thinking about it ever since."

"I see," he said.

"Is that all? Surely you can muster up a better response." She took another sip of her drink and leaned back on the headboard.

Jeff was quiet. When he finally spoke, he did so in such a slow, deliberate manner that the words felt like a speech he'd known and only just remembered. "I've thought long and hard about what I'm—what we're doing. I certainly don't feel good about it and know that Jerry will feel betrayed and may not speak to me for years, if ever. It pains me as much as it pains you. But I've concluded that there is no other way. If we tell Jerry what we're doing before the deal with Charlie is done, it probably would screw everything up. I just can't risk it. We'll just have to live with the fallout."

"What about your parents? They're expecting to get paid back and enjoy their retirement worry-free. What about Kevin and Carolyn? The Foxx deal would set them up for life. Your deal with Charlie will keep your parents, Kevin, and Carolyn at risk. If the company fails, they will lose everything. How can you in good conscience force them to assume such a risk?"

"The company's not going to fail, Salli. The risk isn't that great. I'll handle them. They'll be okay."

"Don't you think you're being awfully cavalier with their futures?"

Jeff didn't respond.

She moved close to him, gently stroked his cheek, and then ran her hand through his hair. She spoke softly. "Jeff, is holding on to the company worth the betrayal, deceit, and general bad feelings that will follow? I could see why you were driven when you thought that you were going to wind up with an empty bag. But we now have a chance to walk away from the whole mess with two and a half million dollars after taxes plus a million and a quarter in transition salary. With my trust, we'd have a net worth of over seven and a half million. We'd be set for life. You wouldn't have to work. We could travel and live like we are right now into a very ripe old age."

He leaned over and squeezed her hand. She was attempting to persuade him, and there was no trace of her former dominance and cruelty. He capped his own discomfort and tried to respond in kind. "What you say is very true. I made the exact same analysis. We'd have an after-tax income of almost four hundred thousand dollars a year without touching principal. We could live very, very well. And don't think I don't find it enticing. I do. But..."

"What 'but?'" she said, her voice rising. "Why does there have to be a damned 'but?'"

"Listen to me." His own voice was rising. He hoped the words he was about to speak did not sound like the demand he was making of her. "This is something I need to do. I will not give up National without a fight. It's been my life. It's what I am. I can't imagine not being part of it anymore. I will not let it go—not as long as there is a small glimmer of a chance to hold on to it. Your dad's deal gives me that chance. I have to take it, Salli. I have to. I need your support. Please."

Jeff noticed that the sun was close to the horizon. He glanced at the clock.

"It's almost six. The kids will be here any minute. We better get up."

Salli didn't move. Sadness came over her face, and tears started to stream down her cheeks. Her eyes reddened.

"What's the matter, hon? Why are you crying?"

She looked at him. "I'm crying because I'm going to support you in this deception even though I know I'm being the worst kind of codependent and I'm helping you sow and nurture the seeds of your own destruction and unhappiness. That's why I'm crying. Because I don't have the guts to kick you in the balls and call up Jerry and blow your cover, even though that would be the right thing to do—the right thing for your folks, for Kevin, for Carolyn, and even for you. It would be the honorable thing to do. But in doing the honorable thing, I'd lose you. So I'm crying because your obsession with that fucking company shuts off every way out of this mess. And I'm crying because I'm frightened that you are a Judas goat and are going to lead all of us over the cliff."

She grabbed her drink off the night table and flung it against the opposite wall. The glass shattered and shards were strewn all over the bedding, the furniture and the carpeting. Jeff stared wide-eyed at the wreckage. He tried to say something to comfort her, but he couldn't get the words out.

The doorbell rang. "Mom, Dad, we're back."

18

"It's Jim Foxx," said Shirley.

"I'll take it in my office." Jerry handed Howard a sheaf of documents and walked into his office. His face was hot and he felt uncharacteristically pissed. Jerry sat down at his desk and took a long drink from his coffee mug. He did not want his agitation to traverse the phone lines to Jim's ear.

"Jim. How are you?"

"I'm okay, Jerry. I'm just getting over a bout of stomach flu. I spent Thanksgiving in bed—but I'm feeling a lot better."

"What a bummer," said Jerry. There was a brief pause. "Well, I'm certainly happy..."

"Look," said Foxx. "Let me get right to the point. I'm concerned about the time it's taking to complete the acquisition agreement. According to the timetable we worked out when you were here, it should be done on Friday, and it's not going to happen. My lawyers tell me that we're still hassling over pronouns and prepositions."

Jerry took a deep breath. He had anticipated this one. "It's somewhat more involved than pronouns and prepositions, Jim. We had a meeting to review progress last Wednesday, and Richard Krimble explained the status of all of the unresolved issues. Ninety percent of them deal with environmental problems. Richard said that your guys are being, well, he used the term 'rigid.' They're insisting that Jeff and Kevin assume a lot of risk for things that they don't know about and can't control. And Jeff is balking, as you might expect."

"It's their risk or my risk," said Jim. "And I'm the one who's laying out the thirty-two million. My lawyers are telling me that your guys are defending your words and sentences like the Russians defended Stalingrad. It's word-to-word combat. The environmental protection we're writing into the deal is no different from the boilerplate we've used on our last five deals. If you're interested, I'll send you copies of a couple of them and you can see for yourself."

Jerry thought for a moment. "That might be helpful. Why don't you do that?"

"I'll have them on your desk by Monday."

"Great," said Jerry. "I'll tear right into them. Anything else?"

"There's one other thing I need to run by you," said Jim. "One of our directors was at a United Way function in Washington D.C. last week and he overheard a conversation between two guys from Wall Street who were talking about a financing that had many of the characteristics of this National deal. Same industry. They were talking about a private placement. I told him it couldn't be National because of your agreement not to shop the deal. But I thought that I'd better discuss it with you. Jerry, is there anything going on that I should know about?"

"Absolutely not." Jerry was surprised at his voice. It sounded a lot more defensive and indignant than the comment merited. "Your deal is the only one we're working on. There is no other deal."

"That makes me feel better, Jerry. The combination of the delays in completing the paperwork and the rumors caused me a little concern. I have a lot of respect for your integrity and I couldn't believe that you would try to fuck us."

"You don't have any reason for concern, Jim. You have my word."

"That's good enough. I'll package up the environmental stuff and get it out to you. Let's give the wordsmiths another three to four days to come up with an agreement we can all live with. Say until Friday. If that doesn't work, I'll fly out to LA with my team, and we'll lock ourselves up in Krimble's office until we get it done. How does that sound?"

"Good plan," said Jerry. "I'll send you a letter confirming that we've extended the deadline until December 7. Take care now."

Jerry hung up the phone and stared at it as if he expected it to say something else. The overheard conversation raced around in his head. He put the phone back to his ear and dialed Ethan Wilson's number. Ethan was traveling, so he left a message on voice mail, and then he buzzed Shirley. He asked her to have Howard come to his office and to call Richard Krimble's office to see if he was available. Within five minutes, Howard was sitting in front of Jerry's desk looking at the speakerphone.

"I just got off the phone with Foxx. He was pretty pissed."

"Yeah?" said Howard.

"He intimated—no, intimated is the wrong word. He accused us of dragging our feet." Howard smiled faintly, but did not offer a comment. "What do you think? Has Jeff been dragging his heels?" Howard didn't jump to answer. Jerry knew him well enough to realize that he was uncomfortable.

"Things did not move very fast while Jeff was in Hawaii. There were logistical problems because of the time change. Then his fax was out for several days. He couldn't get it fixed, so we had to use FedEx, and that cost us time."

"Well, Jeff's been back for two days. Has the pace picked up?" He searched Howard's eyes for some level of comfort.

Krimble's secretary's voice came out of the speakerphone. "Just a few more minutes. He's finishing up a conference call."

"No problem," said Jerry. "We'll wait."

Howard shrugged. "He's been back at work since Tuesday. This is Wednesday. It's more like one day."

"Okay," said Jerry. "Let's not quibble. I'll ask you directly. Do you think Jeff has been dragging his feet? Just your opinion."

Howard loosened his tie. What a lousy witness he'd be, thought Jerry. "No, I don't think so. Foxx's guys are insisting on some pretty onerous language in the environmental area and I think Jeff's just being cautious."

"Hello, Jerry?" Krimble's voice boomed from the speakerphone.

Jerry turned down the volume. "Hello, Richard. I'm here with Howard. I just finished a conversation with an agitated Jim Foxx. He says we're dragging our feet and he's concerned." There was no response. "Richard?"

"Yes?"

"Well, what do you think? Is he justified?"

"I think it's taking longer than I had anticipated. But it's not my risk or your risk. It's Jeff's and Kevin's. Jeff is being very meticulous in his review of the documents."

"You're a real diplomat, Richard."

"I've been called worse."

Jerry told Richard about his conversation with Foxx and the contingency plan for the meeting. He specifically avoided relating Jim's description of the overheard conversation. "I think that a locked-door meeting is a good idea," said Richard. "December 7 is on a Friday. I'll keep the following Saturday open."

Later that day, Ethan Wilson called back and Jerry related the conversation with Foxx. "Can you put out some feelers to see who it is that's involved? My guess is that it's one of our competitors, either Eye Dentity or Identix maybe."

"Could be," said Ethan. "I'll ask around. Mind if I ask my own question?"

"Of course not."

"Why do you care? If either Eye Dentity or Identix was about to pick up a huge chunk of money, it will be a problem for Foxx, not you. He'll just have a tougher competitor to deal with. You and your brothers will be long gone."

"True," responded Jerry, "But just indulge me. Okay?"

"I'll see what I can find out. Meanwhile, I suggest you go kick some ass and take some names and get this deal done. We all have a lot riding on it."

"I intend to do just that," said Jerry. "Talk with you soon." He hung up the phone and went out to bother Shirley.

"Is Jeff around?" he asked.

"He just walked down to see Howard."

Jerry walked along the corridor and headed to the finance department. Along the way, he smiled and nodded at several employees. I should be out of here in thirty days, forty-five days max, he thought. God! His mind wandered to his apartment in New York, attending the Met, working some deals, and going to a Yanks game. He almost collided with a secretary who was carrying a stack of files. Then, he thought of Helen, and his reverie was broken. What in the hell was he going to do about Helen? The time was approaching when she would make the decision for him and take the job in Paris. He needed to decide—and despite all of the good times and intimacy they had enjoyed, he would not make a commitment. He wanted to. He planned to. He needed to. But he simply could not bring himself to say yes.

He reached Howard's closed office door. The department secretary was gone, so he knocked and walked in. Jeff and Howard stopped talking immediately and turned. Both appeared surprised. He noted that as Howard turned toward him, Howard's eyes avoided his own.

"Sorry to barge in," Jerry said, "I hope I'm not interrupting anything important."

"No, not at all," said Jeff. The startled expression was quickly replaced by the broad white trademark smile. Howard still appeared to be ill at ease. "Sit down.

Howard was just briefing me on the unresolved issues in the Foxx deal," said Jeff. "I guess you talked with Jim this morning."

"He was pretty upset, Jeff. He thinks we're dragging our heels. He's extending the deal a week and said that if we don't have it signed by December 7, he'll come out and stay until it's signed. Can you clear your calendar for the next several days, so that we can get this done?" Jerry recognized the supplicant in him, imploring Jeff to cooperate, so that he could get on with his real life.

Jeff reached for his Day-Timer and turned the pages, frowning. "Sorry, bro, I'm leaving for New York tonight. I'll be in New York on Thursday and Philadelphia on Friday. I'm staying in Philadelphia over the weekend. Be in Atlanta on Monday, Austin Tuesday, and Dallas Wednesday. I won't be back in the office until next Thursday, the sixth, at the earliest."

Jerry felt his face flush and a lump begin to develop in his throat. He took a deep breath and said, "Can't you reschedule?"

"No can do, bro. I set all these appointments before I went on vacation. There are simply too many people to coordinate. We'll have to let the meeting with Foxx slide for a week. Sorry." He grinned.

Jerry's head hammered and he felt as if he were about to lose it. Nothing had changed. Jeff could still play his emotions better than any concertmaster could play the violin. Suddenly, he felt very tired. He realized that yelling and screaming at Jeff and punctuating his outburst with various expletives would have absolutely no effect on the outcome.

"Can I presume that you still want to do the deal with Foxx?" said Jerry, trying not to sound sarcastic.

Jeff smiled broadly and laughed. "Of course. I just have to tend to the business. Tell Jim I've arranged all these customer calls. There are large orders at stake. I'm sure he'll understand. After all, we don't want to sell him an empty barrel, do we?"

"Can you clear your schedule for the week of December 9?"

"Of course. I'm marking my calendar now." He jotted some notes into his Day-Timer. "We're all set."

"Fine," said Jerry. "I'll tell Krimble and I'll put Foxx's trip off until December 14." He slowly lifted himself out of the chair. His level of weariness was unexpected. He walked to the door, across the threshold, and closed the door behind him.

19

FRIDAY, NOVEMBER 30, 1990

He arrived at Helen's apartment feeling like a dishrag ready for the garbage pail. An excruciating headache made spots dance in his vision, and he was aware of the first throat irritation that usually telegraphed a developing cold. He told himself that his sluggishness was a result of his inability to get a good night's sleep because Foxx's legalisms kept seeping into his dreams—and that it had nothing to do with Jeff and the emotional letdown following the frisson of the Foxx negotiation. Jim had absorbed the news of further delay with equanimity and good nature, and Jerry had dodged another bullet. Maybe he was being paranoid. But he couldn't shake the discomfort over the Washington D.C. conversation and would feel a lot better when Ethan got back to him.

He had been feeling so bad that he had called Helen to cancel their date, but she suggested—no, she insisted—that he come for dinner and relax and she would nurse him. He asked her if he could bring Chelsey and she agreed with exuberance. "We can be real family tonight—Mommy, Daddy, and Chelsey!"

Chelsey was sleeping in front of the fire. She was on her stomach with her snout on the floor between her two front paws. The white tennis sock that she had been chewing was at her side. "She certainly knows how to make herself right at home," said Helen. "I'm surprised you don't bring her over all the time. She's so darling."

"You'll find out why the next time you vacuum."

"I don't mind," said Helen. "How are you feeling?"

"A lot better. The salmon was fantastic. How did you learn how to be such a great cook?" She had prepared a salmon filet garnished with red peppers and chilies.

"I read cookbooks like you read *Fortune, Forbes* and *Business Week*. I just try different dishes. When one works out, I put it in my repertoire. How about dessert? I have cheesecake with a raspberry topping."

The cheesecake did sound great, but his sick stomach threatened to betray him. He didn't want to take any chances. "No, honey. I surrender. I'll just finish up this glorious wine."

Helen smiled. "Okay, I'll give it to my neighbor. I don't need the fat grams anyway." She took a sip of her wine and set the glass back down on the table. She wiped her lips with the flowered napkin. She moved her chair close, took his hand, and gazed deeply into his eyes. "Jerry, I've arranged for the movers to pack the condo next Saturday, the eighth. I'm planning to leave for Paris on the fifteenth of December."

Jerry sat quietly and did not comment. As he absorbed the words and their implication, he felt a twinge of nausea start to move up his esophagus. He quickly reached for his glass of water.

She grabbed a tissue from the box on an adjacent table and dabbed at her eyes. "I wanted you to hear it from me first. The gallery is insisting that I be there for the Christmas holidays. I can't..." her voice started to stretch thin. "I promised myself I would not cry." She took a sip of wine, and back in control, said, "I can't see any reason for not going."

Jerry started to speak. Helen put her hand over his lips. "You don't need to say anything, darling. Don't need to explain or apologize." Her eyes filled with tears. She let out a high-pitched sob and let her head fall into her hands. For the next several minutes, she cried quietly against her forearms. Then, she raised her head, wiped her eyes with her hand, and said, "Don't make this harder on me than it already is. We both recognize that you're not ready to make a commitment and I'm not going to pressure you into something you're not comfortable with."

They sat quietly for several minutes, holding hands. Finally, she got up and went into the kitchen. When she emerged, she was composed and except for the redness in her eyes, it would have been difficult to determine that she had been crying. She sat down at the table and took another sip of wine.

"I'm planning to stay with Carolyn and Kevin when the condo is empty. They offered me the guest room. The only stipulation was that I not entertain any gentlemen admirers in my room." She smiled. "That means we'll have to meet at your place. Is that okay with you? I'll be welcome, won't I?"

"Helen, you know I love you very much. More than I've loved any other woman in my life, but I…"

Helen was shaking her head. "Don't say any more, Jerry. I'm all right with this. If and when you decide to take the next step in our relationship, you'll know what to do. You're not ready. I'm disappointed, but I'm not devastated. We're still in love with each other and maybe, someday, we'll get married and build a life together. I hope so, because I hope there is more to life than just work, sex, and a kitchen hobby. But in the meantime, I'm not going to drive both of us crazy and become a pushy bitch."

Jerry stood up from the table. He took Helen's hand. She stood up. He pulled her close. He wanted to devour her, to bathe in her smell. He kissed her hair and ran his hands over the parts of her body he could reach while holding her in an embrace. As he kissed her, he recalled the first time they had made love. The fatigue was gone. The sore throat forgotten. "You're wonderful," he said.

"Why don't you take a shower and relax in bed, while I clean up the kitchen. Then how about a massage?"

"Sounds wonderful."

Twenty minutes later, she came into the bedroom. She took off her clothes and went into the bathroom to wash off her makeup and get ready for bed. When she came out of the bathroom, she had the wintergreen scented body lotion she planned to use, and walked over to the bed. Jerry was on his stomach.

Helen climbed onto the bed and kneeled at the end next to Jerry's feet. She pulled off the sheet that was covering his nude body and threw it on the floor. She depressed the plunger of the bottle of body lotion several times until she was satisfied with the quantity in her hands. She set the bottle on the bed next to her and rubbed her hands together to warm the lotion. She lifted Jerry's left foot and began to massage it. She ran her lotion-slick fingers through his toes and grasped his foot in both hands and kneaded it with a firm, gentle pressure.

"That feels good," said Jerry.

"I didn't know if I should just let you go to sleep. I decided that you would prefer the feel of my hands exploring all the nooks and crannies of your body. Was I right?"

"Good decision," said Jerry.

She lifted up his right foot and pressed and caressed it in the same manner. Then, she straddled his feet and began to massage the backs of his legs from his buttocks to his feet.

Jerry continued to lie on his stomach enjoying the sensations. His thoughts bent toward the realization that this excruciatingly sensuous experience would not likely be revisited any time soon. The sadness leached into his mind.

The vast, lofty courtroom was filled to capacity. Jerry sat at the defendant's table, which was to the left of the elevated judge's platform. He slouched in his chair. He looked around the room for support. He saw that his parents were in the front row, smiling benignly. Jerry turned his head toward his attorney, the famous Fetyukovich, who was dressed in a frock coat and white tie. To the right of defendant's table was the prosecutor's table. The prosecutor, Ippolit Kirillovich, appeared nervous and was sweating profusely. Between the tables of the defense and the prosecution was the evidence table that held Helen's ticket to Paris, a photo of Helen and Jerry taken at the restaurant in the marina where they had enjoyed the fireworks, the receipt from their stay at the Cliff Hotel in San Francisco, and Helen's spreadsheets.

The judge announced the hearing of the case of the neglect and abandonment of Helen Knudsen by the defendant Jerry Bascomb. He asked the prosecution and defense to identify themselves. After they announced their names, the judge smiled and said, "Gentlemen, it's good to see you again. I presume you've both recovered from the Karamazov case. To almost everyone's surprise, Counselor Kirillovich pulled that one out of the hat, so to speak. And, I see the entire district is here to observe the rematch in the Bascomb case. So let's get on with it," he said, waving his hand toward the assembled throng.

Jerry sat quietly as the clerk read the charges against him sonorously and distinctly.

Right after the reading, the prosecutor demanded of Jerry, "Defendant, how to you plead to the charge of first degree stupidity?"

Jerry had dozed off. Fetyukovich shook him.

The prosecuting attorney said, "This miserable excuse for a virile, intelligent man is about to allow the most lovely, sensitive, and caring woman, the woman he's loved more than any other woman in his forty years, walk out of his life. Your Honor, we will prove, beyond any reasonable doubt, that Jerry Bascomb is an idiot and doesn't deserve any compassion from this court."

Fetyukovich leaped to his feet. "Objection, Your Honor. The prosecutor must let the defendant plead."

"Sustained," said the judge. He looked at Jerry. "Mr. Bascomb! Mr. Bascomb! Wake up. You need to enter a plea."

Jerry was startled by the harsh voice.

"Yes, Your Honor?"

"What do you have to say for yourself? You stand accused of first-degree stupidity for allowing a wonderful, lovely, sensitive, and caring woman, Helen, to slip through your fingers and walk out of your miserable life. How do you plead? Do you plan to offer a defense? Come on, get on with it."

Jerry stood up. He approached the lectern. He cleared his throat. "You know..." Jerry panicked. He forgot what he was going to say. His mind went absolutely blank. He stood at the lectern, speechless. He appeared to be disoriented and looked to his attorney for help.

Helen's body was moving over him. She straddled his buttocks, and he could feel her body rubbing against his skin. She placed both her hands on his back and gracefully, slowly rubbed the lotion into him. As she learned forward, hands over his shoulders, her breasts glided over his back. He felt a twinge of arousal—just the early stages. But he found he could not focus on it because of the image of himself at the lectern, speechless, grasping for some credible defense of his unfathomed stupidity.

"How do you feel," she said.

"Need you ask? I'm filled with pleasure."

"Good," she said. "Let's see if I can improve on that, just slightly. Turn over."

He turned over on his back and soon all thoughts of his trial vanished from his mind, and he gratefully yielded his mind and body to her.

The following Monday when Jerry arrived at the office, Shirley greeted him with the news that there were two large piles of documents on his desk, courtesy of Jim Foxx. Jerry entered his office. There was a note from Jim on one of the piles wishing him well and advising him that if he needed more information, it would be promptly provided. Jerry smiled to himself. He should have been more careful about what he asked for.

Jerry picked up the top document from the largest pile and scanned it. It was an opinion from a prominent New York law firm discussing the myriad environmental issues that needed to be addressed in any transaction that involved the purchase of real property. Jerry looked over the masthead that listed the attorneys in the firm. He recognized several of the names. That will be helpful, he thought. During the next hour, he looked at each of the documents and mentally assessed how long it would take to read each one and the various lines of inquiry that each might stimulate. As he plowed through the pile, it became clear that Jim Foxx had used his long history in the waste industry to attempt to create a legal shield that would make him absolutely bulletproof with respect to any exposure to environmental liability. He could see how the competence and prestige of Foxx's legal team could easily overwhelm a legal general practitioner like Richard Krimble.

Jerry called Richard and asked him whether he had thought about retaining a law firm with environmental expertise. Richard replied that he had not considered it necessary, and then hastily added that in light of how the negotiations had bogged down, his decision should be revisited.

"I think we need a heavy hitter, both to help us negotiate with Foxx and to give some degree of comfort to Jeff and Kevin. I can read all this stuff, which I intend to do anyway, but at the end of the day, I'll still be an informed layman and have no serious influence on Jeff. He'll still be suspicious."

"You're right," said Richard. "You need the expertise as much for the politics as for the due diligence. Do you have any ideas?"

"Everyone I know is in New York," said Jerry.

"Okay, I'll make some calls in the morning and get back to you before the end of the day."

Jerry buzzed Shirley to see if there were any messages. He returned several telephone calls. Then, he leaned back in his chair, took the top document off of the first pile, and began to read.

During the next several days, Jerry threw himself into the project. He read through everything Foxx had sent. He called various associates in New York to get additional tracts and references. He spent several days interviewing firms that Richard Krimble had identified and during the interview process was able to test his new fund of knowledge about the arcane world of environmental law. A resolution to the environmental controversies and the proper crafting of the related sections of the acquisition agreement was the last hurdle between him and a completed transaction—and a ticket back to New York City. He was determined to do everything in his power to earn it. Besides, he enjoyed the challenge. It was something new to learn and the learning had a clear purpose.

Jerry knew himself well when it came to new challenges. He prided himself in his ability to tackle a new topic, issue, field of knowledge, and in a relatively short period of time, acquire information, insight, and understanding, so that he could speak with confidence to those who were experts in the field. He had done it many times in both his engineering and legal careers. When he went into the knowledge acquisition mode, he would spend hours in the library, digging out books and articles. And he would network among friends and associates to identify experts who might send him information or suggest other paths of inquiry. Jerry always felt that his dogged persistence was the key to the successes that he had achieved.

Adrenaline pumped through his veins, as he devoured the stacks of documents, articles, and books to discover how Foxx had erected his legal defense against future environmental exposure. He looked for clues to how to create enough chinks in the wall to provide some comfort to Jeff and Kevin.

Jerry's days were consumed with environmental law and his evenings were consumed with Helen. The evening she told him of her plans to pack everything up and move to Paris was a watershed. They had come to an accommodation. She would no longer be critical of his reluctance to make a commitment and he would no longer be defensive over his inability to do so. Consequently, they were able to devote all of their energies to enjoying themselves, satisfying each other, and making the most of the time they had before Helen left for France. Jerry felt equanimity about the relationship. "What will be, will be," he kept thinking. For the first time in several months, he didn't feel any guilt.

Ethan Wilson called to report that he had not been able to learn anything related to the Washington D.C. conversation.

Jerry called Jeff at hotels and at customers' offices to discuss the deal, the progress he'd made on the environmental issue, and his negotiation strategy. Jeff was always polite and interested and usually offered insightful comments. Jerry was feeling better about the deal's pace, even if it was slow.

On Thursday afternoon, Jerry was finishing up a memorandum on his negotiation strategy. Shirley buzzed him on the intercom.

"Jeff called from the Dallas Airport. He's arriving at 5:30. He'd like you to attend a meeting with the family at 7:30 at Kevin's home. He's already arranged for Richard Krimble to be there."

Jerry felt a twinge of anxiety.

"Is he on the line? Can I talk with him?"

"No, he called from the gate. He's on the plane now."

Jerry hung up the phone. The twinge of anxiety was starting to grow into a knot. He called Richard Krimble to ask if he knew what Jeff wanted to talk about.

"Your guess is as good as mine," Richard said.

Jerry's call to Kevin elicited the same response. His nervousness started to grow. Calm down, he thought. Jeff is probably just looking for some assurance. He's just being overly dramatic. Jerry called Helen to advise her that he would be busy tonight. He decided to keep it vague, because he didn't want to encourage his growing anxiety by talking about it.

His watch read 4:30 p.m. He'd have enough time to go home, take Chelsey for a walk, and get something to eat. Maybe he would even drink a glass or two of wine to calm his nerves and get him ready for several hours of Jeff's crap.

Kevin swung open the door to a house that smelled of baked goods. "Hi, Jerry," he said. "Come on in and help yourself to peach cobbler and coffee. Mom assured me that it's less than a thousand calories per slice." Jerry greeted his brothers and sisters-in-law and embraced his mother and father. He poured a cup of coffee, picked up a dessert dish, and sat down on the oversized loveseat next to Richard. As Jerry sipped his coffee, he tried to pick up the substance of the discussion between Jeff and Kevin. His mind was still fuzzy from the three glasses of Merlot.

"What are they talking about?" he asked Richard.

"Jeff came home with the Defense Intelligence Agency deal. It's worth about six million."

Jerry let out a low whistle. "No shit. Boy that is something." He turned to Jeff. "You brought back the contract?"

Jeff smiled at him. "Absolutely. The first phase is for six million. I estimate that there'll be at least another ten million at the DIA over the next two to three years. We beat out Eye Dentity and Continental. We now have the inside track to become the gold standard for iris systems." Jerry noticed that Salli was sitting very close to Jeff.

"Congratulations, Jeff. That is one helluva accomplishment."

"Thanks, bro. I'm feeling pretty high about it."

Jeff carried on about his recent trip and the various business prospects for a long time. Jerry could tell that Richard was uncomfortable. He sat stoically sipping his coffee, nodding periodically, and often looked at his watch. Richard finally turned to Jeff and said, "I have to leave by 8:45. Could you please share with us what you have on your mind?"

Jeff's smile disappeared as if the blinds in a room were suddenly drawn. The conversation in the room shut down and all eyes were on Jeff—all eyes except Salli's. Salli put her hand on Jeff's knee.

"Well, yes," said Jeff. "You're right." He opened his briefcase and removed a stack of papers about an inch thick. "Sorry, I got carried away with the war stories." He handed the papers to Salli and asked her to pass them out.

Salli stood and walked around the room handing out the documents. As she gave Jerry his document, she lowered her eyes and whispered, "I'm sorry."

Jerry scanned the three pages. Then, he turned back to the beginning of the first page and read it more carefully. Nausea clamped down in his gut.

"Salli's handed you a document that summarizes the terms and conditions of the financing I've arranged," said Jeff. "The financing group, led by Charlie Knudsen, is going to invest nine million dollars for a 34 percent equity position in National. Kevin and I will each own approximately 25.5 percent of the refinanced company. The sub-debt will be extended for three years, and they will be given warrants to purchase 10 percent of the company at the same price the investors are paying. I will be CEO of the refinanced company, and Kevin will be CTO. Our salaries will be two hundred thousand a year. Kevin will be able to set his own hours. The board will consist of me, Kevin, Charlie, and two people from the investor group."

Jerry's nausea was now fully matured. His head throbbed. He wiped the perspiration from his forehead with a paper napkin. The room was very quiet. The recent clinking of the forks against the dessert dishes and the cups scraping the saucers was a memory. It had been less than five minutes since Salli had handed out the document, but Jerry realized that his life was metamorphosing. He tried to speak, but couldn't get any words through his constricted throat and his dry lips. Jim Foxx's words rang in his ears, "I have a lot of respect for your integrity and I couldn't believe you would fuck us." Wrong, Jim. He looked at Jeff. Jeff's eyes were cold, expressionless. Salli stared straight ahead. His parents continued to look at the document, apparently not comprehending its import. Carolyn and Kevin were whispering. He was living a Franz Kafka novel.

Richard broke the silence. "I presume that this proposed financing supersedes the Foxx deal?"

"Right," said Jeff. "We will abandon the Foxx deal. The investment package includes the one million to pay the breakup fee to Foxx."

"But according to my calculation, the deal is about three million short of what you will need to pay the bank off and to pay Foxx his million dollar breakup fee," said Richard.

"That's correct," said Jeff. "We will only have sufficient funds to pay the bank about 78 percent of what they're owed. They will have to take a haircut."

"Have you talked with them? Have they agreed?"

"No. We will tell them tomorrow as soon as you can arrange a meeting."

Jerry's eyes wandered around the room. He found it difficult to concentrate on what Jeff and Richard were saying. He tried to catch Kevin's eye, but Kevin and Carolyn were still engrossed in a whispered conversation.

"I presume you and Kevin have discussed this situation thoroughly and the two of you are in agreement," said Richard, trying desperately to avoid sounding sarcastic.

Jerry could tell from Richard's tone that he knew that this deal was as big a surprise to Kevin as it was to everyone else. "No, I haven't," said Jeff. "None of the family has been advised or consulted. This is my deal. This is the first time anyone in the room has heard of it, other than Salli."

Richard put the memo into his briefcase. He squirmed in his seat, trying to find a comfortable position. He formed a steeple with his long bony fingers, leaned back in the loveseat and, emphasizing every word, said, "Don't you believe that you're being premature in advising the bank before all the shareholders and note holders have had a chance to mull over and discuss..."

Jeff interrupted him. "Richard, this deal is not negotiable. I vote all of the stock and I'm making the decision to go forward with this financing. Period." As he completed the sentence, he looked at Kevin and Carolyn. "I'm sorry to have to preempt you on this, Kevin, and I regret that I couldn't tell you and Carolyn, or Jerry." He turned and looked at

Jerry, but his glance didn't linger for more than an instant. "But I needed to keep the deal under wraps. I didn't want to put the Foxx deal at risk before I had nailed down the financing with Charlie." Jeff allowed a faint smile to appear. "I knew that neither you nor Jerry would ever agree to participate in such a Machiavellian scheme, so I had to keep you both in the dark. Also, I felt that maintaining the element of surprise would give us the best shot at getting the bank to sign off on the deal."

Kevin sat forward, his head drooped, and he looked as if he had eaten something that did not agree with him. He raised his eyes slightly and stared at Jeff. "Other than you and Salli, who else knows about this deal?" he said.

"Howard, Shirley, Allen, and Sam Trinkle, my personal attorney."

"Howard? Shirley?" said Jerry.

"Yes," said Jeff. "I needed them to help prepare the due diligence information for the investors. They both felt pretty lousy about having to keep you in the dark. Don't be angry with them. They were following my instructions."

Jerry knew he was going to lose it. The room was spinning. His first reaction was to scream at Jeff, but he couldn't muster the energy. Speaking to no one in particular, he said, "Can we take a break. I need some air." Without waiting for a response, he stood up and hurried toward the French doors that led to the side patio. He opened the doors and felt the clear cool night air on his overheated face. He took a deep breath. His right fist was clenched so tight that he had dug his fingernails into the palm of his hand. Tears welled up in his eyes. He thought about Adlai Stevenson's quip, "It hurts too much to laugh and I'm too old to cry." The enormity of Jeff's deception beat against his brain. His own brother had organized a conspiracy to betray him. Jeff had used Jerry's trusted confidants to carry out the scheme. His promises and assurances to Sheila Crown and Jim Foxx weren't worth a damn. No one would believe that he had not been part of it. His reputation would be ruined. The very brother for whom he had sacrificed the last six months of his life would destroy him. He wanted to yell "fucking bastard," but he constrained himself in deference to his parents and the neighbors. He walked around the patio once, twice. He sat down in one of the patio chairs and held his head between his hands, pressing against his throbbing temples that were threatening to blow his head off.

"Jerry," his father called. "We need to get started again. Richard needs to leave in ten minutes."

"I'll be right in, Dad." He lifted himself off of the bench. He took a deep breath and tried to suppress the urge to vomit. Then, he was on his knees regurgitating his last meal and the three glasses of Merlot. When he recovered, he stood up and inspected his trousers and shoes. His knees were wet from the dew on the patio. There was puke all over his shoes. He took off his shirt and undershirt and used the undershirt to wipe off his pants and shoes. Fortunately, his trousers were black and the wetness would not stand out. He put his shirt back on and deposited the undershirt in the garbage can that was adjacent to the kitchen door. He walked back into the house and into the living room and sat down next to Richard. Kevin looked at him and shook his head slowly.

"Let's cut to the chase, Jeff," said Richard. "You intend to use Kevin's proxy to vote to accept this deal, independent of how Kevin feels about it? Even if he's against it and wants to continue with the Foxx deal?"

Jeff nodded and said, "Yes."

Richard looked at Kevin. "Kevin, as the attorney for the corporation, I am advising you that you do not have to accede to Jeff's plan. You could go to court and seek an injunction. I think you'd have an excellent chance to prevail."

Kevin and Carolyn looked at each other. Carolyn nodded. Kevin turned back to Richard. "I understand, Richard. But I'm not going to start suing members of my immediate family at this stage in my life. I don't agree with what Jeff's done. In fact, I'm very angry with him. He's treated both Jerry and me horribly, and it's going to take me a long time to get over it." Kevin took a sip of cold coffee. He swallowed.

"But he's my brother, and I believe that he thinks he's doing what's best for all of us."

He turned to Carolyn and gripped her hand. "Right, hon?"

Carolyn nodded.

"Mr. and Mrs. Bascomb," said Richard. "Are you willing to go along with this arrangement? You will, as I understand it, continue to receive your interest. Your note will be due in three years, and as a concession for rolling it over, you'll be able to buy 1.5 percent of the company at the same price as the new investors, if you so desire."

"We can't afford to buy it," said Mrs. Bascomb. "All of our money is tied up in the business."

"Mom, you don't have to buy it now. You'd only buy it if it were worth more at some time in the future. It's a gift, Mom. It won't cost you anything," said Jeff.

He turned to his father. "You understand, don't you, Dad?" Sid nodded.

"What if the bank rejects the offer?" said Jerry. "They're expecting to receive one 100 percent of their principal and you're offering 78 percent."

"I'm betting that they'll take it," said Jeff. "Their liquidation value is less than 50 percent of their note. They'll squirm and squeal and yell. But at the end of the day, they'll take it. Don't you agree, Richard?"

Richard didn't respond immediately. Finally, he said, "I've repeatedly stated that I don't try to predict bank decisions. There are always too many variables. But, if your numbers are correct and the bank's only alternative to the two point eight million dollar haircut is a six and one-half million dollar loss through liquidation, they will probably take it. We'll just have to see how they react." He put his papers into his briefcase. "I'll call Bill Bromfield in the morning and try for a meeting later in the day. I'll call you as soon as I firm something up." He turned to Jerry. "I assume you would just as soon stay out of this?"

Jerry glared at Jeff. "You are correct!"

Richard stood up and prepared to leave. "I'll be on my way," said Richard.

Jerry stood up. "I'm not feeling well. I'd better go home and get some sleep."

The living room had a funereal atmosphere. Jeff and Salli appeared cool and reserved. Kevin and Carolyn appeared dejected. The Bascombs continued to look bewildered. No one felt the need or obligation to escort Richard and Jerry to the door.

Jerry started to say his perfunctory good nights and stopped mid-sentence.

"I'd like to ask you one question, Jeff."

"Shoot," said Jeff. He seemed more relaxed now that the ordeal was over.

"In light of the fact that the Foxx deal would pay off Mom and Dad in full and make you and Kevin multimillionaires, and allow all of you to enjoy a high standard of living, free from the risks that besiege 99 percent of the population, why in the hell are you doing this? Why are you taking on the risk and why are you forcing Kevin, Carolyn, Mom, and Dad to take on the risk especially in light of Kevin's health and Mom and Dad's age?"

Richard stood at the front door that was partially opened. The room remained quiet. No one moved. Jeff appeared to be organizing his thoughts. Jerry knew Jeff well enough to know that he had prepared a response for just this type of situation. Jerry really didn't care what the rationale was. It no longer mattered. But he wanted Kevin and Carolyn and his parents to hear it.

"I don't think there is any serious risk," said Jeff. "If I thought so, I would go along with the Foxx deal. The company is worth a lot more than what Foxx has offered to pay. I'm not going to sit by and let him steal the company that Kevin and I have poured our lives into. It's that simple. If you had been here for the last ten years rather than in New York playing investment banker, you would feel exactly the same way."

Jerry shook his head. "I'm sure you don't care a whit what I think, but for the record, I find your argument self-serving and irrational. In essence, you have sold us all out for what will likely turn out to be a mess of pottage." He said goodnight to no one in particular and followed Richard out the door.

When they were outside, Richard turned to Jerry and said, "As a friend, I can say that you certainly deserved better. I'm very sorry."

Jerry struggled to keep back his tears. He shook Richard's hand and said, "Thanks, Richard, thanks. Just keep me informed." He turned away, so that Richard would not see that he had begun to cry, and walked to his car.

20

The drive back from Kevin's was harrowing. His mind kept wandering. He lost his driving concentration several times and only just missed barreling into a dark pickup that was stopped for a light. When he finally pulled into the driveway, he said a prayer of thanks.

Chelsey panted and jumped up when Jerry walked through the door. He grabbed the leash from the kitchen counter and left the condominium to take her for a walk. As he led her through the dark streets punctuated by lighted windows, he felt some slight gratification that at the very least he could count on her loyalty.

By the time he got inside the condo, his head was about to explode. His muscles ached. His only thought was of the large tumbler of Jameson he would soon consume and the shower that would follow. As he walked through the door, he pulled off his clothes and dropped them in the living room on the way to the bathroom. He entered the shower and adjusted the showerhead to create a narrow high-pressure stream. He set it at the highest temperature he could endure, and then stood under the shower for twenty minutes until all the hot water was gone. He put on his white terrycloth robe and walked into the kitchen. He measured out a cup of kibble into Chelsey's bowl and filled it partway with warm water. He poured six ounces of Jameson into an eight-ounce tumbler and added crushed ice until the glass was full. He took two swallows and called his voicemail. There was a message from Helen, asking him to call before he went to sleep, no matter what the time. There was a message from Kevin asking him to call in the morning. He debated whether to call Helen immediately. It was 10:45 p.m. He definitely did not feel like talking long and wanted to avoid relating anything that had occurred at the meeting.

She'd hear about it soon enough. He decided to return the call and get it over with. He needed the rest of the night to think about what happened and what if anything he could do about it.

He dialed Helen's number. She answered on the second ring.

"I've been thinking about you all night," she said. "How did your meeting go?"

"Fine," he lied. "Routine matters."

"I hope you don't mind my being so possessive. Time is running out and I want to stock up on your presence. It will help carry me through the lean times."

"I understand," he said. He knew he was sounding abrupt. "Honey, I'm exhausted. Can we just say goodnight?"

"I understand. How does tomorrow look?" she said.

"As of now, I'm clear. How about I call you around noon?"

"I'll be out shopping. Just leave a message on my voice mail. Try not to disappoint me."

"Not seeing you is a disappointment for both of us. I love you, Helen. Don't believe for a moment that I'm not wracked with anxiety over your move."

"That's sweet," she said. "Goodnight. Have a good sleep."

He placed the phone on the cradle. He picked up his half full glass of Jameson and ice and walked into the living room. He sat down on the sofa and clicked on the TV. It was almost time for the eleven o'clock news. He gave himself permission to watch the news and then Ted Koppel's Nightline before he started to seriously think about the implication of Jeff's revelation. The news came on at eleven, and ten minutes later, he was asleep.

A blaring infomercial for an abdominal exercise machine awakened him. He looked at his watch. Two thirty-five. He felt refreshed. The headache was gone. Then, he remembered the meeting and sagged back into the couch. Chelsey was snoring at the other end, oblivious to the television. He turned on the mute button, and as the silent male and female images cavorted in their quasi-erotic spandex gym attire, he tried to organize his thoughts. But no sooner did he resolve to stop thinking about the effect of Jeff's action on his reputation and his career, and to discover the options available to deal with it, that his mind drifted into the victim status that he now shared with all the other betrayed brothers in the Bible, history and literature.

There was Cain who murdered his brother Abel because God preferred Abel's sacrificial calf to Cain's. Then, there was Jacob, who with his mother's help, masqueraded as his brother Esau to deceive the blind Isaac and steal the blessing that was intended for Esau. Jerry was feeling better. Somehow it was comforting to know that his misery had also been experienced by others—what the Germans call *Schadenfreude*. He was into the game. It was like a personal version of a TV quiz show. How many cases of betrayed brothers could he identify? Ah-ha! Joseph and his coat of many colors. His brothers were jealous of him, so they sold him into slavery, the bastards. He looked for his glass of Jameson. It was about one third full. He walked into the kitchen and added some ice from the refrigerator, swished the ice around in the glass, and then drank the remaining liquid in one long gulp. Who else? He reached into the recesses of that portion of his memory that housed what remained of his Sunday school education.

The bible was full of stories of brothers betraying brothers. He remembered that Aaron, Moses' brother, created the Golden Calf for the Israelites to worship, while Moses was on Mount Sinai receiving the Ten Commandments. Was that a betrayal or was Aaron just a weakling who couldn't provide leadership while Moses was away? No, thought Jerry. He doesn't qualify.

He picked up a yellow tablet and pen. He sat down on the couch and switched off the television. As he thought, he jotted down notes. Was there anything he could do to stop Jeff? What were the options? There was no talking Jeff out of the financing. That was clear. And he couldn't do anything that would increase the stress on Kevin. His health couldn't handle it.

He paused with his pen in midair. George, the Duke of Clarence. Richard III's brother whom he had murdered to clear his path to the throne. That's rich, he thought. In many ways Jeff is a perfect clone of Richard III—ruthless, deceptive, and callous. Jeff's a Richard III without the physical deformities. The fucker! And I'm George—loyal, trusting, and slick of tongue. What about Salli? She didn't seem very happy. Wouldn't work. She's been part of the plot. She's sold out. And she was supposed to be Carolyn's best friend.

Anyone else in Shakespeare? Brutus conspired with Cassius to murder Julius Caesar. *Et tu, Brute?* But Brutus was just a colleague and a "friend," not a blood brother. Who else?

"Ah-ha! Yes!" he yelled. Chelsey awoke and perked up her ears. Claudius murdered his brother, Hamlet's father, to steal the throne. And then he married his sister-in-law. Ruthless and reckless, just like Jeff. Why am I shocked? Jeff betrayed Salli during their engagement and during their marriage by screwing Helen. And who knows how many other women he fucked during the marriage. And the nude photos of him and Helen with Maurice and Maya. Mindless! Insane! My brother has thought with his cock for his entire adult life. How the hell can we be related? He's not at all like Kevin or Dad or me. No. He's more like Dad than me. Maybe Mom had an affair while Dad was in Korea and Dad's not my biological father. Possible. Mom was real attractive when she was young, and Dad was away a lot, and she certainly had the opportunity. That would explain it. He shook his head. This wasn't helping. The fact was, it was a *fait accompli*. There was nothing to be done.

"I'm fucked and so are Kevin, Carolyn. Mom, Dad, and the bank. The cocksucker has done a number on all of us."

He got up from the sofa, picked up the clothes he had dropped in the living room, woke Chelsey, and went into the bedroom. He set the alarm for eight a.m. He took off the bathrobe, threw it on the rocking chair in the corner, and climbed into bed.

As he lay in bed, he tried to think of other examples of betrayed brothers. As he drifted off to sleep, he remembered that John, the brother of Richard I, plotted against Richard, while he was in Jerusalem on the Third Crusade.

The phone rang. Jerry sat up in bed suddenly. He looked at the clock. It was 6:35 a.m. He had dreamed about Jeff's deception throughout the night. His head ached. He reached over to his night table and lifted the receiver from the cradle. His throat was dry.

"Jerry, it's your Dad. Sorry to wake you, but we need to talk."

"Hold on for a minute. I need to get some water."

Without waiting for an answer, he climbed out of bed and went into the bathroom. He urinated, drank an eight-ounce glass of water, and then returned to the bedroom.

"Sorry, Dad. What's up?"

"Your mother and I have been up all night. We're both devastated by what Jeff's done. For Christ's sake. We're halfway to Florida. After you came back from Utah, we made up our mind to move. We've put a deposit on a place in Ft. Myers, right on the beach."

Jerry just listened. What was there that he could say.

"And I can't keep your mother away from the bottle. She's going to drink herself to death. She's done nothing but wail and drink."

"Have you talked to Kevin?"

"No, there's no point. I know his situation. He and Carolyn were planning to split as soon as the deal closed. I'm sure he's told you about their relationship.

"You mean lack of relationship. Yeah, it's a damn shame."

Sid didn't respond. Silence.

"Is there anything I can do to help, Dad? I can give you and mom some money if you're strapped."

"No, we're okay. For now. I think I'll be able to get the deposit back. What I need from you now is to meet Jeff and myself for breakfast at Dinah's. We need to talk him out of this craziness. Will you do that, Jerry?"

Jerry didn't answer immediately. He knew he wouldn't turn his father down. But he knew the effort was futile.

"Jerry?"

"Sure, Dad, I'll meet you. Just don't get your hopes up. Okay?"

"I hear you," said Sid. "I really appreciate it. You certainly don't deserve being screwed over. Christ. You delivered a miracle. A fucking miracle."

"Don't worry about me, Dad. I'm not the issue. Kevin, Carolyn, Mom, and you are the ones at risk. We'll do what we can with Jeff. I'll see you soon."

Jeff and Sid were already sitting at a table when Jerry arrived. He said hello to his father, nodded at Jeff, and sat down across from his father, so that Jeff was seated between them. He immediately picked up the menu. "Have you ordered yet?"

"Just coffee," said Sid.

Jerry looked around the crowded restaurant and tried to get the attention of a waitress. After two failed attempts, he got up from his chair, walked over to the receptionist, and handed her a five-dollar bill. "We're really in a hurry," he said. "Can you help us?"

"Of course, sir." The five-dollar bill disappeared in her blouse, and one minute later, there was a waitress at the table taking their orders.

As the waitress left the table, Sid moved his chair closer to Jeff. He spoke so softly that it was hard for Jerry to hear above the din in the restaurant. No matter, he thought.

"Jeff," said Sid. "You gave us a helluva surprise last night. You know that, don't you?"

Jeff sat back in his chair, trying to put a little distance between himself and his father. He ignored Jerry. "I know, Dad. I didn't want to do it that way, but we had no other choice. I'm really sorry. I hope I can make it up to you."

You supercilious asshole, thought Jerry. How the fuck can you ever make "it" up?

"That's not the point," said Sid. "The shock and surprise will pass out of our memory. The point is that your plan is putting your mother and me and Kevin and Carolyn in a terrible spot. We can't move ahead with our lives. Kevin and Carolyn will not have enough money to go their separate ways, and your mother and I will not be able to relocate to Florida."

Jeff took a sip of coffee, wiped his lips, and put the napkin back on his lap.

Jerry was impressed at how calm and reasonable his father appeared. He rarely saw him this way.

His father continued. "Your mother and I have always been there for you, Jeff. I pulled the strings to get you into West Point. You asked me to come to Vietnam to help you with that Rodrigues thing and I dropped what I was doing and traveled eight thousand miles. Your mother and I have put up the money you needed to send your kids to a private school. Now I'm asking for you to stand by us. Am I being unreasonable, Jeff? Can't you empathize with our situation? Mine and Kevin's?"

Jeff looked down. His napkin had fallen off his lap. He bent down to pick it up, replaced it on his lap, and slipped the corner under his belt.

He's playing for time, thought Jerry. He couldn't help but be amused to see Jeff squirm. Not much satisfaction, but at this point Jerry, would take anything he could get. Before Jeff could respond, the waitress arrived with their breakfast sand. Soon the table was covered with plates of eggs, bacon, toast, hash brown potatoes, and marmalade.

As soon as the waitress left the table, Jeff started eating. "I'm starved," he said as he sawed into the three-egg omelet that was oozing with cheddar cheese. Jerry started to attack his eggs benedict. But as the first bite of food was moving from the plate to his mouth, he looked up and saw that his father was sitting with his hands folded, looking directly at Jeff.

"Aren't you going to eat, Dad?" said Jerry.

"I'm waiting for Jeff to answer my question. You did understand my question, Jeff?" His father appeared to be struggling to maintain the appearance of calm, but underneath that veneer, Jerry knew he was seething.

Jeff set down his fork and took another swig of coffee. "Dad, I'm really sorry that you can't see my situation. This is my chance to do something significant with my life. I mean, you got your four stars." He turned to Jerry. "Jerry's got his face plastered all over *Barron's*, the *Wall Street Journal*, and the *New York Times*. Kevin started a company that is worth over thirty million dollars. I'm nothing but an aging peddler, a Willy Lohman. Dammit," he said as he pounded on the table, "I want my chance to be somebody. And I'm going to have it. I need to do this, Dad. I was hoping that you and Kevin would support me. I'm disappointed that you won't."

A flush was enveloping Sid's face. Perspiration appeared on his upper lip. He wasn't moving.

"Dad," said Jerry. "We're not getting anywhere. There's no point in rehashing this. Jeff's going to do what he wants to do, and the rest of us can go piss up a rope."

"Be quiet," said Sid, his voice rising. He turned back to Jeff. "Are you really willing to mortgage our lives to achieve your dream? Don't you think you're being selfish, Jeff?"

"Me, selfish?" Jeff's voice was low, but each word was enunciated carefully, so that each word would hit its mark. "You're a fine one to talk about being selfish. What about you? Weren't you being selfish when you sought out the overseas assignments that would get you a vacation from fathering and husbanding? And let's not forget those extracurricular female entanglements that created so much stress on Mom that she became an alcoholic. Weren't you being selfish?"

No sooner did the last word pass from Jeff's lips, than Sid screamed, "You'd commit patricide? I'll kill you first, you *fucking ingrate*!" Sid lunged across the table and grabbed Jeff's throat. Jeff's chair fell back, and he fell to the floor with Sid on top of him. The table turned over, and the eggs, hash browns, marmalade, broken cups, and plates, were scattered on the floor. Jeff was gasping for breath.

"DAD! DAD! STOP!" Jerry got down on his knees next to Jeff and tried to pry Sid's hands off of Jeff's throat. But Sid's fingers held tight like steel bands. "Dad, *stop*! You're going to kill him!" All of a sudden, Jerry experienced some success in loosening Sid's grip. He looked up and saw that a uniformed LAPD policeman had placed Sid's head in a hammerlock, which finally induced Sid to let go.

The policeman lifted Sid off of Jeff and while he held him, his partner handcuffed Sid and led him out of the restaurant to the parking lot. The second policeman and Jerry helped Jeff get up off the floor. Jerry noticed that Jeff's right arm was limp, and he winced when Jerry touched it.

"Do you want me to call 911, sir?" asked the second policeman.

Jeff was feeling his right arm with his left hand, and was apparently in great pain. But he shook his head. "No, my brother will drive me to the emergency room. I think my right shoulder is dislocated." He looked at Jerry. "Can you drive me?"

"Of course."

The manager of the restaurant came over to talk to the policeman. The policeman nodded, and the manager motioned to a busboy to start cleaning up the mess.

"Sir," said the policeman. "Do you know the gentleman who attacked you?"

"Yes, he's my father. We had a disagreement that just got out of hand."

"Do you want to press charges?"

Jeff made a sour face. "Let him go on his way. My brother and I will settle up with the manager for any damages to the furniture and the crockery." Jerry nodded in agreement. "Will that be sufficient to end this?"

"Assuming your father has no outstanding warrants, and his car isn't stolen."

Jeff and Jerry both laughed. "Please check, but I am absolutely certain that he's clean," said Jeff.

The policeman handed Jeff his card. "I'll talk to my partner, and if he is clean, will escort him back to his vehicle and send him on his way. Good day, gentlemen." The policeman left the restaurant and headed in the direction of Sid and his partner who were standing in the parking lot. Sid was still in handcuffs. Jerry walked over to the manager. They talked briefly, and Jerry took out his wallet and handed him several bills. They shook hands. Then, Jerry led Jeff through the entrance of the restaurant, and they stood just outside the restaurant door and watched while the two policemen talked. The second policeman went over to the squad car and sat inside.

"How are you feeling?" said Jerry.

Jeff was holding up his right arm with his left hand. "Not so good, bro. My arm hurts like hell. I think it must be dislocated."

"Then, let's go now," said Jerry.

"Not yet," said Jeff. "I want to make sure they release Dad. We'll wait."

Five minutes later, the second policeman emerged from his squad car and walked over to Sid and his partner. They talked briefly. Then, the first policeman removed the cuffs from Sid, and both policeman led him to his car, helped him inside, and then watched as he drove away. Jeff and Jerry looked on, immersed in the temporary peace that grew from no more than the long habit of tolerating each other.

"Let's go, said Jeff.

Jeff emerged from the hospital emergency room just before eleven a.m. His right arm was in a sling. His face was pale as if all the blood had been drained from it. Jerry thought, the son of a bitch! But he was still his brother and he hated to see him suffer.

Jerry put aside the magazine that he had been reading and walked over to Jeff.

"How do you feel?

"Better. They gave me some pain pills. I'm lucky. The rotator cuff isn't torn. The doc says if I'm a good boy and baby my arm, I'll be able to play golf in about a month."

"That's great news," said Jerry. "You'll just have to learn to masturbate with your left hand."

Jeff laughed—genuinely, for this was his brand of humor. "That's the least of my problems. I talked with Salli and she's going to arrange to pick up my car from Dinah's parking lot. Can you drive me home?"

"Sure. Are you ready to go?"

"I'm all checked out."

The drive between the hospital and Jeff's house took about a half hour. Traffic was light. As soon as Jeff got into the car, he closed his eyes and was soon sound asleep. Jerry was grateful for the drugs that obviated any necessity for small talk. He wasn't sure what he would talk to Jeff about if he weren't sleeping. What a goddamn mess. Jeff's rogue operation had torn the family apart. He looked over at his sleeping brother. Damn him!

Jeff was still asleep when they arrived at the house. Jerry got out of the car, walked around to the passenger side, and opened the door. He tapped Jeff on his good shoulder and said, "We're here." Jeff immediately awoke. He seemed confused. "Where am I?"

"In front of your house, Jeff."

Jerry helped him out of the car and walked him to the front door. Jeff asked Jerry to get his key out of his left pants pocket and open the front door.

"Is anyone home?" said Jerry.

"No, the kids are in school. But Salli will be, shortly."

"Do you want me to stay with you until she gets home?"

"That's not necessary, Jerry. I'll be fine. Thanks for all your help. I really appreciate it." He walked into the house and shut the door behind him.

Jerry remained on the doorstep, surprised, feeling that perhaps he should have insisted upon staying with Jeff until Salli returned. He turned and walked down the stairs and over to his car. As he opened the car door, he had the epiphany that Jeff's betrayal had washed away whatever feeling of affection he may have had. At best, they would spend the rest of their lives tolerating each other.

21

NOON, FRIDAY, DECEMBER 7, 1990

Jerry returned to his condo tired, hungry, and dejected.

He took Chelsey for a walk around the block. The sun was shining and he relished the warmth on his face. When he returned to the condo, he decided to treat himself to the lox and bagels that he had purchased in anticipation of Helen's sleepovers. He toasted the bagel halves, spread each half with a liberal amount of non-fat cream cheese, and placed two large slices of lox, a slice of onion, and a slice of tomato on each half. He took the plate containing his feast into the living room and turned on the television to watch the news and eat his breakfast. At 1:00 p.m., he called his office. Shirley answered.

"Hello. Shirley, I'm not planning to come in today. I'm feeling under the weather and I'm just going to stay home and relax. I'll call in for my messages around noon."

"Jerry," she said, tentativeness revealing her discomfort. "Jeff told me about your meeting last night. I just want you to know how bad I feel about—about—you know."

He felt his diplomatic skills drain away like water in a tub. "Save it, Shirley," he said. "I don't want to talk about it. There's nothing that you can say that will make either of us feel better."

There was a long silence. "I understand," she said. "Richard called and wanted me to tell you that the meeting with the bank is at three. He just wanted me to advise you. He stated that he assumed that you're not going to attend. And Kevin called looking for you."

Jerry hung up without saying goodbye and dialed Kevin's number.

Carolyn answered the phone. "Hi, Jerry. He's anxious to talk with you. He's out back." Several minutes later, Kevin came on the phone.

"Salli called us and told us what happened at your breakfast meeting. She was crying. She didn't have many of the details, because Jeff had called her from the hospital and was in a lot of pain. I called Dad, but there was no answer."

"It was an unmitigated disaster. Jeff was snide, sarcastic, and full of himself, and Dad exploded. He would have killed Jeff, I mean literally killed him, if the cops had not been there to break it up."

"Salli didn't tell us that part," said Kevin.

"Did she tell you that the cops put Dad in cuffs, and checked him out for outstanding warrants before they let him go?"

"No," she didn't."

"I'm sure Jeff did not tell her the gory details," said Jerry. "He was in pretty bad shape.

"So, how is he?"

"Dislocated shoulder. No damage to the rotator cuff. He's hurting, but he should be fine. Which is a hell of a lot more than I can say for us, you, Dad, and myself."

"How are you feeling?" said Kevin.

"Lousy," said Jerry. "I think I'm getting the flu. I've decided to stay home today. I've got a date with Helen this evening and I want to save myself."

Kevin laughed. "You better get it while it's available. She's leaving soon, isn't she?"

"They're going to pack up her apartment tomorrow, and she's leaving for Paris on the fifteenth. I guess she arranged to bunk with you guys until she leaves."

"Why don't you just ask her to marry you and stop the nonsense? Anyone can see that the two of you are crazy about each other."

"It's complicated, Kevin. Anyway, I'm sure you didn't call me to talk about my love life."

"No, but it's a lot more pleasant than talking about Jeff. He's played all of us for fools. He's lied to us and capitalized on your contacts and reputation to…"

Jerry could tell that Kevin was getting worked up. "Calm down, Kevin. This won't help. Jeff's just being Jeff. He's always been Machiavellian, but until now, we haven't been the victims. Now we are and it sucks."

"Do you see anything we can do? Carolyn and I really like the Foxx deal. We thought you had achieved a miracle. We don't really want to spend the next several years under Jeff's thumb."

"I don't think there's much we can do. Jeff's holding all the cards. As my Jewish friends say, we've got bubkiss. Let's see how the hand plays out. I think you and Carolyn have made a wise decision not to pursue a legal action, but anything short of that won't get Jeff's attention."

"I don't like this, Jerry. He's fucked us over. Our own brother."

"Let it alone, Kevin. Getting worked up over this is the worst thing you can do to yourself. Let's just see what happens."

"Okay. I hope you feel better."

Jerry called Ethan Wilson on his direct line to bring him up to date on what was going on. "The sleazy bastard," said Ethan. "Now it all makes sense."

"What do you mean?"

"Remember the Washington D.C. conversation that Foxx was so concerned about? The two guys talking were probably part of Charlie's deal. The reason I couldn't find out shit about it was because all the investors probably signed a non-disclosure agreement, so that Jeff could keep the deal under wraps."

"Yeah, I had forgotten about that." Jerry had not forgotten about it. He had thought about it over and over since Jeff first announced his deal the previous night. He had dreamed about it. And it was on his mind now.

"What do you want me to do, Jerry? Do you want me to call Foxx or do you want to do it?"

Jerry let the question hang for a moment. "No, let's not be hasty. The Foxx deal isn't over yet. The fat lady's still in the wings, gargling." He smirked. "Jeff still has to convince Sheila to accept a two point eight million dollar haircut, and then she has to sell it to senior management. That's not going to be a walk in the park. If the bank balks, Jeff will beg for the Foxx deal."

"I see your point," said Ethan.

"Let's keep mum on the Jeff deal until the bank responds. We have until the fourteenth before Foxx is scheduled to come out. I'll arrange for the lawyers to continue to work on the environmental issues and we'll all operate as if the Foxx deal is going to happen." Jerry wanted to come across as being merely prudent and not overly optimistic. "If the bank tells Jeff to go fuck himself, we can still save the Foxx deal. Are you cool with that?"

"I'll give it a burl," said Ethan.

Jerry checked his watch. It was almost 1:30 p.m. Jeff's meeting with the bank would be starting in an hour and a half. He decided that now was as good a time as any to call Sheila.

He called Sheila on her direct line. She picked up the phone on the first ring.

"Hi, it's Jerry."

"I was waiting for your call."

"That's funny, I didn't leave a message that I would be calling."

"You didn't have to, Jerry."

"You know me too well."

"I know you a lot better than you know your brother." She did not sound angry, just resigned.

"What can I say?"

"Nothing, Jerry. I know you did your best."

"What do you think the bank will do?"

"I'm not sure. This case has such a high profile within the bank that senior management will think long and hard about their options. I think you should tell Jeff not to give up his day job. He may have just outsmarted himself."

"You don't really think the bank would foreclose?"

She was quiet for what seemed like an eternity.

"I wouldn't bet against it," she said. "What do you plan to do now?"

"I'll be going back to New York in about two weeks."

"Call me next week, say Wednesday. I'll have a better perspective by then. Also, I want you to know that I have enormous respect for you, independent of how this works out. We should have lunch before you leave."

"Thanks, Sheila, your opinion means a lot to me. I'm looking forward to lunch."

As Jerry put down the receiver, a sudden feeling of nausea came over him. He started to sweat and became concerned that he would not be able to keep down the lox and bagels that he just consumed. Maybe he was really coming down with the flu—a self-fulfilling prophecy. He sat down on the couch and closed his eyes and WHAM! It hit him. He had gone to bed the night before wallowing in a pit of despair over how Jeff had betrayed Kevin, Dad, and himself. He had attempted to think through the options for stopping Jeff. But he had been so emotionally distraught that he could not think clearly. He saw the yellow tablet and the pen on the side table of the couch where he had left it the night before. He'd been distracted all morning with the breakfast, the melée, taking Jeff to the hospital, walking Chelsey, eating lox and bagels, talking with Kevin, Ethan, and Sheila. What he hadn't done was to give some serious professional thought to whether there was any plausible strategy to stop Jeff. He needed some quality time to think through the situation.

He called Helen and left a message that he'd be there tonight. He assembled his relax-on-the-beach paraphernalia, slipped into his swimsuit, put on his jogging outfit, grabbed Chelsey's leash and his yellow tablet and the pen, called Chelsey, and headed to the car. He drove down Pacific Coast Highway to Manhattan Beach Boulevard, turned west toward the beach and found a parking space two blocks from the pier. He walked Chelsey to the beach and over the sand, and picked out a spot twenty feet from the water and about forty feet south of the pier. He spread out his blanket, opened the bottle of water, and filled up Chelsey's dish, spread suntan oil over his body, and sat down on the blanket, next to Chelsey, his pen and tablet ready for action. He checked his watch. It was just after three. The bank meeting had started. He smiled as he thought about the possible explanations Jeff would offer for his injury.

During the next half hour, he made a number of lists, all designed to stimulate his creative juices. He started by listing the people who had influenced Jeff in the past and might influence him now. That led nowhere. The only persons on the list were Salli and Charlie, neither of whom would dissuade Jeff. Then, he made a list of potential intervening events that might upset Jeff's plan. That list was also short, consisting of three items: (1) the bank refusing to go along with Jeff's proposal, or (2) the group of investors that Charlie assembled either breaking up or not actually closing the funding, or (3) Charlie suddenly becoming disenchanted with the deal and closing it down. He had to admit that none of these intervening events was likely. The bank would probably go along with Jeff's deal, because they would achieve a better outcome than a liquidation. If the investor group came apart in the next several weeks, it wouldn't matter, because Jim Foxx would have withdrawn his offer. And it was unlikely that having invested so much time, money, and reputational capital in the National deal that Charlie would lose interest and scuttle it.

His head hurt. The sun's heat made him sleepy. He got up and walked to the water with Chelsey. He walked partway into the surf and then dove in. Chelsey was close behind. They bobbed in the water for several minutes and then returned to the beach blanket. He toweled himself off, sat down, and looked at his yellow pad. Fucking hopeless! He stretched out on the blanket and closed his eyes. His mind wandered. He relived the scene in the restaurant when his father had attacked Jeff. His father had yelled, "You'd commit patricide? I'll kill you first." Patricide. That's what Dimitri was accused of, and falsely convicted for—killing his father, Fyodor Karamazov.

Jerry remembered the plot of the novel. Dimitri, the oldest Karamazov son and his father, Fyodor, were estranged because Dimitri believed his father owed him money and his father was trying to seduce Dimitri's love object, Grushenka. Dimitiri breaks into his father's house and beats up his father in front of Alyosha, Jerry's hero, and then runs around the town claiming that he plans to kill his father. Rather than go after Dimitri and try to reason with him, Alyosha ignores the threat to his father and goes back to the monastery. When Fyodor's bludgeoned body is discovered, Dimitri is arrested, tried, and convicted, although he is innocent of the crime.

So, Alyosha might have been able to influence Dimitri, had he not gone back to the monastery. Dimitri loved and respected Alyosha. Jeff doesn't love or respect me. I can't influence him. But this Alyosha won't go back to the monastery.

Jerry put his pen and pad down, set his watch alarm for 6:00 p.m., stretched out on the blanket, and immediately fell asleep.

His alarm went off at 6:00 p.m. Chelsey was snoring quietly next to him. The wind had come up while he was asleep and left him chilled, but he felt rested, relaxed, and almost serene. All traces of somnolence were gone. He was alert. His mind was unfettered. He had solved the problem. He knew exactly what to do.

He quickly gathered up his beach stuff and walked to his car, stopping only to allow Chelsey to go potty, and then drove back to his condo. He went straight to the phone to call Helen and tell her that he was going to be late and they would have to skip the Woody Allen movie that he had wanted to see.

"That's okay," she said. "I'll just keep the things that are supposed to be warm, warm, and the things that are supposed to be cold, cold. Drive carefully. You're precious." He hung up and hurried anyway—into the shower, shaving, and feeding Chelsey. He dressed in beige Dockers, a green plaid button-down shirt, Rockport walking shoes, and a black cashmere sweater. Before he left the condo, he picked up a package of documents about six inches thick and he and Chelsey headed for his car.

Jerry drove to the Del Amo Shopping Galleria in South Torrance. He located the Circuit City electronics store, parked his car, and walked in. A half-hour later, he emerged, carrying a large bag. He brought the packages back to his car, stowed them in the trunk, and drove to the west side of the shopping center. He located the luggage store he was looking for, parked the car, and went in. Fifteen minutes later, he emerged, carrying an oversize briefcase similar to the ones lawyers lug to depositions and trials. He opened the trunk of the car and stuffed the sheaf of documents into the briefcase. He opened the package from Circuit City and placed the video camera in the briefcase. He shut and locked the briefcase, got into the car, and drove out of the parking lot toward Helen's.

Jerry led Chelsey up the stairs to Helen's condo, carrying the briefcase. Chelsey was carrying her leash. He rang the bell. Helen came to the door with her wide smile and threw her arms around him.

"Whoa," he exclaimed. "Let me set down this load, so I can greet you properly." He patted Chelsey's head. "Go in, girl."

He placed the briefcase inside the door and folded Helen into his arms. He kissed her and pressed his hips against hers.

She glanced at the briefcase. "Plan to stay awhile?"

He laughed. "Tomorrow's project. I need to get up early and get started on it."

"Well then, we'll just have to get on with the evening, so that you have your dinner, walk your dog, fuck your woman, and get back to work. Do I have the drill right?" Her smile said sarcasm, but the rest of her face told him to take it in good humor.

"You have it down pat."

By 9:00 p.m., Jerry and Helen were in bed under her comforter, actively engaged. By ten they were both asleep. At five, Jerry's wristwatch alarm went off. He was awake immediately. He shut off the alarm and looked over at Helen. She was still in a deep sleep. Chelsey was curled up at the foot of the bed. He climbed out of bed and gathered up his clothes that had been strewn around the room. He went into the living room, dressed, and made a pot of coffee.

While the coffee brewed, Jerry inspected the bookcases in the living room. He carefully scanned the shelves. He located the photo album Helen had shown him the evening of the spreadsheets. He carried the photo album to the dining room table and turned on the table light to its brightest setting. He opened the photo album to the pictures of the Black's Beach excursion. He smiled to himself and retrieved his new briefcase. He took out the video camera and video taped all ten photographs of Helen, Jeff, Maurice, and Maya, dwelling on each picture approximately fifteen seconds. He had completed the operation within five minutes. He rewound the tape in the camera and viewed the photographs. He placed the video camera back into the briefcase, locked it, and placed it beside the couch.

He headed to the kitchen, poured a cup of coffee, and sat down at the kitchen table with a thick stack of reports and analyses related to the Foxx deal, and a yellow pad. He slowly sipped his coffee and waited. At 7:30 a.m., he looked in on Helen and Chelsey. Both were still asleep. He crawled back into bed, woke her, and they made love.

At 9:00 a.m., on the way back to his condo, he stopped at a park, so that Chelsey could have a long run. When he returned to his condominium, he immediately opened the briefcase, removed the video camera, ejected the tape, and inserted the tape into the VCR of his entertainment unit. He waited, keeping his anxiety in check. Finally, there they were, the very nude Jeff, Helen, Maurice, and Maya, romping on Black's Beach.

"I can play hardball too, Jeff," said Jerry, although no one was around to hear him.

He rewound the tape, ejected it from the VCR, inserted it into a blank case, and carefully wrapped it in plain brown paper. He affixed the three dollars in stamps required for Priority Mail and addressed a plain white label to Charlie Knudsen at his office address in Century City. He printed "Personal and Confidential" in several places on the package. He drove south on Highway 405 to the post office located near the Los Angeles Airport. He drove into the lot, up to a mailbox, and he tossed the package into the box.

22

THREE MONTHS LATER—FRIDAY, MARCH 1, 1991

The National parking lot was deserted when Jeff pulled into his assigned space shortly after 7:00 p.m. It was cold. It had been raining for two days, and by now, the weather thoroughly matched his mood. Kevin's car was already in the adjacent stall. The building was dark, except for the light coming from Kevin's office. Jeff mused how quickly things change. Before the announcement of the sale to Foxx, this place would have been lit up like a Christmas tree until 11:00 p.m.

Jeff got out of the car and opened the rear door. He rummaged around the empty soda cans and McDonald's bags and wrappers that littered the back seat, and eventually dug out a notebook. He walked along the cobblestone pathway to the front door. He unlocked the door and entered the deserted reception area and locked the door behind him.

There was a small nightlight across the room that provided sufficient illumination, so that he could navigate through the reception area and into the executive suite. As he stood inside the door and his eyes adjusted to the low light, the emptiness of the building seemed to echo the emptiness of his life. "Gone," he said softly. "Done and over."

His eyes started to tear up. He shook his head and stood at attention as if he were addressing troops under his command. "Gentlemen, sometimes, you have to lose a battle to win a war. Remember that! At ease and dismissed," he said. He relaxed his posture and headed toward Kevin's office. There was a light under Kevin's door. He hesitated for an instant, knocked, and opened the door. His brother was pouring over some papers at his desk.

"How are you doing?" said Jeff. The walls had been stripped of all the photos, degrees, awards, and mementos that had evidenced Kevin's successful career and standing in ACS industry and the Southern California technical community. The bare walls and empty nail holes attested to the fact that the dreams that were nurtured in this office were dead.

Kevin looked up from the piles of paper on his desk, startled.

"I didn't hear you come in. I thought you weren't coming until about nine."

"Jessie decided to ditch me in favor of her newest love—so I didn't have to take her shopping."

Kevin laughed. "I know how disappointed you must be, missing an opportunity to shop with a thirteen year old. I'm surprised that you let Salli pawn that job off on you."

Jeff sat down in the chair in front of Kevin's desk, leaned back, and put his feet up on the desk. "Salli's in Hawaii getting ready for the big move. I'm babysitting."

Kevin's face showed his surprise. "I didn't know she was moving."

"Yeah. As soon as the kids are out of school. Probably in early July."

"How are you handling it?" said Kevin. He put the document down and leaned back in his chair.

Jeff noticed something had changed in Kevin's demeanor. He couldn't quite put his finger on it. There was an odd light in his eyes and his speech seemed to be more brisk—more like the Kevin of five years ago.

"I'm doing better. It took some getting used to after the initial shock. But a split was in the making for years. I just wasn't prepared for it when she dropped the bomb—especially with the bullshit that you and I have had to deal with. And I never expected her to move and take the kids away." He took out a handkerchief and blew his nose.

Kevin got out of his chair, came around the desk and placed his hand on Jeff's shoulder. Jeff put his hand over Kevin's and held it while he wiped his face with the handkerchief.

"I'll be fine—I keep telling myself," he said. "But I'm already missing them and they haven't even moved. It will be a big fucking adjustment." He put his handkerchief back into his pocket.

Kevin went back to his desk and sat down. They were both silent for several minutes. Finally, Jeff said, "So, why are we meeting, Kev? I thought we had everything wrapped up the other day. Driving into this place is as much fun as a visit to a grave."

Kevin placed the document he was holding on one of the piles of paper on his desk. He attempted to straighten out the pile, so that it would fit into the banker's box at the side of his desk. The awkwardness and delay meant that Kevin was preparing himself for what he expected would be a difficult conversation. What the hell was there to talk about? They had hashed it and rehashed it. The company was gone. Monday was the effective date for the transfer. Foxx had decided that he did not need either one of them and was content to just pay them off. It was time to move on. After what seemed like an eternity of Kevin's paper organizing, Jeff said, "Come on, blurt it out."

Kevin put the final pile of paper in the banker's box, swept the bent paperclips and miscellaneous office offal into the wastebasket, and looked carefully at his desk that was devoid of anything but the phone. "My desk hasn't been this clean for five years. Anyway, I'm ready to go." He leaned across the desk and looked into Jeff's eyes. His jaw was set, his voice firm. "I signed a contract with the agency—a contract to set up facility security systems in the Kurdish areas of Iraq." He picked up a sheaf of papers from his desk and shoved them across to Jeff. He was smiling and his voice conveyed exuberance and determination. "I fly out to Washington next Wednesday for two weeks of orientation and training, and then it's off to Irbil."

Jeff picked up the papers, glanced at them, and tossed them back on the desk. When he saw that Kevin wasn't joking, his reaction was swift and undiplomatic. He jumped out of the chair and leaned over the desk, pushing his face as close to Kevin's as he could manage. Vietnam flooded him—using the bodies of his dead soldiers as a shield, the choppers, the smell of napalm, the noise of the bombardment, the filth, the blood, and the death.

"You are out of your fucking mind! Where the fuck did this crazy idea come from?" His face was beet red, and he realized he was yelling. "What business does... does an old fart like you have traipsing around a conflict area playing spy? You could—no, you will get yourself killed." He wanted to beat some sense into Kevin. "And with your health problems. Shit, what is the matter with you? You've got a wife. You've got kids, responsibilities."

Kevin was silent. He cleared his throat, placed both hands on the desk, and leaned forward, looking directly into Jeff's eyes. His lips and eyes formed up into a hint of a smile.

"I knew that would be your reaction. That's why I wanted some quiet time to talk.

I contacted several of the guys in the agency that I worked with during the seventies when I was the manager of the Code Matrix Reader project. I asked them if they had something that would fit with my talents and experience. They came up with the Iraq assignment. The agency is well aware of my medical problems. They still think I am the best person for the job." His face lit up. The hint of a smile had turned into a broad grin. "Think about it, Jeff. Someone actually thinks I'm the best person for something. You don't think so, and Jerry doesn't think so." The grin had evaporated. His voice was flat. "Carolyn and my kids don't think so. No one in this company that I've devoted fifteen years of my life to thinks so. Everyone in my life, as you put it, thinks I am a failure and a fuck-up, a perennial victim."

Jeff eased some of the weight off his hands and stood down a fraction of an inch. "Dammit, that's not true. You're being melodramatic."

"It is true. Let's cut the bullshit. I'm a has-been. Yesterday's newspaper. No one really gives a shit about me other than Mom and Dad. The offer from the agency was like a shot of oxygen. I can breathe. The testosterone is starting to flow. I've got something to look forward to."

Jeff pulled back from Kevin's desk. He paced around the office for a few moments and tried to formulate arguments that might make an impression, although he knew that the die was cast. He moved back to the front of the desk and placed his hands on it again, this time to steady himself. He would try appealing to the engineer with logic and facts.

"I've been in a war zone. It isn't pretty. You don't know what in the hell your signing up for. Don't you read the papers? Saddam is going to crush the Kurds—and anyone else who gets in his way. We're not going to send troops. You guys will be on your own. You could get killed."

"I'm dead already. The agency job is a second chance at life. If I die, I die." He paused, and then, speaking slowly, "At least I won't die a loser. What did you always say? Better to die with your boots on. Like the title of that old Errol Flynn movie about the Battle of Little Big Horn."

Jeff straightened up, removed his hands from the desk, and paced around the office again. He stopped and looked at Kevin and his fucking beatific calm. "Goddammit, you're depressed. You're not thinking clearly."

"I've been depressed for years. That's what my shrink tells me."

"What does he think about this? I mean you're putting yourself at risk. Doesn't he see it as suicidal?"

"He's happy to see me stop wallowing and take some action. He doesn't pass judgment on the decisions I make."

"Have you told Carolyn?"

"That's tomorrow's project. I don't expect it will be a problem. She'll probably tell me to shut the door on my way out—and be sure to keep the checks coming. You know our situation. We're just roommates, Jeff. There's nothing left."

The brothers were silent. Kevin had made up his mind, and there was no purpose in analyzing, criticizing, or rehashing it. There was a part of Jeff, a really big part, that envied him. Kevin was right. Who would want to die in a nursing home, eating pabulum, and pissing in his diaper?

"When are you going to tell Mom and Dad?"

"I've told Dad. He's cool. He respects my decision. He understands. He'll tell Mom after I've left for Washington. I think it will be easier that way."

"What do you want me to do?"

"Just three things, Jeff. Look after Carolyn and the kids." He handed Jeff a large manila envelope and pointed to the banker box that he had been working on. "Everything you'll need is in the envelope and the box. They contain all of our financial information, bank statements, copies of trusts, life insurance polices, and so on. Go through it and get back to me with any questions before I leave for Iraq."

"What's the third thing?"

Kevin rose from his chair and walked around the desk. He grabbed Jeff's arm and pulled him out of the chair and wrapped him in his arms. "Tell me you love me and wish me good luck."

Two weeks later, the telephone woke Jerry from a deep sleep, and by the time he got himself oriented, it had rung four times. He turned on the light and saw that the time was 1:45 a.m. EST. He picked up the receiver.

"Yeah," he said.

"Jerry?"

"Yeah, who's this?"

"It's Jeff."

Jerry's heartbeat accelerated. He knew that Jeff wouldn't call him early in the morning unless there was a crisis.

"What's up? Anything wrong?"

A long silence. "The CIA called me an hour ago. Kevin passed out during a training exercise. The paramedics were not able to revive him."

"No! I thought he was doing..."

"So did we. So did he. I talked to him two days ago, and he sounded so excited and positive. He was confident that this deal with the agency was going to let him turn his life around." A dry sob. "Can you come today? If not, please get here as soon as you can. There's a lot to do and I really need your help. We all need to be together. I've got to go. So long."

Jerry replaced the receiver in the cradle. The loss was unbelievable, immeasurable, incomprehensible, and the grief unfathomable. So, he conducted himself as always. He showered, shaved, packed, and confirmed a nine o'clock departure for Los Angeles. At 5:30 a.m., he called Lisa to arrange to pick up Chelsey and take her to the kennel. He then called Dave Dezube, his junior partner, to take over for the next week.

As the aircraft gained altitude, he leaned back in his seat. He tried to remember just how he felt last time, flushed with the knowledge that he was flying back home, like a Paladin, to save the family from financial ruin. Now he was a pallbearer.

He arrived in LA around noon. He picked up his bag and walked out to the arrival curb. Jeff was waiting for him. Jeff got out of the car and threw his arms around him. "God, I'm happy to see you. Mom, Dad, and Carolyn are inconsolable. Everyone's at Carolyn's waiting for us. You'll be staying there if that's okay with you. We don't want her to be alone."

"That's fine."

"Tired?"

"I slept a little on the plane," Jerry said. "I'll be all right. How are you doing?"

Jeff had gained weight since he had last seen him—twenty to thirty pounds. Even more surprising was that Jeff, impeccable in his appearance no matter what the occasion, was unkempt, disheveled, and unshaven. He fumbled with his keys and dropped them in the gutter beside the car. He got down on his knees to retrieve them, oblivious to the fact that in the process, he was soiling his pants. Seeing him, Jerry felt a surge of disgust—at his brother, and at himself, coupled with a feeling of guilt.

Jeff staggered back to his feet. "I feel like shit. This is a nightmare." He climbed halfway inside the car and collapsed in the driver's seat, one foot still dangling out the side. "I always thought that the three of us would always be around, that we'd bury Mom and Dad, and get to enjoy each other in the mellowness of our old age." He pounded on the steering wheel. "God *fucked* us!"

Jerry averted his gaze as his eyes welled up with tears. "I know, I know..."

The car trip to Kevin's house passed in silence.

Shortly before they arrived, Jeff said, "After you spend some time with Mom and Dad, you, Salli and I will get together and figure out what we're going to do about the funeral. Salli has talked with Carolyn and has her input. Is that okay with you?"

Jerry nodded.

"Also, I hope that you'll take charge of the financial part of this. You know, figure out what Carolyn's assets will be, make sure the money's invested, and help her work out a budget. Salli says she doesn't have any clue about their financial situation, or what they have. Kevin gave me a banker's box full of files and stuff before he left for Washington. I haven't had the chance to look at it. You're a lot better at that stuff than I am. Are you willing to take that on?"

"Of course," said Jerry. "Carolyn will need a lot of handholding on a bunch of fronts." Jeff shut off the car. As Jerry walked through the front doorway, his mother appeared on the stairs. She was still in her dressing gown, her hair disheveled, and for the first time in Jerry's memory, she looked like an old woman. He climbed the steps and held her tight. She moaned, "It isn't fair. He was so young. I'm empty, empty."

Jerry held her more tightly. She looked him over, and down the stairs at Jeff. Her sons—two of them, the only two she had left.

She turned away, sobbing. Jerry could not fathom what to say, so he helped her down the stairs and into the living room, where his father sat on the sofa, hands inert on his knees. He looked more exhausted and haggard than when Jerry last saw him. There were used coffee cups, dirty plates, with half-eaten Danish pastries covering the tables. Newspapers and magazines were strewn all over. Someone had spilled a drink on the rug and the spot was still wet. The Bascomb clan was devoid of any of its old pretense of maintaining appearances.

"Where's Salli?" said Jerry.

"She's in the kitchen making sandwiches. Carolyn is upstairs talking with the children," said Mr. Bascomb. "Why don't you go up and say hello? I know she's anxious to see you."

"I'll wait until she comes down. I need a drink. You? Jeff?"

"Best idea I've heard all day," said Jeff. "You want to make them, Jerry?"

Jerry went into the family room and busied himself with the drinks. Sid came in a few minutes later. He put his arms around Jerry, hugged him, and held him tightly. "I'm so happy you're here. We all need you."

"I couldn't be anywhere else. We all need to give each other strength."

He moved closer to Jerry and spoke just above a whisper. "It's more than that. Jeff can't really handle this. He's had a very hard time since it became obvious that National was going to be sold. When Salli announced that she wanted a divorce and was moving to Hawaii, he seemed to crumble. He hasn't tried to find another job or do anything. Salli says that he's really depressed and that he mopes around the house all day, drinking and watching television. He doesn't work out anymore. You saw him. Jeff's never been fat. I've tried to talk with him a few times, but he just won't say much. He's just not himself. I just don't have any idea how Kevin's death is going to affect him."

Jerry placed his hand on his father's shoulder. "Nor do the rest of us. Kevin was such a big presence in all of our lives. There's going to be a big hole in our world." Since there wasn't any Jameson, Jerry fixed Absoluts on the rocks for Jeff and himself, and a scotch on the rocks for his father, and then headed back into the living room.

Jerry handed Jeff and Sid their drinks. Jeff raised his glass and said, "To Kevin. His tie was usually stained, and he always had pencils and pens sticking out of his shirt. But he always had his head on straight. He was the best of us and he leaves a hole in our lives that can never be filled."

Jerry, Jeff, and Sid clinked their glasses.

Salli entered the living room, carrying a tray filled with sandwiches and sodas. She set it down on the coffee table, and then she and Jerry embraced. "Thanks for coming."

"Of course, Salli. I need to be here. What do you want me to do?"

"Let's you, Jeff, and I go into the family room while Carolyn's upstairs." The three of them went into the family room, and Salli opened a notebook. "I've made a list of action items. I'd like to go over it and divide up the tasks. Neither Carolyn nor Mom and Dad are in a condition to help, so the three of us are going to have to plow ahead. Is that okay?"

Jerry was impressed. She always had her steno notebook at the ready. He wondered whether she carried her director-like behavior into the bedroom. It would explain some things.

"I am writing the obituary. Jerry, I'd like you to review and edit it. It will be published in the *L.A. Times*. I've set up a meeting with the people at McCormick Mortuary in Hawthorne. Carolyn said that she and Kevin had talked about funerals and burial sites after his heart attack. He said he thought he wanted to be buried at Hillsdale Memorial Park—the place where Howard Hughes is buried."

"Are you going to have the service at the church or the funeral home?" said Jerry.

"Carolyn wants it at the church—even though Kevin wasn't big on religion. He knew and respected the minister. Also, the facilities are larger. The church can seat fifteen hundred people."

Jerry was surprised. "How many people are you expecting?"

"Quite a few. I called Jim Foxx to tell him about Kevin and they're going to shut down the plant and offices, so that any employee who wishes can attend. He was really shaken up. Anyway, Carolyn and I are going to meet with the minister after we finish up with McCormick's."

"What is the schedule?" Jeff asked.

Salli answered quickly, without looking up from her notebook. She ticked off the date Kevin's body would arrive, the obituary publication date, and a likely date for the funeral, along with phone numbers for the minister and florist. Under the influence of her skills, the meeting had all the emotion of a florist's cold case: Jerry's grief was distinct but distant, as if shut behind a heavy glass door. His thoughts tried to wander further, but Salli snapped her pencil against the notebook. "Get enough food for three hundred people. We'll freeze what's left over and she can use it for sandwiches the rest of the year. Jerry, can you arrange for tables, chairs, plates, and utensils?"

"That kind of spread will cost several thousand dollars," said Jerry, shaking his head.

"I know," said Salli. "But that's what she wants to do. Now, for the service. Jerry, will you do the eulogy? Carolyn wants you to and we all think you're the logical one to do it."

Jerry was not surprised. He had been thinking about the problem of the eulogy while he was on the plane. Then, he had been genuinely concerned about his ability to deliver the eulogy without breaking down; now, he wondered if his mind would remain present long enough to be convincing.

"I'm not sure I could get through it," he said. "How the hell am I going to deliver a twenty-minute speech about Kevin before fifteen hundred people? It would take me two hours to deliver it. I think we should come up with another idea. How about you, Salli? You're eloquent. You'd be fine."

Salli shook her head emphatically. "No, I'm not the one to do this, Jerry. I knew Kevin as a brother-in-law for maybe fifteen, sixteen years. You've known him intimately your entire life. You can do it. I know it will be hard. But Bobby Kennedy did it for Jack and Ted Kennedy did it for Bobby. You can do it for Kevin." Jerry looked intently at Salli, then to Jeff, who nodded his agreement. He realized that further resistance would be fruitless. He swallowed hard.

"All right, I'll do the eulogy."

Jerry was seated on the aisle seat of the first row of the section of the church reserved for the family and very close friends. Carolyn sat next to him. Seated along the row were Carolyn and Kevin's children, Mary, John, and Kevin, Jr. Then, Salli, Jeff, Jessie, Michelle, Mrs. Bascomb, and Sid. Every seat in the church was occupied; and approximately one hundred people were standing along the side aisles and the back aisle. The full choir was on stage, dressed in light blue and white gowns. The minister stood in the pulpit.

The dark mahogany casket was embellished with brass handles. It contained the remains of Kevin Bascomb. It sat in front of the stage, five feet from Jerry and Carolyn. She had decided that a closed casket service would be more dignified, so Jerry was spared having to "view the body" in front of a full church.

The service had been in progress for about ten minutes when the choir sang "Amazing Grace." Jerry had been composed and stoic during the entire morning. But when they started to sing, he lost it. Up until now, he had only lost pets to death. But as devastated as he had felt, he was unprepared for the enormous grief that enveloped him. Kevin's death had shown him that Shakespeare was right, that "life's but a walking shadow, a poor player, that struts and frets his hour upon the stage, and then is heard no more."

Carolyn held his hand and comforted him. He sobbed during the minister's blessing and the sermon.

The minister told the audience what a kind and loving father, son, and brother Kevin had been, how proud everyone was of his accomplishments, and how his efforts had created a fine company that employed over two hundred and fifty people, and how much he loved his wife and his children, and what a good life he had made for them. The minister made sure that each member of the family was mentioned by name and had a sentence of acknowledgment.

The minister reminded those who were Christians that Kevin was now with the Lord and in a better place than the rest of us, so that there was no need to worry about him anymore—he was being taken care of. He said that we all now had to heal each other because Kevin's departure had created a great void for those who loved him. He asked the congregation to pray, and led them in the Lord's Prayer.

The choir sang, "Nearer My God to Thee," and Jerry realized he was next at bat. He took a few deep breaths to suppress the panic that had begun to zip through his veins. It shuddered against the last of his defenses, and he lost control. He bent in half. His forehead was on his knees and he was sobbing in silence. The choir finished the hymn and the minister introduced him to the congregation—Jerry heard his name. He dug down as deep as he could to find the strength to stop crying. He remained seated for a minute or so. The church remained silent. The minister's face began to show a hint of concern. Jerry turned to Carolyn and hugged her to draw strength from her body.

Jerry approached the podium slowly, clutching his notes. He placed them on the lectern, took out a tissue, and wiped his face. He briefly looked around the church, nodding at and acknowledging employees and friends. Then he said, in a strong, measured voice, "Carolyn, Jeff, Salli, Mom, Dad, Mary, John, Kevin, Jr., Jessie, Michelle, relatives, and friends, I will always remember this day as the saddest in my life, sadder than on Monday, when I first learned of Kevin's death. Because then, I was in a state of shock. I knew I had lost a brother, a mentor, and a friend. But I was so overcome with the suddenness of the event that I did not have the time to think much about what Kevin's life meant to me, and to you, and how his departure will affect us. I've had four days and four sleepless nights to think about Kevin's life. Organizing my thoughts in order to deliver the eulogy has proved to be a difficult challenge. How do you choose a set of words and string them into sentences that will convey to you what I know of the brother that was Kevin Bascomb? What he stood for, what he believed, what his life meant. How do you sum up a life in a short speech? Shakespeare described man as a marvelous 'piece of work, noble in reason and infinite in faculty.'

"My brother, Kevin, was such a great piece of work! He was my beacon. He lighted my path. He was my teacher. He took the time and effort to impart to me the skills that helped me achieve success on the ball field, in the classroom, and on the corporate battlefield. He was my mentor, my confidant, and my conscience.

"When I screwed up, he would call me Alyosha, the name of the hero in the *Brothers Karamazov*, and he'd look sternly at me and say: 'That is not the behavior I would expect from my brother, Alyosha.' And it would be like I'd been hit by a freight train.

"Everything that I am today and every significant achievement I've accomplished emanates from Kevin's inspiration and guidance. Losing him has covered me with sorrow as it has many of you who come to show your respect.

"I'd like to close with a quote from the *Brothers Karamazov*. A peasant woman whose young son had died is suffering inconsolable grief. She goes to see Alyosha's teacher, the highly respected monk, Father Zosima. Zosima tells her: 'Every time you weep, you must know that your little boy is one of God's angels; he sees you from heaven and is happy because of it. He sees your tears and draws God's attention to you. In your sorrow, you will continue to weep for a long time to come. Then, you will attain the purity of heart that delivers from Sin.'

"God Bless you and God bless our brother, Kevin."

23

TWO MONTHS LATER, WEDNESDAY, MAY 15, 1991

Jerry gazed out the window at the East River. He desperately wanted to close his eyes and sleep. He checked his watch—7:30 a.m. He'd been up since 2:30.

Since he returned to New York following Kevin's funeral, he rarely slept past three. He'd tried various over-the-counter sleeping pills and Valium that he'd gotten from Lisa. Nothing helped. No matter what time he'd go to sleep, he'd awaken between 2:30 and 3:30. Immediately upon awakening, he was aware of a deep, unremitting sadness coupled with fear for which he could discern no basis.

He'd lie in bed for several hours, unable to fall back to sleep. His mind wandered, but inevitably focused on National, Kevin, Jeff, and Helen. He'd remember how, in his dreams, he'd analyze, reanalyze, and then analyze again the events surrounding the sale of National. The drama he played out in his dreams took place in a courtroom in which he was on trial for copying the Black's Beach photos and sending the tape to Charlie. He was the prosecuting attorney and the defense attorney.

As prosecuting attorney, he'd heap scorn and ridicule on Jerry for betraying his own brother and deceiving Helen. He cast Jerry as a modern Cain who destroyed his brother's reputation and future. He'd refer to him as a villain, a Judas, a traitor. Memory tormented him, conjuring up the horrible image of the tattered, overweight vagabond of a brother who picked him up at the airport.

As defense attorney, he'd make the argument that it was absolutely essential that Jeff be prevented from pursuing a reckless plan that would tie up most of Kevin's assets and make him dependent on Jeff when he was weak, ill, and defenseless, and ruin his mother's and father's life; and that the only way to stop Jeff was to alienate him from Charlie, and the only way to do that was to wring Charlie's racism for all it was worth, and make Jeff repugnant in his eyes. Jerry had no choice. He had to act. The photos were the only way.

The prosecuting attorney would respond that it was Jerry's animosity toward Jeff and his commitment to the bank that they would be paid in full that motivated his actions. His narcissistic vainglory caused him to undermine Jeff's deal, so he could sell the company to Jim Foxx and be a hero to the bank.

The defense attorney would respond by enumerating Jerry's virtues of honesty, integrity, and prudence, arguing that it was only his deep loyalty and affection for Kevin and his parents that prompted him to take such a drastic action. Each night, in his sleep and in his ruminations when he wasn't sleeping, he replayed the courtroom drama with himself as the defendant, prosecuting attorney, and defense attorney. Each night, he would review the arguments again.

He would ask himself what other alternatives he had and attempt to assess their practicality, ultimately concluding that he had no alternative. Upon awakening, soaked with perspiration, he'd lie in bed, dejected, and exhausted from the ordeal and knowing that the next night would be no different. As he'd lie in bed in his wakened, but somnolent state and try to recall what transpired in his dreams, he would invariably think of a new fact that was relevant and might enhance or diminish the case against him. He would then attempt to integrate this newly discovered fact into the arguments of both the prosecution and the defense.

Finally, at about 7:00 a.m., Chelsey would put her front paws on the bed and bark. That would finally get Jerry going. He would walk Chelsey, feed Chelsey, shower, shave, dress, and go to work. In between his feeble attempts to attend to business, he would ruminate and ruminate.

Jerry's social life had deteriorated to an occasional sleepover with Lisa. He had resumed the relationship with her after he returned to New York, because it was convenient and non-threatening. All he wanted was companionship, an occasional dinner, and some recreational sex. That was about all he had the interest and energy for, and Lisa seemed fine with it.

He went to the gym regularly. When he worked out, his mind was unoccupied, so he'd use this opportunity to ruminate some more about his past, the various decisions he had made in his life that turned out well, the ones that turned out poorly, his parents, Helen, and so on. His mind never stopped, yammering on like the 24-hour cable news channels.

Perhaps he should have threatened Jeff. No, that wouldn't work. Jeff never responded to threats. Maybe he should have enlisted Helen's help. How? Suppose he and Helen had gone to Jeff and threatened to send the photos to Charlie if he didn't go along with the sale to Foxx. Preposterous! He couldn't reveal to Helen that he would stoop to blackmail. Helen would have been horrified and that would have ended their relationship for good. Maybe he should have just walked away from the situation and let Jeff and Charlie go ahead with their deal? Like Alyosha going back to the monastery. NO! NO! He couldn't do that. He could not abandon Kevin. Kevin had looked out for him all his life. He couldn't abandon his father and mother. It was clear. He had to scuttle Jeff's deal. And the only way was to send Charlie those photos of Jeff, Helen, Maurice, and Maya, romping in the nude on Black's Beach. I did what I had to do, he said to himself. No further point in thinking about it. Case closed! But he knew that it would only be a few minutes or a few hours before he would rethink it all again.

Birney noticed and spoke with him several times about his job performance. Jerry responded that he had not been able to get over Kevin's death. He was reading Elisabeth Kubler-Ross's book *On Death and Dying* and understood that it was going to take a while for him to work through the various stages of grief. When Birney inquired about Helen and suggested that perhaps Jerry should take a week off and visit her, he said that he'd talked with her a few times by phone, but didn't feel he'd be very good company.

Two months after Kevin's funeral, depressed and exhausted, Jerry called the local chapter of the American Psychiatric Association and asked for therapists who specialized in treating depression. He was given the name of Ben Goldfarb, whose office was two blocks from Jerry's office.

Fifteen minutes before his appointment the next day, Jerry entered the reception room of the Cognitive Therapy Clinic. He filled out the application form, his medical history, and a "Depression Inventory" that seemed to be typical of the various surveys he'd seen in popular magazines to tell you how good your sex life was or how good your current relationship was. Jerry quickly circled his answers, calculated his score, and thumbed through the current *Newsweek* until his name was called.

Dr. Goldfarb was waiting for him at the door of his office. He was on the short side, portly, and wore a full grayish black beard. Jerry estimated that he was in his early sixties. Dr. Goldfarb ushered Jerry to a plush chair beside his desk and took the seat by the window. The office was cluttered with piles of books and documents scattered around the room, covering every available surface. There were floor-to-ceiling bookcases on every inch of wall that didn't have a window, and the bookshelves were stuffed to sagging. On the wall behind Dr. Goldfarb's desk, hung framed diplomas, certificates, and awards attesting to the fact that Dr. Goldfarb was well educated, well certified, and well respected.

"Give me a few minutes, while I look over your history and inventory. Comfortable?" He had a low-pitched soft mellow voice that reminded Jerry of Mel Torme.

"Yes, very," said Jerry.

After a few minutes, Dr. Goldfarb asked, "How are you feeling now?"

"Weary, sad, helpless, guilty."

"No surprise. You got a forty-five on your inventory, indicating you're extremely depressed. But you know that already. Can you pinpoint when you first became aware of these symptoms?"

Jerry relaxed. The chair was very comfortable. He had closed his eyes, while Dr. Goldfarb was reviewing the paperwork, and kept them shut. "Sure, in fact exactly. It started a few days after my brother's funeral. I thought I was doing okay, you know, I was sad, teary-eyed a lot. But then about three days after I was back in New York, I awoke early, about 2:30 in the morning and I was overcome with such a feeling of total despair and hopelessness. It was unlike anything I had ever experienced." He chuckled, "And it's gone downhill from there..."

The first thirty minutes of the session was Jerry telling Dr. Goldfarb the background information, keeping it whitewashed. Finally, Dr. Goldfarb went quiet for what seemed to be a long time, and Jerry opened his eyes.

"You say that you get up early every morning and lie in bed, unable to get up. Is that right?" said Dr. Goldfarb.

"Yes. Every damn morning," said Jerry. "Between two-thirty and three-thirty, as if I had an alarm. I just lie there and think and think. If I didn't have a dog who needed to be walked in the morning, I'd probably never get out of bed." Jerry laughed, nervously.

"What do you think about when you're lying in bed?" said Dr. Goldfarb.

"Think about?" Jerry raised his eyes. Dr. Goldfarb was staring at him. The stare made him feel uncomfortable. He looked around the room as if searching for the answer in one of the books on the sagging shelves. He mumbled, "Not sure what you mean, Dr. Goldfarb."

Dr. Goldfarb's eyes had not moved. "Tell me the thoughts, images, daydreams. Whatever fills your mind when you're lying in bed and feeling like shit?"

Jerry did not know how to answer. Somehow, in all his ruminating, he had done no preparation. He never considered the possibility of confessing his sins to another human being. He started to perspire. He loosened his tie and unbuttoned the top button of his shirt. He felt nauseated. He realized that Dr. Goldfarb was studying him intently. "Anything wrong?"

"I'm not feeling well," said Jerry. His face was slick. His throat was dry. "Can we take a break, so I can go to the restroom?"

"Sure. Turn right when you walk out the door to the reception area. It's about twenty-five feet down the hall."

Jerry fled. He walked out the reception door, turned left, and pushed the button to call for the elevator. After he left the building, he stopped at a corner phone booth and called Ben Goldfarb's office and told the receptionist that he was too ill to continue the session and that he would call Dr. Goldfarb during the next several days to set another appointment.

During the next three days, Jerry only left his apartment to walk Chelsey. He called in sick and had Lisa rearrange his appointments. He handed off the matters that couldn't be delayed to Dave Dezube. Lisa asked whether she could come over and nurse him. He declined, saying he needed to rest. He slept intermittently for two to three hours at a time. He ate very little, but went through two bottles of Jameson. He listened to a few operas, watched old movies on TV, and tuned into CNN. But mostly he sat, thought, and analyzed how the events of the last year had brought him to the state where he simply could not function. By the following Monday, he saw clearly that he could not deal with his problems without help. He called Dr. Goldfarb's office and got an appointment for the next day.

"Its good to see you again," said Dr. Goldfarb. "Are you feeling better?"

"Not really." Jerry was sitting in his comfortable chair, his hands folded on his lap. He was wearing jeans. He hadn't shaved. His eyes were red.

"Is there anything you want to tell me?" said Dr. Goldfarb.

"I want to apologize for running out last week. I did have some physical discomfort, but the primary reason I left was that I simply wasn't prepared to go into certain matters. Certain events that occurred that—well, I wasn't ready to talk about, and I was surprised and frightened when I realized that I would have to talk about them if I was going to answer your questions truthfully."

"Based on our previous conversation, I take it that you are an avid reader," said Dr. Goldfarb.

"That's right," said Jerry. "I've always been the major reader in our family. Mainly fiction, classics. I probably read more books than everyone in my family combined."

"So, what authors do you prefer?

"Hemingway, Salter, Updike, Joyce, Henry James, Kafka, Dostoevsky."

Dr. Goldfarb leaned back in his chair and was silent. He leaned forward and said, "I think I have something that might help you process the information you're holding tight to your vest."

Dr. Goldfarb went over to his bookcase and scanned the shelves. He found the book he was looking for and removed it, a battered hardback edition of *The Brothers Karamazov*. "Since you're an avid reader of Dostoevsky you may already be familiar with this quote." He read from the book as Jerry listened intently. "This is from book two, chapter two, Zosima's speech to Fyodor: 'Above all, do not lie to yourself. A man who lies to himself and listens to his own lie comes to a point where he does not discern any truth either in himself or anywhere around him, and thus falls into disrespect toward himself and others.'"

Dr. Goldfarb smiled. "You haven't murdered anyone, have you?"

Jerry was startled by the question. "No, no, I..."

"Or raped a small child, or set a fire surreptitiously?"

"Of course not." Jerry was indignant and he wanted to sound indignant.

"Good," said Dr. Goldfarb, grinning. "I think I can handle your case. Now, tell me why you left my office."

Jerry took a deep breath. He realized he was about to step out onto a plank suspended between two skyscrapers. He was frightened and wasn't at all sure that he would survive. Then, in a very low voice, and very slowly, he told Dr. Goldfarb all the events and circumstances surrounding the workout of the bank loan and the sale of National. He told Dr. Goldfarb about how his father had attacked Jeff during their breakfast meeting. He explained why the refinancing that Jeff and Charlie were promoting would tie up most of Kevin's assets as well as those of his parents, and that Kevin would become in effect an indentured servant to Jeff and that he had to "stop Jeff" in order to "save Kevin and his parents." Sure, Kevin could have sued to block Jeff's plan, but Kevin would never do that. His heart condition had made him passive. It was up to Jerry to stop Jeff. He would not, like Alyosha, go back to the monastery.

It was as if Jerry was a reporter dispassionately and objectively describing a series of events in which he was not a participant. He did not feel any emotion, guilt, shame, or remorse. It felt good to get it all out. Dr. Goldfarb made an occasional note, but for the most part, listened with a poker face.

Jerry then went into his relationship with Helen and how he learned about the existence of the nude photos of Jeff, Helen, Maurice, and Maya. He told him what he knew about Charlie, including his relationships with Jeff and Helen and his attitude to blacks and how it was common knowledge in the investment banking circles that Charlie was a bigot. Finally, he described how he videotaped the photos in the middle of the night when he slept over at Helen's, and sent the videotape to Charlie. Like a criminal confessing to the detectives on NYPD *Blue*, he explained every step of his thinking and the rationale for taking every action. He wanted to be sure that Dr. Goldfarb understood why he did what he did—why he felt it was so important to stop Jeff and to save Kevin and his parents. Why there was no other choice. Just no other choice. Kevin was sick. Jeff would take advantage of him. It was up to Jerry to stop Jeff.

"So, what happened?" said Dr. Goldfarb.

"Jeff called me within the week to tell me that Charlie was not able to complete the investment package that he had proposed and he was terminating his efforts to finance National. Jeff asked me to advise the bank that he, Jeff, would complete the deal with Foxx. Jeff was beaten down. We closed the sale about seventy-five days later. The bank was paid off, the personal guarantees were released, my parents received their money back, and Kevin and Jeff each walked away with a pile of money."

"What's Jeff doing now?" said Dr. Goldfarb.

"He took a job as a broker with a small trading firm here in New York. If it works out, he plans to use the money he got from National to buy into a partnership. He started working there about three weeks ago."

"And the other characters in the drama, Salli, Helen, Carolyn?"

Jerry told him about Jeff and Salli's divorce and that Salli was moving to Hawaii with the children; that Helen had moved to Paris to work in a gallery, and that Carolyn had pursued her own social life during the last few years and that the only change in her lifestyle was that she could do openly what she had previous done surreptitiously.

Jerry saw Dr. Goldfarb look at his watch. "Excuse me for a minute, Jerry." He left the office, returned a few minutes later, and sat back down, this time at his desk. "Our scheduled time is up, but I want to keep going for a few more minutes." He looked at his notes, and then looked back at Jerry. "So," said Dr. Goldfarb. "You tried your hand at playing God. You didn't like the world as you found it, so you rearranged it, so that it would be in accordance with your desires. Things worked out, for the most part. The Foxx deal went through, the bank was paid in full, and you emerged from the ordeal with you reputation intact."

"I guess so," said Jerry.

"Then, why are you so unhappy? Why do you feel helpless? Why can't you sleep?"

Jerry closed his eyes and leaned back in the chair. "There's a part of me that feels terrible—feels guilty, over having betrayed both my own brother and the person I love. I can't seem to sort it out. I think about it over and over again, trying to figure out some other way I might have stopped Jeff without betraying him."

He explained that for several months, he didn't even think about National and the events surrounding the Foxx deal. When he returned to New York to resume his job, it was like returning home after a long vacation. Then Kevin died. Shortly thereafter, it suddenly hit him that he only had one brother left. The one he had betrayed. "And I was lonely, I missed Helen. I wanted to call her and visit her, but I realized I couldn't. I had betrayed her, too." His voice trailed off. He took out his handkerchief and wiped the tears away from his eyes. His head hurt. Jerry drank some water. It felt cool and refreshing going down his throat. He poured some water on the handkerchief and pressed the compress against his aching head. He leaned back into the plush chair. He was exhausted, but relieved. He had shared his burden with another human being. They both sat quietly for several minutes. He leaned forward and put his head in his hands and stared at the floor. He looked up at Dr. Goldfarb and pleaded, "How can I deal with this? How do I live with myself? What should I do?"

Dr. Goldfarb replied that his job wasn't to tell him what to do. It was to guide Jerry, as he developed the knowledge and skills to deal with his depression and achieve some insight into his thought process, so he can decide for himself. He said that Jerry's depression is typical of people who are dealing with cognitive dissonance.

Jerry responded, "Cognitive dissonance? I know all about cognitive dissonance. I don't see how that applies to my situation."

Goldfarb sat back in his chair, smiled, and said, "Yet, that is the problem, Jerry—the source of your courtroom dreams. It's your inability to reconcile your image of yourself as an honest, ethical, courageous, dedicated person who believes in truth, justice and the American way with the ruthless manipulator who sent the photos to Charlie.

"During the period between the time you sent the tape to Charlie and Kevin's death, you didn't think about what you'd done. You were too busy closing the National deal and getting back to the job in New York and the lifestyle that you enjoyed. The problem you created for yourself was under the surface. Even if Kevin hadn't died, it would eventually have burst through your resistance. Kevin's death caused you to focus on your loss and what you had left in life that you could hang on to. That started you thinking seriously about Jeff and Helen and what you did to them. And when you thought about it and reflected on what you did, you recognized that your actions in sending the video to Charlie were imprudent, insensitive, and reckless. That is the second fact, or belief that you have in your mind. So, we have on the one hand Jerry the paragon of integrity and on the other Jerry the ruthless Machiavellian. The two self-images are in total conflict. Cognitive dissonance."

Dr. Goldfarb continued, "Did you consider that Charlie might show the video to Salli, so she would know what Jeff was doing when he wasn't home playing Dad?"

Jerry was stunned. He simply hadn't thought about it. He told Dr. Goldfarb that he just assumed that Charlie would look at the video and terminate his efforts to finance National.

"Why not?" said Dr. Goldfarb. "He didn't sign a confidentiality agreement with you, did he? If Salli were my daughter, I think I'd want her to know that her husband was having an affair with her sister. Didn't Salli announce her intention to divorce Jeff shortly after Charlie's deal aborted? Isn't it likely that your video gambit precipitated Jeff's divorce?"

Jerry could not respond. It was incredible that he never considered the possibility that Charlie would show the tape to Salli and that as a consequence Salli would divorce Jeff.

"You're not making me feel any better, doctor." His voice was loud.

Dr. Goldfarb parked his mellifluous voice and therapist manner. He leaned forward and spoke in a firm, polite manner, like a traffic cop advising a driver that he is going to give him a ticket. "I'm not trying to make you feel better. I'm trying to get you to stop bullshitting yourself and face up to your actions and their potential ramifications. This is the only way you're going to get well."

Jerry sat in the chair shaking his head. Until today, he had never thought about the unintended consequences of sending the photos to Charlie. He had been an idiot.

Jerry looked down at his hands. He leaned back in his chair and looked up at the ceiling.

Dr. Goldfarb said, "I don't think you'll find any answers up there, Jerry."

Jerry burst out in tears and he shouted, "Why are you torturing me?"

Unfazed, Dr. Goldfarb said, "Did you hope that what you did would remain a secret that you could take to the grave?"

Jerry was sobbing. He held his head in his hands. He whispered, "I don't know."

Dr. Goldfarb leaned back, placed his hands in the form of a steeple, and closed his eyes. After several minutes, he said, "Jerry, we've done enough for the day, and I really have to get to my next appointment."

"I'm so ashamed," Jerry said. "I can't live with this. What am I going to do?"

"The first thing we're going to do," said Dr. Goldfarb, "is put you on medication to deal with the depression. I'll write you a prescription. Start out with the smaller dose and build up the heavier. You should start feeling better within a week. You'll also sleep a lot better. Then, I want you to make copies of the BDI, the Beck Depression Inventory, and take it once a day, sometime in the late afternoon. Calculate your score and make a graph to show how it varies every day."

He reached over and pulled a cassette out of the audio recorder next to his desk and tossed it across the desk to Jerry. It made a slight thunk as it hit the desk. Jerry, surprised, looked at the tape and then back to Dr. Goldfarb. "I've taped the session, so that you can review what we've talked about and can start dealing with all the issues that you've been avoiding. I should see you at least twice a week for a couple of months."

Jerry picked up the tape and examined it as if he were seeing a cassette tape for the first time. He felt a tinge of fear, as he thought about the possibility of the tape falling into the wrong hands.

He stood and headed toward the door. Before he opened the door, he turned to Dr. Goldfarb and said, "Where does all this lead, doctor? I need to know what to expect."

Dr. Goldfarb let out a hearty laugh. "Mr. Investment Banker wants a silver bullet. There are no silver bullets. The psychiatry business is like the investment business. You get to spend a lot of money, and make choices based on flimsy facts and questionable theories, and hope for the best. I can't tell you where this will ultimately lead. What I can promise you is that you'll feel better. The pills will do that. And if you work hard, read a lot, keep your appointments, track your BDI, you'll discover whether Jerry Bascomb is an honest and honorable man whose actions were the consequence of immature and inadequate thinking, or he's a sociopath who will exploit any relationship and abuse every trust in order to achieve his objectives. You'll discover how much all this had to do with protecting Kevin, heaping vengeance on Jeff, or enhancing your ego."

As Jerry opened the door, Ben put his arm on Jerry's shoulder and said, "This is like a course. You read the assignments, do the homework, pass the tests, and eventually graduate. Just like college."

"Thanks," said Jerry. He turned and went down the hall, clutching his cassette tape, BDI, and prescription to his chest.

Jerry returned to Goldfarb's office on Mondays and Thursdays. Then, one Monday, in the clutch of a Manhattan snowstorm, he stamped the snow off of his shoes and entered the room to be confronted with a new apparatus. Goldfarb had erected a whiteboard on an easel, and on it, drawn an outline of a head with a brain and an eye. The drawing included three colorful scribbles inside the brain, labeled "Jerry's thalamus," "Jerry's amygdala," and "Jerry's prefrontal cortex."

He stared at the whiteboard and said, "I hope you're not going to give me a biology lecture. I hated biology. It was my worst subject."

"Well, you'll soon have real motivation to learn some. Meet your brain." Goldfarb pointed to the drawing on the whiteboard. "These are the key parts of your brain that are involved in decision making."

As Jerry shed two layers of winter clothes and seated himself in the now-familiar plush chair, Dr. Goldfarb acquainted him with his brain—specifically, the workings of cognition, logic, and emotion—that age-old jousting match between the head and the heart. Goldfarb's manner was familiar now, too, a pleasant balance between the windy academic and a wry, self-effacing guru.

He stopped and looked at Jerry. "Are you following me?"
Jerry frowned at the whiteboard. "Basically."

"Okay," Dr. Goldfarb said, turning back to the whiteboard. "When life is good, you have the right blend of thinking and control from the prefrontal cortex and the right amount of emotion from the amygdala, and your brain is your friend. That's how you normally perform, Jerry. You get out your yellow tablet and your pen, you list all your options, evaluate the benefits and negatives of each alternative, you choose either the best or least worst option, and then you take appropriate action. Now, when you were at the beach on December 7, you had a lot on your mind, didn't you? I mean just before you took your nap."

Something in Jerry stirred. He was anxious, he realized suddenly and inexplicably. "Of course, I had a lot on my mind. Jeff had just hung our family's future out in the sun to dry."

"And in this instance, you didn't reach for your yellow tablet and pen, did you? When you woke up from your nap, the plan to stop Jeff was firmly in your mind, and you never went back to your tablet and analyzed the potential unintended consequences."

Jerry was stunned. He did not know how to respond.

Goldfarb uncapped his pen again and scribbled on the whiteboard, dictating to himself: "Question one: Why did Jerry Bascomb fail to fully analyze his plan to stop Jeff before he executed it?

"Question two: If Jerry Bascomb had analyzed the plan using all of his skills as a banker and engineer, and all the knowledge that he had at the time, would he have carried out the plan?" He capped his pen. "Hmm?"

And so began the appointment that changed Jerry's life.

Twelve hours later, Jerry slumped is his favorite chair, nestling an untouched glass of bourbon against his chest. With the other hand, he held Dr. Goldfarb's appointment card, suspended on its corner between his finger and the surface of his living room end table. He flicked it once, twice, making it do pirouettes beneath his fingertip.

The good doctor had explained that stressors are cumulative, like a series of waves. He also pointed out that one event could create multiple stressors, one for each time that he ruminated about it. For example, in the case of Jeff's betrayal, Jerry experienced the stress at the family meeting, he experienced it when he was driving home, he experienced it when he was identifying all the brothers in literature and history that had been betrayed...and so forth. And this was only one of the stressors.

"When we add in the other fourteen," Goldfarb had said, tracing his marker up and down the list of fifteen stressors that Jerry had indentified as harrying the days of his National assignment just prior to December 7. "It is clear that you had mixed a high-octane stress cocktail for yourself. Can you recall any prior time in your life that you had experienced these levels of stress from so many diverse sources?"

Jerry shook his head. "No. Never."

"So, what happens when the owner of the brain—you—is subjected to high stress is this. The initial result is that a cascade of hormones initiate elevated heart rate, nervousness, rising blood pressure, aggression, constriction of capillaries, and forgetfulness." Goldfarb poked the whiteboard with the butt of the marker, and stared Jerry down. "You don't *think straight*. So, there you have it, Jerry. The answer to Question 1. You, the consummate analyst, failed to perform the most rudimentary analysis of your plan to stop Jeff, because of the large number of stressors that you experienced between November 30 and December 7. You blundered into your evil twin—an illogical, angry, resentful, frightened, and humiliated Jerry Bascomb, who hijacked your thinking processes."

Jerry continued to stare at the whiteboard. He shook his head. "That's it? Is that all there is to it?

"What were you expecting?" asked Goldfarb.

"I don't know. Maybe something more complicated."

"The human brain is damn complicated, " said Dr. Goldfarb. "But the explanation for its misfiring in your case is straightforward. It misfired a few of months before, too."

Jerry was perplexed. "I don't remember that. Are you sure?"

Goldfarb let out a roar. "Come on, don't you remember your behavior during the meeting in Utah when you damn near strangled poor Phil Bourge?"

It was as if a light in Jerry's mind suddenly turned on. "I was out of control."

"Your evil twin took over, Jerry. It's that simple." Goldfarb went back to the whiteboard, and pointed to Question two: 'If Jerry Bascomb had analyzed the plan, using all of his skills as a banker and engineer, and all the knowledge that he had at the time, would he have carried out the plan? Would he have made a video of the photos and sent them to Charlie?'"

"Of course not," said Jerry. "There's no way I would have sent Charlie the photos had I done the analysis. Not only no, but hell no!"

"Why not?" said Goldfarb. "Was there another way to stop Jeff that you hadn't previously thought of?" He set his hand on Jerry's shoulder and said in a gentler voice, "Don't answer me, Jerry. Question two is for you to take home."

"But I answered no," said Jerry. "I would have concluded that there was no acceptable way to interfere with what Jeff was determined to do."

"And what about your concern for Kevin and your parents?" said Goldfarb. "And your own good reputation?" He held up his hand. "Think about it. Maybe there is no answer. Question two is hypothetical, irrelevant now, purely for thought." He squeezed the cap back on his marker and tossed it on the desk. "We covered a lot today, and our time is up."

As he was leaving Goldfarb's office, they agreed to meet for one more session. They would talk again about the basics, how to manage stress and prevent the overload condition that has caused so much grief. Now, at home, Jerry took his first sip of bourbon in months. He had flushed his prescription down the toilet and was resolved to be healed. The problem had been laid bare, demystified, and recast in sensible and logical terms. Yet Question two still haunted him, and he suspected Goldfarb was wrong: There was an answer, and it had eluded him, and his project now was to solve it on his own.

24

Shortly after Jeff moved to Manhattan to start his new job, Jerry invited him to dinner at Luigi's, an Italian bistro located in Soho. The atmosphere was strictly Southern Italy with checkered tablecloths, yelling waiters, and loud arias on the sound system. Luigi's eighty-five-year-old father sat next to the disc player and played selections by request by the patrons. Occasionally, a singer with one of the small opera companies would sing along from a spot next to the bar. That dinner gave rise to a monthly ritual that Jerry diligently kept up, frequently rearranging his own schedule to accommodate Jeff's. Although Jerry looked forward to the visits, he found that he had to arm himself with sufficient material beforehand to minimize lulls in the conversation. Once they got beyond exchanging news about the family, they really did not have much to talk about. That's why Jerry liked Luigi's—there was enough going on, so that the silences were interrupted by some restaurant action.

Four months after Jerry's first meeting with Ben Goldfarb, Jerry arranged to meet Jeff for their dinner ritual. Jerry arrived about twenty minutes early, so he could get a table in the back, away from the speakers. He ordered a glass of Chianti and some cheese and crackers and reviewed in this mind what he planned to say and how he planned to say it. He had practiced for two weeks. First, he wrote out the statements and read them back into a tape recorder and revised and re-recorded his statements several times until he was satisfied. He then committed them to memory. He wanted to be sure he said exactly what he meant to say.

At about two minutes after 8:00 p.m., Jeff walked in. He was dressed in a dark blue pinstriped suit. He wore cordovan wing-tipped shoes, a light blue shirt with a white collar and a matching club tie. A carefully ironed matching handkerchief protruded from the breast pocket of his jacket. He carried a beige trench coat.

Jerry rose and embraced him. Jerry took a few steps back and exclaimed. "You look great. You've lost some weight."

"Thanks. I've got a ways to go. But I'm back in the routine. I feel a lot better."

The waiter came over to get their drink order. Jeff looked quickly over the wine list and selected a bottle of '90 Freemark Abbey Chardonnay. He still could do it in his sleep. In the course of six months, he had descended into the bowels of his own purgatory and recovered. Jerry envied him.

"Well, how are things going?" He attempted to sound casual, but his voice was strained.

Jeff grinned and made a fist and held it up. "Good. Better than I could have hoped. I've worked out a routine and I'm building a pretty decent client base. God willing and the creek don't rise, I should at least equal my National salary this year." He laughed and shrugged, apparently surprised by his own success. "The partners seem to like me. I'm taking it day by day."

The small talk was just preparation for exploding the bomb he had carried to the restaurant. "How's the divorce going?"

"A done deal. All issues have been agreed to and I signed off the settlement documents last week." His face was expressionless. "Frankly, I'm amazed that it went as smoothly as it did. We were able to keep our combined legal fees to fewer than twenty-five thousand dollars. Salli was so pleasant, rational, and accommodating that I felt a sudden twinge of regret that we were divorcing."

Jerry was taken aback. "You're not serious—or are you?"

Jeff laughed. "I'm kidding, Jerry. What did you think?"

Jerry smiled sheepishly and took a sip of water. "Are you happy with the settlement?"

"She wasn't that accommodating," he said.

The waiter returned to the table with the wine. He opened it, poured a small amount for Jeff to taste, and Jeff gave him the thumbs-up. They ordered their dinners and the waiter disappeared.

Jerry raised his glass. "To life after divorce." They clinked glasses and drank. "Good selection," he added.

Jeff sipped his wine with dramatic relish. "I still have the touch, don't I?" He laughed at himself and set the glass aside. "How are things going with you, Jerry? You look a little drawn. Have you spoken to Helen recently?"

"About ten days ago. She's working very hard. She's taking two fairly difficult courses in addition to working about fifty hours a week. She says she loves it. She asked me to tell you hello."

Jeff smiled. "I miss her. Are you planning to visit her soon?"

"I want to, but—but I need to deal with some matters before I..." Jerry stopped. He realized he was procrastinating. He took a deep breath and reached down into his gut for the courage to do what he knew he must. "Jeff, I need to talk with you about something that involves you and me." His voice was hesitant. It was difficult prying the words from his dry mouth through his dry lips.

A look of mild amusement played on Jeff's face. It said he was expecting a pedestrian confession, despite his little brother's melodrama.

"It has taken me several months—" he took a sip of wine—"to summon the courage to tell you and I have no idea as to how you will take it. After I finish, you may hit me over the head with that bottle of wine, beat the shit out of me, or get up and leave the restaurant and never speak to me again. I hope you don't do any of these things, but if you do, you'd be perfectly justified."

Jeff's grin remained in place. "Pretty dramatic introduction, bro. Go on."

"I'm the guy who screwed up your deal to refinance National."

The grin disappeared from Jeff's face. He leaned back in his chair, as if he'd been shoved. Jerry looked directly into Jeff's eyes and during the next ten minutes laid out the entire story. The memorized sentences flowed automatically, and Jerry was calm enough to watch for some reaction from Jeff. There was none. Jeff just sat, listened, and was inscrutable.

Just as he finished, the waiter brought their dinner. Jeff pushed his chair back and rose. "I need to use the john."

Jerry sat quietly at the table, inspecting the huge dish of veal piccata and angel hair pasta. He sipped his wine. He felt drained. He couldn't imagine what Jeff was feeling. There was the distinct possibility that he wouldn't even return to the table. He might just leave and not give Jerry the satisfaction of a response. He would deserve it. He felt as if he were waiting for the guillotine blade to drop.

Ten minutes later, Jeff returned. "Well, let's eat," he said.

"I thought that you might be going to retrieve a gun you had hidden in the restroom, like Al Pacino did in *The Godfather*. You know when he killed The Turk and McCluskey in the Italian restaurant."

Jeff laughed, genuinely amused. He smiled, "I wouldn't shoot you. That would be too easy on you."

They ate their meals in silence. Jeff consumed every morsel that the waiter had placed before him. Jerry had no appetite. After the waiter had cleaned away the plates, they silently drank their coffee. Three of the singers had gathered at the bar and were singing the trio from the last act of *Faust*, and conversation was both impossible and unnecessary.

When they finished, Jerry said, "I have been wrestling with the remorse and guilt over what I did. I'm so ashamed. I've agonized and agonized over it. There is nothing I can ever do to undo it. I'm sorry, Jeff. I know it sounds hollow, but I don't know what else to say."

The waiter cleared off the dishes and glasses with the exception of their wineglasses and left. Jeff's eyes were half closed. He shook his head as if he were having a hard time believing this strange tale.

"You know, this is the first time in many years that I really wished I hadn't given up smoking. It would give me something to do with my hands, so that I wouldn't use them to strangle you." He opened his eyes and looked at Jerry. "I never suspected that you were such a ruthless bastard."

Jerry had started to perspire. He wiped his forehead and his face with the napkin. "I've been doing a lot of work on myself with the assistance of a therapist. I'm not the Boy Scout I thought I was."

Jeff shook his head again. His face was grim. "Have you told Helen?"

"No," said Jerry.

"Do you plan to tell her?"

"Yes, eventually," said Jerry. "I'm trying to screw up the courage. It will probably end our relationship. I certainly wouldn't blame her."

"Are you still thinking marriage?"

"Yes. But that plan may all go up in smoke when she discovers that her Mr. Clean is a ruthless bastard who betrayed her trust." Jeff divided the last of the wine between his glass and Jerry's and then drained his glass. Jerry let his sit. Now that he had unloaded his burden, he really wanted to leave and go back to his apartment and get drunk. Sitting in the restaurant, hanging on Jeff's every word was excruciating, but he was trapped. Jeff had control.

"I wonder whether Charlie showed the tape to Salli," said Jeff. He squeezed out a sardonic laugh. "It certainly would have made an entertaining evening for them." He seemed about to say something and changed his mind.

"I don't know how I'm ever going to make this up to you."

Jeff looked at him intently. He spoke slowly, choosing his words with care. His voice was devoid of anger or hostility. It had the flat tone of a policeman describing the scene of an accident. "You can't and you don't have to. You did a terrible thing to both Helen and me, not to mention all the other people who would be hurt if the tape ever came to light—like Mom and Dad and my kids." His voice broke, and it took him a moment to recover. "You had to be fucking insane to pull that stunt, Jerry. Was it worth it?"

"Of course not. And you're right—I was insane. All I could focus on was how to stop you. I never thought about the consequences. I don't have any excuses."

"Good," said Jeff, "because I don't want to hear them. Besides, you may have actually in retrospect done me a favor."

Jerry was startled. He gulped. "You're joking, of course."

Jeff leaned back in his chair.

"I shouldn't tell you this because you deserve to spend at least ten years in purgatory for being such a prick. But, doing the deal with Charlie would have kept me tied to Salli. We were kidding ourselves. It would not have been in either of our interests. The sale of National to Foxx eliminated all the business entanglements. The money I got out of the sale gave me enough of a stake to live comfortably and buy a partnership interest in the investment bank where I'm working. Sure, I miss the kids. But they'll grow up and get on with their own lives. My affair with Helen during the time I was engaged to Salli should have been the clue that my marrying Salli would be a mistake, which it was. It was good that we ended it." There was no rancor in his voice. He was resigned to his new situation and he was moving on. "Actually, we get along a lot better now that we're divorced."

The waiter came by and presented the check. Jeff picked it up, and looked at it, and then took out his wallet, extracted his American Express card, and set it on the tray. "I think it's my turn." When Jerry started to protest, Jeff shook his head and gave the tray to the waiter. When the waiter left the table, Jeff said, "Look, I'm not telling you this so that you'll feel better. But you're the only brother I've got and I think it's time that we were honest with each other. I really think it's time. It's the least we can do for Kevin." He looked at his watch. "Anyway, I've got a date, so we'll have to talk later." Jeff stood up, signed the American Express receipt, and retrieved his coat. Jerry remained sitting at the table, unsure of what to do. He hadn't expected Jeff to end the conversation so abruptly. As Jeff was putting on his coat, he pushed his chair back, stood up, grabbed his coat off of the same rack, and followed Jeff out the door.

When they were outside, Jeff gave the claim check for his car to the valet, turned to Jerry, and said, "I'm headed uptown. Can I drop you anywhere?"

"No," said Jerry. "I want to walk a bit. You go on. Remember to wear a condom."

Jeff laughed. "You better believe it. I need to stay alive a long time to ensure that you suffer appropriately." Jeff embraced Jerry. "Take care, bro, I'll see you."

As Jeff released him, Jerry said, "I love you, Jeff. I am really sorry."

"I know. Take care. I'll call you."

Jerry stood on the sidewalk and watched Jeff get into his car and drive away. In his wildest dreams, he could not have predicted any of it.

25

ONE MONTH LATER

Paris in the fall is the second most romantic setting for a tryst—bested only by Paris in the spring. Well-traveled lovers will also include Christmas in London, New Year's in Vienna, and Munich at Oktoberfest. But if you've been in Paris in the early fall with your lover, you'll never forget the experience. It's a theme park Disney would have created, less tastefully of course, if it did not already exist—the Parisian women in their finery, walking along the Bois de Boulogne, and the young boys sailing their final races in the pond in front of the Louvre before the weather turns, and the *gendarmes* in their crisp uniforms, directing the bumper car brigade around the Arc de Triomphe and the Eiffel Tower, glistening in the sunlight.

Jerry had not planned to go to Paris to meet Helen. It was Dr. Goldfarb's idea. He told him that as part of his therapy, he needed to meet face to face with Helen and confront all the issues he'd finessed. Phone calls and letters were not adequate. He had to meet her, talk with her, and level with her. Doctor's orders.

Ever since their last evening together in Los Angeles ten months ago, they had exchanged a few letters and talked by phone less than a half dozen times. All the interactions had been superficial, more typical of the kind of communications Jerry had kept up with travel acquaintances over the years. His letters and phone conversations dealt primarily with family news and work. She talked about her work and her traveling. Jerry did not know whether she was involved with anyone. He didn't ask and she didn't tell. He hadn't mentioned anything about the absence of any romantic involvement in his life.

Jerry had called her and asked if he could visit her in Paris, and she shrieked with glee and said, "Yes, YES!" They agreed to meet the following Friday for lunch at the Jules Verne restaurant in the Eiffel Tower. Jerry's plane landed at Charles De Gaulle Thursday at noon. He exited the airport and took a cab to the Hotel Splendid, a three-star hotel in the seventh arrondissement, a few blocks from Napoleon's Tomb. His travel agent had described his hotel as "marginal" with a fantastic view of the Eiffel Tower. By the time he got there, it was after 2:00 p.m., and he was tired and hungry. He took a quick shower and lay down on the bed. He quickly dozed off, unfazed by the smell of old cigarette smoke, Lysol, and the traffic noise outside his window. He awoke at 5:30, dressed, and walked across the street to a brasserie. He carried a yellow notepad. He chose a table in the back of the restaurant, ordered a glass of the house red and a shrimp salad, and took out the pad.

He had made a few notes during the plane trip, but they were disjointed and unfocused. He couldn't wrap his arms around the project at hand, namely, how to comply with Dr. Goldfarb's final order without destroying his relationship with Helen. He had wrestled with this problem since he had started his therapy, and had not made any progress in solving the dilemma since he had quit. Now he was out of time. He would be seeing Helen in eighteen hours.

In response to Goldfarb's book recommendations, he had assiduously worked to improve his empathy skills and had invested a good deal of time and intellectual effort imagining how Helen would react when she saw the full extent of his betrayal. He fully expected that she would simply write him out of her life. True, Jeff's response was certainly counterintuitive. He had been lucky. He didn't really expect to draw two aces in a row. Hopeless. As he turned to a fresh page of his yellow tablet and began to outline his presentation, he fingered the case in his pocket that contained the engagement ring.

He returned to his room at 10:00 p.m. He opened the window and saw the Eiffel Tower bathed in glittering lights. The travel agent hadn't oversold it, after all. He stood watching the dancing lights, reviewing the elements of the story he planned to tell Helen.

He awoke ten minutes before his scheduled wake-up call. He shaved and showered and dressed in blue slacks, a blue button-down shirt, a red and blue club tie, and a gray camel's hair jacket. He opened the window. The temperature had dropped about ten degrees since yesterday afternoon. He threw his lined topcoat over his arm, grabbed an umbrella, exited the hotel, and walked over to Rue Clare. All along the street, the various merchants were opening their stalls. He passed the meat store with its hanging carcasses. The distinctive smell of chocolate wafted along the street, and the shop from which it emanated was soon visible. He found a café and ordered an American breakfast. He motioned to the waiter for more coffee. It was the one thing he hated about France. The coffee cups were so damn small and you had to beg for a second cup, and they charged you for it.

And what if she asked him whether prior to sending the tape to Charlie, had he spent one minute thinking about how this would affect her life and her relationship with Charlie and Salli if Charlie showed Salli the tape? He would have to admit that he did not. Helen would be horrified. Suddenly, his appetite waned, he put down the fork, and stared at the half-eaten greasy mess on his plate.

He was planning to walk to the Eiffel Tower. He estimated that it would take him about forty-five minutes. As he left the café, he felt sick to his stomach. On his way to the Eiffel tower, he stopped at a flower stall. He looked through the various buckets and chose a bouquet of pink and white roses for Helen. He took the elevator up to the restaurant, situated four hundred feet above the street. The receptionist advised him that there would be at least a half-hour wait. He left his name with the hostess and asked her to look out for Helen. He walked into the bar and ordered a double Jameson to fortify himself. The bar looked out on the Hotel des Invalides. He had read that Louis XIV built it to house wounded veterans. He sat down at a small table next to the shiny black piano, placed the bouquet of flowers on the table, and reviewed the notes on the yellow paper.

As he silently mouthed the key points, he felt a warm hand on his neck, and smelled the perfume that was Helen's favorite. Lips brushed his cheek, and in his ear, a voice whispered, "The hostess told me that there was a sexy American businessman in the bar. Could that be you, sir?"

He turned into the glistening black eyes and the white smile. He stood and, taking advantage of the license that Paris grants to lovers, kissed her passionately.

They sat silently for several minutes, holding hands and scanning each other's faces, remembering who they were and who they had been.

"I've missed you," said Jerry. "I really missed you." His eyes misted over and tears started to stream down his face. God, he loved her. He was overwhelmed by the prospect of losing her.

She leaned over and kissed him and wiped his face with her hand. "Me, too."

"It's been almost a year," he said.

"Nine months, three weeks, and five days—approximately."

"I never knew you to be that precise."

"I'm usually not. You bring out new skills in me."

"Do you still like your job?"

"It's okay. It's a good stepping-stone into the gallery business. I'm learning a lot on the job and taking some courses in art history and sculpture. I think I'll be able to make a living at it."

Jerry thought he had remembered exactly what she looked like. He had several photographs to refresh his recollection. But seeing her for the first time after more than nine months, he needed to discover her all over again. He took a sip from his drink and moistened his lips. He dreaded asking the next question.

"Are you—seeing anyone?"

She smiled at him and patted his hand. "I dated a few guys when I first arrived, but I've discovered I'm either too old or too mature for recreational fucking. I've become a celibate drone. Job, school, cat, garden, and a daily workout to get rid of my sexual frustration."

"You look fantastic," he said. "How do you fend off all the studs at the gym?"

She laughed. "I work out at a women's health club."

"What about your plan to settle down and have kids? Is that on hold?"

The smile waned. Her voice was firm but soft. She stopped turning the jade bracelet on her wrist. "Look, I've found the man that I want to settle down with and be the father of my children. I'm looking at him." Tears welled up in her eyes. "I'm hoping he decides he wants the same things I do before my biological clock runs down. Until then, I don't want to complicate my life. As you say, kapish?" She squeezed his hand.

Jerry became warm. His face was flushed. He took her left hand and held it. He reached into his jacket pocket with his right hand, retrieved the ring, and slipped it on her finger, all the time looking into her eyes.

"I want to marry you Helen—it's the thing I want most in my life. Will you have me?"

Helen looked down at the ring. Her eyes widened. "Oh, Jerry. WOW. I'm shocked and thrilled and..."

He held up his right hand, indicating he wanted her to stop. "Wait, don't answer me. Don't say anything. I need to tell you something very important before you respond and I'm not sure that after I do, you'll want to keep the ring. I hope you do. I pray that you do. Let's take a walk on the platform and look at the scenery while I tell you a story."

Helen, confused, apprehensive, and excited got up from her chair, took her jacket, and followed Jerry to the elevator that would take them up to the upper platform. On the way, Jerry gave the host his card and said he would be back later. He gave the host fifty euros for his trouble.

They took the elevator up to the upper platform and began walking hand in hand—Jerry looking at the scenery, and Helen admiring the ring. As they walked, Jerry asked her to please not interrupt him until he was through saying what he had to say. Then, he told her all the events starting from the evening that Jeff revealed that he had secretly been working on a deal with Charlie: the disastrous breakfast meeting with Sid and Jeff the following day, how he had videotaped the Black's Beach photos, while she was sleeping, how he had sent the tape to Charlie, Kevin's funeral, his subsequent depression, his treatment by Dr. Goldfarb, and his confession to Jeff.

When he was through, he stopped walking, turned to her, and held both her hands.

"I betrayed you. I used you to stop Jeff. I had plenty of justification for stopping Jeff, but using you was beyond the pale. I have plenty or reasons why I did it. But I have no excuses. I hope you can forgive me for what I've done and I hope that you will marry me. I think we could have a wonderful life together."

Tears were streaming down Helen's face. She tried to talk, but she couldn't. Finally, in a hoarse whisper she said, "Let me walk by myself for a while. I need some time to absorb all of this. Wait for me here." And without waiting for a reply from Jerry, she wandered off.

He watched her walk around the corner of the platform. He walked over to the railing and looked at the view toward the east. It was a beautiful cloudless day and the view was stunning. The platform was nine hundred feet above the ground and the panorama stretched out before him for miles. He tried to distract himself from the enormity of his situation. He tried testing his knowledge of Parisian geography.

Southwest and directly in front of him, not more than six-tenths of a mile away, were the Hotel des Invalides and the Ecole Militaire; and further west, Notre Dame and the Pantheon. To no avail. The remarkable vistas did not prevent him from thinking about the emotional rollercoaster that he'd been on for nine months. The Zosima quote from *The Brothers Karamazov* was the tipping point.

Although he had arrived at the end of the ride, he still felt like the criminal who, in order to plea bargain, must confess his crime and lay out the sordid details three times. He had confessed to Goldfarb, his defense attorney, to Jeff, the prosecutor, and finally to Helen, his judge, who would be the ultimate dispenser of solace and closure.

Jerry looked at his watch again. She had been gone over twenty-five minutes. He identified the glistening white Sacré Coeur, but then he fell back into rumination. He could only think about the possibility of her giving the ring back. No, he needed to face facts, be realistic. It was more than a possibility; it was more like a probability, but...

He felt a tap on his shoulder. He turned. Her face was bright and lustrous. She had renewed her makeup and wore a hint of a smile.

"Mr. Bascomb, I think I'll keep the ring."

Jerry felt the tension in his throat vanish. He smiled and said, "I'm relieved. I'm ecstatic."

As she threw her arms around him and pressed her body against his, she said, "Neither of us is perfect. We should make a great team."

He felt that for the first time, he could see to the center of her, and all of her was smiling at him. She harbored only one mystery now, and it was nothing more than how completely she forgave him. He closed his arms around her, and their lips locked together. They were oblivious to the people who were staring at them. Finally, she tilted away and whispered in his ear, "Let's forget lunch and go to my place. You know, to seal the deal."

"*D'accord,*" he said.

She took him firmly by the arm and steered him toward the elevator. He was more than happy to follow her lead into his new life.

THE END